DETOUR

James Wharton

ISBN-13: 978-0615568416 (Desert Wells Publishing)
ISBN-10: 0615568416

To my wife, Carol, with deepest affection.

ACKNOWLEDGEMENTS

Special thanks to the following individuals for their tremendous help. Edna Wharton for her advice and counsel. Jordan Mack for her detailed edits and narrative observations. Dr. Brent Sebold for his comments on content and specific technical points. Many thanks to Carl Earl for his patience and for illustrating the cover.

"Do not peer into the mind of God to comprehend the Universe," saith the Lord. "The Universe is time, space and evil. Righteousness dwells only in my house."

Louis, Bishop of Avignon, 1286-1342

Prologue

It is accepted fact that in the closing days of World War Two Adolf Hitler retreated to his Fuhrerbunker in Berlin. Surrounded by thousands of Russian troops, no escape was possible. Hitler committed suicide on April 30, 1945.

However, never accepting that Hitler was dead, the Russian leader Josef Stalin repeatedly sent SMERSH (Russian Intelligence) agents to Berlin to verify the facts. In June of 1945, SMERSH obtained a bullet pierced fragment of Hitler's skull and the definitive proof he died in the Fuhrerbunker.

In 2003, the remains of a building destroyed by the 1945 Allied bombing of Berlin were unearthed at a construction site. Documents found at this previously unknown installation indicated it had been a top secret Nazi laboratory. The German government immediately secured the site and completed the excavation under total secrecy. A blackout on all information related to the laboratory continues to this day.

In May, 2005 a journal discovered in the 2003 excavation was anonymously sent to a German newspaper reporter. The journal belonged to scientist Dr. Monika Wagner who worked at the laboratory and was killed in the wartime bombing. Dr. Wagner's journal revealed the laboratory was developing highly advanced technology, which, if completed, would have allowed Hitler to escape from his Fuhrerbunker.

In February 2006, Lena Hoch, a German intelligence agent, was assassinated while vacationing in Rome. The German government maintains it was she who sent Dr. Wagner's journal to the reporter. It is believed the German government reacquired Dr. Wagner's journal and the whereabouts of the newspaper reporter are unknown.

In 2009, a DNA analysis by the genetics laboratory of the University of Connecticut revealed the "Hitler skull fragment" actually belonged to a woman less than forty years old. That discovery eliminated the only proof Adolf Hitler died in the Fuhrerbunker in 1945.

PART 1

BERLIN, THE OBERSALZBERG –GERMANY

POLAND-BELARUS (North of the Pripet Marshes)

MAY 20, 1935 - MAY 2, 1945

1

Montag Morgen
(Monday Morning)

May 20, 1935   Berlin

Dr. Peter Krause was running late. As he drove his motorcar into his customary parking space behind the Science and Technology Building, he was silently cursing the time consuming departmental faculty meeting he was about to attend. Monday mornings were always difficult however not even the weather was congenial today. Although the sixty-degree temperature wasn't unusual for May, the gusty breeze and early morning rainfall made the day seem especially unpleasant.

The gray concrete glistened from the rain, reflecting the illuminated lights, which squatted atop the twelve-foot poles evenly spaced around the rectangular parking area. The lot was only half full, with approximately sixty cars parked in random spaces across its puddled surface. The black trunks of trees were glossy from the blowing showers and the green leaves and grass shined with an exaggerated brilliance.

Peter was very happy with his professorship at the National University of Berlin. Being a scientist of the most pure type, and a man who possessed both a brilliant mind and formidable education, he found university life suited him well. Although he was only twenty-eight, because of his research skills he was recognized as one of the most promising physicists in Germany. But, this recognition meant little to him. It was his love of science and the possibilities of discovery and invention that consumed his interest and most of his waking hours.

Peter despised doing anything but his science and abhorred the all too frequent meetings as being a waste time. It was his science that kept him up so late Sunday night causing him to oversleep this morning. He was irritated he had to skip his daily exercise routine because he was half an hour late for the faculty meeting. His regular workouts kept him energetic and alert and he could spend more hours on his research. At five feet, ten inches and one hundred sixty pounds, he was in good condition. Because of his long hours of research, he needed to be.

Twenty-four hours was not enough time in the day, he brooded. The administration wants to waste my precious hours sitting around talking about future projects and who is working on what. The day should be longer and there should be no meetings. Now there's a project I could recommend at the meeting. How do we make the day longer?

It was probably not a good idea to push that suggestion too aggressively, however. Doctor Johanna Neisner, the Dean of the Physics Department and a woman with whom Peter had become infatuated, would definitely not support that suggestion. Doctor Neisner, four years older than Peter Krause, was an inordinately disciplined woman and she adhered to "policy" in everything. It all must be done according "to the book."

She had become aware of Peter's romantic inclinations several months earlier, although she had cautiously expressed her own interest in him even before then. Peter noticed she had begun to request that he do little assignments and departmental errands which would require their spending time together. When Peter came to her department just over a year ago, she didn't go out of her way to even say "hello." She seemed purposely condescending whenever they happened to interact, especially at faculty meetings. Peter assumed this was because of his relative youth and even more youthful appearance. The round lens glasses he wore didn't make him look any older. His light brown hair, brown eyes and cherubic face projected the expression of idealism and intellectual purity so frequently possessed by the young and uninitiated.

For Peter, however, this was a precise description of who he was. Peter also concluded her inattention and little regard for him was probably due to the fact that he hadn't really discovered or created anything noteworthy. His reputation was based solely on his brilliance as a student and researcher, not for any results he had actually achieved.

But that had changed in the last several months as their cautious feigns and advances ascended to the level of a genuine romance. It was all rather sudden but, not really. Each of them knew how they felt but neither of them had actually told the other. A big part of the reason, Peter had assumed, was because university protocol was not sympathetic to the idea of the dean of a department being involved with a faculty member.

But that day in her office, a Thursday Peter recalled, they were standing next to each other looking at a student's thesis when Johanna suddenly turned and kissed him. "It was on the lips, too!" he laughed to himself. He remembered her smiling and telling him "You better wipe off the lipstick, Dr. Krause."

As he walked toward the Science and Technology Hall with its three stories of oppressive nineteenth century architecture, the dark, gothic towers and ponderous battlements caused his thoughts to shift. The increasingly intrusive role of Adolf Hitler's Nazi regime in everyday life in Germany had begun to trespass on the comfort on his cloistered world. In 1933 all German universities had become Nazi educational centers. Across Germany, "non-German" books were being burned in public by the Nazi's. Although the general political climate did not affect Peter, he felt an unexplainable anxiety with the increasing repression of freedoms.

He soon reached the building, quickly pushed open the heavy, wood door and rushed through the entrance. As he hurriedly walked down the hallway, his eyes had to adjust from the outside brightness to the dim, artificial indoor lighting. He would get a lecture from Johanna because of his tardiness. He chuckled to himself that he would have difficulty keeping a straight face when Johanna scolded him for being late.

Because he was rushing, he failed to notice that although he locked his office at the end of every day, the door was slightly ajar and the lights were on. He was pulling off his overcoat as he hastily threw open the door.

He gasped in shock as he entered the office. Instead of finding a normally empty room, Peter was confronted by three men in German Army uniforms. The apparent leader of the group, a slightly stout, gray haired Nazi Colonel with a ruddy, bulbous face was sitting at his desk. The leader immediately stood up to greet him.

"Professor Krause, I am Colonel Armin Huber," he said tersely. "I am a Special Aide to General Bellinghaus. This is

Captain Speicher and Captain Braeden. You will please come with us, Professor."

Although he was apprehensive as to why the three Nazi officers had come for him, Peter half-heartedly joked, "I hope you're not here because I'm late for the faculty meeting." But, his sense-of-humor was unappreciated by the un-smiling Nazi officers. It was one of those times when comedy was not appropriate.

"That you are late for work is of no concern to us, Professor," Colonel Huber replied. "However, your disregard for punctuality has greatly inconvenienced us."

Peter looked at the three men. The two captains were much leaner than Colonel Huber, but their similarity ended there. Captain Speicher was tall. Captain Braeden was short. The tall one's face displayed an intense, impatient expression. His mannerisms indicated he wanted to quickly get on with whatever it was they were here to accomplish. The short one was more relaxed. With his calm manner and pleasant face, he was a reassuring presence in this distressing situation.

"Professor Krause, you will please read this message," Colonel Huber announced, as he handed a sealed envelope to Peter.

Peter picked up the letter opener from his desk and slid it beneath the sealed lip of the envelope, sliced it open, and pulled out its folded contents. He worried that he had done or said something wrong, but he couldn't imagine what it might have been. It was not often that a university professor received a visit from three Nazi officers, especially one with the rank of Colonel. Their formality and military demeanor were intimidating.

He unfolded the single sheet and stared at the short note: "The following instructions are issued regarding the national security of the German State and are of the utmost secrecy. You are directed to immediately accompany Colonel Armin Huber upon receipt of this message. You will travel to a destination which will not be revealed to you at this time. You will tell no one of your departure nor reveal the contents of this message. Signed, General Hans Bellinghaus."

Peter's face paled and he was visibly unnerved by the fast moving events. "I must speak with Dr. Neisner. I can't just leave. I must put in a request to the Dean of the Department."

"That detail has already been taken care of," replied Colonel Huber. "I have spoken with Dr. Neisner. We must leave now because there is little time, Professor."

"And, what if I refuse to go with you?" Peter asked defiantly. But, his shaking voice betrayed him, revealing his fear and resignation that resistance was futile.

"Then I shall place you under arrest and you will come anyway. It would be best if you cooperate, Dr. Krause."

Peter knew he had no choice. He followed the Colonel out of his office and was in turn followed by the two Captains. They reached the end of the hallway and exited the building through the same door, which Peter had entered.

In his haste to get to his meeting, Peter hadn't noticed the black limousine to which the Colonel was now leading him. Captain Speicher asked Peter for the keys to his car as he would drive it and follow the limousine. A troubled Peter Krause, impatient Colonel and a very quiet Captain Braeden got into the ominous looking vehicle. The driver, a military man of lesser rank, started the engine and drove the car slowly out of the parking lot and onto the city street. It was still raining.

2

Ungeplante Reise
(Unplanned Journey)

May 20, 1935   Berlin

Dr. Johanna Neisner stood at the window of her second story office and watched the two vehicles driving away. Colonel Huber's unannounced seven-thirty arrival at her office that morning left her shaken. That he refused to tell her why Peter must immediately leave with him added to her distress. As the vehicles disappeared into the Berlin traffic, she could only wonder why and where Peter was being taken.

As she looked at the overcast sky and gusts of rain she reflected on the rapidly moving events of the 1930's. Germany was filled with exhilaration and new inventions. Scientists were working on all sorts of ideas. Discoveries were constantly being made. A jet engine being developed would propel airplanes at the incredible speed of 350 miles per hour. Wernher von Braun was creating liquid fuel rockets. Heinrich Focke was inventing the twin rotor helicopter. The Hindenburgh, the largest airship imaginable, was soon to be constructed. And the 1936 Olympic Games would be held in Berlin, less than a year from now. Berlin nightlife was a never ending celebration, an endless parade of happiness and laughter.

However, Germany was still recovering from its painful defeat in World War 1 and the economic and political chaos which plagued the country after the war ended in November of 1918. True, the country was moving forward, but it was not moving forward fast enough for certain powerful men. Like many Germans, Johanna was becoming concerned with the unstable political situation. Initially, Hitler's promises seemed like wonderful ideas. But, she had become suspicious of the Nazi's motives and their ultimate objectives.

As recently as yesterday, Sunday afternoon, Peter had complained about the same dilemma. On one hand, he told her, there were more resources available for him to pursue his science.

The Nazi regime not only supported science and technical development, they strongly encouraged it. This was particularly the case in the area of weapons development. While his own research did not fall into the weapons development category, Peter nevertheless benefited from the financial support the Nazis were providing nearly all scientific research.

On the other hand, she remembered Peter complaining several times about the burning of books and the university takeovers by the Nazis and their supporters. Johanna knew Peter followed in the footsteps of his parents when he became a university professor. His father, Raynard Krause, was a professor of Philosophy and his mother, Sophia, was a History professor. Both were well known and respected in their fields. Throughout his life, they had constantly instilled in Peter the value of knowledge and intellectual freedom. One of his father's abiding quotations was from Heinrich Heine, "Where they have burned books, they will end in burning human beings." On more than one occasion, Peter reminded Johanna of this quotation when he read of the incidents of book burning reported in the newspapers.

Johanna shook her head. She finally found someone she loved and the Nazi's had just taken him away. All she could do was wait and hope something good would come of it.

****

"Where are we going Colonel?" asked Peter.

"We are going to the small Army base a few kilometers from the University," the colonel replied. "There is an airplane waiting for us there."

"I meant, where are we ultimately going? Where do we end up?"

"I can only answer that once we're airborne Herr Krause," responded Colonel Huber. "Relax Professor. You will find this to be a very interesting trip, I'm sure."

Peter was already finding it interesting, but in a nerve wracking sort of way. After twenty minutes the limousine pulled up to a gate guarded by two military policemen.

"I didn't know there was an Army base this close to the University, Colonel," Peter said.

Colonel Huber explained, "This base is a very small facility with an equally small airstrip. It's only used for the special

14

movement of high priority personnel and materiel. Since it's used infrequently, most people don't realize it's here."

One of the two military guards motioned for the limousine to enter through the open gate. The car drove ahead and pulled around to the back of the large building which resembled a warehouse but was probably a hanger. There was a single airplane sitting on the concrete apron behind the building. It was a smaller two-engine transport with military insignia on the fuselage. Before the limousine rolled to a stop, the propeller of the airplane's left engine began to slowly turn. There was a loud rumble as the engine suddenly caught and a cloud of smoke belched from the rear of the nacelle. The number two-engine propeller was now slowly turning on the right wing. There was a loud backfire as the second engine lurched to life and expelled a similar burst of smoke.

Both engines were idling smoothly as the three men walked from the limousine toward the open door on the left side of the airplane's fuselage behind the wing. The pilot throttled the engines down to a quieter rpm (revolutions per minute) as the three men walked up the portable staircase and into the plane.

Captain Speicher, who had followed the limousine in Peter's car, ran across the small concrete apron and up the steps of the portable boarding ramp. He came inside the fuselage and reached outside to pull the airplane's door shut. Looking through the window to his left, Peter noticed a soldier pulling the boarding ramp away from the airplane. The airplane began to slowly roll toward the take-off end of the runway.

Like nearly all airplanes of the time, the airplane was a "tail-dragger," meaning it had three wheels, two located under the right and left wings respectively and one located under the tail. The front of the plane, which had longer struts to which the wheels were attached, was higher than the tail section. The tail had a very short strut to which a single "tail dragging" wheel was fastened causing the back of the airplane to sit much lower to the ground. Upon boarding, passengers had to walk "downhill" toward the tail section to get to their seat.

In a few moments the airplane stopped at the runway and the pilot gave the two engines a final run-up and then released the brakes. The plane rolled forward, slowly at first, but the pilot steadily throttled up to full power in order to get airborne as quickly as possible to accommodate the short runway. The plane was now moving much faster and the tail gently rose as the flight surfaces began to take effect. The runway and take-off roll was smooth but then, the plane briefly shuddered when the front wheels lifted off and left the ground behind. They were airborne.

****

Peter turned anxiously to Colonel Huber, his eyes asking, "Where are we going?"

Colonel Huber, who was sitting to Peter's right across the narrow aisle, immediately replied to the unasked question, "The Obersalzberg. We are going to the Obersalzberg."

"Thank you, Colonel," replied Peter. "May I further ask you why I am going to the Obersalzberg?"

"Yes, you may ask," laughed Colonel Huber. "But unfortunately, I cannot answer your question."

"You mean you will not answer my question," replied Peter, with a tone of impertinence in his voice.

Sensing the impudence in Peter's voice, Colonel Huber retorted brusquely "No, Professor, I mean exactly what I said. I cannot answer your question because I do not know myself why we are taking you there. Again, I'm sorry. You have been a very good sport about all of this. But, as you know, there is much going on in Germany right now. There are things happening of which many of us are not aware. Our orders are simply to escort you to the Obersalzberg." With that comment, Colonel Huber looked away to stare out the airplane window.

The airplane was now making a steep climbing bank to the right, providing a panoramic view of the city. "Berlin is a beautiful city," Peter observed, "even when it is raining. "But, I like it better when viewed from the ground."

Colonel Huber nodded, "Yes," he said.

The plane was coming out of its turn and settling in on a southerly heading. As raindrops splashed on the plane's windows, the water blew across the glass to the rear edge and formed shivering little puddles.

Peter knew the Obersalzberg was a mountain retreat in the Bavarian Alps which had been converted to a large Nazi installation. It was situated just above the nearby town of Berchtesgaden which is where Peter assumed the plane would land. The Fuhrer had a home

16

at the Obersalzberg, as did many other high-ranking Nazi leaders such as Herman Goring (Commander in Chief of the Luftwaffe) and Albert Speer (the official Nazi Party architect). Party Secretary, Martin Bormann, the Nazi Reichsleiter (national leader), who ranked second only to Hitler, also had a home there. It was Adolf Hitler himself who "discovered" the area much earlier in his career. He wrote part of his "Mein Kampf" while visiting what was then a mountain vacation spot. Now, however, the Obersalzberg had become an important Nazi complex, a second command post with a large number of administrative buildings, an SS Guardhouse, and numerous other support buildings. "What do they want with me?" Peter wondered.

It was going to be a three or four hour flight. Peter wasn't sure exactly how many miles the trip was, nor how fast the plane flew. Besides, he thought he heard Captain Braeden mention something about a stop to re-fuel. This was necessary because the runway was so short the plane had to take off with a smaller fuel load in order to get safely airborne.

Peter remembered he had been up late working the night before. This was a good opportunity to get some sleep. He put his head back in the seat and immediately nodded off. Sometime during his long nap, he felt the plane land and heard voices. It must be the refueling stop, he concluded, and fell back asleep. He felt the plane rumble down the runway and take off and he dozed soundly for two more hours.

The next thing he felt was a heavy thump as the wheels touched down on a runway. The plane grumbled down a bumpy landing strip and quickly came to a stop. Peter was awake and sitting up.

"Did you have a good rest?" asked Colonel Huber.

"Yes, thank you, Colonel," replied Peter, who was in a "just woke up, slightly bewildered" mode.

"Are we in Berchtesgaden?" asked Peter, expecting "yes" for an answer.

However, as he looked through the plane's window he could see nothing but pine trees. There were no buildings, no other planes, just pine trees.

At the same time, Colonel Huber replied, "No, we are not in Berchtesgaden, Herr Krause. We landed at a secret runway in Obersalzberg."

Colonel Huber then stood up, as did Captain Speicher and Captain Braeden. Peter got up and followed Colonel Huber to the door of the plane. There was no ramp with steps. Rather, the military man who served as the flight steward attached a ladder to the plane for the four men to climb down. Peter descended the four steps of the ladder and looked around. The landing had been rough because the runway was not made out of concrete, but dirt. It was a long, narrow strip cut into the forest. There were pine trees on both sides of the runway. There was nothing else to be seen. The four men, led by Colonel Huber, walked away from the plane and over to the edge of the runway. Neither the pilots nor the flight steward got out of the plane.

The four men waited for a few minutes and then heard the sound of a motor car coming up the narrow road. The "road" was little more than a path through the forest which led to at the end of the runway. The car slowly rolled up to where the four men stood and stopped in front of them. There was a driver and someone else in the front seat of the car but, they were discussing something and remained where they sat.

Colonel Huber turned to Peter and said, "This car shall take you the rest of the way, Professor. It has been nice meeting you. Good luck."

He then turned and walked back toward the waiting airplane followed by Captains Speicher and Braeden. Peter, now feeling even greater anxiety, watched the three men climb into the plane. He then walked over to the car. The two men in the front seat were still deep in conversation so Peter waited, assuming they would exit the car when they were ready. After another minute or so, the driver got out and walked over to Peter and introduced himself. "Did you have an enjoyable flight, Dr. Krause?" he asked. "We are only travelling a short distance," he added, and motioned to Peter to climb into the back seat.

The passenger in the front seat spoke to the driver and gave him several instructions, and then the engine started. The car turned around to go back down the narrow road on which it had just come. As they drove away, Peter saw the propeller on the plane's left wing

18

begin to turn, followed by a puff of thick, dark smoke as the engine growled and came to life.

3

Die Sitzung
(The Meeting)

May 20, 1935   The Obersalzberg

The car followed the narrow path through the thick forest of pine trees, some which were only inches from the slowly moving motor vehicle. The other passenger in the front seat who had been preoccupied with his open brief case and stacks of paper turned to Peter and extended his hand to introduce himself. "Professor Krause, I'm General Bellinghaus. I want to personally thank you for taking time from your busy schedule to come to Obersalzberg to meet with us." The two men shook hands.

Peter was shocked that General Bellinghaus himself, one of Germany's highest ranking generals, would even speak to him, let alone personally come in a vehicle to pick him up. Not that I had a choice, Peter thought to himself, but wisely decided on a more diplomatic reply. "Not at all, General Bellinghaus. I'm very honored and delighted to be here. Thank you for personally coming to meet me."

"The pleasure is mine, Professor. We'll arrive at your quarters in just a few minutes. You'll have some time to freshen up and I shall come back for you in about an hour, at exactly three o'clock. Our meeting begins promptly at 3:15 pm. Please make sure you are ready."

"Of course, General Bellinghaus," responded Peter. He wanted to know whom he would be meeting with and what the meeting was about, but he thought it wiser to not ask questions. He had no doubt the questions would be answered soon enough.

The car passed out of the forest and entered onto a concrete road. The snow covered mountain peaks towering over Obersalzberg and Berchtesgaden were now visible and Peter marvelled at the view. He was asleep when the plane landed and hadn't seen the mountains. But now that the car was out of the forest the breath-taking scenery was all around him. Breathtaking was the only word he could think of.

Obersalzberg was a small village situated at an elevation of 3200 feet, 1400 feet above Berchtesgaden, which was located two miles west. He could see the latter town as he looked out the car's window and down the steep, forested slope of the mountain range. Berchtesgaden was the larger of the towns however, from the higher elevation it appeared as a tidy, miniaturized city snugly nestled in a pine covered valley of a child's toy train set. Instead of railroad tracks however, there was a mountain stream winding through the city. In a few minutes, the car was passing through the small village of Obersalzberg.

There were only a few shops and homes in the little burg and it was the perfect scene for the idyllic painting of an alpine village. Everything was neat and clean and the locals waved at them as the car passed through their small town. On the other side of the town Peter could see the Obersalzberg compound, a monumental undertaking and the Nazis' second headquarters. The great number of buildings and their large size surprised Peter.

The car slowed and turned right off the road, stopping in front of a cozy Bavarian style cottage with a front porch. General Bellinghaus got out of the car before his driver had time to run around and open the door for him. The driver opened Peter's door and he stepped out. General Bellinghaus walked up to the front door of the cottage with Peter, unlocked it, and walked inside with him. "I hope you will be comfortable here, Professor."

"Thank you, General. I'm quite sure I shall be very comfortable."

"I will be back for you at precisely 3:00 o'clock. You must be ready then," he reminded Peter.

"Of course, General. I shall be ready when you arrive. Thank you for your courtesy, Sir."

General Bellinghaus smiled and nodded, then walked out of the cottage leaving Peter to wonder what exactly was going on. It was nearly 2:15. There wasn't much time however Peter took off his overcoat and suit coat and neatly draped them over a chair. The cottage was beautifully appointed with heavy, rustic furniture, colorful drapes, and an incredible view of the scenic valley from the back porch.

This is very nice, thought Peter. He went into the bathroom to wash his face. Again, he encountered a handsome room with modern conveniences. Yes, this is very, very nice, he thought. He splashed some cold water on his face and rubbed his wet hand on the back of his neck. "I guess I'm refreshed," he voiced to the mirror. He dried himself and went back into the main room of the cottage. He noticed there were several bedrooms in addition to the main sitting area. He rolled his shirtsleeves down and walked over to sit on the chair next to the bed. All he could do now was await General Bellinghaus' return and wonder what was to come.

****

Three o'clock finally came. Although it had been only forty-five minutes since Peter arrived at the cottage, it seemed like a much longer time before he heard General Bellinghaus' car roll into the driveway. Peter had already put on his suit coat and immediately came out on the small front porch and walked down the steps to the waiting car. The driver stood by the opened back door and once Peter stepped inside, closed it behind him.

"Good! Right on time," said General Bellinghaus, as the driver climbed in, shut his own door and started the car to begin the trip.

The drive was to be very short, however. The driver had shifted the car into third gear but it remained there only a few minutes before the vehicle began to slow. The driver down shifted into second gear and the car rolled even more slowly. The car merged left from the main road onto a white concrete driveway which ascended for several hundred feet and ended in front of a grandiose estate. While the driveway was not steep, the driver had to leave the car in second gear for its entire length. The driver stopped the car at the end of the driveway directly in front of a large staircase, which Peter later learned was called the "grand staircase."

Although Peter was already enjoying the exhilarating view of the mountains to the northeast of the estate, General Bellinghaus commented on the beautiful scenery anyway. He pointedly mentioned that the area visible behind two mountains at the center of the vista was Austria. "That is, of course, where the Fuhrer was born," he said. "Alright, Professor, we have arrived."

The driver quickly exited the car and scurried around to the passenger side to open the general's door. He then opened Peter's

22

door. General Bellinghaus led Peter up the impressive staircase onto the promenade at the entrance to the house. He stopped and turned to Peter.

"This is the Berghof, Dr. Krause. This is Adolf Hitler's home and headquarters." Peter's anxiety grew. General Belllinghaus knocked twice on the door and it was promptly opened by a smartly uniformed lieutenant colonel. He respectfully greeted General Bellinghaus but did not introduce himself to Peter.

The lieutenant colonel led General Bellinghaus and Peter down a hallway and into a large room with a massive oak table surrounded by twelve leather chairs. At each place on the table there was a glass for water and paper and pencils for notes. Six large pitchers of ice water were positioned around the large table's surface. They must have been very fresh because the usual condensation had not yet formed on the outside of the pitchers. The rest of the room was richly decorated with leather couches and four leather armchairs, as well as a large number of very expensive paintings adorning the wood paneled walls.

"Please sit down, gentlemen," said the lieutenant colonel, and he motioned for the General to sit in the second chair to the right of the head of the table. He then motioned Peter to sit in the same position chair directly across the table from General Bellinghaus.

"The meeting will begin in just a few moments, gentlemen," said the lieutenant colonel, as he exited into the hallway and closed the door behind him.

Peter noticed his hands had become damp. He felt intimidated and the uncertainty of his situation troubled him. Who would he be meeting with? He hoped his nervousness was not obvious to General Bellinghaus.

The sound of heavy footsteps and voices of several men in the hallway signaled the meeting was about to start. The door abruptly opened and an SS officer with a holstered side arm stepped smartly into the room and snapped to attention by the door. It was then Peter experienced the greatest shock his life. Adolf Hitler entered the room, followed by Martin Bormann, head of the SS, and Heinrich Himmler, head of the Gestapo. General Bellinghaus had already gotten up and snapped to attention and Peter, recovering from his initial amazement, quickly rose to also stand at attention, although he had never been a military man.

Peter realized these three individuals were the most important men in the Nazi establishment. His eyes were focused on Adolf Hitler. Peter, who was five feet, ten inches tall, judged Hitler to be slightly shorter than him, possibly five feet eight inches. However, Hitler seemed to be heavier than he appeared in newspaper photos, probably weighing one hundred and eighty pounds. While his hair was dark with hints of gray and his skin had an unhealthy pallid tone, these bland features were offset by the intensity of his blue green eyes. Hitler's legs seemed to be disproportionately short, and despite his military background in World War One, he was round shouldered. Peter thought all military men carried themselves with their shoulders back and chest out however, Hitler did not. He also did not appear particularly graceful in his walk. His face had a stern, malevolent look about it. Peter remembered he had rarely seen a photograph of Hitler smiling. This was not a man to be trifled with, he immediately surmised. However, he already knew that from the newspaper reports.

Once the Fuhrer was seated at the head of the table, the rest of the group sat down.

"Hello General Bellinghaus and welcome, Dr. Krause," Hitler said. "This is Mr. Bormann and Mr. Himmler."

Both men nodded politely, their faces devoid of expression. Friendly group, Peter thought, before responding, "Hello, gentlemen."

The Fuhrer continued. "Professor Krause, I have been following your work with great interest for some time. I have always been intrigued with the possibilities of moving backward or forward in time. As that has been the focus of your research, would you please tell me the precise status of your project today? Is it possible to travel in time?"

Peter was stunned Adolf Hitler was aware of his work and astonished he said the words "travel in time." But, he was also disturbed Hitler was speaking of time travel in such a casual manner. This suggested to Peter the Fuhrer had been misinformed about the nature of his research. Time travel was only one aspect of his work, never its sole objective. That the Fuhrer wanted a presentation specifically about time travel caught him unprepared and he feared Hitler had preconceived expectations which were unrealistic.

With considerable apprehension, Peter struggled to organize his thoughts. What could he tell the Fuhrer? How technical could his presentation be? Get it together, Peter, he thought to himself. His mind racing, he slowly rose to his feet and paused, looking at the group of powerful men taking stock of him.

"Meine Fuhrer," Peter began, "I will do my best to summarize the main points of my research and progress." Hitler leaned forward slightly while Bormann and Himmler sat erect, listening carefully.

"Sir, since you have been following my work, you know the primary focus of my research is to increase mankind's knowledge in order to eliminate hunger, disease and war. The basic premise of my research is to develop a framework by which we could study the millions of species which evolved and went extinct. If trees, plants, and vegetation which no longer exist could be recovered and analyzed, new medicines and foods would be made available to those of us living in the present time. If ancient knowledge written and lost, or never written at all, could be rediscovered, we could learn from past civilizations. As an example, if we could recover the learning from the great library at Alexandria before it was burned, a huge volume of knowledge would be accessible to us.

The basic question is how we go about recapturing this lost knowledge. If a means could be developed to travel through time to other ages, this could be achieved. From that standpoint, my work has been highly theoretical because the reality is that time travel is impossible. I am hopeful that at some time in the distant future someone will discover the means to accomplish this goal. I view my work as laying the initial groundwork."

"Your work is very admirable," said Hilter, an enthusiastic expression on his face. "I'm appreciative or your objectives, Dr. Krause, and support what you're trying to accomplish. But I'm also most interested in how you would accomplish these objectives."

Peter thought for a moment, realizing Hitler was interested in his work and also shared his goals. Unfortunately, Peter had spent only a small number of his research hours in the theoretical realm of time travel.

"Fuhrer," Peter continued, "I have gathered the limited existing research and theoretical conclusions to create a rudimentary database which would serve as a foundation. Other scientists would add more information to this bank of learning as it is further developed in the future. This is a very long-term project which will be continued by future generations. Eventually, possibly hundreds of years from now, a practical method could possibly be developed to bend or circumvent time. Of course, we would have to confront the parameters of physics in order to visit other times in the past or future."

"But, exactly how would you travel back in time if it were possible, Dr. Krause?" Hitler asked.

Although delighted the Fuhrer was enthusiastic about his work, Peter wasn't sure what he was getting at. He hesitated before speaking, contemplating how to respond. "The challenges are insurmountable at this time," Peter replied. "Even if we developed a method to travel in time, the technology does not exist to do so."

Martin Bormann, who had been especially attentive, suddenly spoke. "What are you speaking of specifically that would make time travel impossible, Dr. Krause?"

"Mr. Bormann," Peter replied, "theoretically, in order to travel in time, incredibly high speeds are required. We refer to that particular theory as the 'high speed hypothesis.' But, we don't have the technology to create the fuels necessary to achieve these speeds. Even if we did, the materials do not exist to build a transport device that could withstand the incredible heat generated. These are two basic examples, but the list of technology shortcomings is far more complex and extensive, I assure you. We are many years away from achieving the goal of time travel, if it is actually possible in the first place."

"But, by researching time travel, are you not acknowledging that it is possible," Heinrich Himmler countered.

"Sir," Peter replied, "Einstein proved that, mathematically speaking, time travel is possible. But, that is only a theory. As I said, technology limitations make time travel completely impossible in the foreseeable future. Not to be impertinent, Sir, but flying to the moon is also mathematically possible. But, it's impossible to do so today."

Himmler laughed. "We shall never be able to fly to the moon." Hitler pursed his lips, suggesting he wanted to hear something more positive. Although Peter wanted to provide a more optimistic assessment of the possibility of time travel, he was cautious to be realistic and precise. He wasn't sure why Adolf Hitler had chosen him instead of a more experienced scientist to discuss the prospect of time travel. That in it-self was very strange.

However, these powerful men were obviously hopeful time travel could become a reality. If Peter implied that the means to travel in time could be developed in the near future, he might find himself charged with the responsibility of making it happen. He wanted no part of such an impossible scheme.

"Come now, Dr. Krause," Hitler replied. "Can you give us nothing more promising?"

Again, Peter answered cautiously. "I have also considered some type of inter-dimensional transference as a possible means of time travel," Peter added. "However, I have not gone very far with that theory because the high speed hypothesis is the only one which may be confirmed mathematically. Inter-dimensional transference is a completely subjective theory with no substance."

"And how does inter-dimensional transference differ from the high speed hypothesis?" asked Himmler. He spoke as if he were challenging Peter.

"Sir, please understand," Peter replied defensively," we are speaking of highly theoretical concepts and that is all. I'm not arguing for one idea or the other, or even that time travel could ever be possible. We know next to nothing about it. I'm only attempting to answer your questions."

"We realize that," Hitler said. "But, you are not telling us what we want to hear, Professor."

Peter was stunned. Hitler was apparently insisting that Peter agree that time travel was possible. He continued, hoping the meeting would end quickly. "Inter-dimensional transference is punching through the walls of the time dimension in which we now exist and stepping into the dimension of another time. As I said, it's a purely subjective theory and cannot be supported by mathematical proof."

Peter could see Hitler was becoming frustrated. The Fuhrer wanted to be told the impossible was possible but Peter was avoiding telling him that.

"Anything else you can tell us, Professor?" Hitler asked. "Where does your research stand today?"

Peter shifted uncomfortably in his chair. "At the present time, Fuhrer, I have developed a set of approximately half a dozen theories. I want to stress these are only academic hypotheses, not practical possibilities. But, I'm hopeful at least one of my theories will be valid to the point of possibly advancing to the next step."

Peter heard that Hitler rarely smiled and was introspective and moody. Also, Hilter's demeanor could change immediately from one of contentment to absolute rage. Peter was trying to be very careful to not say anything that would test those rumors. He also knew Hitler was abrupt and became agitated if he did not immediately get what he wanted. Unfortunately, he had not gotten the answers he wanted. Before Peter could continue, the impatient Fuhrer interrupted.

"You are speaking double talk and saying nothing, Professor. Exactly how far has your research taken you? That is the key point. Can you develop a practical means to travel through time within the next three years? The next five years? I need facts, Professor. Do you understand? I must have facts! We both know you are a very smart man, Professor, but, you have wasted our valuable time and told us little we did not already know."

Peter felt the blood rushing to his head and his face flushing. Beads of sweat were forming on his skin. He had managed to irritate the most dangerous of men. That was not a smart move for a supposedly very smart man.

"You are right, Fuhrer," Peter quickly replied. "But, the fact is Sir, I have not achieved a breakthrough in any part of my investigation," he added assertively. "The work is complicated. There are many obstacles and I devoted the greatest part of my time to other aspects of my research. I wish I could give you a more encouraging assessment of the possibility of time travel, but unfortunately, I cannot."

Peter, surprising himself, would not let Adolf Hitler bully him into agreeing that time travel was a possibility. He had no desire to be given the job of making it happen and that, apparently, was what this meeting was all about. Peter glanced at the door, wishing he could somehow escape.

"I already know all of that, Professor Krause," replied Hitler. "But, I have a question. If you were given the resources, could you achieve the goal of time travel within the next three to five years? That is what I need to know, Professor."

Peter was now becoming frustrated. Although he feared he would lose the funding for his research if he didn't agree time travel was a possibility, he had repeatedly told Hitler and the other two Nazi leaders that it was not possible. That was the simple truth, which Peter had always felt was the most honorable and wisest course to follow. He also knew if he agreed with Hitler and said traveling in time was possible, he most likely would be assigned the task of developing the means to do so. But, Peter knew he could not produce the desired end result and feared the consequences would be even more unpleasant. Peter had decided, as he knew he would, to tell the Fuhrer the truth because it was the right thing to do. It was not what the Fuhrer wanted to hear and Peter dreaded his reaction.

"Fuhrer, your question may be answered this way. As to whether time travel is possible, it comes down to this. Time travel is completely impossible. This is because in order to 'break the time barrier,' as I describe traveling in time, a vehicle must reach velocities approaching the speed of light, 186,000 miles per second. As I mentioned, these are unattainable speeds from the standpoints of the non-existence of materials needed to withstand such speeds, propulsion limitations, trajectory control mechanisms and countless other obstacles. No, Fuhrer, time travel is absolutely impossible. I am sorry, but that must be my answer because those are the facts."

Hitler, who was once again becoming impatient, got up from his chair and stood with his hands clasped behind him as he often did. For the man who smiled rarely, today was no exception. He stood a few feet from Peter, his head cocked downward. He was wearing his customary tan uniform coat but, for some reason, black pants. Peter thought he always wore a tan uniform including tan pants. But, he did not today. The Fuhrer had a severe look on his face. He seemed to be carrying a great weight on his shoulders. As Hitler stood near him, Peter could see he was deep in thought.

After a long, uncomfortable pause, the Fuhrer finally spoke. "Professor, what is delaying you in your research? What are the biggest challenges holding you back in your work?"

Without thinking, Peter replied, "Time and money are always the problem, are they not?" He immediately realized it was the wrong answer because it implied time travel was possible if enough time and money were spent to develop it.

"I'm asking you, Professor!" a very upset Adolf Hitler yelled loudly. "You tell me what obstacles you face. You tell me what you must have to succeed in this endeavor. This is a matter of the utmost seriousness and urgency. We must create the means to travel in time. Period!"

As Hitler screamed just inches from his face, Peter could feel tiny drops of the Fuhrer's saliva hit his cheeks and lips. He could see little beads of white spittle curling in the corners of Hitler's mouth. Peter was sweating profusely, paying the price for saying all the wrong things to this powerful man who would not accept "no" for an answer.

This guy's got terrible breath, Peter thought to himself. He remembered someone telling him that, as a youth, Hitler craved pastries, candies, any kind of sweets at all. His poor eating habits caused him to have very bad teeth which in turn gave him trouble his entire life. This was probably the cause of the bad breath.

"Professor Krause, you will be provided with an unlimited budget. I would like you to assemble a team. It doesn't matter how large or how expensive. We will see to it that you have every person you request working on your team. You will also be provided an adequate facility in which your team will conduct their work. You will report to General Bellinghaus and coordinate your needs with him. General Bellinghaus will see that you have all the resources, everything you need, to accomplish our goal. Is that clear?"

Peter wanted no part of a project which was certain to fail. And, he wanted no part of working for Adolf Hitler under the intense pressure he knew would exist.

"But, Mein Fuhrer," Peter replied, "many scientists are far more accomplished than me. There are men who have achieved great things. I am barely out of graduate school. I have accomplished nothing. Surely there are many men far more able to lead such a project. I have done nothing but research."

Hitler looked straight at Peter. "I have already talked to some of these men. Like you, they say time travel is impossible. However, unlike you, they are not working on a project that includes time travel as a necessary element. Therefore, you must think time travel is possible because, if you didn't think so, that would make you a hypocrite. Certainly, you are not a hypocrite, are you, Dr. Krause?"

Martin Bormann and Heinrich Himmler chuckled. "Are you squandering the research funds you have been allocated on something you know is impossible?" Hitler continued. "I already know how many hours you spend each day, each week, and each month working to create a way to travel in time. Therefore, Dr. Krause, you must think time travel is possible."

Peter had never thought about his work in quite that way. He was doing research for the sake of knowledge, assuming he would also make countless other discoveries as he progressed. Very few of his research hours had been devoted to time travel, which, he assumed, would be a project for future generations when more advanced technology was available.

Hitler added, "The only difference between your vision and mine is the time frame in which the time travel puzzle must be solved. If time travel is possible to achieve in the future, Dr. Krause, then it is possible to achieve now. You are the right man for this job because you are the only scientist in Germany who believes time travel is ultimately possible. It is my wish that you lead this project Dr. Krause. Do you have an objection to doing that?"

Peter realized there was no changing the Fuhrer's mind. He had already been selected for this impossible job and he could not refuse Adolf Hitler. He must tell Hitler yes.

"I will be happy to accept the responsibility to lead this project, my Fuhrer," responded Peter. "I will do my very best to achieve the results the Fuhrer desires."

"I am happy to hear you shall accept this position, Professor," Hitler said. "Now, I wish you to provide to me a timeline on exactly when you will have achieved our goal of a practical means to travel in time?"

Peter thought for a moment. He knew time travel was impossible to achieve in the lifetimes of every person sitting in the room. It might not be possible to achieve ever. Although he knew the Fuhrer wanted it to be a reality in the very near future, Peter knew he would need all the time he could get. Maybe Hitler would die before the deadline by which he expected Peter to create a method to travel in time. "Sir," Peter replied. "I would need at least ten years."

As Peter suspected, that turned out to be the wrong response. Hitler now became red in the face, signaling his increased frustration. Clearly very angry, he leaned over, his face only inches from Peter's, and looked him directly in the eye.

"I want your work successfully completed exactly four years from today, Professor," he demanded loudly. "That will be May 20, 1939. Have I made myself clear?"

"Yes, Fuhrer," responded a visibly shaken Peter. He was beginning to feel that Hitler transferred the weight he had been carrying onto his shoulders. Peter knew the goal of time travel could never be achieved if he worked for another one hundred or one thousand years. He also knew that was not the answer the Fuhrer wanted. However, he had no choice. The man is insane, Peter thought, but he must do what the Fuhrer directed.

Being caught between the proverbial rock and hard place shattered Peter's cloistered world of academia. Suddenly, the Monday morning faculty meetings seemed very attractive. They were familiar, safe and comfortable. Peter wanted to remain in this very secure environment. He wanted nothing to do with high-pressure government ventures.

On the other hand, the Fuhrer had provided an unlimited budget for Peter to pursue his dreams of rescuing humanity from the miseries of disease, hunger and war. Maybe something good will come of it, Peter hoped. I just hope I'm alive when that happens, he reflected. Unfortunately, the conversation did not end well. Peter had handled this meeting very poorly. He promised himself he would do much better when speaking to Adolf Hitler in the future.

Hitler now turned to General Bellinghaus, who had an expression of deep concern on his face. "Do you understand I want this project successfully completed by May 20, 1939 General?"

General Bellinghaus, who appeared to be carrying a weight as heavy as Hitler's, crisply responded, "Yes, of course, Meine Fuhrer."

Hitler then said, "Gentlemen, the work you are required to perform is absolutely the most important goal we must achieve. It is our first priority. As you know, I expect nothing less than one hundred percent success within the four-year deadline I have given you. General Bellinghaus, you are to spend one hundred percent of your time on this project. I want a weekly progress report from you personally. Is that clear?"

"Yes, Fuhrer," replied General Bellinghaus.

Hitler, standing with his hands clasped behind his back, slowly paced back and forth across the room several times. His head was cocked forward and he stared at the floor. His face was still flushed and he was breathing heavily, almost snorting. The Fuhrer stopped directly behind the spot where he had been sitting, placed his hands on the back of his chair, and looked toward the other end of the table. Tension weighed heavily in the room, pressing down on the shoulders of Peter and General Bellinghaus. Hitler stared toward the far end of the room for what seemed to be a great deal of time.

Then, without looking at anyone, he abruptly declared, "This meeting is over."

4

Auf der Platterhoff Hotel
(At the Platterhof Hotel)

June 14, 1935   Berchtesgaden

Peter had been at the Obersalzburg working with General Bellinghaus continuously for over three weeks. The pace had been brutal, and even though he was used to working long hours, he was nearing the point of exhaustion. General Bellinghaus had turned out to be an affable enough fellow to work with, but both men clearly realized the urgency and felt the pressure for results.

The first task had been to identify and select critical personnel required for the different scientific and research fields and then design an organization structure. The Fuhrer directed that General Bellinghaus would have broad oversight responsibility and budget approval, and Peter would report to him. Peter would have complete management and control of the entire organization and direct all scientific and research endeavors. He would have an Organization Director as his second in command. This position would manage day-to-day operational support, including management of the facility. There would also be a Security Director reporting to General Bellinghaus. This person would be an SS officer.

Work had already begun to renovate the building which would house the laboratory. Oddly enough, the facility allocated for the task of producing what was now called the Chronometric Teleporter, or time travel machine, turned out to be the very Army base from which Peter had flown out of Berlin three weeks earlier.

Most of the preliminary organization work had been completed and nearly all key-personnel had already signed on. Over one hundred and fifty scientists and support personnel were on the team. The Interior Ministry had worked with the various universities to arrange leaves for academic personnel. Also, to induce prospective employees to volunteer, the financial rewards for working on the secret project were very attractive.

However, for anyone, and there were a few, who did not take advantage of the attractive offer to join the team, the government had other options to "encourage" them to rethink their decision not to participate. Peter would never have approved of strong-arm tactics had he been aware they were being used to coerce people to join the team. He was not to learn of this unpleasant tactic until much later.

Peter wanted the Organization Director's position filled as soon as possible however he procrastinated on choosing the person to fill this critical spot. The person performing this job would necessarily be tough, able to set up and enforce operating policies, and assure compliance by all personnel. Also, that person must know how to effectively interact with and manage highly educated people. While he had considered half a dozen people, including several of General Bellinghaus' recommendations, he knew from the very beginning what person would be perfect for this crucial role. It's a no-brainer, Peter thought to himself. However, he was hesitant to make the decision for one reason. He was in love with the person he knew would be the best choice for this position.

Doctor Johanna Neisner, his department head at the National University of Berlin, was by far the most qualified person for the job. But, he wondered if he could effectively work with Johanna because of his romantic involvement with her. He was also hesitant because he wondered if his decision was truly objective. Did he prefer her for the job because of his feelings?

But, he finally became certain his objectivity was intact after interviewing five other candidates. While all of them were good prospects, none appeared to have the comprehensive qualifications and toughness that Johanna, Dr. Neisner that is, possessed. It has to be her, Peter decided, regardless of how I feel about her. He would just have to learn to work with her and make sure the project ran smoothly.

There was one other concern. Peter had formerly worked for Dr. Neisner and she would now be working for him. He hoped this would work out satisfactorily. But, he concluded, with the intense pressure and the Fuhrer's interest in this project, it had to work out well. There was no other option. On Friday morning, June 14, Peter telephoned Dr. Johanna Neisner, his former boss and the only romantic interest he ever had. He asked her to join his team to work on a secret government project. He needed to know her answer right away and they would talk later that day after she had time to think about the offer.

"I don't need to think about it, Peter," she said. "I want to join the team." Peter insisted that Johanna give it more thought, just to be sure, and he would call her later that day.

****

At 3:00 p. m. the following Monday, Peter was pulling his car into the parking lot at the Berchtesgaden airport where he would meet Dr. Johanna Neisner. She was on the team.

Dr. Neisner's plane arrived a few minutes early, and as Peter walked into the terminal, he spotted Johanna walking toward him with a porter carrying her two suitcases. When she saw him, a smile came across her normally serious looking face. They shook hands warmly, but formally, not wanting to inadvertently reveal their relationship to anyone who might cause a problem. Peter was sure that neither General Bellinghaus, nor the Fuhrer himself for that matter, would tolerate a romantic relationship between the Chief Scientist of the "Time Travel Project" and his Organization Director and second in command. The two scientists walked to his car, loaded her bags and headed toward the hotel.

The trip from the airport to the Platterhof Hotel took only a few minutes. Because they had been separated for nearly a month, their discussion began a bit formally, mainly centering on the beautiful scenery surrounding them and that Johanna had not been to the area since she was a young girl. However, the conversation quickly changed, with Johanna speaking first.

"Peter, I must confess I missed you terribly," she said. "I'm so happy we will be together again."

"It makes me very happy to hear you say that, Johanna. I've missed you just as much, if not more. I'm looking forward to being with you however, I don't know if you will like the circumstances under which we shall be working."

"Why do you say that, Peter?" she responded.

"There is constant pressure from the Fuhrer to complete the project," he replied.

"Quite frankly, time travel is impossible, as I'm sure you agree. I tried to tell the Fuhrer that, but he wouldn't listen. I'm not sure I'm doing you any favors asking you to get involved in this insane scheme which is doomed to failure."

"Peter, I want to be with you no matter what the situation. That's why I didn't hesitate when you asked me to join this team."

"I love you Johanna," Peter replied.

"And, I love you too," she said. Then, changing the subject, Johanna added, "You know, Peter, the political climate in the country is getting much worse. Things are very unsettled. Even in the three weeks since you left the University, the situation has deteriorated."

"I've been too busy to follow things, Johanna," Peter said.

"You don't follow things even when you aren't busy," Johanna said laughing. "I keep track for both of us."

Peter laughed. "You see, I need you, Johanna. We must be together, if for no other reason than I shall always know what is going on."

Johanna laughed, but once more became serious. "You know, there is talk of war, Peter. Does your project have anything to do with that?"

"Of course not, Johanna. The Fuhrer personally assured me he shares my goals of helping all of mankind. He understands that by being able to access the knowledge of other times we can help people live better and become wiser. I truly believe his greatest wish is to avoid wars. I understand it is other countries that are causing problems for Germany."

"I don't know about that, Peter," Johanna replied guardedly. "Germany has violated the terms of surrender the country agreed to at the end of World War One. Hitler has increased the size of the Army and Navy. Germany is also building airplanes. Frankly, it scares me."

They arrived at the hotel and Peter drove the car into the driveway and to the front door of the lobby. A bellboy quickly walked over to the car and took Johanna's two suitcases from the vehicle's trunk.

Peter walked to the front desk with Johanna and she quickly checked in. Always the model of efficiency, Peter thought. He decided to go into the hotel bar while Johanna went to her room to get refreshed from her long airplane trip. They would have an early dinner and discuss what her role would be and also outline the week's activities. After dinner, they would visit.

While Peter never allowed himself much relaxation, he did, on occasion, enjoy a good martini. This was his plan as he walked into the Platerhoff's agreeable looking cocktail lounge. It was one of those atmospheric places with a heavy oak bar, large rustic furniture and huge greenery, even several small trees, strategically placed around the room. What a great place to have a martini, he thought.

A martini is one of those drinks that demands precise ambiance if it is to deliver maximum enjoyment to the person drinking it. The right atmosphere, such as Peter was now enjoying, is the first requirement. Next, it goes without saying that the drink must be properly mixed. Peter's preference was English gin, Beefeaters to be exact, with just a touch of vermouth so the martini was quite dry, and one drop of Scotch. The "Scotch thing" was his own invention and he had to instruct every bartender to be careful to add only one drop. Then, the martini had to be shaken vigorously to get the mixture cold enough to achieve a thicker consistency to become almost syrupy. At that point, it would turn a grayish color and form ice crystals which would float on the surface. Then the mixture was poured into a stem glass, which was the final requirement. A ceremonial olive was served on the side, not in the glass. Now that was the perfect martini!

Having had little rest in the past three weeks, Peter enjoyed his first martini and was sipping his second when Johanna walked into the bar. He smiled as she strolled toward him and he asked if she would like a drink. Peter's attraction to Johanna was both intellectual and physical, in that order. He found her mentally disciplined and knowledgeable, and her coal black hair and green eyes boldly contrasting with her ivory skin proclaimed a strong, forceful woman. Johanna was five feet seven inches tall and, though not stunning, she was beautiful. The way she carried herself with precise posture and purpose, and the efficient manner in which she moved about, projected an inner strength and incorruptible character. This greatly appealed to Peter's ever present need for order and honor in the universe. Johanna was the perfect match for Peter.

She asked for a gin and tonic and took a seat to his right. Once again, the conversation was cordial, but formal. They were being especially cautious to not seem overly friendly. Then Peter asked her if she would be comfortable working for him since their roles were now reversed and she would no longer be the supervisor. She smiled and said this situation did not bother her in the least. While Peter was happy to hear this, he could only hope that this was the case. There could be no discontent on the team, as they had to operate at the highest efficiency at all times. They finished their drinks and moved into the dining room to the table Peter had earlier reserved.

The dinner was pleasant and, while Peter and Johanna shared the greater part of a bottle of wine, the conversation remained formal and polite, not hinting at any kind of intimacy. She still referred to him as Dr. Krause and he addressed her as Dr. Neisner. They continued to talk about the more mundane aspects of her new position and the organization, carefully avoiding any mention of the highly classified nature of the project itself.

Dr. Neisner then mentioned that she had something very confidential she wished to discuss with Peter. She further suggested that, since her room was quite comfortable and commanded a beautiful view of the mountains, they might adjourn there to take advantage of its outside balcony. Peter agreed to this although he was worried what her "confidential matter" might be. As they walked through the hotel lobby to board the elevator, Peter was thinking the last three weeks of organizing and team building had gone amazingly well.

The elevator swiftly carried them to the third floor. Peter had never been to the Platterhof Hotel. Its luxurious atmosphere and modernistic decorating style were impressive. A university professor's salary is not enough to pay for things like this, he thought. But Dr. Neisner was on a government expense account so these costly accommodations presented no problem. Johanna opened the door to her room and asked Peter to come in.

Johanna's room was just as luxurious as the rest of the hotel. As Peter walked into the room from the hallway, he saw a sitting area with a separate, large bedroom to the left. Large glass doors opened onto the outside balcony which extended the entire length of both the sitting room and bedroom. She was right. The view from the balcony was incredible, with a huge panorama of snow-capped mountains covered with pine forests.

However, instead of going out on the balcony, Johanna asked Peter to have a seat on the large sofa in the sitting room. Johanna took off the black suit coat she was wearing and laid it across the back of one of the two armchairs. She sat down in the other armchair directly opposite Peter on the other side of a large glass coffee table.

"What is it you wish to talk about, Johanna?" Peter asked apprehensively. He was concerned Johanna might present some sort of problematic issue.

Johanna, with a great deal of composure, responded, "You are in love with me aren't you, Peter?"

Peter was caught off guard by her question. He thought Johanna might have had an organizational concern of some type. But, she was talking to him as his lover, Johanna.

"I thought we settled that, Johanna," he said, relieved. "Of course, I'm in love with you."

"Have you thought about that thoroughly, Peter? Are you really in love with me?"

Peter was trying to figure out what exactly she was getting at. He had answered her question. What else could he say?

"Johanna, I told you I love you. I've been telling you I love your for several months now. Do you think something has changed?"

"Something has changed, Peter, not between the two of us, but the situation in the country has changed. I know we must keep our feelings for each other secret but, how long can we do that?" She then added, "Are you prepared for what might happen if we are found out?"

I see what you're getting at," he responded. "You mean, what is to become of us in this new organization we'll be working in?"

"I mean," Johanna continued, "are you prepared to possibly sacrifice your career when we are found out, which we both know will surely happen?"

Peter had thought a great deal about that since he called Johanna on Friday. In fact, he had agonized over the situation. He realized that having her join the team was a great risk, even though she was the most qualified person for the Organization Director's position. On the other hand, he knew how strongly he felt about her.

He had struggled greatly with the situation and the risks if they were discovered. Like Johanna, he knew that eventually their romance would be found out.

Could he work effectively with someone he loved on a top secret, high priority, stress laden project? Was it possible to do this? Would their relationship compromise the mission? Would the mission compromise their relationship? And, regardless of what he and Johanna thought, General Bellinghaus, or even Adolf Hitler himself, would probably not tolerate such a situation once they found it out. Yes, he thought, he had given the whole matter thorough consideration.

He had no choice but to go forward as the Chief Scientist of the Chronometric Teleporter time travel Project, knowing this project would not be of brief duration. His choice of Johanna as the Organization Director was driven by the necessity to select the best people who would have the greatest chance of completing the impossible project. The fact that he loved Johanna was something the Nazis would have to accept. If they chose to fire him, so be it.

Instead of the eloquent response he prepared, Peter simply blurted out, "Johanna, I have considered everything very carefully. I know the risks and I am sure we will eventually be found out. For me, it is an impossible situation. I have no choice but to do what I have been ordered to do by the Fuhrer. But, I also must have you. I don't give a damn about the Chronometric Teleporter Project and the possibility of time travel if I can't be with you. The Fuhrer will have to accept that or find someone else to lead this project."

There hadn't been any doubt in Johanna's mind that Peter must do as he had been ordered by the Fuhrer. She was not sure, however, that he would sacrifice his career for her. She knew he loved her but their relationship could destroy his career, or worse. But, he was willing to take that chance. In her heart, she hoped that he would. And he did. He loved her that much.

Johanna got up and walked the few steps around the coffee table over to the sofa where Peter was sitting. She sat down next to him. "You have made me very happy, Peter. That is exactly what I wanted to hear but, I was not sure I would," she said.

He was in love with her, and now that he told her that he loved her with absolutely no reservations, he found himself even more attracted to her. They both agreed that they would do their jobs but, they would always put each other first. "I'm so happy we're in love, Peter," she said.

"So am I," replied Peter.

She moved closer to him, putting her right hand on his left cheek. "So, what are we going to do about that?"

5

Keine Fortschritte
(No Progress)

August 10, 1939   The Obersalzberg

Dr. Johanna Neisner and General Hans Schneider were
sitting in a vacant meeting room at the Berghof, Hitler's office and
home at the Obersalzberg. General Schneider had replaced General
Bellinghaus on the time travel project or, "Zeit Reisen Projekt," as
the Fuhrer called it. In late 1937, the Fuhrer had become impatient
with the lack of progress and he decided that General Schneider
would deliver concrete results where General Bellinghaus had failed.

Like General Bellinghaus, General Schneider had regularly
traveled to whatever geographic spot the Fuhrer might be located to
brief him on the status of the project. At first, the briefings were
weekly. Then, as it became more difficult to schedule an
appointment with the Fuhrer, the briefings were scheduled every two
weeks, and then monthly. But now, it had been nearly four months
since the last briefing.

Johanna Neisner and General Schneider had been scheduled
to see the Fuhrer on May 20 because that was the deadline he had
given the laboratory for completion of the four-year project.
However, all prior briefings had reported no progress. Hitler seemed
to want to avoid the May 20 meeting, and then the meetings the next
two months. Johanna guessed Hitler didn't want to hear the
predictably bad news. It was now August 10, 1939.

General Schneider sometimes brought Peter or Johanna along
to help in the briefing, but most often he would come alone.
However, the briefings had settled into mundane routines regularly
concluding with the Fuhrer shrieking his dissatisfaction in his
excited, high-pitched voice. After four years, the one hundred and
fifty person Chronometric Teleporter Project (time machine) team
had accomplished nothing. Depending on who attended the meeting,

either Peter or Johanna admitted to that fact at the end of every briefing.

The team had no better idea of how to build a Chronometric Teleporter now than when they started four years earlier. At best, they had developed a great many side projects and a lot of interesting theories, most of which were not particularly relevant to time travel. Today's status report would be the same. Four years and three months had passed and everyone had worked long and hard and a great deal of money had been spent. However, there had been no results.

On the personal side however, Peter had secretly married Johanna. One of the scientists at the laboratory was also a deacon at his church and he officiated at the wedding. With the intense pressure on the Zeit Reisen Projekt, Peter and Johanna wouldn't dared have a formal wedding. Hitler would consider such an event a distraction from their work. But, after that memorable night at the Platterhoff, marriage was inevitable. They just had to keep it on the quiet side.

Peter and Johanna had separate living quarters on the grounds of the laboratory however, they discreetly spent their nights together. The pressure to complete the project had become so intense, no one really cared about who slept with whom. Both Peter and Johanna guessed SS security personnel were keeping close track of things however.

As they waited to meet with Adolf Hitler, both Johanna and General Schneider were deep in their own thoughts. Johanna was to give the briefing but still had not figured out what she would say to the Fuhrer. She knew what she had to tell him, but she worried about how. She also knew from past experience he was extremely impatient and direct. He was not interested in the process, peripheral discoveries or technical jargon. He simply demanded to be told the bottom line.

Johanna was concerned over what she knew would be the Fuhrer's reaction when she could show him no concrete progress. Hitler would be unhappy. Also, she knew that the team had exceeded the project's four-year time deadline by nearly three months. In a gallows humor reflection she thought, if we only had a Chronometric Teleporter we could go back in time and start the project to invent a Chronometric Teleporter all over again. Not really funny she decided.

Johanna was also worried because the laboratory grounds were swarming with SS personnel. Hitler must have found out about her and Peter's marriage by now. If he did, he might blame their relationship for the failure of the project. She worried about what consequences might come from an enraged Fuhrer.

General Schneider assumed he would be fired. While he felt he pushed everyone on the project as hard he could, he was concerned today's zero progress report would be the end of his job, possibly his career. "What else could I do?" he asked himself. He saw everyone putting in grueling hours, doing all they could. Like Dr. Neisner, he had no idea what to say to the Fuhrer other than to express his deep regret and offer to resign. He assumed the Fuhrer would fire him before he could offer his resignation anyway. He already cleaned out his desk and packed his personal belongings at his quarters on the laboratory grounds in Berlin.

Their morning meeting with the Fuhrer had been scheduled for nine o'clock. It was nearly ten-thirty and they were still waiting. While Johanna and General Schneider had a cordial relationship, neither of them said more than a few words since they arrived. Both knew it promised to be a tense, unpleasant meeting.

Their thoughts were interrupted by voices in the hallway. The door was opened briskly by a military attendant and the Fuhrer entered the room followed by Martin Bormann. Both men took their seats. Hitler sat at the head of the table and Bormann sat to his right. Noticeably, Heinrich Himmler was not in attendance.

"All right, General, what good news will we hear today?" the Fuhrer asked. His voice suggested a reluctance to ask the question to which he already knew the answer.

General Schneider rose and spoke. "Meine Fuhrer, I regret I am unable to report progress on the Zeit Reisen Projekt. I am aware that we are three months past the generous time you have allowed for us to complete this assignment. However, we have failed you. I take full responsibility for that failure. I offer my resignation to you in the hope you will find someone else to successfully execute this mission. With that, General Schneider saluted the Fuhrer and sat down.

Hitler, surprisingly, did not react to General Schneider's comments. Rather, he sat in his chair staring toward the far end of the table, seemingly resigned to having heard precisely what he anticipated from General Schneider.

"And what do you have to report, Dr. Neisner? Perhaps you shall have some good news for me?" he questioned.

"My deepest regrets, Fuhrer. I too have failed you and the German people. After four years and three months, we have nothing. It is my fault. I take full responsibility for our failure, Sir. I, too, offer my resignation." Johanna was attempting to shield Peter and General Schneider from the Fuhrer's rage.

Again, Adolf Hitler stared toward the far end of the table and said nothing. He was in deep concentration. An overbearing stillness filled the room. Adolf Hitler, Martin Bormann, General Schneider, and Dr. Neisner sat in silence. If anyone were to speak, it would have to be the Fuhrer.

Hitler finally broke the silence. "So, we have two people who claim the responsibility for failure is theirs alone. How nice that is," he remarked sarcastically. "Dr. Neisner, I presume you would not attribute the lack of progress to the fact that you and Dr. Krause have an 'arrangement,' shall we say?"

As Joanna suspected, the Fuhrer knew about her and Peter. "Meine Fuhrer, we have worked many hours on this project. We have little or no relaxation. Our only pleasure is that which we derive from each other. Even when we are together, the phone is constantly ringing. We are working even then. The lack of progress is not due to a lack of time invested by Dr. Krause or myself. As I said, I take full responsibility for the failure we now face. Unlike General Schneider, I have been working on the project since it began and logically, the fault is mine."

"Then where is the problem?" the Fuhrer retorted, a dark expression on his face.

"The problem is our inability to comprehend the physics of time travel mechanics," Johanna said. "The hypothesis on which we have been proceeding is that time travel must involve impossibly high speeds and the means to attain them. As we have often said, in order to achieve these speeds we would need some type of vehicle which is capable of tremendous propulsion capability, and the materials which would be able to withstand incredibly high temperatures and innumerable collisions with debris it would encounter. The physics for this hypothesis are completely beyond our understanding. Quite frankly, Meine Fuhrer, using this hypothesis, even if we worked for another four years or four hundred years, we could never be successful." Johanna thought the Fuhrer would come out of his seat and unleash a torrent of fury after her brutal assessment.

Instead, his response was simple and conclusive. "Dr. Neisner, we have been through all of this before. I think the answer is for you to find another hypothesis. You have two years, Dr. Neisner. Tell Dr. Krause I want this project completed in two years. Do you understand Dr. Neisner and do you understand General?"

Without waiting for an answer, he abruptly dismissed them with his customary, "This meeting is over."

Coincidentally, the laboratory recently put a small team together to work on exactly what the Fuhrer had just demanded, the development of other hypotheses. This had been done many times before however, for various reasons, each new hypothesis was always rejected. The conclusion each time was to return to the "high speed hypothesis" because it was mathematically verifiable.

As Johanna and General Schneider walked toward the door, the Fuhrer, in almost an afterthought, said, "Oh General, may I speak to you for a moment?"

Johanna, who was passing through the doorway, walked into the hall and sat down just outside the meeting room. The door was partially open and she could hear Hitler speaking in a very low but excited tone. "General, I know you have been working very hard on this project and I commend you for all of your labors. We must clear up several points, however, General. First of all, I don't give a damn about the knowledge of the past and helping make mankind better. That fantasy is the exclusive property of the naïve Dr. Krause."

Johanna was not surprised to hear these words from Adolf Hitler. She never trusted him nor did she think his motives for creating a time machine were for the betterment of mankind. He had been playing Peter for a fool, just as she had suspected.

The door to the meeting room suddenly closed. Although Johanna could still hear the men talking, it was unclear what was being said.

Johanna had a feeling of deep foreboding. On several occasions she thought of the destructive potential of the Chronometric Teleporter if it were used as a weapon against mankind. But, she dismissed these concerns because she hoped that no one would ever use the time machine as a weapon. She also knew she was fooling herself.

The Furher dismissed General Schneider who then joined Johanna in the hallway. A brief glance at each other was all it took to communicate the concern and danger they both felt. As they were driven back to the airport, neither of them talked. Both sensed the danger they would unleash on the world if their project was successful.

They arrived at the airport and boarded the airplane for the flight back. Johanna was controlling her urge to confront General Schneider about his conversation with the Fuhrer. The General was a professional military man and she assumed he would say nothing about that discussion. But, she sensed the General seemed troubled and wanted to talk with her.

As the airplane lifted off the runway, General Schneider turned to Johanna and whispered, "Dr. Neisner, there are some things I must tell you, terrible things."

6

Offenbarung
(Revelation)

August 10, 1939

As the plane gained altitude, General Schneider looked at
Johanna and began to relate what took place in his closed door
meeting with Hitler. He told her Hitler said the Chronometric
Teleporter was not going to be a philosophical toy to provide
serenity for mankind. Instead, it would be used for the conquest of
the rest of the world to be dominated by the Aryan master race. "It
is to be used as a weapon," Hitler said. "Surely you are aware of the
military and political possibilities of such a weapon, General."

"Those are his exact words, Johanna. He also said, 'the
purpose of the Chronometric Teleporter is to allow us to alter the
events of history. We will go back into time and change the past
and, by so doing, we will change the future. We can conquer our
enemies without firing a shot. Can you not see the potential here,
General? The Chronometric Teleporter will be the ultimate military
weapon. Now do you understand why there is such urgency to have
it completed?"

"It is very disturbing, is it not?" General Schneider said.
"But, quite frankly Johanna, I don't believe it surprises either of us
to hear these are Hitler's true motives for wanting a time machine."

"You are right, General," Johanna replied. "I never believed
Hitler's promises on anything, let alone his sharing Peter's goals of
helping mankind. He's an evil man, General. I fear the worst as
long as he is in power."

"There is one other thing, Johanna," General Schneider
interrupted. "Hitler is very unhappy the project was not completed
within the four year deadline because Germany's neighbors are
threatening war."

Johanna noticed General Schneider spoke mockingly,
knowing very well it was Adolf Hitler who was pushing for war.

"I don't need to tell you that I am distressed to hear the Fuhrer actually speak these words," General Schneider continued, "even though we both these were his motives all along. You and Dr. Krause are good people caught in the whirlpool of a mad man's fantasies."

Johanna was shocked that General Schneider had spoken so frankly with her. "General, you are a professional military man and I appreciate how difficult it was for you to speak to me about this. I will say nothing of our conversation to anyone and I thank you for being honest with me. General, you also are a good man and I know your loyalties are to Germany and not the Nazi Party. We shall always be good friends, General. I pray for your future safety as well as Peter's and my own."

The talk of war was rampant and hung heavily over the entire country. Germany had completed the massive mobilization of its military though its peaceful neighbors posed no threat. General Schneider and other military leaders saw no reason to go to war, but the politicians were creating excuses for expansion and conquest.

General Schneider, though deeply upset after the meeting with the Fuhrer, had become greatly concerned about the immediate danger of war. Hitler's final comments to General Schneider before dismissing him added to the General's distress. "I need that Chronometric Teleporter, General, and I need it very quickly. You shall see why soon enough." General Schneider already knew why.

Two weeks later, on August 23, 1939, Germany and the USSR signed the German-Soviet Non-Aggression Pact which stated that the USSR would not defend Poland if Germany were to attack that country. On September 1, 1939, less than three weeks after General Schneider's August 10 meeting with Adolf Hitler, Germany invaded Poland. A few days later, Britain and France declared war on Germany. World War Two had begun.

7

Barbarossa

0400 hours, June 22, 1941

Poland-Belarus (U.S.S.R.) Border
North of The Pripet Marshes

Sergei Kaparov's lungs were searing with pain as he ran furiously down the remote, muddy country lane. The recent rainfall had made the road, little more than a wide path through the farms and woods, extremely slippery. It was late afternoon on June 22 and he knew the German invasion from the west would start at any time. On the previous day he left Bialystok, which was located approximately twenty-five miles west of the Polish/Belarus border. He had come nearly forty miles east and crossed over into Belarus in the darkness of the early morning. From Bialystok, he had gotten rides on trucks, horseback, horse drawn wagons, and walked. But now he was running. He was running as hard and fast as he could.

He heard from his friends that the Germans had mobilized huge forces and there were rumors Germany was going to invade Russia soon. In recent days, German reconnaissance units had boldly entered the Russian sector of Poland (In 1939, Germany and Russia had divided Poland between them under the Molotov-Ribbentrop Non-Aggression Pact). German reconnaissance units were also probing towns near the Poland Belarus border. The local population knew the attack was imminent, as did the Soviet troops stationed in the area. Joseph Stalin, however, had refused to believe there was going to be a German invasion and the bureaucracy straddled Soviet military had specifically not taken defensive measures in accordance with his direct orders.

Sergei, as well as everyone else in Bialystok, knew that nothing was being done by the Russian Army to stop the German attack. Sergei was also well aware of the brutality of the Nazi forces. Now, as he ran and slid down this little used rain slicked mud road, his only hope was that he could reach his father's farm before the invading Germans. He had to warn his family to find a hiding place before the attack. It was an eerie sensation as he frantically ran on the puddled dirt road which was still shining from the rain. He felt like his body was not moving forward but remained in one spot with his legs and arms wildly flailing in the air. However, the deep green trees on both sides of the road were flying by him. It was the trees which were moving it seemed, racing toward him and past him and then disappearing into the distance in back of him.

Sergei was startled by the muffled sound of car engines coming from the road behind him. No one ever uses this road, he thought to himself, as he instinctively bolted to his left and jumped over a water-filled ditch separating the road from the wooded area. He glanced to his left but could see nothing down the road from where he had come. He ran forward a few steps and threw himself to the ground behind some underbrush on the far side of a large tree. From there, he could clearly see the road and anything which would pass.

About a quarter mile behind him, there was a gentle curve in the road. The vehicles must be coming around that curve. The trees on the side of the road hid the vehicles from his view, but also shielded Sergei. The cars or whatever they were still hadn't rounded the corner.

The sound of engines was much louder now, and he could hear the splashing of water as tires thumped into the road's holes which formed the puddles. In a few anxious seconds, the vehicles making the sounds had nearly reached him. Germans! Six motor cycles followed by an open car with several officers and two large trucks loaded with soldiers rumbled by his hiding place. They were here. The invasion must have begun.

In fact, the German attack, Operation Barbarossa, had commenced at four a.m. This was one of the advance units of the German's Army Group Center. Sergei watched as the column passed fifteen feet from where he was hiding. He hoped this unit, which like him, was headed east, was not one of the mobile killing units he'd heard about.

He guessed his father's farm was seven miles away. He could run no faster. He had to stop and rest often, but not for long.

Finally, after nearly two hours, he was approaching his family's farm. The road curved to the right just before it reached the farm. The woods on the right side of the road offered a short cut and cover to hide his approach to the farm. He decided to take the short cut just in case the Nazis were in the area. Sergei left the road and trotted into the woods.

He couldn't run because the trees and undergrowth were so thick. In fifteen minutes he reached a slightly elevated point where the trees ended at the edge of his father's western field. The tidy field was covered with a healthy crop of wheat. From this point, he could see the farmhouse and the large wooden, unpainted barn. The Russian winters had turned the natural wood color of the barn dark gray within a few years of its construction.

As Sergei looked down at the farm site, his worst fears were realized. A group of soldiers from the German unit, which earlier passed him, was stopped in front of the house. One of the trucks and two of the motorcycles were parked at the side of the road. The rest of the detachment had continued up the road. Sergei counted more than a dozen soldiers milling around the front yard of the farmhouse. His entire family, his father Vitaly, mother Galya, two teenage sisters Gema and Biana and his little brother Georgy stood in a line with their hands raised in the air. Three German soldiers pointed rifles at them. The farm hand, Dimitry Kerensky, and his wife Lyeta also stood with their hands lifted. Sergei, who had no weapon, could do nothing but watch.

The three Nazi soldiers motioned the two men and his little brother Georgy to move over to their right, away from the women. As the three walked over five paces and stopped, the Nazi soldiers, one holding a tommy gun, started firing. The two men fell to the ground immediately however, Georgy turned and started running toward the barn. He was shot before he had gotten ten feet. Sergei held his mouth with both of his hands so he wouldn't scream. He pounded his head on the ground, still holding his mouth. He wished he had a weapon, even though he didn't know how to use a gun. He held himself in place, fighting the powerful urge to run across the field and try to save his family. But, he knew that he could accomplish nothing other than to be shot himself.

The next minutes would only worsen the nightmare. The four women were made to strip off their clothes and lie down on the ground on their backs. As his mother, sisters, and Lyeta were being repeatedly raped, other soldiers ransacked the house and set it afire. Then the barn was torched. The Nazis tried to set fire to the fields however, because it had rained, they were too wet to ignite.

As the soldiers finished with the women, they began to shoot them. His mother Galya was the first. The last soldier got up off of her and another soldier pointed a pistol at her and pulled the trigger. She was shot as she lay on the ground, sobbing and naked. Lyeta, like Georgy, tried to run. She started toward the western field in the direction where Sergei was hiding. She only got a few paces and several pistol shots brought her ravaged body to the ground. Sergei, his body shaking, was silently screaming and cursing into his hands which were cupped over his mouth so tightly his lips were cut and bleeding. His two sisters, Gema and Biana, were on their knees naked, pleading for their lives. He could see the Nazi soldiers laughing. An officer stepped forward with a pistol and fired his weapon twice, once at each girl.

Sergei, his hands still tightly cupped over his bleeding mouth, was sobbing into the floor of the forest. The little twigs and branches on the ground cut into his forehead and inflicted one larger gash which trickled blood into his eyes and over his face. He lay crying and shaking, afraid to look at the horrific carnage that once had been his family. He heard the truck's engine start up and he raised his head to see the Nazis depart. The two motorcycles rolled forward followed by the truck with the soldiers sitting in back facing each other.

Sergei didn't move for an hour. He lay on his back sobbing, looking up at the trees' tangled branches. Their dark leaves were blurred by the tears in his eyes. The forest's canopy seemed to be holding the swollen gray clouds like columns supporting a roof. The dark clouds threatened more rain. "Nothing good is coming from the west today," he bitterly mumbled to himself.

As rain began to fall, the dense roof formed by the tree branches captured the heavy drops and transformed them into countless, streaming drizzles which spattered on the ground and formed little puddles in the forest's floor.

Sergei, exhausted from his strenuous journey and the horrifying loss of his family, drifted into a tortured sleep as the rainwater fell from the trees to soak his clothes and wash the dirt and dried blood from his face.

****

Wet clothes and cold roused him and he awoke to darkness and the light of a full moon. The clouds had disappeared and the night sky was clear. Sergei had no idea what time it was. But, with the cover of darkness, he got to the task of taking care of the bodies of his murdered family.

Though only twenty-six, he struggled to stand. His body was stiff from the torturous run and long hours lying in the rain and cold. Easing his body forward, he walked out of the woods and began crossing his father's wheat field. He was trembling, dreading the task before him. In a few minutes he reached the east side of the field and walked onto the soaked grass area between the smoldering house and barn.

The women's naked bodies, shining silver in the glowing moonlight, appeared as angelic figures posed in a contorted portrait of evil. The rain had cleansed the blood from the small, deadly black circles where the bullets entered their bodies. Sergei wanted to cover the women, but there was nothing he could use as a temporary shroud. Everything had been burned by the Germans. All that remained of the house and barn were skeletons with their smoking wooden bones pointed at the sky.

He planned to dig seven graves but it was an impossible task for his weakened body. And he didn't have time for such a task because if the Germans returned, they would kill him too. As he stood near the bodies in front of the ruins of his home, he also realized the larger tools had been in the barn anyway. His only option was to burn the bodies.

The small wooden shed near the barn was not burned. Father kept his boots, gloves and a few tools in this building, including a hammer and nails for miscellaneous repairs. He also kept a can of kerosene for the lanterns. Sergei walked over to the shed and opened the door. The moon provided all the light he needed. He stepped in and picked up the five-gallon can of kerosene, which was nearly full. With bitter irony he thought, "This is the only good thing that happened today."

He retrieved large pieces of charred planks from the barn and house and built a platform inside the shed three feet above the floor.

55

He would place the bodies lengthwise on this shelf. He gathered other smaller pieces of wood and stacked as many as he could below the platform. He went out to collect the bodies, father and mother first, and laid them side-by-side on the platform. Then he collected little Georgy and the two girls, gently placing them side-by-side so the whole family was together. Lyeta and Dimitry were next. Everyone was together now, lying on the platform in the small shed.

Above the bodies he crisscrossed others planks to form a second platform on which he stacked more pieces of wood from the house and barn. He climbed to the roof of the small shed, bringing the can of kerosene with him. Using the heavy hammer, he knocked a hole in the center of the roof then poured the kerosene into the shed and climbed down to the ground. He had no matches so he walked over to one of the little fires which still burned in the remains of the house and pulled out a piece of flaming wood.

He began to cry again as he walked toward the shed holding the flaming stick of wood in his right hand. He was shaking with grief as tears streamed down his cheeks. The whole thing seemed a surreal ceremony.

He said a few words, prayers he invented. The flame on the piece of wood had become hotter as it burned closer to his hand and the ceremony abruptly ended. He threw the burning wood through the open door of the shed. The dense pile of kerosene soaked wood exploded with a loud puff and flames engulfed the shed.

As he stood looking at the fire burning his family's bodies, he promised "I will learn how to fight, to kill the men who did this. I will avenge these senseless murders and I will also kill Hitler." That was the mission he vowed to accomplish as he walked away from his father's farm.

****

He walked east on the road. Every farm he passed was a similar atrocity. Everyone was dead and many of the women lay naked, raped by the Nazi intruders. He stopped at a few farms to help a survivor bury his or her loved ones. But he left the rest of the bodies to the large black birds and snarling dogs which were pecking and chewing on the bullet riddled corpses.

He would no longer be a simple farmer. He would join the Russian army and become a soldier. He would learn how to shoot and kill. He would get even these with the barbaric invaders who killed everyone in their path. Across the western Soviet Union, the story continued to unfold. The Germans pressed the advantage of their surprise attack.

What Sergei and the rest of the Soviet Union did not know was this carnage was all in Hitler's plan which he long ago revealed to the world in Mein Kampf. The breadbasket of the Soviet countries was to be owned by prosperous Nazi farmers who would feed the Aryan Nation Hitler was building. The Russians themselves needed to be dealt with and pushed aside to provide needed breathing room and food for the Aryan expansion.

****

To that end, Operation Barbarossa was the largest military operation in history. The German invasion force's military assets numbered three million troops, six hundred thousand vehicles, thirty three hundred tanks, twenty eight hundred aircraft, seven thousand artillery pieces and over six hundred thousand horses. Approximately twenty five million Soviet citizens and military personnel would die in the invasion. From its inception, the operation was noted for its barbarity and lack of regard for the treatment of civilians as well as soldiers.

**Note: On August 31, 2009, in preparation for a visit to Poland, Vladimir V. Putin, Prime Minister of Russia, published an article calling the 1939 Molotov-Ribbentrop Non-Aggression Pact, which divided Poland between Germany and the Soviet Union "immoral." Mr. Putin declared this pact similar to the acquiescence of France and Britain (in the Munich Agreement of September 29, 1938) to the German invasion of Czechoslovakia.

8

Durchbruch
("Breakthrough")

May 20, 1943   Berlin

It was a beautiful May afternoon when Peter walked into Johanna's office. He didn't have any project business to discuss with her. He just needed a break and he suggested they go for a walk. She agreed, and soon they were outside enjoying the sunny Berlin afternoon. Another four years had passed, much too rapidly, it seemed. They had been working continuously for eight years on "Zeit Reisen Projekt" and still did not have even a modest proposal for a machine which would allow travel backward or forward in time.

There were no more meetings with Hitler now. Instead, due to the Fuhrer's increasing preoccupation with the War, General Schneider would brief Hitler on the project's status at irregular intervals. With the creation of the Tripartite Agreement, Germany, Italy, and Japan had become allies. The United States had declared war on Japan on December 8, 1941, the day after Pearl Harbor was attacked. On December 11, 1941, Germany and Italy declared war on the United States because they were allies of Japan. These onerous developments distracted the Fuhrer from his personal project of building a Chronometric Teleporter. As a consequence, there was less pressure from the Fuhrer on General Schneider and laboratory personnel.

Peter and Johanna, as well as the other one hundred and fifty people working at the secretive Berlin compound, had long since passed the point of burnout. The physical demands of the job as well as the mental stress had taken its toll. The simple fact was that people could not work at the intense pace indefinitely. Over the last eight years, there had been nine deaths of scientists whom were critical to the team's success. At least half of these deaths were due to the work schedule at the laboratory. There had also been five mental breakdowns.

Four years prior, just after General Schneider and Johanna briefed the Fuhrer on August 10, 1939, the working schedule at the laboratory had been cut back from twelve to nine hours per day and there were no more seven day work weeks. No one informed Hitler of this fact but, General Schneider, who would be the one to apprise Hitler of the reduced work schedule, knew there was no choice. If everyone died from overwork, there could be no success anyway.

Johanna had never told Peter about what she heard Hitler say to General Schneider regarding his real motives for building the Chronometric Teleporter. And she had asked the General to not tell Peter about his conversation with Hitler. She believed that withholding this information from Peter was critical in order to protect him. She knew that if he found out Adolf Hitler wanted to use the Chronometric Teleporter for a military weapon Peter would immediately terminate work on the project. Peter's doing so would endanger his life.

But, there was another reason she never told Peter of Hitler's true motives for building the Chronometric Teleporter. She felt there was no chance that the laboratory would ever succeed in building one. The technology needed for propulsion, heat resistant metal, and countless other requirements, was still non-existent. Even now, after eight years of excruciating effort, there had been virtually no progress.

But, that was about to change.

****

Peter and Johanna walked for fifteen minutes before returning to the laboratory. As usual, when Peter walked into his office, there were several phone calls to be returned and several people who "absolutely must see him immediately," as his secretary would say. General Schneider must see him about something. Dr. Becker had some kind of problem over in Propulsion. And, Dr. Monika Wagner in the Mathematics Group had been by his office twice in the last fifteen minutes.

"Dr. Monika Wagner," pondered Peter. "I wonder what in the world she wants." Peter knew she was an outstanding scientist and mathematician. She always completed her work expeditiously and thoroughly. She kept very much to herself and was an extremely hard worker. She would often stay at her office late into the evening. While there was some minimal social life in their compound, Monika had absolutely none. All she did was work, but she seemed to enjoy it. Peter was quite curious about why this woman, with whom he rarely spoke," needed to see him so urgently.

He knew that General Schneider probably wanted to discuss something of a routine administrative nature. He went next door to Johanna's office and asked her to see the General and also Dr. Becker. Peter instructed his secretary, Erna, to ask Dr. Wagner to come to his office.

Less than a minute later, Dr. Monika Wagner rushed into Peter's office. Monika was a rather plain looking woman with blue eyes that pierced and questioned. She was of average height and clearly didn't dress to please anyone but herself. She favored loose fitting dresses for their comfort but, as Peter's secretary continually pointed out, her slip was always hanging an inch or two below the hem of her dress. "She's far too sloppy to be a scientist," Erna insisted. Monika's blond hair never seemed to be in place either, which was another irritation for Erna.

Monika was soft spoken, but a very effective speaker. What little she did say always made a lot of sense. Peter remembered that on one of his few trips walking by her office, he happened to look in to tell her "hello." What he saw were stacks of papers on her desk, what seemed like a carpet of paper across her office floor, and a blackboard covered with a dizzying array of equations, formulas, arrows and lines drawn in every direction. There were papers tacked to the wall around the office. He remembered thinking that Erna had a point about Dr. Wagner's organization, or rather, disorganization.

"Come in Monika," Peter smiled. "How is it that I can help you today?"

"Dr. Krause, I am very excited about something which I have discovered."

Peter had many conversations of this nature with other colleagues. They had been working for eight years and many discoveries had been made. Countless new ideas had been formulated. New ground had been plowed, and so on. But, the main reason they were all working together was to develop a method to travel across time. No one in the laboratory had even begun to approach a solution to that challenge. Now, here was Monika, with another exciting discovery of interest to probably no one but her.

Peter was thinking how bored he had become running the laboratory. He still did his research, but too many of his precious hours were taken up with mundane things like personnel matters, meetings with General Schneider, planning meetings, and so on. This was not the life he planned for himself. He had become disillusioned with Hitler and hated the war Hitler started.

"Wonderful Monika," Peter replied, pretending to be interested. "Tell me what you have found." He knew he had to act like he was interested for reasons of morale.

"Well, Dr. Krause, as you know, we have repeatedly considered other possibilities to expand our thinking beyond the high speed hypothesis approach. But, every time we return to where we began with no solution. And then we go to the re-work phase, and end up yet again, with the high-speed hypothesis. We continuously return to where we started, but for different reasons. It is an endless circle of futility, Dr. Krause."

"Yes, Dr. Wagner," replied Peter. "I am painfully aware of that frustrating cycle which repeatedly ends with nothing. However, even though it has produced nothing, brainstorming alternatives for other hypotheses is all we have if we don't pursue the high speed hypothesis."

Dr. Wagner continued. "I have taken a different course than the rest of the team. I have done this on my own time, mind you. I mean, I completely supported the group and did my part every time we went through one of these laborious repetitions on the high-speed hypothesis. You see, my numbers and the rest of the data on that hypothesis are precise and correct. Nothing has changed in my data from one repetition of the high-speed hypothesis analysis to the next.

So, I finally concluded, to hell with it. This is a dead-end street. What I then decided, however, was to apply the same repetitive analyses method we had been using on the high speed hypothesis to one of the other hypotheses we had already put forward."

Monika paused, waiting for Peter to respond. "That's interesting, Monika," Peter acknowledged on cue, struggling to be enthusiastic.

Monika continued. "As you no doubt recall, Dr. Krause, in one of our brainstorming sessions we conjectured that specific points of time were defined by specific dimensions. Our conclusion for that opinion was that time is really many billions of dimensions arranged like the pages in a book. As you know, we named that the multi-dimensional hypothesis.

Peter nodded. "Yes, I remember."

"In re-analyzing that hypothesis however, I realized a very basic error in the working group's approach. While we had defined what time was, I mean, what time really consisted of, we had completely overlooked the cosmic referential delineation.

"Just a moment, Monika," Peter interrupted. What do you mean by the cosmic referential delineation?"

"I'm sorry, Dr. Krause. I should explain that."

"Yes, please do, Monika."

"What I mean by overlooking the cosmic referential delineation is that we did not establish a method by which we might reference specific time dimensions by quantitative designations or mathematically generated dimension descriptors. An example would be numbering the pages in a book.

In other words, how do we identify specific points of time in order that they correspond to specific years, such as they are defined by the Gregorian calendar which we presently use? I mean, the Gregorian calendar is a silly system. We all know the Gregorian calendar is a subjective, distracting reference inserted at a random point in cosmic time. From that perspective, it is completely irrelevant. However, we may continue to use it as long as we understand its limitations and that it is of no mathematical value in our hypothesis.

"Go on," said Peter, now becoming more interested in Dr. Wagner's monotone explanation.

"Using the multi-dimensional hypothesis developed by the working group, and developing a method to identify specific time dimensions, I made a remarkable discovery. We know there are trillions of radio waves continuously bombarding the earth and the rest of the universe. Radio waves are themselves the product of the juxtaposition of time and space and their ultimate intersection.

As such, each one of the trillions of radio waves is an essential component of time itself. Also, as the working group hypothesized, time is constant. All time exists at the exact moment of all other moments in time. Events which have happened in what is called "the past" or will happen in what is called "the future" are actually occurring now, in what is called "the present." The past, present and future all occur together at exactly the same moment but, in different dimensions."

"But, that is only a theory, is it not Monika?" he interrupted.

"I don't think so, Dr. Krause. What I discovered is that each dimension possesses its own specific radio frequency or time vector. Therefore, if a machine could be developed which would cross reference specific radio wave frequencies or time vectors with dimensions of time, then specific time dimensions would be identifiable. A vector enumeration calculator could be developed to categorize radio wave frequencies according to their specific period in time.

Then a vector transference module could transmit a radio signal at the specific frequency for the time vector, or time period targeted, and a portal would open into that dimension. Moving from one time period to another then would simply mean moving from one dimension to another. A person could simply step from their current time period into the new time period made accessible by the vector transference module.

"I'm listening, Monika," said Peter, realizing she might actually have something.

"Don't you see, Dr. Krause?" she said. "To move about in time, you must have two devices, a vector enumeration calculator and a vector transference module. Those are the essential components of a time machine, Dr. Krause. I have invented a Chronometric Teleporter, a time machine!"

"Yes, Monika," replied Peter, excitedly. "I think you are on to something very important. Did you carefully check your calculations?" he asked, although, knowing Monika Wagner, that question was unnecessary.

"Of course," she said. "I have re-checked them many times. And here is some more good news. A vector-enumeration-calculator can be developed very simply by using existing technology. This device would provide a specific radio wave length description to every possible time dimension. The smallest time descriptor would be the second.

A vector transference module is a little more complicated and must be invented. But, I am sure we can do that. Although a Chronometric Teleporter would be a fairly complex machine, it would be small enough to be carried in a suitcase. It would be powered by batteries, so it could be taken into other dimensions to enable the operator to return to our own time. The final details are challenging, but definitely achievable. The Applied Mechanics Group should get on this immediately and a completion date should be established.

Dr. Krause, I believe I've had a real breakthrough. The answer is so simple you cannot believe it. We don't need to accelerate to an impossible velocity to travel in time. We simply need to be able to step out of our own dimension and step into another."

Monika could see she had Peter's complete attention. "Please come with me to my office, Dr. Krause, and I will show you."

As Peter followed Monika out of his office door, he knocked on Johanna's open door and motioned to her to follow them. The next hour was spent in Dr. Wagner's office. "She's definitely got something here," Peter concluded.

"Monika, let Johanna and I take your data home tonight and we'll go over it once again. We'll meet with the full staff in the morning. I think you really have achieved a breakthrough. Thank you for all the time you have put in on this. We shall talk in the morning."

As they walked on the sidewalk toward their home, Johanna was tempted to tell Peter what Hitler said to General Schneider about his true reasons for wanting a time travel machine. But, as before, she was concerned for Peter's safety. She reassured herself that if he learned the truth about Hitler's motives, he would stop work on the project. And, she was certain that Peter would be in grave danger if he did so because this project was so important to Hitler. There was no question in her mind about that. Besides, she thought, they could never get a Chronometric Teleporter put together anyway, even if it was theoretically possible.

But, there was another reason she didn't think she needed to tell Peter about the Adolf Hitler-General Schneider conversation. The war was not going well for Germany. The invasion of Russia, while initially successful, had turned into a disaster. Hitler had ignored the advice of his generals and directed the invasion himself. All Hitler proved was his incompetence as a general. Unfortunately, he killed many millions of people in the process. Although Johanna realized Monika Wagner may have solved the time travel puzzle, Germany would most likely lose the war before a Chronometric Teleporter could be built. She again decided not tell Peter about what she heard Hitler say at the August 10, 1939 meeting. That time now seemed so long ago.

****

It was Friday, May 21, 1943. Johanna and Peter stayed up late the night before and completely analyzed Dr. Wagner's data. They could find nothing wrong with the calculations and conclusions. Peter had also instructed Erna to set up a full staff meeting for eight a.m., assuming Dr. Wagner's data checked out. The staff was now assembling as Dr. Wagner stood at the front of the meeting room organizing notes for her presentation. Attendees included General Schneider, Johanna, and all eight department heads. When Dr. Wagner completed the presentation of her results, the rest of the staff would then discuss the validity of her proposition and ask questions. If her conclusions were correct, the staff would then develop a plan for the next steps to be taken.

Dr. Wagner began the presentation of her findings. In a blunt admission, she reiterated what she had initially told Peter and Johanna. While she dutifully fulfilled her part of the numerous laboratory wide re-examinations of the high speed hypothesis alternative, she had long ago concluded that achieving time travel through this means was completely impossible, at least within their lifetimes. Therefore, she began developing propositions on her own. Dr. Wagner passed out a packet of her data to each member of the staff.

"What I am going to tell you," Dr. Wagner stated, "will initially not make any sense to you. However, you will see that the mathematics I present completely support the hypothesis and prove the theory. At first, I thought I made some kind of key error or fallacious assumption. But I have checked and re-checked the formulas, equations, and all of the numbers. The results are the same every time."

Dr. Wagner gave a comprehensive, convincing analysis of her findings. When she concluded her presentation the entire room, which initially was dumbfounded and silent, suddenly erupted in a standing ovation. The remainder of the meeting went very quickly as everyone was in complete agreement with Dr. Wagner's results. Each department was given specific assignments for their respective part of the plans for the design of a prototype Chronometric Teleporter. After eight years, Zeit Reisen Projekt was finally underway. The laboratory had now begun building an actual time machine.

9

Luftangriff
(Air Raid)

March 4, 1945   Berlin

Peter Krause's speeding car dodged mountains of rubble which once were buildings as it careened wildly through the bomb cratered Berlin streets. Before the phones went dead minutes earlier, Peter, Johanna, General Schneider and three scientists had arrived at the Fuhrerbunker to give Adolf Hitler a dramatic briefing. Final tests had been successful and the Chronometric Teleporter (time machine) was now operational. In less than two years, the laboratory had successfully produced three working machines.

However, Peter received a call from a friend at the Luftwaffe who told him intelligence reports indicated an American bombing raid would hit the laboratory in approximately half an hour. Before the conversation ended, the phone lines went dead. Because he could not call and warn them, Peter would drive to the laboratory and evacuate the staff. He told Johanna, General Schneider and the three scientists to stay at the Fuhrerbunker and brief Hitler.

Peter immediately left the Fuhrerbunker and began racing his car toward the laboratory. While the basement of the laboratory had been modified to act as a bomb shelter, Peter never thought it was completely safe. Besides, with the phones out, the one hundred and fifty member team might not get the warning in time if the air raid sirens failed to go off.

Up to this time, either because of Allied operational planning or just good luck, the laboratory had never been bombed. What made this fact even more incredible was that there was an airplane runway on the laboratory site. Peter was beginning to think the rumors about Adolf Hitler could be true. He seemed to have some supernatural connection which protected him from death. Was the fact that Hitler wanted the Chronometric Teleporter completed and had help from some "supernatural friend" the reason the laboratory had never been bombed? In a moment of gallows humor, Peter wondered about that possibility. But there was no time for that, he quickly concluded. He had to focus on his driving.

Actually, the facility with its runway had been on the "secondary target list" of many Allied bombing runs. However, the runway was so short it couldn't handle German bombers, and the tiny airport was so small, there was no room for a "staging area" for Luftwaffe fighter formations. Besides, aircraft activity at the laboratory had virtually ceased several years before. Only one or two planes a month now used the facility.

The building, which was once a hanger, had been converted to Peter's laboratory for building the Chronometric Teleporter. Allied aircrews were told not to bother bombing the facility because of its location in the middle of the city in a heavily fortified sector. Also, it had little military value and it wasn't worth exposing the bombers to the nearby flak towers with their 128 mm anti-aircraft guns.

But now, with the war ending, nothing was being spared. This was partly due to the fact that German air defenses had crumbled. The Luftwaffe was nearly obliterated by the loss of pilots and airplanes, neither of which the German military could replenish. Also, German factories had been bombed out of production and pilots were not being trained because there were no planes to fly.

Peter wanted to shut the project down many times before and move it out of the city because of the danger of aerial raids, but Hitler would not hear of it. In fact, he absolutely forbade it. He needed the Chronometric Teleporter and that was the number one priority. And he wanted the project to stay where it was because his Fuhrerbunker was also in Berlin. If the war went badly, which it had, the Fuhrerbunker was Hitler's last refuge. If the Chronometric Teleporter were completed, Hitler would be able to access it and escape.

As Peter raced his car past the destroyed buildings and hills of wreckage in the streets, he tried in vain to avoid the smaller pieces of debris so densely scattered they might as well have been grains of sand on the beach. The car's tires ran over broken bricks, wood, and other chunks of devastation, throwing them upward to strike the underside of the car with solid thumps. They were occurring with such regularity that Peter imagined the constant thump, thump,

thump sounded like the car's second engine. "How long before I get a flat tire?" he wondered.

Suddenly, Peter slammed the brake pedal down while simultaneously pushing in the clutch with his left foot as he came to a main intersection he could barely recognize. The street on which he was traveling west was blocked by rubble on the other side of the junction with the street running north to south. His only choice was to turn left and go south to try to get around the mountain of destruction. He punched the accelerator with his right foot and released the clutch sending the car whirling around the corner.

"My god!" he screamed, as he immediately stomped on the brake pedal.

An American B-17 bomber was flying directly toward his car! When he slammed on the brake he killed the car's engine. He was so shocked to see the huge plane coming toward him he neglected to push in the clutch. He frantically tried to re-start the car but immediately abandoned that effort, throwing the door open and leaping from the driver's seat. He fell into the litter on the street.

He jumped to his feet and began running, looking back toward the plane just before he darted around the corner from which he had just come. The plane was less than a half-mile away but, it was coming fast. The pilot struggled to keep the plane in the air as its thunderous engines roared like a primitive beast in its death throes. But, the plane would crash onto the street in front of his stalled car in seconds. He thought the plane was going to drop bombs on the already devastated area around him until he saw smoke pouring from the two engines on its left wing. "Either flak or the Luftwaffe must have gotten it," he thought.

He had furiously sprinted past a half block of mangled buildings when the earth heaved violently beneath his feet. A tremendous explosion roared through the canyons of ruined buildings and twisted vehicles as the airplane crashed and its bomb load and gasoline tanks exploded simultaneously. The monstrous blast leveled buildings and walls, sending out an immense concussion, which collapsed even more structures.

Peter was thrown to the ground, landing in the doorway of what had been a department store. As he lay on the sidewalk, the covered doorway of the building provided a partial shield as debris rained down on him. The ground continued to shake as buildings around him collapsed inward or fell onto the street. He thought he felt the wall sway as he lay next to it.

He didn't go back to his abandoned car because he knew it had been destroyed. There was no way he could get to the laboratory now. It was still four miles away and he had no car. As he walked east re-tracing the route he had just traveled, he heard the explosions begin as the American aircrews dropped their lethal cargoes. He knew the laboratory was being struck at this very moment. He hoped his friends at the laboratory got the warning in time and would be safe in the modified basement bomb shelter.

There had been Allied bombing strikes near the laboratory before, two of them causing minor damage. Prior to this day, the laboratory had been only a secondary target for Allied bombing missions. However, because it was located at a former German Army base with an airstrip, it was finally upgraded to a primary target. The other reason for this upgraded target status was that there were fewer primary targets left as most of them had already been destroyed. On this day, there were many Allied bombing missions over Germany. Over two hundred total airplanes were destroyed, nearly three fourths of them German.

The personnel working at the laboratory felt relatively secure as the increasing air raids and artillery strikes blasted targets near the facility. The designated bomb shelter for the laboratory was the basement underneath the massive facility. Whenever an air raid siren sounded, all personnel would proceed directly to the four stairwells and descend into the basement converted to a bomb shelter. While the government had begun building bomb shelters in the city before 1939, only a percentage of the number planned had ever been completed. The basement was not an actual bomb shelter structure but it had been reinforced to supposedly withstand explosive strikes. It had been certified by the Interior Ministry as being capable of withstanding a concentrated bombardment.

On this early morning bombing raid the laboratory complex was bombed. While the air raid sirens gave ample time for laboratory personnel to move to the bomb shelter, a B-17 dropped its entire six thousand pound bomb load straightaway on the facility. The multiple direct strikes obliterated the laboratory and blew in its floor, which was the roof of the basement bomb shelter. The entire one hundred and fifty-person laboratory group was killed instantly.

The exploding bombs set off a raging firestorm, which consumed the entire laboratory complex and buildings immediately surrounding it.

Peter, Johanna, General Schneider and the three scientists were all that remained of the laboratory team. Had they not gone to meet with Adolf Hitler in the Fuhrerbunker that morning, they too would have died in the bombing raid. Peter lost many good friends that day. They were people he had worked with for ten years. They were good people, brilliant people. Although Peter had repeatedly asked, Hitler would not let him move the complex to the countryside because it would cost too much time. Now, the laboratory was destroyed and the people who worked in it were dead. Peter would never recover from this tragedy. And he had come to hate Adolf Hitler, even more than he did before.

Peter, Johanna, the three scientists and General Schneider were distraught that their long time friends had been killed. It made no difference to Hitler, however. He was driven by sheer panic, perhaps madness. The war was coming to an end and Germany's defeat was certain. He vowed to continue the Third Reich.

General Schneider found a house in the residential section of Berlin where he, Peter, Johanna and the three scientists could stay. Also, German planners had long made a point of trying to predict which sites had the greatest likelihood of being targeted for Allied bombing. It was this information which led the SS Commandant at the laboratory to establish the nightly procedure of moving all new information and the Chronometric Teleporters to a different, safer location each evening. His caution had paid off. While the entire laboratory team was killed, all the records, blueprints and the three Chronometric Teleporters had been saved.

10

Fuhrerbunker

April 30, 1945   Berlin

"Good morning, General Schneider, and Dr Krause," came the stern faced greeting from the young German Army guard standing at the meeting room door in the Fuhererbunker.

Peter, Johanna, General Schneider and the three scientists had been summoned to the Fuhrerbunker for a special meeting with Hitler this morning at ten thirty. The war would end within days, perhaps hours. Hitler and his closest confidantes had retreated to the safety of their underground command post in January and remained there since.

Peter nodded, unable to force a smile. Although nearly two months had passed, he was still grieving over the deaths of his friends and the destruction of the laboratory. He was pondering what had led Germany to this time and place. He was sick about the role he had played, and his naïveté in believing in Adolf Hitler. He was sick of the war, the daily bombings, the air raid sirens and the destruction of the city. He was sick of it all.

He was reflecting on the German military defeats and other events that happened in the last year. On June 4, 1944, Allied Forces defeated the Germans and captured Rome. Paris was liberated by the Allies on August 25, 1944. On January 12, 1945, the Russian offensive in Eastern Europe began. Hitler, seeing that the end was near, moved to his underground bunker on January 16. On March 19, Hitler issued his "Nero Decree" which ordered the destruction of Germany's infrastructure. All transportation, communication, industrial and military complexes were to be demolished. Two weeks earlier on April 16, the Russians launched the Battle of Berlin.

It was now April 30, 1945. The situation had long since passed the point of hopelessness for the Nazi's. An atmosphere of foreboding haunted the Fuhrerbunker from the very first day. A murky shroud of depression thickened the air, making every breath a conscious effort. The Fuhrerbunker's dispirited inhabitants, senior staff, doctors and security people, walked through the doomed headquarters in a trance- like slog, their faces reflecting the grave situation. Even Hitler's dog Blondi seemed to sense the gloom.

For the first two months after moving to the Fuhrerbunker, Adolf Hitler also seemed distressed by the grim predicament. Although an optimist in public, he turned inward and appeared aged and desperate. His perpetually round shoulders seemed even more so as they sagged under the gravity of what had occurred and what was to come. As he passed people in Fuhrerbunker he would smile and greet them, however, his eyes acknowledged the inevitable annihilation, the extinguishment of the Third Reich and himself. He knew he had orchestrated the deaths of tens of millions of people, destroyed countries, cities, and caused immeasurable suffering.

Outwardly, Hitler was downtrodden, portraying himself as the victim of his generals' incompetence. That he was in profound denial was evident to all but him. It was Hitler who ignored sound military strategies and overruled his generals. He refused to listen to their advice not to attack the Soviet Union. He ignored their warnings in the execution of the Barbarossa strategy. This critical miscalculation by Hitler was the turnaround point for the Germans and they suffered a catastrophic defeat by the Russian winter and ultimately the Russian army.

Strangely, in the last few weeks, Hitler's temperament became pleasant and confident. He was no longer depressed nor concerned about his future prospects. On several occasions, he was actually light-hearted, even giddy. It made no sense to the people around him unless, of course, he was losing his mind. But, Peter knew otherwise. Hitler planned to escape using the Chronometric Teleporter.

Along with Adolf Hitler, there were forty other people living in the Fuhrerbunker. While panic had not set in, a siege mentality and the inevitability of defeat had. The constant artillery explosions were affecting the mental state of the inhabitants of the Fuherbunker. Their fear was increasing but no one talked of it. Everyone put on a brave face, but then retreated to private quarters to drink enough to maintain their courage. Some of the lucky ones received "relaxant medicine" from the doctors.

The plush surroundings of the underground complex had been sequestered from the now demolished Chancellery buildings. Expensive paintings, magnificent sculptures and lush carpets intended to exude confidence and hope were an appalling failure, unable to improve the mood in the doomed complex. The grand trappings of former power instead conspired in an eerie counterplot to create a haunted museum whose occupants were living ghosts of a deceased empire.

Of the fifteenth century masterpieces hanging in the bunker's main hallway, one watercolor in particular was noticeably inappropriate, if not bizarre. "The Rape of Adena," a favorite of the Fuhrer, was an odd composition featuring a young woman with her clothing partially ripped away exposing her breast. The woman's grief-stricken blue eyes impart her savage defilement and she struggles to steady her right arm and point an accusatory finger outward at her attacker. The viewer's reflection in the painting's glass cover forces self-reflection, and a feeling that he is the assailant at whom she points.

Because of the painting's location in the main hallway, everyone in the Fuhrerbunker walked past the masterwork daily. Adena was a constant reminder that they themselves were the perpetrators of their own misery. They would look away as they passed the painting which presumed the role of their collective conscience.

As Peter, Johanna, General Schneider and the three scientists stood deep within the bunker waiting for the Fuhrer and Martin Bormann to summon them, Peter could hear explosions from Russian artillery fire and American bombs. Before the explosions started a few weeks ago, other than people working in the Fuhrerbunker, the only sound that could be heard was the continuous humming of the ventilation system. It was a monotonous, whirring-sound which annoyed Peter immensely, though he didn't know why. But now, the drone of the ventilation system was punctured by the explosions. That he could still hear the system's dull buzzing provided a false security.

Eleven days earlier on April 19, the Russians were surrounding the city. At first, the explosions were erratic. But, as the German defenses caved, the explosions became more frequent as the Russians drew nearer the Fuhrerbunker.

Peter, Johanna, General Schneider and the three scientists had been working in a location near the bunker since the March 4th air raid destroyed the laboratory. Peter missed his friends and carried a survivor's guilt that he had lived while they died. He also felt guilty he had not reached the laboratory in time to evacuate the people before the bombing. And, he tortured himself that he had been unable to persuade Hitler to allow him to move the laboratory and its one hundred and fifty scientists to a location outside of the city. And the last ten years of his life had been wasted. All the hard work and sacrifices of the laboratory team were in vain. Peter knew the end was near. The Russians would reach the bunker soon, perhaps within hours.

****

On several occasions, Johanna was tempted to tell Peter about the Fuhrer's real intentions for the Chronometric Teleporter, but she always resisted. She continued to be very concerned for his safety. However, Peter himself, even though he was always the naïve, trusting idealist, had become disillusioned with the Fuhrer in late 1942. He suspected the Fuhrer had other uses in mind for the time machine.

Because the top-secret laboratory was isolated from the rest of the world, the news that did filter in had never been timely and was often unreliable. As everyone was pre-occupied with building the Chronometric Teleporter and time travel, little attention was paid to the infrequent news that found its way into the complex.

However, there had been rumors of mass killings of Jews since the 1940's. At first, Peter did not let himself believe they were true. Although the information he heard was filtered and untimely, the continuous rumors became credible. In 1942 Peter began to pay closer attention to them.

The Fuhrer, the man who said he would do so much for humanity, had become the devil himself. With the war well underway, millions of people were being killed as a result of Hitler's actions. He was killing Jews by the hundreds of thousands, perhaps millions. Peter finally concluded that the Fuhrer, the man in whom he had placed so much faith, was in fact the personification of evil. He kept this opinion to himself however, because if he told anyone, especially Johanna, they might react by speaking out or leaving the project, either of which would be a very dangerous, perhaps fatal, thing to do.

Ironically both Johanna and Peter were protecting each other by not sharing their thoughts on the Fuhrer. Since they were under close scrutiny by General Schneider and the SS, they had no choice but to maintain a reasonable work pace at the laboratory and continue building the Chronometric Teleporter. While Peter's original participation in building the Chronometric Teleporter had been "somewhat voluntary," at least that's what he told himself that for the last ten years, his involvement as well as that of everyone else's, was now clearly mandatory. No one ever said as much but, everyone working in the laboratory well understood the atmosphere changed dramatically as Germany suffered repeated setbacks in the war.

But now, as Peter and the others stood at the entrance to the meeting room, he knew that without a doubt, the end had arrived. The Chronometric Teleporters were operational and Hitler could use one of them to escape into time. Plans were made to be transported to South America to the year 2010. Peter was not told of the specific country, however. That information was only for Adolf Hitler and Martin Bormann.

Perhaps it was his imagination but, for the last several weeks, Peter felt he was out of favor with General Schneider and possibly Hitler himself. For this reason, he was apprehensive about the meeting with the Fuhrer. Peter wondered if Hitler suspected that he long ago lost respect for him, even hated him. Peter had done his best to conceal his true feelings. Hitler would think nothing of killing him or Johanna. He knew he must be very careful.

Peter realized Hitler must escape before the Russians captured the Fuhrerbunker. There was little time left. Everyone in the underground facility knew how much the Russians hated Adolf Hitler and the Germans because of the atrocities they committed during their invasion of Russia.

****

In the closing days of the War, Berlin had become a madhouse. With the Russian Army on the outskirts of the city and food and fuel scarce, panic overtook Berlin and the entire country. There was no way out of the city now. The airports ceased to operate. It would be suicide to try to escape by air anyway as the

Allied air forces controlled the air space. There were a few cars outside the bunker, but the Russians controlled all the roads. The desperation in the bunker was evident. People knew they should have made their escape earlier, but Hitler had not permitted anyone to leave.

Everyone in the bunker was concerned for their safety but, also for a way to keep alive the Nazi ideal of world domination. But, it was obvious there were no options. Within hours, everyone would either be dead or a prisoner of the Russians.

As Peter and the others stood outside the entrance to the meeting room, they heard the Fuhrer screaming and raving. Peter moved away from the door, preferring to hear explosions of Soviet shells rather than Hitler's voice.

Suddenly, the meeting room door swung open and Peter, Johanna, General Schneider and the three scientists were summoned inside. There was complete silence as Hitler told the group what they knew already, the situation was hopeless and escape seemed impossible. However, in what was a shock to everyone, he told them there was a way out. He then introduced Peter, and said, "Dr. Krause, please tell the group of our plan."

Peter began to speak, slowly at first, but then more rapidly as he detailed the escape plan for Hitler's closest confidantes, generals and scientists. Peter told the group that, for the last ten years, he had been working on a highly secret project known only to him, the laboratory staff and the Furher and Martin Bormann. His project was to invent a machine, a device that science fiction writers had only imagined. He must develop a machine which would allow people to go forward and backward in time. There was a collective gasp of astonishment in the room when Peter told the group that he had completed this invention. And, while all the details were not yet ironed out, this machine could be used for their immediate escape. The entire room burst into applause, sighs of relief and laughter.

"There was one condition however," Peter told them. "Those who wish to escape forward in time would not be permitted to go backward in time to the present."

"Dr. Krause," one of the generals interrupted, "if I understand correctly, you are telling us that if we escape by going forward in time, we can never return to our present time and lives."

Adolf Hitler decided to address that question. "Yes, that is correct, General," Hitler replied. "There is a logical reason you can never return to the present time," he added. "Our escape must remain completely secret. The plan must never be compromised. There is a risk that could happen if someone returns from the future to the time in which we are now living. We could be prevented from ever leaving. Have I made myself clear?"

"Yes, my Fuhrer," the General replied, his voice sounding somewhat confused.

"Everyone in this room is one of my highly trusted confidantes," the Fuhrer continued. "I have chosen to include you in my ambitions for a re-birth of the Nazi ideal. Since you have all been apprised of our secret plan, I must insist you go forward with us to begin our new agenda."

"My Fuhrer," the general asked, "what if we wish to stay behind and take our chances with the Russians?"

It was the wrong question to ask. "If any of you choose to remain behind and not escape with the rest of the group, I would need to assure myself you could never tell anyone of our means of escape or our plan."

Everyone in the room knew what that meant. They had little choice in the matter. They would either agree to go or be shot. By escaping, they would at least stay alive. The other staff people who were not included in the group of seventy-two people in the meeting room would remain in the bunker. The SS would begin transporting people through the time machine immediately.

To maintain total secrecy, no one was permitted to leave the meeting room or gather belongings. It was forbidden to talk to anyone in the bunker who was not included in the meeting. Everyone was assigned to a group, which would walk directly from the meeting room to the adjacent room when they were to be transported. Peter completed his presentation and Adolf Hitler and Martin Bormann walked out of the room.

****

What Peter did not know was that the SS had been using one of the Chronometric Teleporters every night for the last four weeks. Over this period, they had transported a huge cache of weapons, a large quantity of gold, and a thousand hand picked officers and soldiers from the S.S. and the army's elite units. They had obtained a large tract of land in the South American country of Tierra Verde, exactly sixty-five years from the present time in the year 2010. Although they would initially live in tents, buildings and housing were being constructed.

The Chronometric Teleporters were suitcase sized and could be carried like a piece of luggage. They were in shiny black metal cases, approximately two feet wide by two feet in length, with a depth of just over one foot. Each weighed about seventy-five pounds. The Chronometric Teleporter they were using for their escape would be transported with them. The other two Chronometric Teleporters had already been sent to Tierra Verde.

The seventy-two people to be transported included fifty SS men who had come to the Fuhrerbunker that morning. Because the room holding the machine was small, the SS assigned each person to a small group of fifteen people. Everyone would go according to the group into which they had been assigned. By their choice, Adolf Hitler, Eva Braun and Martin Bormann, would be in the second last group by themselves. Johanna, General Schneider, and two scientists from the laboratory would go in the first group. Peter, the third scientist and a half dozen SS guards would be the last to go. Their turn would not be long in coming.

Each successive group left the meeting room and walked down the hall to the office housing the Chronometric Teleporter. The explosions from the Russian artillery had become much louder and more constant. The Soviet troops were reported to be only a few hundred yards from the Fuhrerbunker. It would not be long before the Fuhrerbunker was breached.

Now, only Peter, the scientist and the six SS guards remained in the meeting room. Everyone else had been transported. An officer Peter didn't recognize, Colonel Andreas Kohler, came into the meeting room. Colonel Kohler was a serious looking man approximately forty years old with a pale, gaunt face. Even with the Third Reich crashing down around him, he was impeccably dressed and professional. He looked squarely at Peter.

"You will come with me, Professor Krause," he stated bluntly, with no pretense of emotion.

Peter was shocked by this unexpected development, but he followed Colonel Kohler out of the meeting room and down the main hallway with its priceless paintings. They passed "The Rape of Adena" and soon reached the doorway to Hitler's private quarters.

Colonel Kohler, who was standing in front of Peter, slowly pushed the door open to reveal the brighter lights of Hitler's study. Peter had never been to this part of the bunker before. He followed as Colonel Kohler stepped into the room. On the far side of the modest sized study, Adolf Hitler, the Fuhrer, was slumped on the couch, blood running down his cheek and dripping onto the lapels of his tan uniform. A pistol lay on the floor by his feet. To his left, Eva Braun's body lay against the back of the couch, without a mark on her body. Both of them were obviously dead.

Peter was shocked and confused by the scene. "What is this, Colonel Kohler?" Peter asked. "I myself just saw Adolf Hitler and Eva Braun walk through the Chronometric Teleporter to a different time in the future. Besides, I know the Furher well and this is not his body."

"You are correct, Dr. Krause," Colonel Kohler replied. "These bodies are the look-alike doubles used by Adolf Hitler and Eva Braun. However, you and I must convince the people remaining in the Fuhrerbunker that Adolf Hitler and Eva Braun committed suicide and these bodies are their remains. There must be no question that the Fuhrer is dead. Do you understand?"

Peter realized what Colonel Kohler was doing. He was covering up Hitler's escape by making it look like he and Eva Braun committed suicide. Peter waited in the room with the bodies while Colonel Kohler went to find witnesses who would verify these were the bodies of Adolf Hitler and Eva Braun. He soon returned with half a dozen people, including two doctors.

As the six people stared at the bodies, several began to cry, realizing the Nazi dream had indeed come to an end. The others just stared blankly at the two dead people.

"When the Russian troops come, you will tell them the Fuhrer died honorably, by his own hand," Colonel Kohler said. The six people nodded they understood, too shocked by the Fuhrer's death to question whether it really was his body lying on the bloodstained couch.

After they left, Colonel Kohler said, "I suggest you go back to the meeting room and make your escape before it's too late, Dr. Krause."

Peter quickly decided that there was nothing else to do. The time of the Nazi's had passed. Johanna had gone forward in time and he needed to join her. Hitler and the remnants of his once mighty regime had escaped. Peter followed Colonel Kohler to the room with the Chronometric Teleporter. The six SS soldiers and the scientist were waiting for them. As Peter entered this room, the Chronometric Teleporter's blue-orange pulsating threshold, five feet in height and three feet wide, hovered a foot above the ground. Peter stepped to the side and motioned to Colonel Kohler to go through first.

"I shall not be going, Dr. Krause," he said, surprising Peter.

"Alright," said Peter, who then motioned for the six guards to go through before him. "I shall be the last to leave," he told them. The words had barely left his mouth when Peter felt a sharp pain on the back of his head. He slumped, and the floor was coming fast toward his face.

11

Nazistischer Morder
Nazi Killer

0300 Hours, May 2, 1945   Berlin (Potsdamer Bridge)

"What do you have here, corporal?" an exhausted Major
Sergei Kaparov asked the young soldier.

The answer was obvious. Corporal Mihailov was holding his
rifle on Colonel Andreas Kohler of the German Army.

"I picked up this colonel near the Potsdamer Bridge, Major.
I thought you might have a use for him" replied the corporal.

Sergei Kaparov, now Major Kaparov, had joined the Soviet
Army on June 23, 1941, the day after the Germans launched
Operation Barbarossa to invade the Soviet Union. It was also the
day after Sergei lay in the woods watching German soldiers kill his
family after they raped his mother and sisters. On that day, he
vowed to kill every Nazi he possibly could. He joined the army to
learn how to do so.

The limited training he received didn't hinder his abilities as
a warrior, however. The Soviet Army taught him how to use a gun
and when to take cover. That was all he needed. From his very first
day in action, he was a ferocious fighter. In a short time, his exploits
on the battlefield became legendary.

In his first weeks in battle, his reputation was launched.
Screaming like a mad man, he single-handedly charged up a hill and
captured a German machine gun emplacement killing half a dozen
German soldiers in the process. The Germans were firing the
machine gun at him but couldn't find their target before the gun
jammed. As they struggled to get the gun back in operation, Sergei
stormed over the revetment shooting and stabbing the horrified
soldiers.

For this act of insanity which Sergei's commanding officer
called heroism, he received a medal for bravery and a promotion,

neither of which he cared about. In fact, he resented the time he was forced to be away from the fighting to receive the medal.

There were many more heroic exploits as his commanders called them. But, he was not fighting for his country or trying to become a hero. He was driven by the constant nightmares of his family being killed. Every night he woke up screaming as his family was murdered in his dreams again and again.

His fearlessness inspired other Russian soldiers around him. They would follow him anywhere, even before they would follow their own officers. Despite fighting in some of the most deadly battles and daily exposure to artillery and rifle fire, he was never wounded seriously enough to be out of action for more than a few hours.

"Patch me up, medic" became the phrase by which he was known. While some soldiers allowed their wounds to keep them away from the battle, Sergei Kaparov ignored the pain and went back into action. Over the last four years, he was frequently promoted and soon reached the rank of major.

He had a darker name by which he was also known, "The Nazi Killer." He rarely took prisoners, preferring to kill his enemies in the fighting. Despite his reputation, he did have some scruples. He did not allow himself to shoot unarmed or disabled men. However, on the battlefield, his fierce efforts were focused on the total annihilation of the enemy. His intent was to kill them all if he could.

Now, as Major Sergei Kaparov stood in the early morning darkness of devastated Berlin, he had to decide what to do with this Nazi colonel. The young Corporal Mihailov assumed that he was doing Major Kaparov a favor by bringing him the colonel. He assumed Kaparov would take pleasure in shooting Colonel Kohler.

A few hours earlier, the Germans had requested a ceasefire and a meeting with the Soviets at the Potsdamer Bridge. While it was not yet announced, the rumor was that German General Helmuth Weidling would unconditionally surrender the city to General Vasily Chuikov of the Soviet Army. The Battle of Berlin was over. The colonel now held prisoner by the young corporal was captured several blocks from the bridge a few hours later, at 0300 hours.

"I knew you'd want to shoot him personally, Major," Corporal Mihailov announced proudly. "So I brought him to you."

After four years of savage fighting, however, Sergei Kaparov had become sick of the killing and the senseless destruction of towns and cities. He long ago stopped counting how many Germans he had killed. But he kept on killing, more and more of them. The cease-fire at 0100 hours seemed to act as a cathartic switch in his brain, abruptly shutting down his desire to fight and kill any longer. "This madness had to end sometime and the time is now," he thought to himself.

Besides, it was Adolf Hitler that Sergei Kaparov wanted to kill. He was not interested in this colonel. But, it had been reported that Hitler was already dead. Sergei had gotten so close to his final objective. He was only blocks from the Fuhrerbunker and Adolf Hitler had committed suicide, depriving Sergei of the pleasure of killing him. He actually doubted he could ever reach Hitler anyway. He assumed that Adolf Hitler would be killed in the fighting or that someone else would kill him first.

"Can I watch while you shoot him, Major?" the corporal asked.

"Hitler is dead. The War is over," Sergei replied. "Aren't you tired of killing? Besides we are under a cease-fire, corporal."

"But Major, I still hear shooting, the corporal said."

"I know, corporal. I shall talk to the colonel then I'll decide on whether or not to shoot him."

The corporal, disappointed there would not be immediate execution, lowered his rifle to his side.

"Corporal, why don't you get a cup of coffee? If I decide to shoot the colonel, I will call you," Kaparov said.

Looking directly at the captive colonel, Major Kaparov asked, "What is your name?"

"I am Colonel Andreas Kohler of the German Army, Major."

"You mean the Nazi Army, Colonel, do you not?"

"No Major, I mean the German Army," the colonel replied.

"I guess I don't know the difference, Sergei replied."

"There is a great difference, Major," Colonel Kohler said. 'I was a career German Army officer before the Nazis ever existed. Many of us in the German Army have long hated the Nazis. In fact, some of us tried to kill Hitler ourselves."

"I think you are telling me this so I won't shoot you, Colonel," Kaparov responded.

He actually had no intention of shooting the colonel anyway. Besides the fact that he no longer wanted to kill anyone, the orders were to apprehend all German soldiers in the vicinity and hold them for interrogation. But, he would not tell the colonel that. He would see what he could find out from him.

"Major, the corporal has informed me of your reputation. I assume you are going to kill me anyway, cease-fire or not," Colonel Kohler stated bluntly.

"Perhaps I will," replied Kaparov.

"It actually makes little difference to me whether I live or die, Major. My family was killed and my home destroyed and I have nothing left anyway," Colonel Kohler responded bitterly.

Mindful of his own losses, Sergei Kaparov remembered how he had gotten to where he was today. If he chose, he could kill the colonel and no one would really care. But, he had never killed anyone in cold blood. His killing had always been done in battle. And now, he had no intention of killing this man who suffered the same loss of family he himself had endured four years earlier.

"But, you would prefer to live, would you not?" replied Kaparov.

"Yes, I suppose I would."

"Well, maybe we can strike a deal, Colonel."

Colonel Kohler smiled, "I'm afraid I have little to offer you, Major Kaparov."

"You can tell me nothing about Hitler?"

"I can tell you he is dead."

"I know that already," said Kaparov. "I must turn you over for interrogation. It would be better if you told me what you know. They will be much rougher on you."

"Major, I am convinced you are going to kill me. But, there is nothing I can tell you which will save my life. I wish there was."

For the first time in four years, Major Sergei Kaparov felt empathy, faint at first, but, somewhere inside his soul there were emotional stirrings. He hadn't had such feelings for so long he'd forgotten what they were. Suddenly he felt sympathy, maybe even a fondness for this man who had suffered the same fate he had endured.

In an uncharacteristic gesture, Sergei Kaparov said, "Colonel, I'm going to release you. I will take you to where you will be safe and let you go."

"You are probably taking me somewhere to shoot me," responded the colonel. "Why would you release me?"

"Because, I lost my family in this damned war just as you did. I'm sick of war. Now that it's over, maybe some sanity will return to the earth."

Colonel Kohler could see by the expression on Major Kaparov's face that he meant to do exactly as he said.

"There are still some good men, Major. You are one of them. I thank you."

Sergei had Colonel Kohler get into a truck and told Corporal Mihailov that he was taking the colonel to another sector for interrogation. The corporal winked and with a knowing look said, "Shoot him once for me, Major."

It took nearly an hour to travel only a few miles in the city because of the impassable streets piled high with the wreckage of buildings, houses and vehicles. The streets were dark because there was no electricity nor were there any street lights standing after the barrage of artillery fire and aerial bombing. Blown up tanks and upended military vehicles from both the Soviet and German armies were strewn about the city. Unburied corpses littered the streets, having lain for days where they had fallen.

Colonel Kohler had given Sergei Kaparov the directions to a friend's home on the outskirts of the city. He would be safe there.

As they pulled into the driveway, Sergei said, "Get some civilian clothes from your friend and I will take your uniform with me. That way, if our army should decide to search the house, there will be no evidence of who you are."

Colonel Kohler hurriedly walked up to the door of the modest frame house and knocked on the door. His friend and the man's wife embraced Colonel Kohler and he went inside. He returned in a few minutes with his folded uniform, which he handed to Major Kaparov.

"Major, I cannot imagine why you have given me this kindness but I sincerely thank you once again," Colonel Kohler said.

"Good luck, Colonel," replied Sergei. "Maybe we can meet again sometime and have some of your German beer."

"We'll make it a point to do that," responded Colonel Kohler.

"Very well, Colonel, and goodbye," said Major Kaparov as he put the truck in reverse and turned his head to back the truck out of the driveway.

"Major Kaparov, wait a moment," Colonel Kohler whispered. "There is something I wish to tell you. Please, turn off the engine."

Puzzled, Sergei did as the colonel requested and turned off the truck's ignition switch.

"Do you mind if I get back in the truck, Major?"

"No, that's fine," replied Sergei, as the Colonel opened the door to climb into the vehicle.

"Major, you have shown me a great kindness. You could have killed me without any fear of punishment. And, I appreciate that you did not. I feel deeply indebted to you for giving me my life."

"Look Colonel Kohler," Sergei said, "I told you that you owe me nothing. We are both happy this stinking war is coming to an end. I am very happy I could do at least one good thing in this war," replied Sergei.

"Nevertheless," Colonel Kohler continued, "I want to tell you something very important. When I tell you this, your first response will be that it is unbelievable, impossible. But, you must remember that I have no motive other than to repay you for what you have done for me. That in itself provides the only credibility which I can offer for what I shall now tell you."

"I understand. It sounds like this should be very interesting," Sergei said, looking toward Colonel Kohler."

"I assure you it will be, Major Kaparov" replied the Colonel. "Would you have a cigarette?" he asked.

Sergei gave the Colonel a cigarette and flicked on his lighter. Colonel Kohler leaned forward, moving the cigarette in his lips into the lighter's flame. He took a long draw, exhaling the smoke out the truck's open window on his right. Colonel Kohler turned his head to look at Sergei. Then, he looked out the truck's front window, taking another long draw on the cigarette. Sergei, although anxious to hear what Colonel Kohler would say, waited patiently.

"Major Kaparov, we have met on this night in the last days of the War. I realize you don't know me. After I tell you my story and we part ways, you will have second thoughts about what I said. You will wonder if you heard me correctly. You will question why I told you what I am now going to relate. So, please listen carefully."

Sergei nodded that he understood.

"Major Kaparov," Colonel Kohler whispered, "Adolf Hitler is not dead. He is very much alive. And, so is Martin Bormann."

12

General Tarasov's Diary

May 2, 1945   Russian Army Headquarters, Eastern Front

"What?" Sergei exclaimed. "Certainly, you are mistaken, Colonel Kohler. The Nazi leadership announced Hitler's death. Why would they lie about it? There is no reason they would lie. Hitler's death only hurts the Nazi cause."

"The Nazi leadership announced Hitler's death because they think he died. They think he committed suicide in his Fuhrerbunker. But, I assure you. Hitler is not dead, Major Kaparov. I know because I was in the bunker with him.

You see, everyone in the Fuhrerbunker thinks Hitler is dead. The German High Command does not question Hitler's death because they were informed of it by the people in the Fuhrerbunker."

"But, intelligence reports quoted the German High Command saying they found the bodies of Adolf Hitler, Eva Braun and Martin Bormann in the Fuhrerbunker. That proves they're dead," said Sergei.

"But, the bodies are those of their doppelgangers, the people used as body doubles by Hitler, Braun, and Bormann," replied Colonel Kohler.

"I don't understand," replied Sergei.

"The bodies they found are actually impersonators of Hitler, Braun and Bormann. Hitler frequently used his body double to stand in for him when he had to attend events where there was a risk someone might try to assassinate him. The look-alike of Hitler would go to the place and fill in for him. Bormann and Braun often did the same thing."

"Are you sure about this?" asked Sergei, astonished.

"The look-alike doubles of Hitler, Bormann and Braun were executed in the bunker. Hitler and Braun's bodies were positioned to make it appear that they committed suicide. Bormann's double tried to escape and made it to the outside of the Fuhrerbunker. But, he was killed there."

"Major Kaparov, you do not need to believe me," Colonel Kohler continued, "but that is the truth."

"Then where are Adolf Hitler, Eva Braun and Martin Bormann now?" asked Sergei.

"Major, if you have trouble believing what I just told you, then you will find it absolutely impossible to believe what you will hear next."

"I'm sure I will but, please tell me what that is."

"They have escaped in something called a Chronometric Teleporter," replied Colonel Kohler.

"What the hell is a Chronometric Teleporter?" gasped Sergei.

"It's a machine by which a person can travel into another time," the Colonel replied.

"Colonel Kohler, I'm a simple farmer from Belarus," Sergei responded. "What are you talking about?"

"If you had a Chronometric Teleporter and wanted to live one hundred years in the past or future, you could do so. You could travel into another time."

Sergei had heard many tall tales, but never one this incredible. "Colonel, are you joking?" Major Kaparov asked.

"Major, you just gave me my life. I hardly think I would repay you by trying to make a fool of you. We are sitting here in a truck in utter darkness in the bombed city of Berlin. The war is ending. You will leave here in a few minutes. As I said, as time passes, you will question whether I have told you the truth, lied or imagined what I told you. No matter what you think later, you must remember this simple fact. I have absolutely no reason to tell you these things unless they were true."

"How do you know what you have told me is true?" replied Sergei.

"Because, Major Kaparov, I was the one who shot the look-alike double of Adolf Hitler and forced the look-alike double of Eva Braun to take the cyanide capsule. I was also the one who staged the murder scene to look like a double suicide. They chose me for this task because I am in the Internal Investigations Unit in the German Army. In other words, I am like a police detective and I investigate murders within the military organization. As for Bormann's look-alike, an SS officer captured him and offered him the choice of the cyanide capsule or a bullet in his temple. He took the cyanide."

"This is incredible!" Sergei said.

"I don't know," replied Colonel Kohler. "There were over fifty assassination attempts on Hitler. I was involved in two of these. But, there is something about Adolf Hitler that is very unnatural, even eerie. It's impossible to kill the man. I initially agreed to shoot these two people, but my intent was to shoot Hitler himself. Unfortunately, he was constantly surrounded by SS guards. There was no chance for me to kill him.

After I killed the two look-alikes, six SS guards and I took Hitler, Braun, and Martin Bormann into the room where the Chronometric Teleporter was located. I helped them with their belongings, which consisted of only a small suitcase for each of them. Then, Eva Braun, followed by Hitler and then Bormann, stepped through what they called a "portal" which took the three of them away from Germany and the downfall of the Third Reich."

This disturbing new reality pierced Sergei's consciousness. He suddenly realized the colonel was telling him the truth and it was overwhelming. "My god, it is true," he murmured. "Hitler, Bormann and Eva Braun are alive."

"Yes, Major. They absolutely are alive," replied Colonel Kohler. We both may regret that I told you these things, but I believe someone other than I should know the truth of what occurred in the Fuhrerbunker. However, it will probably not do either one of us any good," Colonel Kohler concluded. "Major, I will shake your hand once more. May I call you Sergei?" asked Colonel Kohler.

"Yes, of course. And, I shall call you Andreas," replied Sergei. "Thank you for giving me this information, Andreas," said Sergei. "But, I guess I should be getting back. Don't forget about our beer."

"Goodbye, Sergei," replied the colonel, as Major Kaparov backed his truck out of the driveway.

Sergei Kaparov again drove his truck through Berlin's devastated streets as the sun's morning shadows revealed gruesome collages of death. His battle weary brain roiled from the revelations of Colonel Kohler. He would inform General Tarasov and SMERSH (Intelligence) about this unpleasant development. He knew one of the primary objectives was to either capture or kill Adolf Hitler. According to Colonel Kohler, this had not happened.

It was late morning before Sergei could see General Tarasov. As Sergei walked into his commander's office, General Tarasov stood up and smiled, shaking hands and embracing him.

"Well Major, it looks like the war is nearly over!" the general exclaimed. "That should make you very happy. You can return to your home and get back to a real life."

"Yes, General," Sergei replied. "I am looking forward to that."

"What brings you to see me today, Sergei?" the general asked.

**General Tarasov recorded the following earlier conversation with Colonel Lev Demidov of SMERSH, as well as the subsequent conversation with Major Kaparov, in his diary:

General Tarasov's Diary:
Headquarters: Russian Army Headquarters, Eastern Front
Commanding General Georgy Tarasov
2 May, 1945
0800 Hours: Meeting with Colonel Lev Demidov, SMERSH
Security Level: Top Secret
Attendees: General Georgy Tarasov, Colonel Lev Demidov

I met privately with Col. L. Demidov, SMERSH. Meeting duration was two hours. Demidov was highly agitated and under great stress. SMERSH conducted an analysis of the burned bodies purported to be those of Adolf Hitler and Eva Braun. It was concluded with absolute certainty the bodies were not those of Hitler and Braun.

I was shocked that Adolf Hitler and Eva Braun had escaped. SMERSH and Army Intelligence reports indicated with 100% certainty that Adolf Hitler was located in his Fuhrerbunker. All roads and all airports were controlled by the Soviet Army. Rail lines were destroyed. To escape on foot through Soviet Army lines was impossible. Additionally, both Demidov and I thought German High Command radio broadcasts that Hitler was dead were highly credible.

Demidov was terrified that if Josef Stalin learned Adolf Hitler had escaped, he and I would be sent to a Siberian prison camp, or even executed. For my part, I was weary of war. I fought against the Germans in Russia during the bitter winter of Operation Barbarossa and have been fighting for five years. I was not interested in being rewarded with imprisonment in Siberia or executed because Stalin's archenemy Adolf Hitler was alive and we let him escape.

For our own-well being, we devised a story that would prove Hitler was indeed dead, as the Nazi High Command had reported. Several weeks prior to my meeting with Demidov one of my officers, the famous writer and poet Ruslan Fedoseev, told me a very tragic story. He brought to me a picture of Brigitte Vogel, the beautiful German singer. She and her fiancé were caught in an aerial bombardment. Bombs were falling all around them as they ran down a street. Suddenly, a nearby explosion caused a building to collapse and fall into the roadway. Part of the building fell on Brigitte Vogel and she was trapped in the fire. As she lay underneath the burning rubble screaming for help, her fiancé and some German policemen tried to free her, but it was impossible. Water lines had been destroyed by the bombing and there was no way to extinguish the fire. In order to end her suffering, her fiancé pulled a gun from the holster of one of the German police officers and shot her.

Several days late, her fiancé and some friends searched through the charred wreckage of the building to find her remains. The only part of her body they could find was a piece of her skull. Eerily, it was the piece of skull with the bullet hole caused when she was shot by her fiancé. This bizarre event overwhelmed the poor man and later that day he committed suicide. When his friends found him, he was holding a picture of Brigitte Vogel and the piece of her charred skull with the bullet hole in it. Colonel Fedoseev had given these items to me.

As Demidov and I continued to talk, I turned to the cabinet in back of my desk and opened the drawer. Pulling out the picture of Brigitte Vogel and the piece of her skull with the bullet hole in it, I said to Demidov, "You and I know Hitler has escaped however, I agree with you. It will go badly for us if Stalin should find out."

I looked at Colonel Lev Demidov and handed him the piece of Brigitte Vogel's skull. "This is the piece of Adolf Hitler's skull which proves he is dead," I said. "You write a letter to your commander in Moscow which he will give to Josef Stalin. This proves Hitler killed himself as our initial reports stated. Now, my friend, will you share a bottle of this very high priced vodka I have been saving for our victory celebration?"

Headquarters: Russian Army Headquarters, Eastern Front
Commanding General Georgy Tarasov
2 May, 1945
1030 Hours: Meeting with Major Sergei Kaparov, Russian Army
Security Level: Top Secret
Attendees: General Georgy Tarasov, Major Sergei Kaparov

I met privately with Major Sergei Kaparov. Meeting duration was one hour. Major Kaparov, one of my most trusted officers, detailed a conversation he had with a captured German Officer, Colonel Andreas Kohler. Colonel Kohler maintained that Adolf Hitler was not dead. I was greatly disturbed to receive this information because it corroborated information I had just received from Colonel Lev Demidov of SMERSH.

Because of my agreement with Demidov, I attempted to convince Major Kaparov that Hitler was indeed dead. I berated Major Kaparov because he had no tangible proof Hitler had escaped. However, Major Kaparov was absolutely convinced the man was telling the truth. I responded I would not dare relay this information to Moscow without credible evidence, not just the word of a German Colonel.

I gave Major Kaparov a direct order to never tell anyone what he had just told me. Moscow does not want to hear that Hitler is alive. It would not beneficial to cloud the Soviet victory in Berlin with a claim that Hitler had escaped

"Major Kaparov," I said, "I need your word both as an officer and as a personal friend you will never speak of this insane story again." Major Kaparov realized it was of no use to pursue the subject any further as he had no proof other than Colonel Kohler's word.

I could never admit that I let Adolf Hitler escape because the consequences were too severe to consider. Colonel Demidov and I would stay with the version of events as they were.

Note: In 2009, DNA tests on the bullet pierced skull fragment (now held by the Russian State Archive) were conducted in the United States at the genetics laboratory at the University of Connecticut. Although long claimed by SMERSH (Soviet Intelligence) to belong to Adolf Hitler, DNA test proved the skull actually belonged to a woman less than forty years old. This discovery eliminated the only "proof" that Hitler had actually shot himself while in his Fuhrerbunker. Brigitte Vogel was thirty-two years old when she was killed by her fiancé's bullet.

PART 2

ARIZONA DESERT

MAY 14, 2010—MAY 15, 2010

13

Stone Woman Mountain

May 14, 2010   Arizona Desert

Some days are better than others to explore the desert. One never knows what kind of day it's going to be until he or she is on the trail. Those who have experience with the desert know one thing is certain. All days are different. For that reason, when in the desert they walk with caution.

Across the immensity, myriad hues of green are continually re-shaded by the sun rotating in its southwesterly arc. The unending expanse of desert plants fuses into a sage colored blanket of tangled thorns and velvet. Intense heat and the absence of movement underscore the dramatic solitude. There is no sound. It's hard to comprehend the aloneness as one ponders the reality of this place.

People in the desert are often fooled that way. There is nothing out there but the cactus, weeds and the vastness, they think. The desert won't tell them they are wrong. The desert won't tell them they could soon discover that in a most unsettling way.

There are others. But, the desert does not willingly share its secrets. If you listen closely you hear the sound of a distant bird, a call you do not recollect. You look but see nothing. You hear a faint noise to your right. You look again, but there is nothing, only the unseen bird in the profound distance.

You feel the slightest draft across your face, but there is no wind. Leaves on a solitary, tree do not move. Bushes don't rustle. Was there a breeze?

It is a timeless land of astonishing beauty and ancient mysteries. Twisted cactuses seem like ghostly acrobats frozen midway through gymnastic movements. A ruined wall crumbled centuries before calls out in an ancient, forgotten language of a people who long ago vanished from this place.

There is a gentle intrusion into your soul. In the powerful heat, there is a chill along your spine. You wonder if other eyes are watching.

****

On this day, David Kelly was just beginning to get into the rhythm of his hike. He already walked several miles from the trailhead and was ready for a brief rest stop and a drink of water. There was a tree a quarter mile up the trail. It looked like a good place to escape the sun for a few minutes.

David was a Professor of History at Arizona State Teacher's College and something of an introvert. It wasn't that he didn't like people. He enjoyed getting together with his small circle of friends. Besides, a liking for people was part of his Irish heritage, a courtesy of his father. On his mother's side, he was part Navajo. That was why he also enjoyed his "alone time" when he could be in the desert. He described himself as "a gregarious introvert, if there were such a thing." He liked people, but he liked his "alone time," a little more.

At thirty-four years of age, David had never married. He spent most of his adult years teaching history at the college. An Arizona native, he was born in Yuma but grew up in Ramona Springs, a small town seventy-five miles north. His father owned a farm and ranch supply store there for thirty-five years.

David was an athletic man and spent most of his spare time out doors. While not muscular, he was fit and carried little fat on his one hundred and sixty-five pound frame. At five feet, ten inches he was average height. Although not tall, he had been a better than average basketball player in high school and even got some playing time at Pecos Junior College. He could have been an outstanding athlete but sports were not important to him. Because he was a Navajo, there were more important things in life.

Hiking in the desert was one of those things, actually his favorite pastime. As he stopped to rest, he knelt on one knee to take maximum advantage of the meager shade of the small tree. It was nearly ten o'clock. The morning was drifting quickly toward the noon hour. The temperature was also drifting, quickly toward the one hundred degree mark.

David knew hiking in the desert imposes certain rules that must be followed if one is to have a pleasant experience. And that's always a good idea because an unpleasant experience in the desert is likely to be extremely unpleasant. One of those rules is to hike early to "beat the heat," as David liked to say. "Hike as far as you can before the sun takes command of the sky and your hike," he would tell people. "Everyone must race the sun before it gets too high."

When midday comes, the hiker surrenders the day to the sun for the sun is now in charge. The hiker must find shade and rest and wait for late afternoon when the sun tells him "It's your turn now. You can have the rest of the day."

But, it's only grudgingly that the sun returns the day to the hiker. As it begins its slow exit from the western sky, the sun leaves its heat to remind the hiker it still demands respect. Ignoring his waning presence is to risk trouble. He will punish those who do not respect him. In the desert, the sun is in charge. David learned the rules well. He made mistakes along the way and learned from them. It's best to not make mistakes.

In the desert there are others. The desert hides them. It hides every imaginable description of life. They are small and large, running, crawling, slithering, creeping, plodding, hopping, jumping, flying, walking, springing, and waiting. They too must obey the sun. So they wait. Most of them wait for the night when the sun is gone. Night helps them hide. Night is cool. They find food. They are hunted because they too are food.

David got a late start on his hike. For several reasons, namely a long phone call from one of his students, he was delayed and found himself putting aside his own early start rule. His destination, which he hiked several times before, was Stone Woman Mountain. The small mountain was located six miles off County Road 136.

While Stone Woman Mountain seemed an odd name for a mountain, it brought to mind several difficult females David had known in his past. While he didn't have much of a romantic history, his few brief encounters were not "made in heaven" as the saying goes. In fact, he thought these particular encounters might well have been manufactured in quite the opposite place. He did not, however, wish to ponder these individuals any further.

This was to be a relatively short "day hike" with a return to the trailhead before six p.m. This would get David out of the desert before the rattlesnakes came out to hunt. This was his usual routine because he didn't like snakes. He planned to take a morning hike to the base of the mountain and then the one-mile trail to the rocky peak. There was a small shelter at the top, just a few benches under a roof, which provided some shade. There were also some large rocks, which provided additional shade. There was no water along the trail but he could easily carry all that he needed. While the elevation of the mountain was five thousand feet, the surrounding desert was twenty-five hundred feet. That meant the mountain was only twenty-five hundred feet above the desert floor. David was not sure the mountain could even be called a mountain. It was not high, but it had a nice view. Even with the late morning start, it would be an easy hike.

Although David was only two miles in, he could reach the base of the mountain and get to the top before noon or shortly after. While he had come this way before, he checked the map at the trailhead. It showed most of the trail to be over flat land, with the last mile consisting of a narrower path with several switchbacks winding gently up the mountain to its summit. David rested in the sparse shade of the small tree for only a few minutes, but the day was getting noticeably warmer. It was time to go.

The dirt trail was wide, about six feet across, bounded by smatterings of light green scrub and brush on either side. He stayed to the center of the trail as a precaution. There was always a chance a stray rattlesnake might be hiding at the side of the path in the shade of a bush or rock.

In the next twenty minutes, David hiked another mile and had almost reached the familiar fork in the trail. If he stayed on the shorter main trail, there was more shade and he would reach the mountain sooner. If he took the narrower footpath, there was less shade but more dramatic scenery as it ran along the rims of steep gorges. It was also a mile longer than the main trail. Because the sun was high, David opted for the main trail because he would reach the mountain and the shade sooner.

Walking fifty yards further, David could now see the fork. However, he also saw there was a sign posted in the middle of the main trail, which cut to his left. As he got closer, he could read the sign. "Trail closed for maintenance," it said. "Use the Gorge Trail."

David had only used the Gorge Trail once. He didn't like it because it was narrower and there were more snakes. But, he had no choice so he turned right and headed up the trail. In another half mile, David would reach the two hundred feet tall pink rock formation looming ahead. That's where he had encountered snakes before.

As he walked, he was thinking about snakes and an experience he had when he was eleven years old which caused him to fear them. He remembered stopping on a small hill on his way to a creek about fifty yards from where he stood. There was a one hundred feet wide boundary of lush, green grass between him and the shore of the creek. The grass was two and a half to three feet tall. He knew this was a bad snake area. He could smell them, or at least imagined that he could. I was afraid of snakes even then, he thought to himself.

He didn't know what possessed him then and still didn't all these years later. He stood on the hill alone, daring himself to run through the deep grass. He didn't have to prove anything. But, he decided to run through the lush grass to the creek. He took off running as fast as he could, crashing through the high grass and struggling to keep up his speed as the thick growth pushed back against his legs.

As David ran, his fear was increasing to near panic that he was going to step on a snake. Two seconds later, when he had run half way through the dense grass, his left foot came down hard, directly on something that lurched and twisted. He knew exactly what it was and it was big. He didn't break stride and maybe even increased the length of his paces. He dashed another ten or fifteen yards and stopped to look back and catch his breath. His chest was heaving with frantic breathing, caused more by his fear than his jog through the grass.

He could see the snake, rather its head, weaving hypnotically above the blowing grass. It looked like a sea serpent floating on the waves of an emerald ocean. This was a very unhappy snake. It glared at David for a long time. It was a terrifying experience for a young boy because he had never experienced any animal or person mad enough to want to harm him.

He broke eye contact with the furious snake and ran, jumping across the creek. When he looked back, the snake was still watching him. David thought that was eerie and he got out of there fast. The snake had given him a good scare. David was careful about where he walked ever since.

He was now walking the wide curved path toward the area in back of the large pink rock where the ground sloped slightly to the east. The area directly ahead of him, between where he was walking and the back of the big rock, became more rocky and brushy. The trail changed course sharply to the right, extending its arc and winding around the back of the big rock.

His direction was now east to northeast and he slowly advanced to the area in back of the rock. The ground was beginning to slope away to the right, gradually turning into a much steeper drop-off. From where he stood, the ground sharply descended approximately one hundred and fifty feet downward at a sixty-degree angle. At the bottom of this steep, rocky hill were several high walls of pink rock spires reaching three hundred feet into the sky. As David looked across the steep valley, the tops of the spires towered two hundred feet above the elevation where he now stood. He knew well this was not a place to lose his footing. While the trail had faded to a trace, he could see the narrow walkway that went past the drop-off. He started walking along this tight path, being careful to avoid a misstep.

But, trouble began a few yards in. David, who had never fallen on his desert hikes, stumbled and fell forward on the narrow pathway, his right foot coming down on uneven ground just off the edge of the steep slope. The daypack on David's back held one of his canteens and the second canteen hung at his waist. Their combined weight caused him to lose his balance and fall sideways.

He was suddenly tumbling uncontrollably down the rocky hillside. He banged his head a couple of times even though he was trying to shield it with his arms. He seemed to collide with countless rocks and, after tumbling for what seemed like a long time, his fall ended at the bottom of the slope. He slowly sat up to take a look around, wondering if there was any part of him that didn't hurt.

Suddenly, there was a loud cracking sound as wood shattered directly underneath him and the earth gave way. David slid downward, grasping for a handhold to avoid sliding into the earth itself. But, everything he grabbed was sliding with him. Then the ground collapsed completely and he plunged through a gaping hole along with broken timbers, dirt, and rocks.

He braced himself to hit the ground just before he landed on the side of another steep slope. He was tumbling again, struggling mightily, but futilely, to stop his plummeting. He reached level ground and his fall stopped as abruptly as it started. "That was well done," he mumbled, in a weak attempt at humor. Other than bruises and cuts, he didn't suffer any damage.

He recovered his senses and began to survey the situation. It looked as though he had fallen into some sort of huge, natural grotto. There was plenty of light. He could see other wide patches of blue sky as he looked toward the rear of the cavern from where he sat. There were high towers of vertical pink rock forming the sides of the grotto, while many levels of flat, horizontal rock slabs jutted out in every direction providing a multi-layered roof. The grotto, which he estimated to be about two hundred feet wide by two hundred feet in length, was almost a perfect square. As he looked up at the ceiling, he could see the hole through which he had fallen. It was one hundred feet above the floor where he sat along with the broken wooden poles that had fallen with him. It was then he noticed the shattered timbers were rounded and very old.

He thought he could climb out of the grotto if he could find a rock with some handholds. Or maybe he could find a natural path out of the large room. However, as he walked around and inspected the sheer, rose-colored rock walls surrounding him, he could find no exit points or routes which he could climb. He felt as if he were at the bottom of a huge, square toy box, a place where a giant's child put his toys when he was finished playing. His only chance at freedom was the giant child reaching in and picking him up by the back of his shirt and lifting him out. As he looked about the huge grotto, it almost appeared that it had been purposely created.

David brushed aside that thought as he explored the cavern. There were many rock formations in the desert with geometric shapes randomly designed by ice, wind and water. The horizontal outcroppings forming the roof of the grotto cast dark, precise shadows over the far wall, the only one David hadn't yet inspected.

He walked across the grotto's rock floor toward the shadow-covered wall, his only remaining chance to find a way out. As he walked along the side of the huge rock, he noticed three large petroglyphs that had been obscured by the shadows on the wall.

The ten-foot high wall paintings depicted three coal black, mummy-like images, eerie and unearthly. While the images bore a resemblance to more traditional rock art, there was a notable difference in the precision of their designs and intensity of their coloring. The strange obsidian silhouettes seemed to speak to him in language he didn't know. The images must be two thousand years old, he figured.

David had written a book about Indian wall paintings and was considered an expert on the subject. But, he had never seen any like these. These were unique, in a style completely apart from all other wall art. The three phantoms were a frightful sight which captured the essence of every supernatural story he had ever heard. He was living a horror movie he thought.

The heads of the spectral shapes were not supported by distinct necks, rather flowed downward and merged onto their shoulders. From the shoulders, the body was shaped like an inverted teardrop. The slightly wider, rounded shoulders of the ebony silhouettes tapered downward, momentarily enlarging to include the arms. The arms flowed into and were a part of the torso on either side, concluding at the waist. Below the waist, the figure again slimmed as the legs continued the downward taper of the form. The lower portion of the legless bodies faded into a ghostly mist, which gradually dissolved into nothingness.

But there were other unnerving features of these phantom-like images. The three figures cast an unworldly bluish glow, giving them a lifelike appearance. The eyes were eerie, narrow white slits, widened at the center to frame intense yellow eyeballs, which peered into David's soul. More unsettling was their otherworldly gaze. The figures' eyes followed David as he moved from one side of the specters to the other. Wherever he stood, their eyes glared directly at him, seemingly comprehending his very thoughts and growing fear.

The glowing images on the wall were unnerving and frightening. It wasn't that David was immersed in supernatural beliefs, however his mother was a full-blooded Navajo and she often told him stories, legends about things he did not understand. The three wall paintings were disembodied beings, disquieting and mysterious, an unwanted link to the mystical. If they were created to invoke fear, they had succeeded. Undoubtedly, it was thousands of years since anyone had come to this place. The people who painted the wall figures must have used ropes to descend from the top of the rock summit.

And that was David's main concern. Without assistance from the top, there was no way to climb out. Screaming for help would be wasted energy. As it was Thursday, a weekday, there would be no one else on the trail today or tomorrow.

David had taken a detour and it had gone very badly. He had fallen into a hole in the ground and nobody would find him for another thousand years. While David could easily see parts of the sky from where he stood, if someone climbing around the rocks above and looked directly downward, they couldn't see past the multilayered, horizontal rock slabs of the "roof." No one would realize there was a huge room below. What had begun as a simple hike had become a life-threatening situation. David was trapped in the grotto.

14

Ghost

May 14, 2010   Arizona Desert

David walked across the grotto floor to the spot where he landed when he fell through the hole in the roof. He sat down to sort things out. He was trapped in this huge room and there was no escape. As the grotto's temperature was much cooler than the desert above, he wouldn't need to drink as much water and had enough for several days. But what would happen after that was something he didn't want to think about. He had been inside the grotto for only five minutes but that was already much too long.

Suddenly, from across the grotto in the shadows of the pictograph wall, a strong voice shattered the silence. "Hello David. I hope you weren't injured in your fall."

David, badly startled, instantly looked up, focusing his eyes in the direction of the pictographs. Though he could see nothing, he recovered his composure and came back with "No, I think I'm okay." He then stood up, but he was struggling to control his fear. Things have gotten much too weird, he thought.

He strained to see through the shadows but, just as he had not seen the pictographs on the wall, neither could he see the source of the voice. Where had this person, if it was a person, come from? David had searched along the wall for a passage out but had found nothing. There had been only a sheer wall and the three frightening pictographs with their haunting eyes. Had one of the black silhouettes come to life and stepped down from the wall?

David could now see the faint outline of a figure in the shadows seventy-five feet away. "My god," he exclaimed to himself, "one of the specters has come down from the wall." However, the silhouette in the shadows was closer to six feet, not ten feet tall like the wall figures. Nevertheless, the figure moving toward him was an exact image of the mysterious shapes. His head flowed into his shoulders and his body was the inverted teardrop shape. And, the dark outline in the shadows seemed to float as it advanced toward him.

All the stories his mother told him about ghosts and the supernatural fused into an increasing horror of his predicament. He had stumbled into a place of evil, an earthbound outpost of Hell. What in God's name have I gotten myself into? David wondered fearfully. The spectral figure drifted closer now, its black outline more defined as it reached the lighter outer edges of the shadows.

"Relax, David," the voice said. "You're safe here."

As the figure emerged from the shadows, David gasped with relief. He realized his imagination and anxiety overrode his judgment. The dark figure floating through the shadows was not a grotesque fiend but a man, who was not gliding but walking on legs.

The man was about forty-five years old and had a square jawed, classic Indian face. His long, coal black hair hanging down past his shoulders accounted for the "veil-like silhouette" David saw in the shadows. He was dressed in faded blue jeans, an equally faded denim shirt and cowboy boots. But, he wore no hat. The man's face was more elegant than handsome, resembling an idealized sculpture. As he walked, his definitive movements portrayed a cautious, deliberate manner. His expression was alert and forthright, meditative, yet urgent. David surmised this man belonged to one of the local tribes, probably Navajo, but he wasn't sure.

David, relieved, asked, "Who are you? Where did you come from?"

The man's response was calm and controlled. "I'm here to help you, David, and you're here to help me."

David was puzzled at his reply and wondered how he knew his name. But he was happy the man was here, even though he couldn't understand where he came from.

"My name is Tse. It's a Navajo name and means 'rock.' I live nearby and it's my job to guard Stone Woman Mountain."

David replied, "Stone Woman Mountain is three miles from here. What are you doing in this cave? And, how do you know my name?"

It's not actually Stone Woman Mountain that I guard," he replied. "What I really guard is this rock formation into which you fell. Stone Woman Mountain is a "made up" name we gave the mountain long ago. Calling the mountain "Stone Woman Mountain" makes it the main attraction. People hike to the mountain to look at the rocks and imagine they see the 'Stone Woman.' And that's good because they don't come here. That's the way we want it and why we gave the mountain that name."

"But, why do you want to fool people to keep them from coming here?" David asked.

"Because this place is of great importance to our people and the role we play," Tse said. "This place is holy but also serves a practical purpose. We go to a great deal of effort to keep this location secret from everyone with the exception of a few people in our tribe. We keep outsiders looking for something somewhere else so they don't accidentally find this place. But, you found it anyway, didn't you David?" Tse added wryly."

Not appreciating Tse's humor, David snapped back, "So you lie to them, in other words?"

"Yes, we do lie to them," Tse replied. "But, we like to think of it like the Iceland and Greenland thing. You know, the Vikings named the green island Iceland and the icy island Greenland to confuse people and keep them from coming to Iceland where they actually settled, or something like that. But, who cares? It has worked for many years. Stone Woman is on the mountain, although I've never been able to find her in those rocks," he said, again adding some humor. "However, the real secret is not the Stone Woman but something very different and it's here in this grotto. Are you beginning to understand?" Tse concluded."

"Well, I guess it's not that hard," David replied. "But, I don't see anything here but us."

Tse quickly replied, "But there is a great deal here, and it's much more important than you can imagine."

David, whose only concern was getting out of the cavern as quickly as possible, replied, "Look, Tse," I'm sorry I fell into your grotto or whatever this place is. But, it's getting late and I just want to get back to the trail. I promise not to tell anyone about your sacred cavern or the secret of Stone Woman Mountain. Would you mind just showing me how to get out of this place? I promise to never bother you again."

Tse's mood quickly turned to impatience. "I'm sorry, David, but, this is not about getting you back to the trail."

David interrupted, "Tse, you never answered my question. How do you know my name?"

Tse came back quickly to answer David. "I'll tell you that in time but, not now. There are things happening which are far more important than your questions. So let's not waste any more time with them. Take a moment to think about the events of the day. You didn't arrive at this place by happenstance. I steered you here," Tse laughed. "I'm sorry about your detour and causing you to stumble and fall down the hill. You landed in just the right spot, too," Tse added. "Then you fell through the hole into the grotto. You bounce pretty good," Tse laughed.

"Look Tse," David countered, "are you trying to tell me you controlled my hike by arranging for me to fall through that hole up there? I could easily have gotten killed when I fell down the ridge, or when I fell through the hole in your roof. Are you trying to tell me that was all by your design?"

Tse, looking amused, answered, "Yes, David, I did control your hike. I know that rattles you because you're such a control freak yourself. But, I figured if you survived the falls you were the right man for the job."

"What job?" David asked, annoyed. "What if I got killed?"

"Tse laughed and said, "Then I'd know you weren't the right man for the job after all."

David, who was not amused, replied, "You still haven't answered my question, Tse. What do you mean by some job to be done?"

"Slow down, David," Tse replied, looking more serious now, "I will explain everything as soon as you understand how our relationship will work."

"What relationship?" asked David. "I don't even know you. We don't have a relationship."

"Yes, we do," replied Tse assertively. "Not in the biblical sense, of course," added Tse laughing.

David still hadn't developed an appreciation for Tse's sense of humor. "Funny," he replied.

"Okay, David," he said. "We'll get down to business. Our relationship will work like this. I tell you what to do and you do it. Easy enough?"

"Yeah, I understand," David said. This guy is crazy, he thought to himself, wondering how he would escape from the grotto and this man called Tse.

15

Time Masters

May 14, 2010   Arizona Desert

So far, the only thing David learned was Tse claimed to have manipulated his hike in order to lead him to the grotto. David didn't believe him but wanted to avoid confronting Tse because he thought the man was unstable and didn't want to chance provoking him.

Tse still hadn't answered David's questions of how he happened to know his name and what he meant by the "job to be done." But, the answers to these questions were soon to come.

Tse continued. "David, I have much to tell you."

David thought to himself, this is going to be some bizarre story. He looked around for a route to escape, though he knew there wasn't one.

Tse sensed David's concern. "Don't look so worried, David. We're only going to talk."

"Tse, what is it you want with me?" asked David.

"I'm going to tell you if you'll listen," Tse replied.

David knew he had no choice. "I'm listening," he said.

Tse continued, "I know you'll have trouble believing what I'm going to tell you so I want you to listen closely. When we're done, you'll understand why you're here."

Tse walked over to David and the two men sat down on a flat rock near the center of the grotto. They faced toward the wall on which the petroglyphs were painted.

"David, it's difficult to know where to begin," Tse said. "So," he added, smiling, "I'll begin with me." David figured throwing in a little humor was Tse's way of lightening the conversation and being friendly. Maybe this guy is okay, thought David.

"I'm going to tell you about my tribe," Tse continued.

"You said you're Navajo," David interjected. "I'm also part Navajo."

I didn't say I was Navajo. I said my name was a Navajo name. My tribe was originally called the Quarta. We arrived in North America over twenty thousand years ago. Originally, the Quarta were hunters. We frequently moved as we followed the herds of mammoth and other big game. In those days, very different animals lived in North America than are in existence today. Mammoth, buffalo, deer and antelope roamed the plains by the millions. There were also predators. The big cats, the saber toothed tiger, cheetahs and others lived then. There were huge birds with sixteen-foot wing spans. You should have seen them, David."

David interrupted again. "You talk as if you were there and saw them yourself, Tse," David said, smiling cynically.

Tse looked at David momentarily, and looked away to stare at the shadows hiding the petroglyphs on the large rock wall. He didn't speak for nearly a minute. Then, he turned and said, "I was there, David."

David gasped, his smile quickly fading as cold chills went up his spine. Tse's voice was solemn, its tone reflecting a longing for people once loved and memories made in an unforgotten past. Stunned, David began to sense this man Tse was unlike any he had ever met. There was an aura of integrity about him. He was sincere, genuine. And, yes, he was very eerie.

Tse returned to his narrative. "But, I'm getting off the subject. Over time, more peoples came to North America and the big animals were hunted to extinction. The big cats died off because there was not as much game for them to hunt. Buffalo, deer and a few other species survived.

Twelve thousand years ago the Quarta were still hunting. Nine thousand years ago, the Pre-Anaszi moved to the southwest part of what is now the United States. The Quarta and other tribes were a part of this group. Things get a little confusing because there are no written records. The Quartas were absorbed into the Navajos and other tribes. It's no longer possible to make a distinction between the Quartas and other tribes because together they are all part of who they were and who they have become. We therefore call ourselves by the name of the tribe we are now part of, rather than Quarta. It's just as if someone immigrated to this country and called themselves an American rather than say, an Irishman, no offense meant, he said, grinning."

Although David originally found Tse's humor annoying, he was beginning to appreciate it. He smiled.

"Most Quartas inter-married into the tribes of today. However, some remained together as Quartas to preserve the bloodline and practice the old ways. There are still a few full blooded Quartas living today."

"Why do I need to know this, Tse?" David asked.

"Because your mother was not a Navajo, David, but a full blooded Quarta like me. That makes you half Quarta." Kiddingly, Tse smiled and said, "Of course, your Irish blood combined with your Quarta blood doesn't make the best combination but, it will have to do." David laughed.

Tse continued, "The reason I know your name is because I know your mother. I know all the Quarta people."

"My mother never told me she was a Quarta," David replied. "She considered herself a Navajo."

"That's not quite true, David. There's a very good reason your mother never told you or your father, for that matter, she was a Quarta." Puzzled, David looked at Tse expectantly. "You see," Tse continued, "Some Quartas have a very special ability. If she told you or your father she was a Quarta, it would put you both in great danger. There are people who would try to use your mother's ability in a way for which it was never meant. And they would stop at nothing to be able to do so."

"I don't understand," David replied. "I thought my father and mother knew everything about each other."

"Your father couldn't know about this because your mother was protecting him" Tse answered. "Like I said, that's also why she never told you. Besides, she never had to use this special ability."

David was fascinated with Tse's story and especially curious about the "special ability" his mother had. "It's very intriguing," he thought. Then he asked, "Why are you telling me about these things, Tse? I mean, I'm very interested. It's just that I find it very strange that I'm sitting here in a secret cave with a mysterious guy, meaning you, and being told secrets about my own family."

Tse laughed. "Yeah that is a little weird, isn't it? To answer your question," he said, with a more serious expression, "I'm telling you this because you need to know about your heritage and your mother's secret ability. You see, your mother didn't use this ability because there was never a need for it. However, the time has come when this ability is needed because there is great danger."

"What danger are you talking about, Tse?"

"I'll tell you in a moment."

"What you're saying is that after all these years my sixty-two year old mother is finally going to use her secret talent?" asked David kiddingly."

"No, David," Tse said gravely. "You are."

"What?" replied David, troubled by Tse's answer. "How can I use my mother's secret ability?"

"Because you may have that same ability, David," Tse responded.

David was visibly startled. "What special ability, Tse?"

"Let me ask you a few questions before I answer, David. Okay?"

"Yeah, sure," David replied.

"Alright, I need you to think carefully about your answers."

David nodded that he understood.

"First of all," said Tse, "have you ever found yourself in a strange place and not known how you got there."

"Yeah," David replied. "I fell through the earth and ended up in this big room today. That's the strangest thing that I can remember." Tse laughed.

"I'm talking about other than today," said Tse.

David thought for a moment and told Tse he had not.

"What about people?" asked Tse. "Have you ever met any strange people?"

"You're the strangest one I've ever met," David replied. Again, Tse laughed.

"I don't think you're taking this very seriously, David," Tse said.

"Well, think about it from my standpoint," David replied. "You have to admit, today has been very strange for me. And, what's this special ability thing all about. What do those questions have to do with anything?"

"Be patient, David," Tse said, "We'll talk about the special ability tomorrow."

"Well, do I have the special ability or not?" David asked.

"Not a chance," replied Tse laughing. "I think your Irish genes screwed things up for you."

"Funny," said David.

"Besides, you're here today so I can to tell you about other important things. What I'm going to say will seem incredible," Tse continued. "That's because it is. But, it's very important you believe and understand what you're going to hear."

"Alright," David replied. "I'm anxious to hear what you're going to say.

"David, what do you know about World War Two?" Tse asked.

"I'm a professor of history," David replied. "I think I know quite a bit about that particular subject. But, you already know that, don't you Tse?" he countered.

Tse laughed. "Now you're catching on, David. Yes, I do know, and that's why you were chosen for the task that must be done."

"You mentioned something before about a job to be done, Tse. What exactly are you talking about?" asked David.

"Like I said, I'll get to that. First, I'm going to tell you some things about World War Two of which you aren't aware."

David thought to himself, "This ought to be good." He considered himself an expert on the War.

Tse continued. "During the War, the Germans had many brilliant scientists working for them. These scientists were developing inventions and weapons. If Germany had waited another two years before starting the War, some of these inventions would have been completed and used in the conflict. Several of these weapons were significant enough they may have enabled Germany to win the War. Fortunately, that didn't happen."

David interrupted. "I know about that, Tse. It's common knowledge the German navy and air force weren't ready when Adolf Hitler started the war."

"Hold on, David," Tse said. "I'm aware you know that. But, I'm getting to the interesting part. Before the war began, there was a dedicated scientist, Doctor Peter Krause, who believed his sole purpose on earth was to help mankind. Dr. Krause wanted to find a way to gather all the knowledge of the past. He thought that by assembling all of mankind's past learning he could rid the world of

115

many of its problems and make it a better place to live. And, most importantly, he was working on a practical means of doing this."

"What do you mean?" asked David.

"Well, this is the part you'll find difficult to believe. He was trying to create a machine to go back into time and gather the knowledge of the past first hand. He called this device a Chronometric Teleporter or, time machine."

David was skeptical. "The idea a time machine only exists in science fiction, Tse," David interrupted.

Tse looked at David, not answering. "Adolf Hitler became aware of Dr. Krause's work and he personally took over the project. Hitler convinced Dr. Krause that it was also his objective to make things better for all people. Of course, this was in 1935, long before the World became aware of Hitler's evil."

"I can believe a guy is working on a machine to go back in time but, I can't believe anyone took him seriously," David said.

"On the contrary," replied Tse. "Dr. Krause was a highly respected physicist working at the National University of Berlin. He was taken very seriously. As it turned out, however, Adolf Hitler's true motives were completely different from Dr. Krause's. And, this is very important, David. Hitler's real objective was to go back in time in order to influence or change events of the past which in turn, would change the future. Hitler wanted to change past events in a way that would help the Nazis achieve world conquest in the 1940's. However, he knew that if Dr. Krause should become aware of his actual intentions, he wouldn't build a time machine."

"Too bad Hitler didn't get the Chronometric Teleporter built," replied David. "Things didn't turn out too well for him in the end."

"Are you sure about that, David?" replied Tse. Tse's voice and the expression on his face implied he knew something David didn't.

"Of course, it's historical fact," David replied, disregarding Tse's suggestion there might be more to this story. "Hitler committed suicide and his generals were tried for war crimes."

"Is that so?" replied Tse.

"What do you mean by that, Tse? Of course it's so. As I said, it's historical fact."

"You're wrong, David," Tse responded. "Hitler fooled the world."

"What!" David exclaimed. "I don't even know why we're even discussing this, Tse. What happened to Hitler has long been accepted by historians."

Tse looked at David silently. After a long pause, he spoke.

Hitler's suicide is a myth, David. I'm going to tell you what really happened."

"Tse," interrupted David, "I'm not into conspiracy theories. There's an overabundance of them surrounding every significant historical event."

"Please, David, let me continue," Tse said. "Dr. Krause eventually found out Hitler's actual intentions for the time machine but, had no choice other than to continue working on it. Hitler would have killed him and his wife Johanna if he refused. After working on the device for ten years, several weeks before World War Two ended Dr. Krause successfully produced an operational time machine, or Chronometric Teleporter. Using this machine, Hitler could go forward or backward in time."

David gasped, "Tse, please. Just when I was beginning to think you weren't crazy, you tell me this wild story." Tse didn't respond and his expression remained serious.

"With the German air force destroyed and the army close to defeat, the War was ending," Tse continued. "Using the time machine, Hitler and eleven hundred hard core Nazi officers escaped before the Russian Forces breached the Fuhrerbunker. David, they were transported to another time."

"Tse, with all due respect, I'm really having trouble buying into your story. I'm sorry, but you're right. It's too incredible to believe."

Tse, looking sternly at David, said, "David, neither of us can afford your refusal to believe the truth I'm telling you. There are ominous things happening as we sit here talking. The consequences will be catastrophic if you don't get a grip. Get with it, David. We need to move on!"

David was taken aback by Tse's sudden change in tone. However, he had barely accepted Tse somehow steered him to fall through the hole in the grotto roof. And now, Tse's talking about a time machine and Adolf Hitler not dying in his Fuhrerbunker. It was too much.

Tse knew he hadn't convinced David. "David," he said, "you must know that Hitler's body was never found. And, the bodies of Eva Braun and Martin Boorman were also never found. Nearly fifty years after the end of the War, the Russians said they had Hitler's body but, they could never produce it. It was because they never actually found it?"

"That's not true," said David. "I know there was a lot of controversy about Hitler's body but the Russians had part of Hitler's skull with a bullet hole in it."

"You know Hitler, Eva Braun, and Martin Bormann had 'look alike doubles," Tse continued. "Part of their escape plan was to execute these 'look-alike doubles' and partially burn the bodies to make identification possible, but difficult. There was no DNA analysis at that time. The Russians were the first ones on the scene at Hitler's bunker and they found the burned corpses of the 'look-alike doubles.' They assumed these were the actual bodies of Hitler, Braun and Bormann. Shortly after that, the Russians realized the bodies at the bunker were not whom they thought they were. Even after all this time, no bodies of Adolf Hitler, Eva Braun, and Martin Bormann have ever been provided by the Russians for a proper identification procedure. The real bodies were never found. That is a fact."

David had to acknowledge Tse was right. However, he was about to learn something else.

"David," Tse continued, "in 2003, the remains of a building destroyed by the 1945 Allied bombing of Berlin were unearthed at a construction site. Documents found at the site revealed it housed a secret laboratory which utilized technology highly complex even by today's standards. The partially burned documents revealed Adolf Hitler ordered Dr. Peter Krause to assemble a group of one hundred and fifty German scientists. Their project team was to develop a device that could be used as a means for Hitler to escape.

"But, that doesn't mean it was a time machine," countered David.

"True," said Tse, "it's not a smoking gun but, it's pretty close."

"But, what does this have to do with me?" David asked. "Why are you telling me this?"

"Because," Tse replied, "Adolf Hitler has used the time machine to go back in time."

"Assuming this crazy story is true, what's he going to do, Tse?" asked David, in a skeptical tone.

"David," Tse said somberly, "Adolf Hitler is planning to somehow change events which happened in the past. He is attempting to rewrite history in a way that would drastically change the future time in which we now live. I brought you here, David, because you must stop this insane plot."

David was astounded. "What are you talking about, Tse? Even if this is true, and I still don't believe any of it, who appointed you to save the country? And why would you choose me to try to stop Hitler? I'm just a history professor at a small college in Arizona."

"Ha, Ha," Tse laughed, relieving some of the tension. "You're starting to believe me, aren't you?"

"No, I'm not believing any of this, Tse," David answered.

"Oh yes you are,"Tse laughed. Again becoming serious, he said, "We Quartas were put on the Earth to serve as guardians to make sure the human race doesn't self destruct. We live according to the ancient Quarta rule. 'Everyone must find the Way. But, some are chosen and are themselves the Way.' I have been chosen, David, and so have you. People like us must take the responsibility when it is presented. We have no choice. It's who we are. I want you to think about that and accept the role you must play.

If Hitler successfully changes certain events of the past, all events that occur after that time will also change. He can change events in a way that could allow him to take over the entire earth. Think about it, David. What if Hitler were to change certain events in American history? Remember, the United States was the only country which could stop Adolf Hitler in World War Two."

"Not that I believe any of this, Tse," said David, "but, is that what you think he is going to do?"

"I'm not sure," Tse replied. "But, we're going to find out."

"I think the government must be notified," David replied. "They have trained people to handle this kind of thing."

Tse laughed. "The government doesn't know anything about it," he replied, "because anyone who was aware of the Chronometric Teleporter back in the 1940's is either dead or escaped into time with Hitler. The government assumes Hitler died in the Fuhrerbunker. Even if he didn't, everyone figures he would be dead by now anyway. If you told the government what I just told you, they'd think you were crazy. And even if you convinced the government, it would take them forever to figure out a plan. We must act immediately."

"But why was I chosen?" David persisted.

"There are two reasons," replied Tse. "First, you're a Quarta which is necessary for what you need to do. Second, you're an expert in History. You know about the past and that will be important. Also, you know better than others the potential for disaster if Hitler is successful in changing the events of the past. You understand the consequences if the Nazis restore their power and dominate the world."

Tse could see David was beginning to accept what he was saying. "I think you're starting to 'get it' David. So, here's the rest of the story. The Nazis transported themselves and three Chronometric Teleporters to the year 2010. But, Dr. Krause didn't arrive with the rest of the group."

"Why was that?" asked David.

"Hitler had been suspicious of him for several years," Tse answered. "He knew Dr. Krause had figured out his intent was to conquer the world as he nearly did in World War Two. He worried Dr. Krause might destroy the Chronometric Teleporter to prevent him from doing this. As the last of the Nazis was preparing to go through the time machine and into the future time of 2010, Dr. Krause was separated from the others and sent into a different time."

"Why didn't Hitler just kill him?" David asked.

"Hitler wanted to punish Dr. Krause for no longer believing in him. He felt Dr. Krause had betrayed him. And, to further hurt him, he sent Dr. Krause's wife into the year 2010 with the Nazis. He sent Dr. Krause to a place where he would suffer the most."

"Where was that?" David asked.

"He sent him to Alexandria, Egypt in the year 48 B.C."

"That's the year the Great Library at Alexandria was burned by Caesar. The collected knowledge of antiquity was destroyed," said David.

"Exactly," said Tse, "and that was how Hitler punished Dr. Krause. He forced him to be there when the knowledge of the ancient world was destroyed."

"Unbelievable," said David. "But, why are you telling me about Dr. Krause, Tse? He's dead now anyway."

"No he's not dead," Tse replied firmly. "The first thing you must do is find him and get him to work with you. That shouldn't be hard."

"What are you talking about, Tse?" What do you mean I have to find him? If this time machine business is true and this man actually did go back to the year 48 B.C, how am I supposed to find him? And who said I agreed to look for him?"

"You will look for him, David. Being a dedicated historian, you don't want to miss the opportunity to go back in time to see what things were really like. I've got you, don't I?" Tse said, laughing.

David smiled. "I think I believe what you're telling me, Tse," David said, shaking his head. "And that's what I can't believe. I must be crazy too. Did you say I was going back in time?"

"Remember," Tse continued, ignoring David's question, "Hitler took Dr. Krause's wife Johanna into the year 2010 with the rest of the Nazis. Dr. Krause will want to find her. He'll also want to find Hitler so he can undo the evil that he blames on himself. David, Dr. Krause is a good man and he's brilliant. He's idealistic and naïve as hell but, you need him and he needs you."

"Not that I'm a detail man," replied David, "but, how am I supposed to find a guy two thousand years ago? I don't happen to own a time machine, unless my computer can do things I don't know about."

Tse laughed. "I'll answer that later. Right now, I want to make sure you understand that changing any event in the past, no matter how insignificant, will affect all events which will occur after the original event was changed. That's very important and you must remember that. Just small changes to any historical occurrence can dramatically impact the existence of countries and the lives of millions of people who will live after the event is altered. Nothing must be changed unless it is absolutely necessary. Do you completely understand that?"

David thought about what Tse said, and was concerned he had become involved in something bigger and more important than he could ever imagine. The gravity of the situation was beginning to worry him. What if all of this is true, he wondered.

"David," continued Tse, "whatever Adolf Hitler is up to his goal has always been to dominate the Earth. The time machine gives him enormous power because he can dictate history before it happens. He can create and destroy countries and eliminate civilizations and races. Do you realize the potential for catastrophe, David? Hitler and the Nazis have become the masters of time."

David didn't have to ponder the consequences if such a group of men were to gain control of the earth's history. The Nazis could go back in time and win World War Two, or maybe not have to fight the War at all, and still have control of the entire Earth.

"Tse," David replied, "As crazy as it all sounds, I believe you."

Tse laughed. "Good," he said.

"I'm afraid to ask what's coming next," David laughed.

Tse's expression once again became serious. "Like I said, David, we have to act now."

"I get it," said David. "But, I have one more question."

"Shoot," said Tse.

How did you know about this plot, Tse?"

"My friend had a vision," Tse laughed. "You won't probably believe that, will you?"

"At this point, I'll believe just about anything," said David. "So what do we do now?"

"Let's meet at the Trading Post tomorrow morning at eight a.m.," Tse replied. "You can buy me a cup of coffee and then we'll go see my friend Lomasi Goodwater. She's a shaman and the one who had the vision. We need to find out the details of what she saw. Then we'll figure out a way to stop Adolf Hitler. Pretty simple, huh?"

"I have a feeling it's going to be far from simple, Tse."

Tse looked at David, and then back toward the far wall of the grotto. Again, his eyes seemed to search for something, memories hidden in the shadows. Tse said nothing.

"My God, it's true," David reflected. "It's so completely incredible it has to be true." The idea of time travel had always been a myth. But now, it seemed to make complete sense even though the thought of it was astounding. A sense of foreboding came over him, and quickly turned to horror, the kind experienced in nightmares. "My God, it's really true."

16

Shaman

May 15, 2010   Arizona Desert

Faint yellow hues in the eastern sky floated above the orange glow on the horizon. The early dawn was signaling another day had begun. Lomasi Goodwater didn't feel like eating but she decided to have some coffee. She was troubled because she had experienced the same ominous vision for the past three nights. Fear had replaced her calm disposition. After coffee, she would go see Shimasani, her aunt and confidante. Shimasani was her mother's older sister by over twenty years. When Lomasi's mother Nascha died, Shimasani became her substitute mother. It was Shimasani who told her that the moment she was born, she had spoken and was understood by others in the room. From that day, everyone thought Lomasi was very wise and even at a young age tribal leaders came to her for advice.

Lomasi was born in the small tribal settlement in which her mother and father lived. This settlement was approximately ten miles from the larger community where she and Shimasani now had their homes. While this tiny settlement contained approximately twenty houses, it was known by its own name, which was not common for a place that small. It was called "Ti i akta," a name from the ancient Quarta language name which meant "place of holy persons." Lomasi's mother and father were full-blooded Quartas and both had died four years earlier when Lomasi was twenty-eight years old.

Lomasi sat in her kitchen at the old wooden table that had belonged to her mother. The table, which was centered under the window, was heavy and solid and provided a warm and comforting presence. She could sit at this table and look out the window into her garden which was green with vegetables waiting to be picked. She could also see the small corral and stable for her horse further back in her yard on the right. It looked like it would be a beautiful morning. But, it was one of those mornings that Lomasi wished she didn't have the responsibility of being a shaman. She was a Quarta, however, and felt it was her destiny to become a shaman.

Lomasi was empathetic, caring and a good healer, the perfect shaman. People looked to her for both medical and spiritual guidance. It was thought that shamans had supernatural power and were conduits to the spirit world. It was also said they had the ability to go backward or forward in time. Just before her mother died, she told Lomasi she was a Quarta and, like some Quartas, had the ability to go into the past and future time. She also told Lomasi never to tell anyone of these things.

Three nights ago Lomasi had a disturbing vision. She had the same vision the following two nights. Until she had the visions, she doubted it was possible for anyone to go into another time so she never thought further about what her mother said. Her mother also told her a shaman has a connection with the spirit world and Lomasi didn't believe that was true either. Besides, the possibility of a supernatural connection did not make Lomasi happy. She already had enough responsibility and didn't want to think about it, she laughed quietly. But now, the things her mother told her had taken on new meaning and were suddenly very important.

Lomasi had almost finished her coffee but was still reflecting on the troubling vision and her role as a shaman. Like other Quartas, she lived by a few basic rules. Live a simple life among your people and provide counsel and healing for them. Part of the shaman's responsibility was to preserve the way of life of the past. Follow the established way and maintain strong family and tribal relationships. Although she didn't savor so much responsibility, she accepted it and was dependable. She often thought of herself as being like her kitchen table in that she too was solid. She could be relied upon to be there for others.

Lomasi lived alone and was too busy in her work as a shaman to think about anything else. Although she was a trim and attractive woman with long black hair and brown eyes, she never had a serious relationship. She was thinking that because she was so strong mentally and physically, those traits had discouraged a romantic interest by anyone. Also, she was very much a controller. She had to lead the way and be in charge. Sometimes she thought she was too intimidating. Whatever the case, while she had many long-time friends, romantic companions were non-existent.

She poured another half cup of coffee. She knew Shimasani would also have coffee so this would be sufficient. She was still thinking about her role as a shaman. She had many dreams before, perhaps even some visions. But nothing was ever as powerful as the vision she had experienced the last three nights. Do shamans really get power from spirits? She should know the answer to that question but didn't. Do spirits really exist? She thought she might have felt them before but wasn't sure. If spirits did exist, she wondered how strong their powers might be. She had many questions.

Some people said that the writing on the walls, the petroglyphs, were drawings of creatures shamans had seen in their dreams or visions. By drawing the pictures on the rocks, the shaman would become more powerful. Didn't her mother tell her that? She couldn't remember. But, what do the drawings mean? Are they just pictures? She wanted to know more about that someday. She took a sip of coffee and got up from the table and slowly walked to her front door. It was time to go see Shimasani.

Lomasi walked toward Shimasani's house as the sun slowly drifted upward in the early morning sky. The rock and mud road, tan like the surrounding houses, was extra dusty this morning. As Lomasi walked, her shoes kicked up little puffs of powdery dirt. She greeted a few of her neighbors who were also out in their yards this morning. Like all people who live in the desert, they had started early to get the outside work done before the sun got too high. By ten-thirty, the temperature would rise to over one hundred degrees. Lomasi liked the community where she lived. People were friendly and everyone helped one another.

She wished her neighbor Vincent would get rid of the two old cars he "stored" in his back yard. They squatted on flattened tires and were framed by dead weeds. The two piles of sun scorched maroon metal and clouded windows were contraptions whose time had passed. Why was it that all old, abandoned cars are always painted maroon? she wondered. That seemed like the color of choice for junk cars. After long years in the desert sun, roofs and hoods bleach out to dirty white. All the neighbors hated Vincent's abandoned cars. Why wouldn't he move them to a junk yard?

Lomasi soon arrived and found Shimasani at work in her backyard hanging the laundry.

"Good morning, Mother," Lomasi called.

Although Shimasani was technically her aunt, Lomasi nearly always called her Mother. On certain formal or more serious occasions, she might refer to her as Shimasani.

"Good morning," Lomasi. "What are you doing up and about so early?"

Shimasani knew Lomasi was never one to sleep late and Lomasi knew that Shimasani realized why she was visiting so early this morning. She had visited Shimasani on the two prior mornings for the same reason she had come today. She wanted to ask her about the vision.

"I wanted to come and ask your advice," Lomasi answered.

"Let's go into the house and have some coffee," replied Shimasani.

Lomasi knew the coffee would be ready as Shimasani also enjoyed her morning break. Both women went into the house through the back door. Shimasani's house, like Lomasi's, was an ordinary reservation type house. Both houses were stucco construction with a light tan, earth tone color. The houses each had half a dozen trees that served both decorative and functional purposes. They provided shade and made the houses cooler by preventing the desert sunlight from radiating through the windows. The houses were not large but they were adequate with three bedrooms, a kitchen, living room and a bathroom. Both women were alike in that they maintained neat, orderly homes and tidy yards with small gardens in their backyards.

Shimasani went into the kitchen to get the coffee as Lomasi sat down on her favorite living room chair. The chair was dark green with a huge back and soft arms. She could go to sleep instantly in this chair, except that today, she was "out of sorts" as Shimasani would say. Shimasani reappeared in the living room with the coffee and a "tell me what's wrong" look on her face.

"What is it, Lomasi? Did you have another vision last night?"

Of course she would have already known, Lomasi thought. She knew even before I got here.

"Yes," said Lomasi. "It was the same one. I've had that same vision the last three nights."

Shimasani looked at Lomasi with an understanding smile.

"Why do I keep having this same vision, Mother?" Lomasi asked.

"I told you Lomasi," replied Shimasani, "the visions come to you because you were chosen to receive them. Now, tell me about last night's vision and write it down like you did with the other two. Then compare it with them. I want to make sure you don't forget anything."

Shimasani handed Lomasi a tablet. Writing the visions down and comparing them was a good idea, she thought. She'd been very careful to record every detail in the first two visions and she would do the same for this third one. Then she would combine them all into one final copy.

"Who makes these choices, Mother?" Lomasi asked. "Who decides that I should receive these visions?" She hadn't wanted to ask Shimasani those questions because she knew her reply would involve spirituality and she didn't want a lecture from Shimasani. Lomasi always believed there was a God but had begun having doubts. "Perhaps it's all superstition," she mentioned to Shimasani one day. It was the wrong thing to say and the sermon was forthcoming.

However, today, Shimasani paused before speaking. She seemed different, like she understood Lomasi's doubts. "Just before my mother, your grandmother, died, she told me that spirituality was not only about God. There are other forces at work in the universe. These forces counter-balance each other. There is good and there is evil and these forces are independent of our earthly existence. You and I have talked about this before.

However, what my mother also told me was that she often felt the presence of 'others.' 'They are a part of these forces of good and evil,' she said. 'These others are always watching. In my old age, I sometimes think I see them but then I decide it's my ancient eyes imagining things.' She died shortly after she told me this. I have talked with many old people. I think when you are older and near death, you begin to see these spirits. They are there, Daughter. And you might think differently about things after this is over. You must find the answer to these questions yourself, Lomasi. But, don't worry. The answer, whatever it is, will come to you," she said smiling. But, Lomasi also wondered what Shimasani meant by "after this is over." After what is over? she wondered.

Shimassani would never admit that she was nearly eighty years old. Her long gray hair and wrinkled face didn't make her look old. These features established her authority as a holy person and one who should be greatly respected. She stood straight, moved quickly, and had more energy than many younger people. Everyone in the community presumed Shimasani had a spiritual connection, but she spoke with authority on every matter, religious or otherwise.

After nearly an hour, Lomasi had completed writing the description of her third vision for Shimasani. They both compared her notes and then created one final copy. The morning sun had a good start and it was getting late. Lomasi had a strange feeling she must leave.

As Lomasi looked toward Shimasani, she was surprised to see her crying. "What's wrong, Mother?" she asked.

"I don't want you to go," replied Shimasani. "It is dangerous, very dangerous. Very bad people are awaiting you. I wish you could just not go."

"What do you mean, Mother?" Lomasi asked, suddenly distressed.

Shimasani looked directly into Lomasi's eyes, the expression on Shimasani's face providing the unspoken answer, "We both know there is no choice."

Lomasi sat in her chair without speaking. It was slowly dawning on her what Shimasani meant, but in a way, she already knew.

Without speaking, Shimasani had risen from her chair and walked out of the living room. In little more than half a minute, she walked back into the room with a small box.

"I want you to take this," said Shimasani, as she un-wrapped the box.

"What is it?" Lomasi asked.

"It belonged to your grandmother," was her reply, as Shimasani handed Lomasi a beautiful knife in a soft leather sheath. The knife had a small, white bone handle and an eight-inch double edged blade. It was very old. This was not a hunting knife meant for animals but a "people knife" meant for self-defense. There was a small leather strap about fifteen inches in length attached to the sheath. "The strap holds the sheath around your thigh," Shimasani said. "The knife remains out of sight until you need it. Your grandmother had much good luck with this knife. Take it. It will keep you safe."

Lomasi had never used a knife or any weapon against another person. She was reluctant to accept it but Shimasani insisted.

"Lomasi, look at me. I am an old woman and I know many things. Remember what I am saying to you. You are to trust no one. You will not understand many things. You will not understand why people do certain things. But, you must always remember this. Trust your instincts. If you do not feel you can trust someone, then do not trust that person. But, always trust yourself. Let your instincts guide you.

If you are in danger, you must use the knife. Do not hesitate. When you pull the knife out, you must use it swiftly. There is no time to decide once the knife is out because you already decided. Use the knife to kill. Your life depends on this."

Lomasi embraced Shimasani and said, "I will, Mother."

Lomasi walked through Shimasani's front door, the knife in her hand. The moment has come before I'm ready, she thought to herself.

17

Visions

May 15, 2010   Arizona Desert

David pulled his old Chevy pick-up truck into the parking lot of the Trading Post. It was Tuesday morning and he had asked his department head for a few days off. Tse said to be there at eight o'clock and David was right on time. Usually, there were a lot of trucks in the parking lot by this time of the morning. But today, David's truck was the only one in the lot.

As Tse had not yet arrived, David decided to remain in his truck and try to remember all that happened the day before. He had lain awake and gone over everything last night and slept very little. He was trying to remember the trail he and Tse used to exit the grotto but couldn't. He couldn't even recall leaving the grotto. Didn't Tse say something about his friend Lomasi being a Quarta with the ability to go backward or forward in time?" David, who was normally clear headed, was finding everything blurred. There was a lot going on, a heavy load, he thought, and it had kept him tossing and turning all night. His mind felt like the tangled conglomeration of debris at the forefront of a flash flood crashing through a desert canyon.

Why was Tse late, he wondered. He said to meet him at the Trading Post at eight a.m. David checked his watch. It was eight a.m. exactly. A crisp knock on the truck's passenger side window jostled David from his thoughts. It was Tse. He opened the door and got in. "Let's go," he said.

"What about your coffee?"

"I don't drink coffee. I just wanted to make sure you were here early, and you are."

"Well, where's your truck?"

"Don't have one. A friend drove me here," replied Tse. "

David started the engine and the truck started rolling across the parking lot toward the main road. "Which way?" he asked.

"Take a left. We're going into the housing area."

David pulled the old Chevy truck on to the road and had only gone a few hundred yards when Tse said, "Take the first left, that road over there."

David turned off the main road and on to the dirt street leading into the small settlement of approximately fifty houses. "Take the next right," said Tse. "Stop at the second house on the right."

David turned the truck into the dusty street and it rolled to a stop directly in front of a small, neatly kept, earth tone house.

"Lomasi lives here," said Tse. "Let's see if she's home."

"You mean to tell me you didn't call her to tell her we were coming?"

"She doesn't have a phone. Come to think of it, she doesn't have a television either. She doesn't care for too much for modern conveniences," Tse said. "You'll like her a lot, David" Tse added as he knocked on the front door.

There was no answer. "She'd make a fine wife, too, David," Tse said laughing. "You ought to remember that. You're not gettin' any younger. Is that gray I see in your hair?"

"No, it's not gray and I don't need your help in the romance department," David replied.

"You need somebody's help. Your love life is a train wreck," Tse chided.

David shook his head in mock disgust. As they stood on the front porch, he could feel the sun warming his back.

Tse knocked on the door again, but there was no answer.

"Let's go," Tse said, turning around. Both men walked to the pick-up.

"Where to?" asked David.

"Take a U-turn," said Tse.

David turned the steering wheel hard and slowly rolled the truck back in the direction of the street leading from the main road. Instead of taking a left however, Tse said to go right. David pulled the steering wheel hard and slowly rolled onto the dusty street and drove for one block.

"Take a left," said Tse. "Go past the next two cross streets and it's the house on the corner on your right." David steered the truck where Tse told him and stopped at the corner house. Both men got out and walked up on the front porch. Tse knocked on the door.

The door was quickly answered by an older woman, probably in her eighties, David guessed. Tse looked at David and said, "David, meet Shimasani."

"Hello, Shimasani, I'm David Kelly."

Shimasani warily reached out to shake David's hand. "Hello, David," she said. "What is it you want?" she asked, looking at David suspiciously. "How do you know my name?"

"She's hard of hearing, David. Tell her we're looking for Lomasi," Tse said. "I'm all talked out."

"Shimasani, do you know where we might find Lomasi?" David asked.

Shimasani paused for a moment, studying David. "Why do you want Lomasi?" she asked.

David replied, "I need to talk to her. It's very important. Please, can you help?"

"Tell her Lomasi's in danger," Tse whispered.

"She may be in danger," David said to Shimasani.

"Come in," she said.

David and Tse walked into the living room of Shimasani's home. "Please, sit down," she said. Before David and Tse were in their chairs, Shimasani abruptly asked David, "What kind of help do you want from Lomasi?"

David looked at Tse, with a "help me here" kind of expression on his face.

"It's okay to tell her about the vision," said Tse. "She already knows, anyway."

David looked back at Shimasani. "It is very important that I talk to Lomasi about the vision she had.

Shimasani looked away from David again. "Lomasi is not here," she said. "She's gone."

"Where did she go?" asked David. Shimasani was still looking away from David.

Shimasani answered David's question with one of her own. "How do you know about Lomasi's vision? She told no one but me." Then she repeated, "She's gone."

Looking over toward Tse, David said, "My friend told me about the vision."

Shimasani was still looking away. "If your friend told you about the vision, then your friend must be a holy person," said Shimasani.

David saw Tse shaking his head "yes."

"Yes, he is," answered David. "So please, Shimasani, where is Lomasi? Where did she go?"

Shimasani seemed to be more trustful of David but still asked him one more question. "What did your friend tell you about Lomasi's vision?"

David could sense that Shimasani was being extra cautious and wanted to be sure he could be trusted. "My friend told me Lomasi's vision warned of very bad people and very bad things happening," replied David.

This seemed to provide the final reassurance Shimasani was seeking. "We both know where Lomasi is, David." "But, I don't" replied David, looking toward Tse again. "Yes, you do," replied Shimasani. "Because of the frightening things she saw in her vision, where else could Lomasi go but into time?"

"What do you mean?" asked David, the higher pitch in his voice signaling deep concern.

"Did you not say your friend was a holy man?" Shimasani again asked.

"Yes, I did," answered David. "Then, what did he tell you about "going into time?" asked Shimasani?" Once again, Shimansani was being cautious. David looked at Tse for guidance.

"Tell her," said Tse.

"My friend said that Lomasi is a Quarta and she can go forward and backward into other times," said David.

Shimasani was beginning to weep, just slightly, but enough that tears were slowly coming down her cheeks. "She has gone into the Ages." said Shimasani. "She had no choice."

This was bad news. Tse wanted to talk to Lomasi to find out what was in her vision. Also, he wanted her to work with David to try to stop Hitler and his lieutenants from doing whatever it was they were going to do.

David then asked Shimasani, "How much did Lomasi tell you about her vision?"

Shimasani, with a trace of a smile, looked at David. "I knew someone would come, David. I didn't know who would come or when but, I knew someone would. I also think Lomasi sensed that someone would come but she wouldn't wait. She must always be in control."

"But, what about her vision, Shimasani?" David replied.

"I am very old David. I can't remember everything. So, I asked Lomasi to write down what she saw in her vision."

"May I see what she wrote?" asked David.

Shimasani got up from her chair and walked over to the table by the side window of the living room.

Pulling open a drawer, she said "I have been keeping it right here for you, David. Lomasi had the same vision three nights in a row and we combined her notes on all three into one version." Shimasani pulled out the tablet of notes and walked across the room and handed it to David. "You are the other Quarta that can go into the times, aren't you?" asked Shimasani.

David looked over at Tse, an expression of "how do I answer that one?" on his face.

Tse shook his head, "yes."

"I'm the one, Shimasani," David said, hoping the old woman didn't press him on the time travel thing because he had no clue about any of it.

Shimasani went back to her chair and sat down. She looked over at David and said, "These men are very evil, David. Of course, you know that, don't you?"

"Yes, I do," answered David, as he began to read Lomasi's notes.

"Would you like some coffee?" Shimasani asked.

"Yes, thank you," David replied.

Shimasani left the room to make some coffee.

David looked over at Tse. "Did you want something to drink, Tse? I don't know why she didn't ask you too."

"No, I'm good," replied Tse.

"Did you say something, David?" called Shimasani from the kitchen.

"No, just talking to myself, Shimasani," David said. "What do you mean I can go backward and forward in time, Tse?" he whispered.

"I'll tell you later," Tse replied, walking over to where David sat. "Let's see what Lomasi wrote about her visions." Both men were looking at the notes Shimasani had given David.

"Sometimes I have dreams and sometimes I have visions. My dreams are a series of thoughts that run through my head. They can seem very real, but I know they are not because they are things I see in my mind. They can be happy or sad. They can even be nightmares which seem very real. But, my dreams are only images which I am thinking.

It's much different with my visions. In my visions, I actually see and talk to people from another time or place. I see objects such as the chair I am sitting in. I can reach down and feel the fabric of the chair with my hand. I can smell the odors of food cooking, perfume, and tobacco smoke. I can touch the people I see in my vision. What I see and experience is happening right in my room. I see events occurring in front of me.

Visions are much more powerful than dreams. In visions I see actual things that have already happened or that are going to happen, but I am there. The people and things I see are real. The events I see happening are real. When there is happiness for the people in my visions, I feel their joy. When the people in my vision are sad, I feel their sorrow. When there is danger to the people in my visions, I feel their fear. I become a part of the people in my visions and I experience all that happens to them.

What occurs in my visions cannot be controlled and I cannot leave the vision once I am in it. Sometimes I'm frightened and want to run away from a vision but my legs and arms won't move. Just as I cannot make the vision start, I can't make the vision end. All I can do is witness what is occurring. Although I talk to people in my visions, I cannot influence them or the events. Nothing I can say or do can change what is happening in my vision. Visions are often frightening because of this.

Although I had only one vision, I experienced it three times on as many nights. Here is what I saw:

It was on the night of May 11 that I first experienced the vision. There were three parts to my vision and it was terrifying. In the first part, a statuesque man impeccably dressed in a military uniform from another century suddenly appeared. He was lying on a bed and was surrounded by many people. He was coughing

136

violently and blood was coming from his mouth. People were crying. Someone in the vision said it was General George Washington and he was dying. The date was April 19, 1775. The image slowly faded.

In the second part, another man named Colonel Thacher came into my vision. He was an aide to General Washington and was talking with Adolf Hitler and they were laughing. Adolf Hitler talked about George Washington being killed.

Adolf Hitler's objective is to assassinate General Washington. Without Washington, the American colonies never fight the Revolutionary War or, if they do fight the war without Washington, the Americans will lose. That means the United States of America would never come into existence. Adolf Hitler and Germany and Japan would then win World War Two and set up their Aryan ideal master race. However, Germany and Japan will later fight each other with nuclear weapons in World War Three and millions of people will die and the planet Earth will be destroyed. It is too horrible to contemplate."

Shimasani offered more coffee and David quickly accepted. As she left the living room to re-fill the coffee cups, she again ignored Tse. David looked at him and joked, "She must not like you."

Tse replied, "I noticed. No big deal."

Shimasani came back into the room and handed David his coffee and then sat down.

David was still studying Lomasi's notes when Tse spoke. "You must go back into time and find Lomasi, David. She will be wherever Colonel Thacher is located so you need to find him. Be very careful with Colonel Thacher, David. He can't be trusted and Lomasi is in great danger."

Shimasani abruptly jumped in and repeated nearly everything Tse had just said. "You're right, Shimansani. I never thought of any of that," replied David, as he looked over toward Tse and rolled his eyes.

Tse, with a kidding kind of laugh said, "Shimasani's got you covered."

David wrote down Shimasani's thoughts, actually Tse's precise words. He was beginning to think Shimansani wanted to take credit for Tse's ideas. It was "no big deal" to use Tse's words, but she seemed to be going a little overboard in proving her own insightfulness or that she was a very smart person. Didn't Shimasani hear Tse say the same thing? There's something weird here, David thought.

"David, you've got to find Lomasi and help her," Shimasani said abruptly. "You must go now." Shimasani was concerned about Lomasi's safety.

While David hadn't come to grips with time travel being a reality, he was becoming less doubtful that it was a possibility. But, the idea of time travel was still preposterous. However, as he looked toward Tse, he could see him nodding his head, agreeing with Shimasani. David must go backward in time.

Shimasani jolted David from his apprehension. "What's holding you up, David?" she asked. You must leave now. It's extremely urgent. Time is running out."

Before David could ask what she meant, Tse, who had been uncharacteristically silent, interrupted. "She's right, David. There's no time to lose."

Shimasani then spoke. "David, where you are going is extremely dangerous, but you already know this. You must be very careful if you and Lomasi are to come back unharmed."

Before David could reply, Tse gave what would have been his response to David's unasked question. "David, you will be confronting very dangerous people and you must understand the magnitude of what they are trying to do. They intend to change history. You must make sure this doesn't happen. That is, by far, the most important thing. If George Washington dies, there will never be a United States of America. The world you now live in will be replaced by one which is far more hostile."

"Alright," replied David, to both Shimasani and Tse. "I don't mind telling you I'm questioning my sanity. So, what do we do now?'

Shimasani did not hesitate. "Leave now, David."

"All right, Shimasani," answered David. "But there is one more important question. Exactly what date did Lomasi say she would arrive in 1775? Shouldn't I be there on that same date?"

Shimasani already had opened the front door of her house.

"She said she would be there on Saturday, April 15. Bring her back to me, David."

She hugged David and again told him to be careful and not trust anyone. As she stood in her doorway and watched him walk to his truck, she said, "Goodbye, David."

David waved back as he and Tse climbed into the truck. "She sure doesn't care for you, Tse. She didn't even tell you goodbye," said David.

"Naw, she's just so used to me that she doesn't pay attention to me anymore," replied Tse.

"She can't see you, can she, Tse?" asked David.

"Took you long enough to figure that out, Old Buddy. Did you say you're a college professor?"

"Very funny," replied David. "I should have picked up on it when you said you were 25,000 years old but, I thought you were crazy. Now I find out you're crazy and dead."

"Well, the heck with you if you can't take a joke," Tse said, laughing.

David shook his head in mock disgust, a faint smile on his face. "Even though you're 25,000 years old, you don't look a day over ninety-seven."

"Very funny," Tse said. "Turn north. We're heading to the grotto."

David slowed his truck as they approached the stop sign on the main road. He stopped and looked both directions to check for traffic.

"If you're trying to figure out which way is north, we're facing the rising sun in the east so you would make a left turn," Tse said, laughing.

"I can't believe I'm being hassled by a ghost," David chuckled, again shaking his head.

"I'm not a ghost," Tse replied.

18

Revelation

May 15, 2010   Arizona Desert

David was increasingly apprehensive as he drove his pickup toward the grotto. His initial acquiescence to help Tse fight whatever evil was to befall the world had given way to a deep foreboding. If Tse was sane, and David had decided that he was, then he must also accept Tse's claims that Adolf Hitler escaped from the Fuhrerbunker and time travel was possible. These two "facts," as Tse called them, stretched David's sense of reality to the limit. He had read many accounts of Hitler's death and never had reason to question their accuracy. He had also read books on astronomy that dealt with time-space relationships. The conclusion had always been that time travel was not possible.

It was for those reasons that he now struggled. Maybe Tse was not sane after all. Maybe he was not sane himself. The fast moving events of the last two days were too incredible. This whole thing can't be real, David thought. It's got to be a nightmare. However, in his heart, he knew it wasn't a bad dream. Reality was confronting him.

Tse told David to take a left turn off the main road. Now they were driving west down a dirt road that stretched into the distance for several miles before disappearing behind a rise in the desert floor. After ten minutes of bouncing along, the rough road turned into an equally bumpy trail. They drove for another ten minutes before the trail ended at a small hogan and a corral holding three horses. Tse directed David to drive around to the back of the hogan and park his truck.

Both men got out of the truck and Tse led the way over to the corral. Pick out one, David. David chose a brown dappled horse and Tse took the black one. The horses were cooperative enough as Tse and David slipped the reins over their heads. There were no saddles. The men led the horses out of the corral and slung their legs over the horses' backs. They headed toward Stone Woman Mountain and the grotto.

The ride lasted over half an hour but it seemed to be over quickly, at least for David. They stopped the horses and hobbled them at the base of the huge red rock spires. The men started up the hill on Tse's secret path and were inside the grotto in a few minutes.

As they walked through the grotto, David looked up to see the hole he made when he fell through the ceiling. He remembered that, after he fell, he had seen the blue sky through the hole. But, now, there was no hole. This was strange, he thought, however, no stranger than everything else which had happened.

"Come over here, David," Tse called in a somewhat formal tone.

Tse was standing on the other side of the room by the wall with the petroglyphs, exactly opposite to where David stood. David walked across the big room and glanced upward at the one hundred foot high ceilings. As he got closer to Tse, David looked at the three intimidating petroglyphs. They were mysterious and haunting, their eerie blue glow imparting the mystical energy of a supernatural presence.

There were also symbols carved into the wall, which David hadn't noticed before. They were unlike any he had ever seen, resembling Egyptian hieroglyphics or Aztec figures, but not quite either. The black silhouette figures, glaring with fierce yellow eyeballs, seemed to hover above the ground.

Tse motioned to David to stand in front of the third figure from the end immediately to Tse's right. David moved over to where Tse had asked him to stand. What the hell is going to happen now, he wondered.

Tse looked directly at David as he took his knife from its sheath. "Give me your hand, David," Tse said. "This is going to hurt a little." Then he added, "But it could be worse. It could be me that was going to get cut."

David, shaking his head and smiling, raised his hand toward Tse. "What are you going to do?" he asked.

"I need to prick your finger. Sorry, but this knife is all I have. Don't worry. Its sharp and you won't feel a thing."

Tse took David's finger and gave it a slight poke. David felt a sharp pinch but it wasn't painful. Immediately, a small drop of blood appeared. Tse squeezed David's finger and produced several more drops.

"Put your bloody finger directly against the circle on this pictograph," Tse instructed. "Keep it there for just a moment. Oh yeah, and don't faint," Tse laughed.

David didn't faint but he did laugh. He put his finger on the small, black circle on the left side near the bottom of the pictograph.

Suddenly and silently, a part of the wall directly to David's left opened outward, leaving an arch capped door in the red rock. David, though startled, didn't move. He looked over at Tse who was smiling.

"It's okay David. You did well. Now you know the secret of the grotto." Saying nothing else, Tse walked through the doorway and David followed.

Once they were inside, the door silently closed behind them. David couldn't see any lights, but a soft blue glow provided illumination. The small room contained half a dozen flat rock shelves, one of which was a table and four others which were obviously chairs. There was a strange looking machine sitting on one of the other rock shelves. The chairs were grouped together on the opposite side of the room from where the table was located.

"David, I told you earlier about the special powers certain Quartas have. When the need arises those people are brought to the grotto. Their finger is pierced and their blood is put into the circle on the pictograph on the rock."

David interrupted. "Is it some sort of blood brother initiation thing?" he asked.

"Not exactly," replied Tse. "It's a little more scientific than that. What actually happens is when you press your drop of blood into the circle on the pictograph, the blood is absorbed into the rock and analyzed to identify the DNA. If the DNA is the required match the door opens. If it's not, then nothing happens."

"Do I have the special power?" asked David. "Yesterday, you said I didn't because my Irish blood screwed things up."

"You have the DNA which identifies you as a Quarta however you definitely don't have the special power," Tse replied. "Not yet, anyway," he added.

Tse walked over to the strange machine which David noticed earlier. It resembled the machines used at an eye doctor's office, but was a polished metal, three-foot cube. There were two holes on the front wall of the machine, resembling flat eyes, and a head rest attached to the top of the machine. There was a metal plate at the base of the machine, and on each of its sides, there were two larger holes.

"Stand in front of the machine David," Tse said. "Now stretch your arms out and put your hands into those two openings in the metal plate."

As David placed his hands in the openings, he felt his fingers slide into glove like holes. He was startled as the metal gloves contracted, wrapping snugly around his fingers.

"Put your forehead against the headpiece, David," said Tse.

David placed his head against the machine and found himself staring directly into a lens with a white light. He felt awkward and uncomfortable as he stood with his head against the headrest and his hands held tightly in place by the machine.

"Okay David, now look directly into the lens in front of you. You will see a light flash and feel a pin prick in your right index finger," Tse said. "A few seconds later, you will feel a small pain in your right eye and the area of your head behind your right eye. And, you will feel a small pin prick on the back of your right hand."

"What are you doing to me, Tse?" David asked, in a tone of mock alarm.

"I'm getting you prepared to go into time," replied Tse.

David chuckled to himself. For some reason, he trusted Tse, but still wasn't sure about the time travel thing. He was feeling a little ridiculous and began thinking this bizarre man was conducting an elaborate hoax for reasons known only to him.

David saw a tiny flash of light in the lens and simultaneously felt a slight pinch on his right index finger. A few seconds later he felt a brief, sharp pain in his right eye, and then a tiny pain on the back of his right hand.

David now felt the machine loosen its grip on his hands and the screen with the light went dark.

"I just stole your brain, David," Tse said. "But, I promise you won't miss it."

David laughed. "Seriously, what just happened, Tse?" asked David.

"You now have the powers I spoke of, David," answered Tse.

"Great," replied David. "There's just one thing. You never explained what exactly these powers are."

"Oh yeah," responded Tse. "You do seem to like your details. All right David, let's get into your training. Sit down over here," Tse said, as he walked across the small room to the chairs. "This should take about two minutes. Then you have to get to work," said Tse.

"Two minutes, that's all there is?" responded David. Somehow, he didn't think two minutes was quite adequate for the challenges Tse said he would face.

"Two minutes," responded Tse. "You ready?"

David nodded that he was, although he was thinking that maybe he really wasn't.

"Good!" said Tse. "Here we go. David, as I said earlier only a small number of full- blooded Quartas are born with the powers you now have. Lomasi is the only living Quarta with the natural power to go into time. However, a small number of Quartas are born with certain DNA types and you are one of those. When there is a need, such as there is now, a Quarta from the group with the specific DNA type is called upon to confront the situation. That you have that DNA plus a substantial knowledge of history is why you were recruited.

Someone like me guides these people to this place where they receive the powers artificially as you just did. As you can see, we check and re-check DNA very carefully. What you went through today was an initial DNA check before the door in the rock was opened. Inside the room, the machine checked your DNA again. That was the pinch you felt in your right index finger. It also checked your fingerprints and did an eye scan for further identification. But I knew who you were without all that," Tse added.

Tse continued, "After the machine confirmed your identity, it injected two powerful chips, one into your right hand and the other chip directly into your brain."

"You injected my brain?" David interrupted with some alarm.

"Yeah, but don't worry. It won't harm you," replied Tse. "Let me tell you about the powers now, David. Time is critical."

"Okay," replied David, still rattled about a chip being injected into his brain.

Tse shifted in flat surfaced rock chair. The chairs weren't particularly comfortable, but they were adequate. Tse leaned forward toward David and continued. "The first power you have is the ability to see danger coming before it happens. You will use this power but never realize it. It will save you from injury or worse. It could be operating in something as simple as a fistfight, in which case you would be able to sense your opponent's next move. It could occur when there is danger to someone else near you. You'll get a better feel for it as you use this ability. That one is really going to come in handy with your Irish temper," Tse smiled.

"Another thing," Tse added, "is that you'll also get a boost in your athleticism. You won't necessarily be stronger, but you will be able to move more quickly and defend yourself much more successfully." Tse followed up, "That doesn't mean you'll be able to beat up everybody, David, so keep your Irish side under control."

"Well, I do pretty well in that department already," replied David.

"You'll need to do a lot better to be able to handle what's coming at you," Tse emphasized.

"The second power, Tse continued, is the ability to go backward or forward in time."

"This is the big one," said David. "This is the one I still don't believe, Tse. You're going to have a lot of trouble convincing me on this one."

"No, I'm not," replied Tse. "Training's over. You have to go to work."

"Well what about the time thing, Tse?" asked David. "Are you giving up on convincing me that a person can go into time?"

"Not at all," replied Tse. "That's going to be 'on the job' training."

"Okay," responded David, still not convinced.

"Remember Dr. Krause, David?" asked Tse. "He was the good guy who invented the Chronometric Teleporter in the 1940's. You remember, he has the 'idealism" problem. Hey, he's just like you, isn't he?" Tse added laughing.

"What's your point?" asked David, smiling at Tse's humor.

"The point is, your on the job training is going to start very quickly. Like I said, you need Peter Krause and he needs you. You must find him and convince him to join with you. Remember, I said convincing him to work with you shouldn't be hard. He needs to find his wife and he has a score to settle with Hitler and the Nazis. However, finding him and getting him from where he is to where he needs to be is going to be a little more difficult."

"Tse, you said several times that 'you,' meaning me, has to go to work and go find Dr. Peter Krause. What's with this 'you stuff?" asked David. "You mean 'we,' don't you?"

"Sorry, David." Tse replied. "It's time to kick you out of the nest. I'm just the guide, the philosopher so to speak. I can't go with you."

"You mean, you won't go with me," replied David.

"Call it what you will, David. This thing is something only you can do. But, I'll be watching," replied Tse. "Maybe I'll have a couple of beers while I'm at it. Good luck, Buddy."

"I don't like doing this without you," replied David.

"There is no choice for either of us, David," replied Tse. "You must do this alone. The first thing you have to do is find Peter Krause. He will work with you as will Lomasi. You just have to put the team together."

"But, where is he? Won't he be an old man by now? Didn't you say he was in Alexandria Egypt in the year 48 B.C.?"

"He won't be an old man" replied Tse. "And he is in Alexandria, Egypt in the year 48 B.C. In 1945, he was in the last group leaving the Fuhrerbunker. As he was entering the Chronometric Teleporter's threshold, an SS guard hit him over the head and knocked him unconscious. They changed the time and destination on the Chronometric Teleporter and that's how Dr. Krause ended up in Alexandria. The rest of the group went to South America and the year 2010."

Why did you say they wanted to keep him alive?" asked David.

They wanted to be able to retrieve him if they ran into problems with the Chronometric Teleporters at a later time," Tse said. "Although they brought along three scientists who had also worked on the Chronometric Teleporter, they put Krause in storage

146

in case something came up that these scientists couldn't handle. They needed to put him somewhere out of the way where they could find him if he was needed."

"Did you say Hitler was also punishing him?" asked Peter.

"Yes," Tse replied. "You see, Hitler sent Dr. Krause to Alexandria in 48 B.C. As you know, Caesar was also in Alexandria in the year 48 B.C. fighting a war with Egypt. The Library of Alexandria was in the middle of the fighting and caught fire and burned down. In a perverse sense of "justice," Hitler sent Peter to exactly the place he wanted to go, the great Library at Alexandria. However, Peter arrived at the exact time the library was being destroyed."

Tse continued, "David, there are three things you must do. First, you must go back in time and get Peter Krause to join with you. Second, and the most important of these things, is to stop the Nazis from assassinating George Washington. Last, you must also kill Hitler and the Nazis and destroy their two Chronometric Teleporters. Peter Krause will be a tremendous help to you because he knows the Nazis and how they think. Also, he built the Chronometric Teleporters."

"Okay, Tse, I understand. I'll go find Peter Krause. Exactly what does he look like?" asked David.

"He's five feet ten inches, has blue green eyes, very fine light brown hair. He has a light complexion. He just looks, well, I don't know how else to describe it, he just looks honest. If you're a student of physiognomy, his face tells you he's a man who can be trusted. Find him, David. You need him. Oh, by the way, Tse added, one of your powers is to be able to understand and speak other languages."

"What did you do, increase my I.Q.?" asked David.

"You're hooked up with a powerful computer, David," Tse said, "much more powerful than you can imagine."

PART 3

ALEXANDRIA, EGYPT   48 B.C.

AMERICAN COLONIES   APRIL 14-19, 1775

19

Ancient Inferno

48 B.C. Alexandria, Egypt

"All right, David," said Tse, I'm going to show you how to go backward and forward in time. It's really very simple. Remember, you have a chip in your right hand and one in your brain. You simply think of where you want to go and what date you want to be there. The chip in your head will read your brain and communicate with the chip in your right hand and the computer I told you about. When you are ready to go, you simply stick your right arm out in front of you parallel to the ground, your right hand raised at a ninety-degree angle and your palm outward, sort of like waving goodbye."

Simply think of yourself as already there. A door-sized portal will materialize directly in front of you. It will remain there for thirty seconds. That's time enough for you and several others to step through it. To return to your own time, simply do the same thing. That should be easy enough."

"I guess so," replied David, "if it works."

"You know where you're going and when you need to be there. Once you're there, find Peter Krause and get out of there fast," replied Tse.

"Ok, but why," responded David.

"Like I said, Julius Caesar is in Alexandria and there's a war going on. The Library is about to burn down. Go now, David."

"You mean I'll see Julius Caesar?" David asked skeptically, still not convinced he was really going to travel into time. However, he got up from his chair. Carefully concentrating, he thought about Alexandria, Egypt, the great Library, 48 B.C, and when the library would burn. He extended his right arm with his hand at a ninety-degree angle and palm facing outward, just as Tse had instructed. He thought about actually being there and suddenly, a bluish orange portal was hovering in front of him about a foot off the ground. The portal was approximately six feet high and three feet wide. The rectangular borders of the portal were a pulsating bright orange while the area making up the doorway itself appeared as a mist glowing light blue. David took two steps toward the portal suspended in the air before him. He looked at Tse in astonishment.

"Good luck, David. Be very careful," said Tse.

A third step into the portal and suddenly David was choking from thick black smoke enveloping him. Astounded, he thought, my god, I'm here. The Library of Alexandria is burning down around me. Where's Krause?

Colossal flames shrieking fifty feet in the air were consuming the walls of the enormous building in which he now found himself. Pieces of burning debris rained down around him and the fire's thunderous roar sounded like a mortally wounded animal. Men and women in long robes were running every direction, screaming, and cursing the Romans. David could understand the language, even though he'd never heard it before. The computer chips are doing their job, he thought

The enormous flames fanned by the sea breeze leaped skyward, consuming the buildings ceiling. From above, an agonized screech punctured the thick black air and a man's body thudded loudly on the floor to David's right, his white robe still burning. The building was immense, yet the fire was racing through its every alcove and niche. As people ran through the flames, the searing heat ignited their robes.

Where is Krause, he again asked himself. The flames were so intense and the smoke so thick, he could not stand any more and began to run. Smoke billows shuffled and dodged in the fire's drafts, creating fleeting tunnels of light from the outside world. One of these tunnels suddenly opened to a flash of sunlight where a portion of wall collapsed outward into a garden. An escape route was only thirty feet away. The hole, which had opened up when the wall fell away, was immediately filled with black smoke belching through from the Library to the outside. David, covering his mouth and nose with his shirt, ran toward the opening.

As he struggled to reach the opening in the wall, three thunderous cracks above him signaled the huge inner roof was beginning to buckle. The enormous beams supporting the massive ceiling were burned through to the point of no longer being able to hold the overwhelming weight. Within minutes, maybe seconds, the first one or two would collapse triggering a rapid domino effect of failure of the other beams. The ceiling structure would crash to the floor crushing every person and thing in the burning building.

David, gasping for breath and blinded by smoke, could see intermittent winks of daylight. When he reached what he thought was a wall and an opening to the outside, he threw himself forward, thrusting with his arms and hands to try to find his way. Suddenly, there was daylight and he was outside in the courtyard. He was running faster because he knew the roof would collapse at any moment. He had gotten twenty-five yards from the building when he heard the roar of beams cracking and the roof caving in. There was an earthshaking thud as the roof crashed onto the building's floor triggering a fiery eruption. The Great Library of Alexandria was no more.

Gasping for air and choking from thick smoke, David fell to the ground. He could see the swollen clouds of black smoke rising from the burning docks and boats in the harbor. Caesar had torched his own ships, which had then started the fire, and unfavorable winds caused it to quickly spread to the Great Library. It seemed as if the entire city was on fire. The inferno surrounding David contrasted sharply with the serene blue of the Mediterranean Sea.

The scene outside the Library was no less chaotic than it had been inside. Screaming people were running in every direction. How would he ever find Peter Krause? The elegant gardens of the library grounds were littered with chunks of smoking debris. David would search this area first. As he looked back at the raging fire consuming the ruins of the Library, he saw the wisdom of the ancient world reduced to sparks and cinders. The heat radiating from the blazing wreckage was hot on his back.

To his right, the howls of terrified animals rose above the fire's roar. The gardens adjacent to the main building featured a zoo and animals were trapped in cages or pens. Some of the enclosures were burning or destroyed and many animals were running wild. Two zebras and a giraffe nearly trampled David and three deer stampeded past. David abandoned his search for Peter Krause and ran through the dark smoke and showers of sparks. He would try to free as many animals as he could.

He reached a cage holding seven panicked lions, two of which were cubs. They were howling in panic. The heavy door on their cage consisted of large wooden poles over twenty feet tall framed by large planks. David could see into to the cage through the spaces between the long poles. The door was held in place by a similar wooden pole resting in U-shaped metal clamps at each of its ends. The terrified lions were scratching at the door, pushing against it in an effort to escape. The pressure of their pushing held the wooden crossbar firmly in place. David couldn't move it.

He looked around and saw a rock which he could use for a hammer. As he struck the end of the pole, it began to move, and suddenly popped free of the metal U-clamp. The door swung open the lions charged out.

The fire was too intense to go further, but David saw the elephants' enclosure across the path. There were four elephants, all standing behind the same type of door as on the lions' cage. They were terrified and the sound of their cries was more than David could stand. He forced himself to run through the intense heat and across the path to the cage. The elephants seemed to know to not lean against the door and David quickly threw the cross pole to the ground and the door swung open. Three of the elephants ran past however the fourth one, apparently the leader of the group, stopped in front of David. In one of the most amazing experiences he would ever have, the elephant raised its trunk up and touched David's face, as if to thank him. He then lumbered off to catch up with the others.

Where was Peter Krause, he wondered. "And, how did I get into this mess again?" he mumbled, in a half-hearted attempt at humor.

David was startled by a screaming woman running into him, causing them both to fall to the ground. "Come with me," she yelled. "Help me." He could understand what she was saying. "Yes, okay, I will help you," David shouted, in Egyptian. The computer was doing its work, he thought.

He pulled the woman to her feet. Her face was covered with soot and her long robe was burned in spots. There were burn marks on her bare arms and hands. "Come, come, quickly!" she yelled, as she grabbed David's hand to lead him.

They were running toward the burning Library. As they got closer, the heat of the still raging fire was much hotter. David

152

reminded himself he must find Krause quickly but, he could not abandon this woman who needed his help. Since they were running, the smoke made breathing especially difficult.

The woman led David around to the back of the destroyed Library. He felt deep sadness at the thoughtlessness of man and the insanity of war. From his history classes, David recalled that Caesar, who was at war with Pompey, was engaged in battle with an Egyptian fleet. He set fire to his own ships in the harbor and the fire then spread to the Egyptian fleet, also causing its destruction. In what was a major mistake which Caesar never acknowledged, he also destroyed the Library and many other buildings in Alexandria.

Suddenly, the woman stopped and pointed toward a pile of large stone columns lying on the ground. Others lay crossways on top of them. Before they fell, these columns supported the Library's roof and the rear entrance.

"What is it?" screamed David, his voice hoarse from the smoke. He struggled to catch his breath.

"He's in there," cried the woman. "We must get him out."

Someone was trapped under the pile of fallen columns. "Alright, alright," yelled David, trying to calm the frantic woman. "Let's figure out how we're going to do this."

David could see an arm and hand moving under a large column that had come to rest on a second column. The second column prevented the column under which the man was trapped from crushing him to death. However, the columns weighed tons and there was no way to move them. David thought for a moment. If he could dig a small tunnel under the column trapping the man, he could free him.

"Is there anywhere to get a shovel?" David asked the woman.

The woman understood and said she would get something to dig with and return shortly. David tried to talk with the trapped man, but his entire body was held tightly against the ground causing his breathing to be labored. David knew he would have to work fast. The column was pressing down on the man and if David could not dig the tunnel directly underneath him, the man would not live long.

The woman returned with a shovel, and David began digging rapidly. They were still having breathing problems however the wind shifted and was pushing the smoke away from them.

In half an hour, David had dug an "escape tunnel" under the column pinning the man. The ground was not hard and David was now attempting to carefully burrow directly underneath the trapped man without injuring him.

"Tell him to dig with his hands," David yelled at the woman. In a few minutes, a small hole opened and the man's hand came through. David dug upward with cautious thrusts of the shovel, while the trapped man pawed anxiously at the ground around the widening hole.

In another half hour, David grasped the trapped man's hands and gently pulled him into the small tunnel. The woman reached into the small hole and grabbed the man's left arm and they maneuvered his body toward them. As they pulled him out of the hole, she leapt forward and hugged the man. Smiling broadly, she turned to David and said, "This is Didymus Chalcenterus. He is the Head Librarian." David reached forward to shake hands with the man. "Nice to meet you," David said.

"It is my pleasure, Sir," Didymus Chalcenterus replied. "You are looking for Peter Krause, are you not?"

David was shocked to hear this man say Peter Krause's name. He was also astonished that he had actually travelled in time and gone back over two thousand years. My god, he thought, all of this is true.

"Yes," David quickly responded, "I'm looking for him."

Didymus Chalcenterus continued. "He told me someone would be coming to take him away. But, you are not that person. He said a woman called Johanna would come."

"Yes, yes," responded David. "I am here to take him away and I must see him as soon as possible."

"Come with me," said Didymus. As the two men and woman walked away from the burning ruins of the Library, Didymus told David that Peter Krause arrived only two days before. He spoke Greek, which was also spoken by Didymus. Krause immediately came to the library and warned Didymus that the library would be destroyed by fire. They didn't take Peter Krause seriously at first, however, they decided to move many irreplaceable books and papyrus documents as a precaution. They couldn't move everything because of the huge quantity of materials. And, they didn't think the fire would occur so quickly. When the fires began today, Peter took everything he could carry from the Library. Everything that was saved was taken to a nearby cave.

"We will be there shortly," Didymus said.

They arrived a few minutes later. While the fire had destroyed a large part of the city including the royal quarter, the cave, which was located on the far side of a small hill, was untouched. They went inside where several people sorting the piles of ancient texts.

"Peter,"called Didymus. "Your friend is here."

A man about five feet, ten inches tall with light brown hair, just as Tse described, walked over to them. The man was wearing a white shirt and khaki pants. "Obviously, you're not one of the locals," David kidded, as the man advanced toward him.

"They gave me a robe but, I kept tripping over it," the man replied.

David was pleased the man had a sense of humor. "Dr. Peter Krause?" he asked, speaking English.

"Who are you?" the man asked guardedly.

Although Peter Krause was German, he spoke English well. However, David was not expecting his less than friendly reply. He thought Peter Krause man would be overjoyed to have someone "rescuing him."

"My name is David Kelly. I'm an American and have come here from the year 2010 in order to find you."

"How did you know I was here? Have you seen my wife, Johanna Neisner? Have you seen Hitler and the rest of his group?" Have you...."

"Just a moment," interrupted David. "I will answer all of your questions later but right now, we have to get out of here."

"How are we going to do that? Do you have the Chronometric Teleporter with you?"

"Will you stop asking questions?" replied David. "There is plenty of time for that later. Right now, we must go."

Didymus saw the urgency in David's voice. Didymus said to Peter that an Oracle told him that two men from another time would visit him. The one coming first would help him with the important task of saving many of the rare documents of the library. The second man would come and take away the first man because there was great evil in the world of the future and they must confront it.

Peter was calmed by what Didymus told him.

David extended his hand. "Thank you, Didymus."

David bid the woman farewell and she thanked him and hugged him. David turned to leave as Peter bid the others farewell. At that moment however, four heavily armed Roman guards walked into the cave. David knew this was not good.

"You will come with us," said the leader of the four men. Didymus moved to defend the two men from another time. "What is the problem, captain?" he asked.

The captain immediately replied, "These men are spies, Sir, and they are under arrest."

"No, they are not spies, Captain. You must not arrest them," replied Didymus.

"I am sorry sir. They must come with us," replied the captain. "We must go now."

As the guards had surrounded David and Peter, they now turned to leave and Didymus quickly asked, "Where are you taking them, Captain?"

"Caesar has declared all spies are to be immediately executed. These men will be taken to Caesar because he wishes to witness all executions."

"Please captain," cried Didymus, "these men are not spies. Do not take them."

The captain either didn't hear or wasn't concerned with Didymus' protests and they rapidly marched Peter and David from the cave. Knowing the soldiers would not understand, David spoke to Peter in English. "We have to get away from these guys or we'll end up dead."

"What do you suggest?" asked Peter.

David had no suggestions. The Roman soldiers were large, muscular and armed with spears and swords. They also wore metal breastplates. True, they also wore something that looked like a skirt but, David was thinking now was not the time to discuss that particular subject. The group of six men was arranged with David and Peter in the middle, following the two lead soldiers, and the second two soldiers following behind them. They were walking on a path around the side of the hill where the cave was located. There was steep drop-off to the right.

David said to Peter, "When I tell you, turn quickly and push the guy behind you hard. You have to make him fall off the path and down the hill. Okay?"

"I understand," said Peter. "You tell me when."

"Okay, be ready," replied David. "I will not say anything, but watch me closely. When I raise my right hand and scratch my ear, move quickly. Remember hit the guy hard because he's big and strong."

The group had to walk in single file as the path narrowed and the drop-off became very steep for the next seventy-five yards. Both men knew the time to move was now. David raised his hand to his ear and Peter acted immediately. David grabbed the Roman soldier immediately in front of him and he had the advantage of surprise. He threw the astonished soldier to his right and the man was suddenly in mid-air.

Peter, too, had moved quickly and turned to face the guard immediately behind him. However, the guard stepped aside, easily avoiding Peter's attempt to push him off the path. As he dodged Peter's awkward lunge, the soldier swung his left arm, knocking Peter from the trail sending him plunging down the steep hillside.

The captain, whom David was now facing, drew his sword and was coming straight at him. David moved back two steps but, the two soldiers behind him behind were also coming toward him.

David jumped backwards off the trail and landed hard five yards down the steep incline. Figuring the soldiers would use their spears, when his feet hit the sloping ground he bounced from the impact and threw himself sideways, landing another fifteen feet further down the hill. When he hit the ground a second time he began tumbling rapidly downwards. He heard the soldiers laughing as a spear crunched into the dirt, narrowly missing his head. He rolled for another few seconds and suddenly crashed into the motionless body of the Roman soldier he had thrown from the path. He jumped to his feet and heard a loud swoosh on his left as a spear flew past. Running fast toward the safety of the trees, he heard the soldiers yelling. Sometimes it makes sense to retreat, he thought. He hoped Peter was all right.

It's not that he minded rolling down the hill. He was getting used to that. But, he found the spears inconvenient, if not scary. Yeah, scary was the better word, David thought, as he ran through trees. He couldn't see Peter but he heard the soldiers cursing and they were not far behind. My God, these guys are animals, he thought. How'd they get so close to me so fast? He now realized that if he'd known how formidable these warriors were, he wouldn't have tried such a crazy escape.

"Peter, where are you?" he called. The soldiers' voices grew louder as they rapidly closed the gap between them and David.

"Over here, David," Peter yelled back.

David ran over toward Peter and yelled, "Run like hell. They're right behind me."

Although the trees offered safety from the spears, the small forest was not dense. The trees were far enough apart that David and Peter could see the Roman soldiers behind them. Even though the soldiers carried spears and swords and wore a heavy metal breastplate, they were rapidly gaining on Peter and David and would soon be upon them.

David was running ahead on Peter's left in order to push him to run faster. But, the same soldier who had thrown Peter off the path and down the slope had pulled away from the other two Romans and was coming up behind them. He was nearly within reach of Peter and was raising his arm to grab him when David abruptly stopped and jumped toward Peter and the soldier. With a rapid backward chop of his right arm, David's hand slammed against the soldier's throat. As David was running, he was off balance when he delivered the blow and wasn't sure if it was a fatal strike. But, it was enough. As David regained full running speed he glanced over his right shoulder and saw the soldier crumpled, but in a sitting position. At least I slowed him down, David thought.

The other two soldiers were running hard and passed their fallen comrade. The breeze from the Mediterranean had picked up considerably and the smoke from the burning city was pouring into the forest making it difficult to breathe once again. But, the smoke was coming rapidly and was much thicker than before.

What's going on? David wondered. Why is there so much smoke?

His question answered quickly as he suddenly saw huge flames racing toward them from the right. The forest was burning and the wind created a firestorm. Fiery tongues leapt from one tree to the next and jumped over other trees, which immediately

158

exploded in flames. The soldiers saw what was happening and turned to run back from where they came. But, the fire was moving too quickly. They would never make it back to the path before the flames caught them.

"Stop Peter!" David yelled, "and do exactly as I say." David now concentrated on exactly where he wanted to be and at what time period. He extended his right arm with his hand at a ninety-degree angle and the palm facing outward, and thought about actually being there. The portal immediately appeared in front of the two men, just as Peter was going to ask David what he was doing.

Peter knew exactly what it was. The fire was nearly upon them.

"Jump through, Peter," screamed David. Peter instantaneously dove through the portal with David less than a second behind. They felt the fire's heat on their backs as they left the flaming forest and burning city of Alexandria behind.

20

Double-crossed

April 14, 1775   Old Post Road, North of Philadelphia

David's and Peter's dive through the portal brought them from one forest into another. They were again surrounded by trees, however this forest was extremely dense and the trees were much larger. The forest's canopy was so thick they could only glimpse the sun but could see it was directly above them. Wherever they were, it was noon. David rushed the process of escaping from Alexandria. Maybe he hadn't done it correctly. He wasn't sure exactly what time period they were in or even where they were. The forest was so thick they had no clue which direction they should head. David was a desert dweller and had never seen woods this thick. It was also humid and there were mosquitoes. This was definitely not Arizona.

"Where are we, David?" Peter asked.

"Here he goes with the questions again," thought David, who was beginning to think Tse had burdened him with someone who was going to slow him down. He had already shown that he wasn't much in a fight. The Roman soldier had thrown Peter down the ravine with one swipe of his left arm. He couldn't keep up with David when the soldiers chased them, nearly causing them to be caught. Why do I need this guy, he wondered.

David first inclination was to answer, "We're in a forest." but decided that would be cruel. After all, he thought, this guy was yanked out of his own time in the 1940's, lost his wife, and was sent to a place and event that would cause him the most pain. He's suffered enough.

"My plan was to bring us into the time of April 14, 1775, somewhere north of Philadelphia," he replied to Peter. "I'm not sure where we ended up."

"You mean you have no idea where we are?" Peter replied.

"That about sums it up," said David.

"Why 1775, David?" replied Peter. "And how did you get us here without a Chronometric Teleporter?"

"Peter, why do you ask so many questions?" David came back.

"Because that's what I do. I'm a scientist. I want to know everything," responded Peter.

Their discussion was interrupted by a creaking noise and the sound of men's voices. They also heard horses snorting. They quietly crept toward the sounds, crouching to remain hidden. The sounds were much louder, just ahead of them through the large trees. Crouching lower, they crept closer and could clearly hear the men talking. They were speaking English, but with accents and slang with which David was not familiar.

"What do you think, Peter? Should we go talk to them?"

"It can't be any worse than what we just experienced," responded Peter.

"Okay. Let's go," said David.

The two men walked out of the woods toward a group of three men and a wagon and two large horses. They had stopped for a rest in the shade of the trees. From their appearance, David thought they were probably farmers. Only the largest of the three was clean-shaven. The other two had several days' growth. None of the three looked like they had a bath since the last time the two unshaven ones had used a razor. They were a rough looking group but probably typical for the time, David thought.

"Hello," said David.

"G'day, gents," the leader of the group replied. "Were you boys lost in the trees back there?" he asked.

"Yeah, we somehow lost the trail," said David. "I hate to admit it but, I don't know where we are."

"Well, boys, you're on the Post Road just north of Philadelphia. Of course, the Tories call it the "King's Highway." The other two men laughed at this remark, which David knew was meant to insult British rule.

"Are you gents Tories?" the leader continued.

David knew Tories were British Loyalists who wanted the American colonies to remain under British rule. He knew that being a Tory was not a good thing in the company of these gentlemen. He also knew the word "gentlemen" was not an accurate description of the three men. "No, we're not Tories," he replied.

"Well, that's very good, then," said the leader. "Otherwise, we'd have to hang you. And, there's plenty of trees around here to serve that purpose." Once again, the other two men laughed.

"If you want to throw in with us we're headed to Philadelphia. We stick to the Post Road, I mean the King's Highway, and that way we don't get lost." Again, his two companions laughed, apparently greatly appreciative of their leader's humor. David and Peter realized the man was chiding them on being lost when the main colonial "highway" was so close to where they'd been wandering.

"My name is David Kelly and this is Peter Krause," David said.

"My name is Contrary Walbridge," the leader replied. Contrary was a man of average height, probably five eight inches, with a large powerful chest and shoulders. His long brown hair was tied behind his head in a knot. His loose fitting shirt, originally white but now a dingy gray, hung over his black leggings. His large boots bespoke of a working man. Like the other men, Contrary carried a long musket and had a powder horn hanging from his shoulder. His face and hands were tanned from working outside.

Pointing at the two men, he said, "that's Phillip next to the wagon, and that little fellow is John. We sometimes call him "Little John" like in Robin Hood." Actually "Little John, like in Robin Hood" as Contrary said, was a huge man probably six feet four inches and two hundred and fifty pounds. "We're with Brampton's Rifle Regiment, otherwise known as "Brampton's Boys." We're from up north a bit. I'm the captain of this little outfit and we're headed to Philadelphia to meet up with our leader Moses Brampton. He's meeting with General Washington to help us get more supplies and weapons. Don't get me wrong, now. These weapons are only for duck hunting." Again, a laugh came from the other men. David knew that they were going to get weapons to use against the British in the looming Revolutionary War.

"Where are you boys headed?" I mean, now that you found your way out of the woods." Again, there was laughter from the other men.

"We're going to Philadelphia, ourselves," replied David. "If we wouldn't be any trouble, we'll travel with you."

"Okay, then," said Contrary. "Just one thing, up the road a bit is a house of entertainment called the 'Sailor's Haven.' It's a tavern that ain't near any water. Funny thing is that's why the owner named it what he did. A good sense of humor that lad has. Anyway, we're stopping there for the night."

"Okay," David said.

The three Brampton's Boys were anxious to reach the tavern and didn't want to take much time to rest. The group of five men quickly got underway. The road was rocky and filled with deep ruts. If this was the "King's Highway," thought David, the king could have it. In a short time they reached their destination.

The Sailor's Haven didn't look like a ship or bear any resemblance to anything remotely suggestive of the sea. It was a house with an attached large structure which served as the tavern. There was a huge barn to the tavern's right. Carriages, wagons, and a stagecoach sat in front of the tavern and twenty or more horses were tied to a wooden railing. It looked like a busy day at the Sailor's Haven.

John was driving the wagon and he brought it over near the barn where the other wagons sat waiting for their owners. Contrary Walbridge and Phillip, the third member of the group, went into the noisy tavern. Peter and David paused on the front porch of the establishment, looked at each other, shrugged their shoulders and followed the two men inside. They were greeted with strong odors of cooking food, tobacco smoke, beer, perfume, and of course, those who had not bathed in the last month or so. This ain't the Ritz, David surmised.

A corpulent serving maid with a big smile motioned them to a table in the middle of the room. The furniture was wooden, heavy and rough. Oddly, the chairs were comfortable and the table was a good height for an easy reach of a glass of beer. David liked the place and it seemed to be agreeable to Peter too. John finished with the horses and joined the other four men who had already gotten their drinks. It was immediately obvious the most important part of the meal for the Brampton Boys was served in a mug. Contrary, Phillip and John each ordered a New England and molasses, a popular and powerful drink, which consisted of rum sweetened with

163

molasses. However, it didn't sound good to Peter and David who both ordered beers. The beer was warm but, it was strong and the taste was more than tolerable. This could turn into a long night, thought David.

As David and Peter looked around the big room they saw half a dozen British soldiers sitting at various tables. The rest of the clientele appeared to be from every niche of society. There were several well dressed ladies and men, frontiersmen, farmers, businessmen and who knows what else. At any rate, it was very crowded and everyone appeared to be having a very satisfactory time.

The serving maid came back to the table and asked John what he wanted to drink, although she knew it would be a New England and molasses. Contrary and Phillip ordered their second round and also two more beers for David and Peter. It suddenly occurred to that David he had no money, a fact he mentioned to Peter.

To David's surprise, Peter replied, "When I was in Alexandria and Didymus finally decided to believe me about the impending destruction of the library, he rewarded me with a bag of one hundred gold coins. I think one gold coin will take care of any expenses we incur."

Maybe this guy will be okay, David thought. "That's great," he said.

At that moment one of the British officers rose from his chair and raised his glass for a toast. The room immediately went silent. "Long live the King!" he toasted. The other British soldiers and many patrons in the room raised their glasses and shouted, "Long live the King!"

While the talk of war with England was discussed openly, not everyone was enthusiastic about that prospect. Many people in the room, as well as in the thirteen American Colonies, were Loyalists. They wanted the colonies to remain a subject of England. It seemed that the room was divided equally between the "Loyalists" or Tories" and the "Patriots." The Brampton Rifle Regiment Boys were among the most devout of the Patriot group.

Contrary, being a captain in the Brampton Rifle Regiment, took unspoken exception to the British officer's toast to the king. He realized the Redcoat (He sometimes referred to Redcoats as "lobster backs,") was drunk. In the interest of not spoiling a good time for everyone, he kept quiet.

Contrary quickly gulped his second New England and molasses and had grabbed a third one from the serving maid's hand. She obviously fancied Contrary and playfully resisted letting him take the drink, but finally gave it up. He ordered another round and made quick work of his third New England. The next round of drinks arrived quickly. The Brampton Boys, David and Peter, were enjoying the conversation which had become focused on Peter's and David's odd clothing and clean shaven faces. John ordered another round before taking a gulp of the New England just delivered to the table.

A British officer on the other side of the room decided he should also offer a toast to the king and promptly did so. "Long live the King!" he yelled, in an alcohol slurred accent. This was followed by a reply from the Loyalists in the room, "Long live the King!"

Since making the acquaintance of Contrary Walbridge, David and Peter wondered how any man could end up with such a name. They were soon to find out because this second toast was more than Contrary could endure.

Contrary stood up and raised his glass, "To the Patriots!" he exclaimed.

"To the Patriots!" came the enthusiastic reply from the other half of the clientele.

The British were outraged and took Contrary's toast as an insult. The officer who gave the first toast stood up and announced that Contrary and everyone at his table was under arrest for sedition. He then ordered the British soldiers to take all five men into custody. The five British soldiers grabbed their rifles and promptly marched over to the table. The lead soldier stopped next to Contrary. The entire room had become silent.

"Gentlemen, you will stand up and come outside with us," ordered the soldier. Contrary, his patriotism enhanced by six New England and molasses, stood up and looked into the soldier's eyes. "We won't be going anywhere with you today, my lobster back friend," he announced, slurring his words. "In fact, it's you that will be leaving this establishment very directly."

With that, Contrary swung his right arm in a powerful roundhouse punch. His fist landed directly on the left jaw of the surprised soldier, causing him to fall backwards in an unconscious heap across the adjacent table.

The tavern erupted in shouts of support as the Loyalists cheered the British and the Patriots cheered Contrary's group. The local magistrate and two of his deputies who had been having lunch jumped to their feet and were coming toward the table to assist the British. The two soldiers who had been standing near their fallen leader were struggling with Contrary. Phillip and John had begun fighting the remaining two soldiers.

However, the three magistrates and also the British officer who ordered the arrest were converging on the table. David, who had decided to sit back with his beer to enjoy the fight, could see that things were getting a little uneven. There were already four British soldiers fighting with the three Brampton Boys. David wasn't worried about this match, knowing the four soldiers were no match for them. However, with four additional men joining the fray, things had changed.

The tavern was crowded and the three magistrates and British officer had to maneuver around the packed tables in single file. The magistrate was the first to reach David and Peter's table, his two deputies and British officer standing behind him. David had no choice but to get into the fight. However, Peter was sitting next to where the magistrate, two deputies and British officer stood.

As David was getting up from his chair, the magistrate fell to the floor screaming with his hands over his face. His first deputy also fell to the floor screaming with his hands holding his face. Peter charged toward the second deputy and threw himself into the man's mid-section and both men fell to the floor. The British officer was reaching for Peter as David lurched forward and threw a right hand punch. The blow landed above the officer's left eye and opened a wide split as the man fell to the floor. The place was roaring as Loyalists and Patriots screamed encouragement to their respective side.

The British officer struggled to his feet, but David delivered a blow to the man's left jaw causing him to fall backward to his right, taking him out of the fight. The two magistrates, still screaming, had gotten to their feet and were trying to find their way through the crowd to escape the tavern. They were apparently blinded. What the hell did Peter do to them? David wondered.

Contrary made short work of the other British soldiers who ran for the door leaving their rifles where they had fallen. John and Phillip easily handled the other two soldiers who had also retreated through the tavern's front door. Peter was sitting on top of the remaining magistrate and slapping him around.

"Please, let me go!" the man pleaded.

"Will you leave if I let you up?" asked Peter.

The magistrate shook his head yes.

Peter jumped off the man and helped him up. The magistrate then ran toward the door in a crisscross path through the clusters of tables. The fight was over. The Brampton Rifle Regiment men, David and Peter had won and the Patriots in the crowd cheered.

The proprietor of the tavern, a man in his mid-fifties named Jonathan, came over to the table. He wanted to be the first to congratulate the men and slap them on their backs. "That was a great brawl, gentlemen! Thank you for the entertainment. Your drinks are on the house. No charge."

Contrary replied, "Then we'll have another round, Sir." That caused a roar of laughter from the Patriots. Even a few Loyalists appreciated the humor. Jonathan motioned to the serving maid to bring the round of drinks.

"Gentlemen, drink this round quickly," said Jonathan. "Then you must go. The British will be back with reinforcements. I'll meet you outside in a moment."

David, Peter and the three Brampton Boys drank fast and went outside. Cheers followed as they headed out the door. Jonathan was standing over by their wagon with a stable hand. "Where are you boys headed?" he asked.

Contrary told him they were going to Philadelphia, which was about twenty miles away.

"You gents need to stay off the main road because the British will be looking for you. Nobody knows that's your wagon, so Ezra will drive it to Philadelphia on the main road and meet you at a tavern called The Three Rings. If you head directly east through those woods you will come to an old Indian trail. It's barely a footpath. That trail goes south all the way to Philadelphia. The

British probably don't know about this trail and no one uses it anymore because there are several streams that are hard to cross.

But, don't go into the woods here. Those two standing on the porch over there are Loyalists. If they see you go into the woods they'll know you're heading for the old Indian trail. They're watching so they can tell the British where you went. Go north on the Post Road back where you came from. Walk for a quarter of a mile and go around the curve. That will take you out of sight of the tavern here. Once you get around the curve in the road, go into the woods and head straight east and you'll run into the old Indian trail. Go quickly, gents. Good luck."

The group started walking north at a fast pace with the three Brampton Boys in the lead. Because they hadn't been alone since they met in Alexandria, David didn't have a chance to talk to Peter about what was going on.

"Peter," David said, "we need to talk. But, before we do, I have to ask you what did to those two magistrates back in the tavern?"

"I threw pepper in their eyes, David. It's not a new trick but, it always seems to work," replied Peter

"I thought it might be something like that," said David. "It was a great job, no matter how you got it done. But, Peter, as much as you like to ask questions, you haven't asked me where I'm from, where we're going, or anything," added David.

"I figured you were from some future time, David," Peter replied. "I assumed you got hold of my Chronometric Teleporter and traveled into the past to find me. I was hoping it would be my wife who would have done that."

"I've never seen your Chronometric Teleporter," replied David. "Hitler still has it and he's using it. I came back into time another way."

"I guess that should have been obvious," replied Peter. "Hitler sent my wife Johanna into the year 2010, somewhere in South America," he added. "And, you know where he sent me."

"You must have gotten him mad as hell," replied David.

"Actually, it wasn't that I did anything to upset him. I knew better than that," Peter said. "He would have had my wife and I killed had I made him mad. But, I was a fool. I thought he wanted the same thing I wanted. Like a naïve child, I wanted to save

168

mankind. Hitler's goal was to conquer mankind. I finally understood his real objective but by then, my wife and I and one hundred and fifty other scientists were virtual prisoners. We had to do what Hitler wanted or we all would have been killed. It was as simple as that. I thought if I produced the Chronometric Teleporter he wanted, I could destroy it at some later date. Obviously, I was wrong about that."

"But, that still doesn't explain why he sent you back to 48 B.C. I know that seeing the Library burn greatly upset you. But, what did you do to cause him to do that?" responded David.

Peter explained, "I lost faith in Hitler and realized he was evil. I regret it took me so long to figure that out but, I was so completely absorbed in building my Chronometric Teleporter, I ignored everything else. Once Hitler realized I no longer had faith in him, he didn't trust me and wouldn't take me with his group into the year 2010. Unfortunately, he took my wife. I need to find her, David. Will you help me?"

Once the five men walked around the curve in the road they immediately headed into the woods. Getting on the wrong side of the British was not something David wanted but it had happened. Now he and Peter would have to dodge the British as well as the Germans.

The forest was thick and the five men were struggling to get through the fallen trees and brush. However, it gave David a chance to talk further with Peter. He told him that Hitler had come back to the time they were now in for the purpose of assassinating George Washington. If they could kill George Washington, the Revolutionary War would never be fought and there would never be a United States. That would allow Germany to win World War Two and Hitler would achieve world domination. He decided not to get into Lomasi's third vision in which Germany and Japan were to go to war. There wasn't time to explain it all.

Looking worried, Peter told David when he figured out Hitler's true goals he feared the Chronometric Teleporter would be used for something evil. As Tse said, Peter felt a great deal of guilt for making it possible for Adolf Hitler to escape and cause more suffering. "I wanted to accomplish exactly the opposite, to help mankind," Peter explained.

After nearly an hour, the exhausted men reached the old Indian footpath. It was badly grown over from lack of use and they nearly missed it. The small group was hot, tired, and mosquito bitten. They sat and rested for a few brief moments but, the mosquitoes were so troublesome they got back on their feet and headed south.

Contrary led the group with David and Peter alternately walking abreast of him or behind when the trail narrowed. David told Peter all he could while they were walking on the Post Road and through the woods. He also asked Contrary where he might find General Washington's headquarters. He remembered Contrary said their leader Moses Brampton was meeting with Washington. Contrary said the headquarters was in the city and easy to find.

David also asked if he knew General Washington's aide, Captain Thacher.

"I've seen him before but, I don't know him," Contrary replied. "He's a dandy, a fancy pants and not somebody who'll be drinking with me."

"Is he a good man?" pressed David.

"What do you mean by a good man?" replied Contrary.

"I mean, is he honest? Can he be trusted?" David asked.

"I couldn't answer that, to be sure," replied Contrary. "General Washington seems to like him because he's had him as his aide for over a year."

They'd been hiking for three hours and there were only a couple of hours of daylight left. They'd drunk too much, thought David. Everyone was tired.

They heard the sound of water directly ahead. In a few minutes they came upon a small river about fifty feet wide. It looked like it could be deep in spots and there were little islands of rocks and bushes in different parts of the river. A person might be able to jump from one rock to another and get at least part way across the water. However, it didn't appear the river could be crossed completely without swimming part of the way. The group decided to spend the night on the northeast bank.

Luckily, the men brought their rifles and powder horns into the saloon when they arrived. They left everything else, including their rucksacks, which held some strips of salted meat, in the wagon. With the Loyalists watching them from the front porch of the saloon,

170

they had to pretend it wasn't their wagon, which meant they couldn't take anything out of it.

"John, you're the best shot. See if you can get us some meat," ordered Contrary.

"Contrary, how about if I go with John," asked David. "I'll help him carry whatever he kills."

"Good idea," said Contrary. John took his long rifle and he and David followed the river toward the southwest. Following the river northeast back in the direction of the Post Road would not be a good idea. If the British were in the vicinity, they would surely hear his rifle shot if he spotted some game. John was thinking that a fire might not be the best idea either. The woods and sky would be dark before they could get the deer cooked up. A fire glow could be seen for miles. What was Contrary thinking? The good news was the wind was blowing from the south so he wouldn't have to worry about any game picking up his smell.

David and John had been following the river walking in the damp sand on the bank in order to minimize the noise of their walking. Suddenly, John spotted a small deer one hundred yards ahead on his right. The wind was in their favor and the deer hadn't picked up their scent or heard them. John favored a .55 caliber long rifle with an octagonal barrel. It had a blade front sight and an open V rear sight. He could easily hit a deer at two hundred yards but this one at only half that distance was an easy shot. Although they had walked over a mile downstream, John was still worried that the sound of his rifle shot would carry up the river and let the British know where they were located. John squeezed the trigger slowly and the thunderous shot rang out. The deer fell.

David and John gutted the deer and cut a sapling to which they tied the deer's feet. They each took an end of the pole and hoisted it to their shoulders, leaving John's right hand free to carry his rifle. He had reloaded the gun in case they encountered a British patrol. They figured they had gone down river nearly a mile, and as they began to head back, they walked more rapidly because they weren't concerned about being quiet to avoid scaring the game.

In a short while they were nearly back and the camp was about three hundred yards away. As David looked up the river, he thought he saw a flash of red in the stand of trees ahead of them. John had seen it too and both men simultaneously ducked down, throwing the deer into the grass on the riverbank. If it was the British, it didn't appear that they had seen them. Keeping their heads low, they crept through the underbrush and moved higher up the riverbank, quietly slipping into the forest. They would make a semi-circle around the camp, going north and then east, and approach from that point. If it was the British, David and John would be coming in over the same ground on which the British would have approached the camp. If they were waiting to ambush them, the British would not be expecting them to come in from the same way the Redcoats had just come.

They began their semi-circle with a swing directly north but bearing slightly east. They hadn't gone thirty paces when they saw movement twenty-five yards due east of where they stood. They crouched low, nearly crawling, to come up in back of a British officer. The Redcoat was flailing his arms trying to chase away the mosquitoes. He didn't hear John move up directly behind him. The stock of John's rifle hit him hard on the back of his head and he tumbled forward unconscious. David grabbed the fallen man's officer's pistol, a handsome brass barreled piece with silver mountings.

They figured correctly the British captured Contrary, Phillip and Peter and were waiting for them to return. As they cautiously moved further north, they spotted another Redcoat in the brush. He was also batting mosquitoes away. Like John, David sneaked up on this soldier. However, as he was about to thump him on the back of his head, the soldier turned toward David. David pointed the pistol at the man and put his finger to his own lips signaling the man should not make a sound. He motioned for the man to drop his gun and kneel down. John came behind the man and hit him on the head. This was too easy, thought David.

Their luck changed as they heard a third British soldier call to the others. David and John froze where they stood. John answered in a perfect British accent. "Over here, Mate." That was not the right answer and they heard a musket shot and the ball's "whish" split the air inches from their heads.

David crouched low in the brush while John, figuring the Redcoat would not have time to re-load his one shot rifle, charged toward him as fast as he could run. He could see the red coat through the bushes and in the next one or two steps, would throw himself into the air at the soldier. He hadn't expected the soldier would also have a pistol. But, the man was now pointing one at John. "Stop where you are," ordered the soldier. "Hand over your rifle."

John stopped immediately, and surrendered the rifle to the soldier. How humiliating, he thought, I'm captured by a young boy. The boy looked to be no more than seventeen years old. His hands were shaking as he held his pistol.

"Put your hands in the air and walk to the path," he ordered.

John had no choice but to do what he was told. David, still crouching low, quietly followed the two men. The men reached the path in a few moments and John saw his comrades seated on the ground with their hands tied behind their backs and surrounded by a dozen British soldiers. Jonathan the innkeeper was also there and wasn't a Patriot after all. He'd set up a trap for Contrary and the rest of the group. The British waited until the men reached the river and surrounded them. The river was deep and the men couldn't escape. David and John had left to hunt and the British just waited until they returned.

As John walked into the camp followed by his young captor, the British officer in charge, Major Tarpley, greeted him in a sarcastic tone. "Welcome," he said. "Did you have a successful hunt?"

John answered he had gotten a deer which was back in the woods.

"By the way, where is the other member of your party? I believe there were five of you, were there not?"

"He's still hunting," replied John.

"I see," replied Major Tarpley. "And, if I might ask, what did you do with our other two men?"

John told the major that they were fine, other than a lump on their heads.

The major turned to John's captor, "William, would you see if you can find our Lieutenant and our other careless comrade?" The soldier began walking toward the woods in David's direction.

Then Major Tarpley turned toward another soldier, "Corporal, would you be so kind to take two men and escort our great hunter to retrieve the deer and carry it back for us? Fresh meat is always welcome, and Jonathan can prepare the deer for our late dinner this evening. We'll be happy to send some scraps over to the stockade for you four gentlemen and your friend as soon as we apprehend him." The three soldiers and John walked south along the river.

David, who was crouched behind a large oak tree, waited as the British soldier named William advanced toward him. Keep coming my way, thought David. In a few seconds, the British soldier passed, and David jumped out behind him.

"Stop where you are and don't move!" David whispered firmly. "Throw down your rifle and pistol and put your hands behind you."

The young British soldier, shivering with fear, did as he was told. David took the strap off the soldier's rifle and used it to tie his hands in back of him. With the soldier in front of him, both men marched back toward the Indian trail and stopped at the edge of the woods. David looked back to his right toward the south. He couldn't see John and the three British soldiers, and he walked his prisoner back toward the camp.

Major Tarpley and the other soldiers were surprised to see the two men suddenly standing in the trail. With his arm tightly around the British soldier's neck and holding a pistol to the side of his head, David looked directly at Major Tarpley.

"Major Tarpley," David yelled, "I would like to make a trade with you."

Major Tarpley, whose face had turned bright red, was furious this country hayseed had once again gotten the best of a British soldier.

Glaring directly at David, he screamed, "What is it you wish to trade?"

"Would you be interested in three British soldiers in exchange for my three friends sitting on the ground there?" David replied.

Major Tarpley was outraged and screamed, "The Crown does not negotiate with country bogtrotters. You will release that man immediately. If he is harmed, you will hang. Do you understand me?"

"Yes Major, I understand you. But you had best understand me. If you do not release my companions immediately, I will shoot this soldier dead. I will then run through the woods to where I have

174

hidden your other two soldiers and also kill them. If you do as I say, this will end nicely. If you do not, at least three of your men will die, and probably more, as I also have a rifle and can fight in the woods much better than you British. And, you will find out Major, I am the best shot you shall ever meet. Give me your answer, Sir."

Major Tarpley did not wish the incident to escalate into shots being fired and taking casualties. What had occurred at the tavern was embarrassing but no one had to know about this even more humiliating event in the forest.

Still infuriated, Major Tarpley replied, "What is it you wish?"

"Lay down your guns and untie my friends, Major," replied David. "You and your men walk north on the trail for one mile and my friends and I will be on our way. You can come back and pick up your guns later."

The Major knew he lost this battle and wanted the incident to quickly end.

"Cut them loose," ordered the major.

Once the ropes were removed, Contrary, Phillip, Peter and John wasted no time collecting the weapons.

"All right, Major," said David, "start marching your men north on the Indian trail.

As the parade of British soldiers walked out of the camp, Contrary called, "Just a second, Jonathan. You stay with us."

"What do you want with me?" he asked, his voice quaking with fear.

"You know what we want," said Contrary. "We'll relieve you of that bag of gold you received from the major for double crossing us." As he reached toward Jonathan's coat pocket, the frightened innkeeper moved back a step.

"I'll get it for you," he said, quickly reaching inside his breast pocket for the bag of gold coins.

"What else are you hiding in there?" asked Contrary, as he pulled out an even bigger bag of gold coins. This should take care of the two horses and the wagon which I'm sure you kept at your tavern instead of sending it to Philadelphia."

"You can go now, Jonathan," said Contrary. "But, go east through the woods, not north on the Indian path." Jonathan started running east into the trees, happy to be getting off with just the loss of his money.

Contrary complimented David for a job well done. Then he said, "We'll throw the British guns and powder horns in the river. That way, they can't come after us until they fish out the guns and get some dry powder. Then we need to go find John."

John, his hands tied behind his back, had been leading the three British soldiers down the river toward the deer. They reached the place where David and John had thrown the slain animal into the grass. "Cut his hands loose," ordered the corporal.

John stood looking at the three of them, rubbing his wrists. "Well, get a move on. Pick up the deer," ordered the corporal.

"Could one of you gents give me a hand?" asked John. "He's heavy."

"Too bad mate," the corporal laughed. "That job falls to you."

The three soldiers held their rifles parallel to their bodies, with the butts of their guns on the ground and the barrels pointed skyward. John knelt down in the grass with his right side next to the deer and positioned himself between the deer and the soldiers. He untied the deer from the sapling. As the soldiers stood laughing, John slowly moved his hand underneath the one hundred pound gutted body of the deer. Picking up the deer as effortlessly as if it were a glass of beer, in one powerful motion he threw the bloody carcass at the two soldiers standing to the right of the soldier directly in front of him. The force of the deer's body striking them knocked both men to the ground causing them to drop their rifles. John grabbed the rifle away from the astonished third soldier as he tried to raise the weapon.

"I'll relieve you of your weapons, boys," John shouted at the other two soldiers lying on the ground. "Do exactly as I say or I'll put a ball through your heart."

"You there," John yelled at the soldier nearest him, "Tie the hands and feet of your friends, there." Once that was done, John had the third soldier drag his two comrades over to a large tree and tie them securely to its trunk. He left the men's rifles near them in case he might need them later. John tied the third soldier's hands behind his back and they both started walking back toward the camp.

176

Before he had walked a half-mile, he ran into David, Peter, Contrary and Phillip.

"It's about time you came looking for us," yelled Contrary. "We need to find another tavern to finish our drinks. Let's tie this fellow up and be on our way."

They left the British soldier tied to a tree and walked back up the river a few hundred yards.

"Boys," Contrary said, "we've got to split up. David, you and Peter will have to get to Philadelphia on your own. The three of us may not be able to go to Philadelphia directly as the British will be looking all over for us. But, we'll probably get there before you," Contrary laughed. "You boys better be careful too. They hang people for sedition, not to mention assaulting a British officer," he laughed.

Then, the three Brampton Boys were gone, headed northeast into the woods. David figured they were probably going to give Jonathan the tavern owner some more trouble.

David and Peter decided to stick to the Indian path and travel through the night if the moon was bright enough. If not, they would have to sleep in the woods and start in the morning. On the other hand, David had another way to get there. So far, however, he hadn't landed at times and places he considered favorable using the "time travel power" Tse had given him. "It's probably better to walk, he thought.

They had to get on the move as the British would soon be back. Even if they didn't have their guns, there were over a dozen of them. But first, David and Peter had to get across the river.

21

Metamorphosis

February 14, 1775   Boston

When Adolf Hitler initiated World War Two, his assumption was that Germany would win the conflict. Once that was accomplished, the Nazi's could begin racial cleansing on a global scale and the Aryan Race ultimately would become the only inhabitants of the Earth. However, when Germany lost the war, Adolf Hitler and his group of twelve hundred Nazis used the Chronometric Teleporter to escape to South America and the year 2010.

Hitler had already concluded he could use the time machine to go back in time and change past events in a way that would help him accomplish his goal of world domination and the establishment of the master race. Once they were established in South America, Adolf Hitler and the other Nazi leaders then developed actual plans to manipulate history in a manner that would insure Germany would win World War Two.

After researching various historical time periods, they sent SS scouts back in time to determine the most effective way to change past events so Germany would win World War Two. They then developed a brilliant plan that would be very simple to execute.

The plan would require only a small number of people and a contingent of fifty heavily armed SS Troops. The group would go back in time to Boston in the American colonies in the year 1775 and contact the Hessian commanding general Gerhard Muller. (Hessians were German mercenaries fighting for the British.) Working through the general, Hitler would set up an alliance with the British and help them defeat the American Colonies. Once the Americans lost the looming Revolutionary War, the United States would never come into existence. Without a United States fighting in World War Two, Hitler and the Nazis would be assured of victory.

Led by Adolf Hitler the main Nazi group comprised of six key people and fifty SS Troops arrived in Boston on February 14, 1775. They had previously sent three SS men, General Fritz Werner and two spies, to secure accommodations for the main group and gather intelligence on British political and military plans. They would also identify Loyalists who might help them and persons who would oppose them.

General Muller was enthusiastic about meeting with the Nazis because unrest in the American colonies was escalating to the point of armed confrontation. General Muller arranged for Adolf Hitler and the Nazis to meet with the British general, Nigel Pickering, the North American Army Commander.

SS intelligence had confirmed that General Pickering was anxious to put an end to the problems in the American Colonies. He was also under a great deal of pressure from the King and Parliament to do so. He too was interested in working with the Germans to assure a conclusive defeat of the Americans.

Things had not been going well for the British in the American colonies. There had been an increasing number of challenges to British rule by the Americans. While no shots had been fired, groups of armed militia and Minutemen were openly challenging British troops. Throughout 1774, General Pickering realized the situation was getting out of hand and decisive measures needed to be taken to re-assert British control and stabilize the thirteen Colonies. He had sent a letter to the King in October, 1774, requesting a large increase in military forces.

However, instead of sending additional military forces, the King and his advisors devised a plan which they thought would be a more effective way to control the situation in the American Colonies. He responded to General Pickering with the following letter:

My Dear General Pickering,

Regarding your request for additional Army forces, the Royal Colonial Advisement Council has developed the following fair and reasonable recommendations to assure the American Colonies render creditable attention and dutiful respect and adherence to the laws and wishes of England. It was the consensus of this august

179

Parliamentary Council that the following three measures be undertaken with all due haste.

1. The rebels must be dealt several carefully calculated decisive military strikes.

2. The Colonies shall be combined to form a separate country named Dorchester. (You shall be pleased to note that many of the forefathers of the American citizens were born in the town of Dorchester, England.)

3. A monarchy is to be established to govern this new country of Dorchester. This monarchy is to serve as a vassal state and its allegiance is to the throne of England. (You must also note this arrangement would provide the Americans a sense of self rule over the new country's internal affairs. A distant cousin of the King, Madame Rebecca Bettenfield of Philadelphia, would become the Queen of the new country of Dorchester.)

> *His Royal Highness King George III*
> *This Twelfth Day of October of The Year 1774*

The SS spies had learned of the contents of the letter. That the British realized decisive measures were needed and were already moving forward with a plan was a stroke of good fortune for the Germans. They were confident the British would join forces with them to defeat the Americans. A secret meeting with the Hessian commander, General Gerhard Muller, and the British Commander, General Nigel Pickering, was scheduled for ten a.m. on Thursday, February 16, 1775. It would be held at the Nazi compound located at a large estate just outside Boston. Adolf Hitler would conduct the meeting. Other key people of the Nazi group would also attend this meeting. They included Martin Bormann, SS General Fritz Werner, SS Colonel Helmut Wolf, SS Colonel Dieter Kruger, and the scientist Dr. Wenzel Klein. (Dr Klein was along in case there were any problems with the Chronometric Teleporter.) The fifty elite SS Troops, including several other officers, would provide security.

The Nazi group spent Feb 14 and 15 getting organized and securing the compound. The advance group headed by General Fritz Werner had been very careful in selecting a location for the Nazi headquarters. They wanted to have proximity to Boston, but also wanted to be located far enough away from the city that they could operate at the highest level of secrecy.

The main house of the estate was a large, handsome, red brick structure. A formal front porch with white railings complemented the white entrance doors and window frames, accentuating the design of the house. The house was constructed to accommodate a large number of people for formal dinner parties and contained a ballroom which its present occupants could use for meetings. There was a sitting room, library and ample bedrooms to accommodate the higher-ranking people in the group. The furniture was constructed in the colonial style and immense couches and chairs were covered with expensive fabrics of deep red. Imported lace draperies were an added touch of elegance. The ceilings were ten feet high and the large windows allowed maximum outside light.

The grounds surrounding the home enhanced the overall beauty of the estate. Gardens, trees, and stone pathways covered the acres around the house. The gardens were designed around extraordinary white marble sculptures. The large building at the far end of the back yard housing the fifty SS Troops was almost completely hidden by trees and large shrubs.

The SS established a defense perimeter around the house that was easily controlled with their modern weapons which included machine guns, grenades, multi shot rifles and pistols. The perimeter was defined by the white fence winding around the entire estate. The only enhancement was the precaution of loading several wagons with bales of hay from the barn. The hay bales could be placed at strategic points around the white fence perimeter in the event of any hostilities. Any attackers would be limited to single shot rifles or pistols and the firepower at the disposal of the SS Troops would easily overwhelm any force.

It was now February 16 and the Hessian commander, General Gerhard Muller, and the British commander, General Nigel Pickering, had just arrived by horseback. They had been instructed to not use coaches because the drivers might compromise the secrecy of the meeting. As Adolf Hitler and Martin Bormann watched from the large sitting room window, both generals were now dismounting. Hitler looked closely at their horses, large, exquisite animals. "No doubt very expensive," he remarked to Martin Bormann.

SS Colonel Helmut Wolf greeted General Muller and General Pickering at the front door and escorted them into the library where he introduced them to Adolf Hitler and Martin Bormann. They already knew General Werner as he had briefed them that these men were from the future time of 2010. General Werner demonstrated the Nazis' modern machine guns, grenades, pistols and rifles to support this claim. For these professional military men, that was sufficient proof.

Everyone was seated and Hitler, who had been anxious to start the meeting, began to speak. He pointed out that he obviously had the power to go back into time. By doing so, he and his associates could place themselves in a position to change specific events which had happened in past times. By changing these certain events, all subsequent events related to these events would also change. "Do you understand this, gentlemen?" asked Hitler.

Both generals acknowledged their understanding of the potential of this power. General Pickering was very keenly interested in this process. "Commander Hitler, (Colonel Wolf had introduced Adolf Hitler as their commander) I have often thought about the question of time. If certain historical battles had ended with a different winner or loser, what effect would that have had on history? If things had occurred just a moment or two sooner or later, the impact on subsequent events would be horrendous."

"I see you understand completely General," replied Hitler. "I also see that you are a philosopher, just as I am." He continued, "Our objective in coming here is to make certain you defeat the American forces before general insurrection breaks out. If the American forces, which consist of militias and other loosely organized groups, are quickly defeated, the British will have permanent control of the thirteen American colonies."

General Pickering responded, "What is your interest in a British victory, Commander Hitler? Why would you go to such a great deal of trouble to travel back in time and align with us to achieve this victory?"

Hitler replied, "The reason I am interested in a British victory over the Americans is because it will benefit my country in the future. This is because, like Great Britain, Germany shall also be fighting the Americans if they defeat the British at this period in time. You should also know if we do not assist you in defeating the

Americans, it is historical fact that the Americans will defeat you sir."

General Pickering replied, "Sir, this is certainly a most extraordinary situation. You are armed with the knowledge of the past and you can actually alter history. I must decide whether to align with you, not knowing myself, the consequences for future events."

"That is true, general," replied Hitler. "However, future events will be of no consequence to you, sir. You live in the present, the year 1775. You must deal with that which fate has mandated to you. Other men in their own future time will likewise be challenged to address those events which also befall them. Do you not agree?"

"Yes, I do agree," responded General Pickering. "It is not logical to consider the distant future or subsequent events that would be triggered by changing history. To think about such things was incomprehensible."

General Muller then commented, "Commander Hitler, there are many unlawful activities taking place right now, as I am sure you are aware. I fully believe the time to strike the Americans is upon us. A strike must be clearly overwhelming in order to create the greatest impact."

Hitler replied, "You are correct, General. However, I'm more interested in strategic objectives than minor skirmishes to put down demonstrations. Before I provide my plan for you, perhaps General Pickering could detail the British plan now in operation. Our intent is to work in concert with the British plan to achieve our mutual objective. We will adjust our plan accordingly. The British achieving their objective will insure we are able to achieve ours, although not for another two hundred years," he chuckled.

General Pickering was well organized and concise, and quickly covered the three step British plan. The Germans, whom had already learned of the plan through SS intelligence, were very receptive. Even though they had prior knowledge of the plan they could barely control their delight. Their work would be simplified immensely and there was an even greater probability of success.

Hitler then spoke. "Gentlemen, our plan is quite basic. Our strategic objective is the same as yours, to defeat the Americans. While your British Army launches attacks on American arms depots and other military assets, we shall target the one man who can organize an army and lead the Americans in an armed rebellion, George Washington. Gentlemen, we shall assassinate George Washington.

While there was a collective gasp from both generals, both agreed George Washington was of great concern to them. A house had already been procured in Philadelphia to serve as his temporary headquarters.

"The overall plan is very simple gentlemen. On the morning of April 19, your troops shall launch attacks on American military facilities. The evening of April 19, Washington will be assassinated. These two events must be coordinated to occur on April 19. There can be no errors in the execution of the plan. This will insure the greatest demoralization throughout the Colonies and the Americans will realize the futility of further resistance." Hitler's legendary speaking style did not fail him and he had convincingly presented his simple plan to assure British success.

"Sir," General Pickering interjected, "You are going to kill General Washington and that will be to our advantage when that occurs. General Muller and I will coordinate our attacks and they will be executed very smoothly, I assure you. But sir," General Pickering continued, "why do you not assassinate General Washington immediately? Why wait until April 19? With your superior weapons, why not complete this disagreeable task and be done with it?"

"General Pickering," Hitler responded, "we have considered that alternative in addition to many other options. It's true we could walk into Washington's headquarters and assassinate him at any moment. But, killing Washington in that manner would make him a patriotic hero which the Americans could rally around. It would strengthen their resolve to defeat the British. But, coordinating Washington's assassination with significant British military victories will assure that American defeat is total because, as we already discussed, those combined blows would demoralize them. Our strategic objective coordinates nicely with your strategic objectives, would you not agree, General Pickering?"

"Sir, your part of the plan shall tip the scales in either direction. You must also assure us you shall be successful, Commander Hitler?" replied General Pickering.

Hitler's reply was instantaneous. "We will assassinate George Washington at a dinner he is to attend in Philadelphia on April 19. Of that, I assure you."

"I believe it is a good plan, Commander Hitler," General Pickering replied. "By the way, I was already planning a military operation against the Massachusetts Militia and a supply depot they own in Concord. I will change the date of that attack to April 19. We shall begin our attacks by marching through Lexington and then on to the depot at Concord."

Hitler replied, "Gentlemen, then we agree."

Both generals nodded their heads.

Hitler continued, getting ready to conclude the meeting. "Gentlemen, there are two other things we must discuss. First, absolute secrecy is required. There are many spies. The assassination plot must remain known only to those in this room. The fewer people who know of this plan, the greater its probability of success."

Both generals agreed.

"The second matter, General Pickering, I believe you know a Madame Bettenfield in Philadelphia," inquired Hitler.

"Yes, I know her well," replied the general. "As a matter of fact, one thing I did not cover when explaining the British plan was that Madame Bettenfield has been put forth by England to become the Queen of this new country of Dorchester."

Hitler was already aware of that fact. When the SS officers learned she would be hosting the April 19 dinner party to which Washington had been invited, it was obvious the assassination would take place at her residence. She would be a willing participant, as she would become Queen.

"General Pickering," Hitler said, "would you please provide a letter of introduction which I may give to Madame Bettenfield? I shall arrange for a meeting with her in this room on February 20. I ask that you also attend this meeting, Gentlemen."

Both General Pickering and General Muller chuckled slightly.

"What is so humorous, gentlemen?" asked Hitler.

General Muller replied, "Sir, Philadelphia is three hundred miles away. The journey to Philadelphia takes at least ten days or more by coach. How do you propose to contact Madame Bettenfield and bring her to Boston by Monday, just four days from now?"

Hitler smiled and replied, "Remember general, we have a much faster means of travel."

"Yes, I suppose that you would," replied General Muller. "Well, then, Monday shall be fine for me, Sir."

The SS spies had learned Madame Rebecca Bettenfield, a prominent and ambitious woman, had cleverly positioned herself on a fine line between the Loyalists and the Patriots. Both groups thought she sided with their position. In reality, the only side she chose was her own. She always took whatever position gave her the best advantage and opportunity for a profit.

Hitler continued, "General Pickering, after we meet with Madame Bettenfield, most of our party will depart for Philadelphia. We must make the arrangements as to how we will handle the events at the dinner party on April 19. Colonel Dieter Kruger and several of his officers and troops shall remain here to work with you and General Muller. He will meet with you frequently to assure everything is proceeding according to plan. Colonel Kruger will also maintain communication and coordination with me."

"Gentlemen, is there anything else?" asked Hitler.

Neither general had further comment.

"Our meeting is concluded," said Hitler. "We shall see you on Monday at 9:00 a.m."

Immediately after the generals departed, General Werner, Colonel Wolf and two intelligence agents used the Chronometric Teleporter to go to Philadelphia and set up a meeting with Madame Bettenfield at her home on the following day, Friday February 17.

Adolf Hitler and Martin Bormann arrived the morning of February 17 to meet with her. Hitler presented Madame Bettenfield his letter of introduction from General Pickering to assure her that their purpose would be most useful to her.

While she was visibly shocked that she was conversing with people from a future time, she maintained her composure. She had heard some whispers of the possibility that she might become a queen, but was most interested in the fact that an aggressive plan had been put in place to make that possibility a reality. She agreed to go with Hitler and Bormann to meet with General Pickering and General Muller. They would leave for the Nazi compound in Boston on Monday morning and arrive in time for the meeting with the two generals.

In the meantime, Hitler, Bormann, Colonel Wolf and the two intelligence agents would enjoy Madame Bettenfield's hospitality for the weekend. That would also give the Germans a chance to plan some of the details for the April 19 assassination which was to occur in Madame Bettenfield's home. Hitler had purposely avoided telling her this detail as well as other specifics of the strategy. He told her that she would learn about the entire plan at the meeting with the generals.

Madame Bettenfield was amazed on Monday morning when she stepped through the portal in Philadelphia and was instantly in Boston over three hundred miles away. General Pickering and General Muller had already arrived and were waiting for them in the library where the first meeting had been held. They too were amazed when Madame Bettenfield escorted by Colonel Wolf walked through the door and greeted them. Adolf Hitler, Martin Bormann and General Werner, all whom had arrived earlier that morning, were also in the room.

As soon as the greetings were concluded, Hitler began the meeting. He asked General Pickering to go over the British strategic plan once again, which he did. Madame Bettenfield was enthusiastic that the official British plan included her becoming the Queen. Over the weekend, the general had worked on the military attacks to begin on April 19. He had concluded, as he had said, that the action would start at Lexington and Concord. At that point, he returned the meeting to Hitler.

The Germans had worked out most of the details for the assassination of April 19. SS Colonel Wolf was particularly adept at this type of work, and the plan developed was mainly through his direction. However, when he announced that the assassination would take place at Madame Bettenfield's home, she voiced concerns.

"Commander Hitler, you are planning to kill the most important man in the American Colonies at my home. You shall leave me with a grand predicament. How do I explain this man's death?"

That was a question that the Germans had never bothered to think about. She was right. They would be gone, leaving her to

187

shoulder the blame. The Germans weren't concerned about Madame Bettenfield however it suddenly occurred to them that setting up a scapegoat to blame for the murder would be a good idea. If the proper scapegoat were selected, it would further assure the American's defeat.

They now also realized if the murder were to be blamed on the British, it might further inflame the population and still result in a rebellion the British could lose. A scapegoat needed to be carefully chosen, one whom would attach advantageous political intrigue to the assassination. The French were potential American allies who would help the Americans defeat the British. Blaming the French for the assassination of George Washington would destroy France's alliance with the Americans.

Madame Bettenfield, as well as the Germans and the British were satisfied with that idea. Madame Bettenfield would remain above suspicion. The British would not suffer any adverse public reaction, and the Germans had an even greater assurance that nothing would interfere with a British victory.

The meeting was over in several hours. General Pickering and General Muller returned to Boston to their headquarters. Madame Bettenfield, amazed once again, stepped through the Chronometric Teleporter's portal in Boston and into her sitting room at her home in Philadelphia. Incredible! she thought.

The Nazi entourage, Adolf Hitler, Martin Bormann, SS General Fritz Werner, SS Colonel Helmut Wolf, and Dr. Wenzel Klein would not depart for Philadelphia for another week. They wanted to maintain close contact with General Pickering and General Muller in case any unforeseen problems arose. When they arrived in Philadelphia, they would stay at Madame Bettenfield's residence in order to prepare for the assassination on April 19. Forty of the fifty SS Troops would accompany them to Philadelphia. The troops would be housed in a large barracks like structure on Madame Bettenfield's estate. This facility was normally used at harvest time to house additional farm workers.

SS Colonel Dieter Kruger and ten SS Troops would stay behind in Boston to monitor the British and Hessian military preparations for attacking the Americans on April 19. While Adolf Hitler was in Philadelphia, Colonel Kruger could still report to him in person on a daily basis. Doctor Klein would simply create a portal for Colonel Kruger using the Chronometric Teleporter. Hitler would also make frequents visits to Boston, alternating his nights in both places. He still moved between multiple locations as a precaution against assassination attempts, just as he had done in World War Two.

22

Bettenfield Manor

April 15, 1775   Philadelphia

Nathan Bettenfield was a man of solid build, average height and above average cleverness. His gray-flecked black hair and ruddy face betrayed a less than genteel upbringing. He said he was born somewhere in Connecticut however there were no records of his birth. He was a natural charmer and a strong leader. At age eleven, he signed up for duty on the West Indies cargo ships. His early days toughened him and honed an attitude of survival and ruthlessness in his young mind. He was a mean adversary in a fight.

Bettenfield built his fortune during the times before the American Revolutionary War. His business interests included shipping, slave selling and rum importing, agriculture, and horse breeding. He owned thirty thousand acres of land in several colonies including Pennsylvania, Massachusetts, and Virginia. Nathan Bettenfield was never described as a man overly burdened with scruples.

Much of how he acquired his great fortune remains a mystery. Rumor had it he was involved in piracy. The allegations occasionally rose to the level of official inquiry however his shrewdness consistently pulled him from the brink of prosecution and back to the fringe of respectability. He was never immersed completely in the underworld of criminality, nor was he ever totally embraced by the aristocracy to which he aspired. He was a man trapped between two worlds, striving for reputability through disreputability.

There were stories of his ships capturing merchant ships of various countries and selling them, less their cargos and crews, to other countries. The crews would be set ashore at the nearest habitable island if there was one in the immediate vicinity. The humorous stories in the late 1760's were that many ships reported lost in storms were actually lost in "Bettenfield Squalls." The basis of this presumption was that it seemed whenever a vessel was lost in a storm, a Bettenfield ship overladen with cargo would sail into port shortly thereafter. It was also rumored that there were over a hundred tons of gold secured in a vault buried beneath the foundation blocks of Bettenfield Manor.

As clever and charming a scoundrel as he was, he met his match in Rebecca Wellesly, who would soon become Madame Bettenfield. Rebecca Wellesly, like Nathan Bettenfield, also struggled with a nebulous history. However, unlike him, she managed the uncertainty and speculation regarding her background more skillfully.

She was a large woman who indulged in cosmetics and powders, always appearing with outlandishly pink cheeks, shadowed eyes and bright red lips. She was also quite tall at nearly six feet and weighed one hundred and seventy pounds on a "very good day" as she would say.

Rebecca Wellesly was a widow. In fact, she had been widowed twice, each time losing her husband to an unfortunate mishap. One of her late husbands disappeared at sea, which no one on the boat realized until it docked after its three-week voyage. Her second husband was the victim of robbers as he traveled from Boston to Philadelphia. As there had never been a problem with highwaymen along that particular route, there were questions and a bit of scandal began to emerge, but both were soon quieted by the grieving Miss Wellesly. She had acquired through inheritance her late husbands' considerable estates and she was already a wealthy woman when she met Nathan Bettenfield.

She was not nearly as wealthy as he, however. Her great desires were wealth and power. As the matron of Bettenfield Manor she would have both. She sought him out as he did her. He was attracted to her strong, direct personality and found her challenging. She was not attracted to him, finding him obnoxious and tiresome when he was drunk, which he was quite often. She was, however, attracted to his money and the power it would bring. His substantial fortune more than offset his aggravating disposition and his lack of physical attractiveness.

Rebecca Wellesly became Madame Bettenfield at the swift conclusion of a brief courtship comprised of bounteous sex and the revelation she was pregnant. The supposed pregnancy was exactly that, with many ladies of better breeding gossiping that she tricked Nathan Bettenfield into marrying her. Of course, she did.

After one year of marriage, matrimonial bliss would again elude Rebecca as tragedy befell her once again. Her third husband, Nathan Bettenfield, was found lying dead in the barn on his estate. Although an expert rider, he was apparently kicked in the head by his favorite horse which, oddly enough, was named "Swindler."

The grief stricken Madame Bettenfield once again regained her composure and what seemed to be an even greater happiness in a miraculously short time. Speculation was rampant that Nathan was murdered and there was no shortage of other cruel rumors.

One rumor was that Madame Bettenfield established an all time record for the swiftness of her mourning period. Instead of the customary one-year period to grieve for the deceased and dress in black, Madame Bettenfield staged a gala party six weeks after Nathan had been laid to rest. Other than the day of his funeral, she never wore black saying it depressed her. Some people maliciously joked that the anguish of her loss might possibly be offset by her acquiring possession of Nathan Bettenfield's huge fortune, her third but by far most spectacular inheritance. She denied this.

But now, as the matron of Bettenfield Manor, Rebecca relished sitting atop the very pinnacle of wealth, power and respectability, in that order, of course.

****

If ever there were a palatial estate, Bettenfield Manor would be that place. From both its enormity and architectural magnificence, Bettenfield would be the mansion that would never be forgotten by anyone who visited there. It consisted of the main house, a fifty-bed workers dormitory, a fifteen bed maids' quarters, and a large barn behind the house. This large barn was where Nathan Bettenfield's body was found. There were two other barns as well as a carriage house, a blacksmith's shop and several other outbuildings on the property.

The dimensions of the two story main house were monumental for the time. The house, which was constructed of brick and painted white, was two hundred feet wide by one hundred and fifty feet deep. The house faced south and was situated one hundred yards west of Old Church Road and located ten miles north of Philadelphia. Many of the innovations of the house pre-dated features and styles which were popular as much as one hundred years later. As an example, the mammoth front porch was fronted by ten large white pillars. In his travels, Nathan Bettenfield discovered a plumbing system used by ancient Romans. This provided the necessary rooms in the house with running water.

Pre-revolutionary wallpaper and a profusion of plasterwork, floral prints, paintings, handsome walnut veneered looking glasses, and generous wood carving installations graced the interior walls of the house. Broad arches were interspersed throughout the home and round-headed windows with deep seats were generously included in the house's unique architecture. Wide pine board flooring could be seen in the few areas where carpeting and rugs were not utilized.

The largest room of the house was the ballroom, which occupied the southwest corner of the first floor at the front of the house. Across the hallway from the ballroom was the main dining room which was located on the north side of the house looking out on the massive gardens. The black and white diamond pattern floor of the large dining room signaled the progressive tastes of the estate's owner. There was also a small dining room on the east of the house on the first floor.

The huge kitchen contained a five by seven foot fireplace with a beehive brick oven and there was ample room for a dozen or more chefs. All of the twelve bedchambers and offices were located on the second floor of the house. There were also east and west parlors and a library on this level.

The massive basement of the house included a large vault in which was stored over one hundred tons of gold. There were also secret rooms for refuge in emergencies. Also, one secret room was an armory stocked with guns, powder, swords and knives. Secret tunnels led to several of the estate's outbuildings, including the maids' quarters.

The exquisite gardens were designed with symmetrical flower and shrubbery beds, imposing reproductions of ancient statuary, large arbors, clever trellises, and sundials of varying sizes. Bettenfield Manor was an architectural triumph of classic style, grace and civility. Unfortunately, Nathan Bettenfield would only occupy his masterpiece for the last three years of his life.

23

Arrival

April 15, 1775   Philadelphia

After her emotional farewell to Shimasani, Lomasi slowly walked back to her house. She was deeply troubled by the visions of the three previous nights. The visions were ominous warnings of events to come, but they didn't tell her how she could stop them.

When she reached her house, she sat at her big wooden table and stared out the back window into her yard. The garden was heavy with rows of green vegetable plants. A screen like canopy provided a little tent to protect her watermelons from too much sun. Her horse stood in the corral looking off into the vast desert. Lomasi, too, looked into the distance. Red rock spires, mountains and plateaus were the scenic backdrop for her little yard. Although many desert dwellers took the scenes for granted, Lomasi never did. She was always fascinated as the sun moved across the sky creating different colors in the landscape.

But, it was time for her to leave this place. She must go back in time. It was a trip she wanted to avoid, but it was her responsibility as a shaman. She must protect her people and the earth. This task is too much for one person, she thought. She didn't know where to begin but, it must be with Colonel Thacher, she thought.

Her mother told her Lomasi at age eleven she had the power to go into time. However, her mother warned her many times about the dangers of using the power. There were dangers from the people who might be encountered in other times, and there was the danger of altering events which had already occurred. Altering events could set off a chain reaction of unpredictable effects on subsequent events. The power to go into time should never be used except in the most extreme circumstances.

Lomasi looked through the window in her kitchen toward the distant mountains. Reluctantly, she began the process to go back in

194

time. She thought about Philadelphia and April 15, 1775. She raised her right arm so it was level with the floor, and held her right hand with the palm turned outward. She focused on being there. The portal was suddenly hovering before her.

As Lomasi stepped through the portal, the warm, clean air of the desert gave way to cooler air, with a hodgepodge of offensive odors. Manure, tobacco smoke, cooking food, dust, sewage, and perfumes combined to form a stifling aroma proclaiming the habitation of many people. There were sounds of horses clip clopping and carriages clattering over cobblestone streets, people talking and carpenters hammering and sawing. While Lomasi had traveled to cities in her own time, Philadelphia in 1775 was just as busy and noisy but, more smelly.

While she had seen pictures of how people dressed in these times, the women's wide dresses and men in stockings and wigs surprised her. She had taken the precaution of wearing a long, full ankle length dress, which served a dual purpose. It made her appear as just another person in 1775. The dress also allowed her to keep her promise to Shimasani by strapping her grandfather's hunting knife under the dress and around her right leg just below her knee. This wasn't a particularly comfortable accessory however.

As Lomasi walked along the streets past the shops, taverns and other businesses, she noticed the stares of passersby, mostly women. She was not in style, she guessed. However, her dress would have to do.

It was now ten a.m. according to a large clock in the window of a store she passed. Although reluctant to speak to anyone, she knew she would have to ask where she could find General Washington's headquarters and Colonel Thacher. She asked a man walking past where she might find George Washington. The man appeared somewhat surprised this woman would speak to him. However, he quickly gave her the information she requested and, without delay, resumed his walk.

From the research Lomasi had done, she knew Washington wouldn't be appointed Commander in Chief of the Continental Army until June 19. However, a headquarters had been set up for him on the presumption he would play an important role in the coming military confrontation with the British.

Provocative events by both the British and Americans were occurring with increasing frequency. The Tea Act of May 10, 1773 required that tea be purchased only from the East India Tea Company. The Americans thought that this monopoly would harm local merchants and raise prices for tea. On December 16, 1773, American citizens disguised as Indians boarded ships anchored in Boston harbor and threw their cargo of tea overboard in what became known as the Boston Tea Party. Other riots and civil disorder were also occurring.

On March 31, 1774, The Boston Port Act effectively closed the port of Boston to incoming or outgoing shipping until the citizens of Boston paid restitution for the tea destroyed in the Boston Tea Party. This raised the level of tension to the boiling point. Confrontation was imminent.

Lomasi knew she must locate George Washington and warn him that Colonel Thacher was plotting to assassinate him. But, she felt a great deal of anxiety. Shimasani had warned of danger and told Lomasi she must trust her instincts. Lomasi knew she must do everything in her power to prevent George Washington's assassination and whatever evil this man Adolf Hitler was intent on creating. But, she must also protect herself. Finally, she reached her destination.

The headquarters was not a military installation but a stately two-story brick house. A large gate opened to a stone walkway leading from the street to a massive front porch. An ornate white picket fence enclosed the facility. Stone paths wound through large green trees with wide branches and the colorful flower gardens situated throughout the grounds.

The only indication of a military presence was the two sentries on guard on the front porch. They stood on either side of the large, white entrance door. Lomasi pushed open the gate and walked toward the house on the stone walkway. She reached the steps leading to the porch and stopped. The sentry on her right stepped forward and asked, "May I be of service, ma'am?"

"I am here to see General Washington," replied Lomasi.

"Whom may I say is calling?" asked the sentry.

"My name is Lomasi," she replied.

The sentry appeared puzzled as Lomasi had given no last name. However, he turned and went inside the house. He returned shortly and told Lomasi General Washington was not in the building but Colonel Thacher must approve all appointments with General Washington anyway. She could wait for Colonel Thacher in his office and he would join her shortly.

Lomasi followed the sentry into the home. While the outside of the house had been impressive, the inside was magnificent. Handsome wooden furniture and large couches sat on expensive rugs. Fine lace curtains adorned the windows. Silver bowls and delicate glassware adorned every flat surface of the room. Crystal chandeliers seemed to be hanging everywhere. Every nook and corner of the house met the highest standards of grace and loveliness.

Colonel Thacher's office was located just off the living room to the left of the large wooden door leading into the house. The sentry opened the door for Lomasi and she walked into Colonel Thacher's office and sat down by his large wooden desk. The sentry closed the door as he left the room.

Lomasi thought more about Shimasani's advice to trust her instincts. She was uncomfortable waiting for Colonel Thacher. After a few minutes, she got up and walked outside to the front porch. One of the sentries asked her if anything was wrong and she answered that she was not feeling well and she would return the following day. She walked down the steps and onto the path leading to the street. As she exited the front gate and walked onto the sidewalk, she felt much better. She was happy she left his office.

As she walked along the sidewalk and back toward the central part of Philadelphia, she remembered she had seen a sign for a boarding house in the next block of houses. She would go there and get a room. Lomasi had brought along a small leather pouch of silver pieces used in Native American jewelry making. She would use these to pay her expenses.

When she arrived at the house, a large, kindly looking woman answered the door. She was the proprietor, and while she allowed it was unusual for a woman to be traveling alone, a silver piece more than satisfied her curiosity.

Once in the privacy of her room, Lomasi lay down on the bed to ponder the events of the day. She thought about Colonel Thacher and wondered how to handle him. She would think about her next move in the morning. At the moment, she needed to rest. She was asleep in a few minutes and awoke nearly five hours later at the sound of the dinner bell.

****

Refreshed from her sleep, Lomasi decided she must avoid the risk of meeting Colonel Thacher and contact George Washington directly. If Thacher were to become suspicious, he might harm her. But, what was the best way to get to see Washington? And, how could she make a credible presentation to him? She was just a woman of no stature or importance. Would Washington believe her?

The answer was simple in that it was the only solution. She would use her time travel power and simply appear in his office. It was now five p.m. She would go to his office now. Again, she extended her arm with her right hand at a ninety-degree angle. She thought about the present time and George Washington's office in Philadelphia. The orange and blue portal appeared, suspended in the air before her. She stepped through it and into George Washington's office. She emerged from the portal on the far side of the room, slightly to the rear of his big desk. While she expected to find George Washington in the office, she was still shocked and humbled by the experience. Sitting just a few feet from her was a very busy George Washington bent over his desk and studying some papers.

He was just as he appeared in all the likenesses she had ever seen of him. Though sitting in his desk chair, he was obviously a very big man. His graying hair covered his neck but was arranged just as pictures of him had depicted. He had large hands and his profile defined a strong sense of purpose and greatness. Washington shifted in his chair and as he did, he caught sight of Lomasi out of the corner of his right eye. He bolted backward, startled that someone was suddenly in his office without his having noticed their entering.

Lomasi too, was startled. Apparently George Washington sensed her distress as he regained his own composure, realizing the attractive woman standing before him was not a threat. He addressed her in a very kind fashion.

"I don't believe I've had the pleasure of your acquaintance, Madam," he said. "Please, be seated, and tell me the purpose of your visit."

This was odd, she thought. He asked me to have a seat as if I had an appointment, ignoring the fact that I just suddenly appeared in his office. Assuming that George Washington's intent was to put her at ease, Lomasi sat down. Her apprehension was lessened, but her mind was racing. She realized she hadn't thought out how she would approach General Washington. Should she explain to him she was from the future? She wasn't sure.

Meeting George Washington as a real, living person instead of seeing pictures of him as a mythical legend triggered a comprehension in Lomasi of the reality and seriousness of her task. But, her concern was if she actually could do anything to stop the events which seemed certain to occur?

She decided to simply tell Washington the truth, as difficult as it might be for him to understand and accept. The truth is always the best and the easiest path to follow, she thought. She would skip the fact that she had come from a future time, unless it became necessary to tell Washington this.

"General Washington, what I am going to tell you will be quite unbelievable but, it's very important and I ask that you please hear me out." General Washington nodded, reassuring Lomasi he would listen to her.

"Sir, I am a shaman, a healer and caretaker of people. Shamans have visions which tell of actual events."

George Washington interrupted Lomasi. "I am familiar with the term "shaman" Madam. They are similar to a medicine man if I am correct."

"Yes, that is correct General Washington."

Washington, smiling kindly, interrupted once again. "I appreciate your calling me 'general,' Madam. However, my present rank is colonel. I have not yet been promoted to general but, I'm certain I will be soon. You can continue calling me 'general' if you wish," he laughed. Then he sighed, "It's a task I would not choose to perform but, I surely must."

"Thank you, General. In my vision, you were dying. You were assassinated by a man named Adolf Hitler."

To her surprise, he didn't appear moved by what she had just said, seeming to take everything she told him for granted.

Lomasi continued, "General Washington, I thought you would be astonished by my story yet, you don't appear at all phased by it. I don't understand your reaction. Do you not believe what I'm telling you?"

Smiling, he replied, "My dear woman, I am an educated and liberal man. I believe in the likelihood of any and all possibilities. While your story is extraordinary, I am inclined to believe it has some measure of credibility. I am not taken aback by what you told me because a man called Adolf Hitler arrived in Philadelphia several weeks ago. He has an unusual group of men with him and we have been watching them to determine their intentions.

What I question is how you were able to suddenly appear in my office and where you are from. I'm quite positive I was not so engrossed in my work that it would have escaped my notice had you come through the door. Also, you would not have gotten past the sentries. Therefore, you didn't walk into my office."

Lomasi decided she had no choice but tell General Washington she was from a time in the future. "All right, General," Lomasi said, "I hadn't intended to tell you this, but I will. As incredible as it may sound, I actually live in the year 2010. I have the ability to travel backward and forward in time. This is the first time I have used this power because it is forbidden to do so unless it is absolutely necessary. I've come back to warn you that Adolf Hitler and his men are plotting your assassination and to try to stop them from succeeding with their plan. They are also from a time in the future."

"These men have weapons far more advanced than anyone has ever seen," Washington replied. "I tend to believe what you say because that would explain the sophistication of their weapons. However, because of the gravity of the events of which you are forewarning me, I would ask your indulgence on one matter."

"What is that, General?"

"Madam, I would like you to prove to me that you truly are from another period in time," General Washington said.

Lomasi thought about what General Washington was requesting. She could not blame him for asking for proof of her claims. Although he was suspicious of Hitler's presence and the sophistication of his soldiers' weapons, he had not allowed himself to completely believe Hitler had come from another period in time. She must think of a way to convince him she had come from the future.

"All right, General," replied Lomasi, "I will give you the proof you demand however, you must agree to some rules."

200

"Agreed, Madam," he replied.

"General, you and I shall go into the time in which I live, the year 2010. We will go to Boston, a city with which you are very familiar. We will arrive at Faneuil Hall, which is also called Quincy Market in 2010, but you will recognize the building. You may not talk with anyone and we will not go inside any buildings. We will observe for a few minutes and then return to where we are now. Will that be satisfactory, Sir?"

"Quite satisfactory, Madam" Washington replied.

Lomasi created the shimmering portal in Washington's office. He was awed by the orange-bordered, blue threshold hovering in the air.

"Please follow me closely, Sir," she instructed him.

Lomasi stepped through the portal and onto the pavement in front of Faneuil Hall accompanied by George Washington. He was amazed at the number of people scurrying about, and from his frame of reference, the unique clothes they were wearing. There were several pick-up trucks unloading merchandise for the nearby marketplace. Lomasi was explaining that they were wagons but didn't need horses. The roar of an airplane's jet engines caused him to look upward.

"What is that silver tube in the sky?" he asked.

Lomasi responded by saying the thing moving through the sky above them was like a stagecoach, but it carried many more people and could fly. One of the pick-up trucks drove away as Washington watched. He did not speak, obviously astonished at all he was beholding.

Several people slowed to stare as they walked past, assuming that the Lomasi and her guest were in period costume as they were standing on Boston's historical Freedom Trail. No one stopped however.

"Sir, we must return if you don't object," said Lomasi.

"No, I don't object at all Madam. It is what I agreed to. Thank you for giving me this opportunity to look into the future," replied George Washington.

Lomasi asked him to follow her around the side of a building and she created the portal to return to the year 1775. She and Washington stepped into the portal and onto the rug in his office. That was a fast trip, she thought.

"Madam, I am truly astounded," said General Washington. "You have given me more than enough proof that you are who you claim to be. Thank you again for you indulgence but, it was necessary for me to be positive about what you say."

"Let me ask you a question now," Lomasi interjected.

"Of course," he responded. "Anything."

"How did you know about Hitler and his weapons?" she asked.

"Adolf Hitler and his entourage are quartered at Bettenfield Manor. Madam Bettenfield is a good friend of mine and she keeps me informed as to what is going on there. It was she who arranged for me to meet Adolf Hitler in order to purchase weapons from him. I believe she is an ally however she is very motivated by wealth and power. With the confused state of affairs in the thirteen colonies, it is difficult to determine where everyone's sympathies lie. Therefore, I'm not positive she is telling me everything she knows nor am I completely sure whether she will ultimately align with the British or the Americans. She also informed me that Hitler and his men are aligned with the British and Hessians so I naturally questioned why they would wish to sell weapons to the American Army. I was not aware of their assassination plot."

"General, they intend to assassinate you on April 19, at Bettenfield Manor," Lomasi said.

"Well, the easiest solution is for me not to go to their dinner and never see Adolf Hitler and his yokemates (cohorts)," replied Washington.

"I'm afraid it is not that simple, sir," replied Lomasi. "Adolf Hitler is the most brutal man in history. He started a war we refer to as the Second World War in which seventy million people died. He has come here to kill you and he will not leave until he has done so. You must kill him if you are to survive. With far superior firepower, he would win any armed conflict. But, we must find way to destroy him."

Lomasi continued. "Sir, I think it would be wiser to go to the dinner and confront him there. If he doesn't know you are aware of his intentions, surprise will be with us."

"Lomasi," said Washington, "I could write a letter to Madame Bettenfield and have her employ you as a maid in the kitchen. You could work there and monitor what is going on and advise me. With your magical power, you can travel to where I am and we can talk. In the meantime, we shall consider a plan of attack. However, you must be very careful. Don't trust Madame Bettenfield or her chief housekeeper, Miss Chattenborne."

The fact that Washington was aware of some of what was going on was reassuring to Lomasi. Also, he said he would consider a plan to counter Hitler. That was also of some comfort. However, she knew that she was the one with primary responsibility for making sure Washington was not killed.

"There is one other thing sir," said Lomasi. "Colonel Thacher is involved in the plot. He can't be trusted."

"What?" replied Washington, astonished."

"He is involved in the plot to kill you," Lomasi reiterated.

A visibly shocked George Washington replied, "I find it difficult to believe I was wrong about him. I won't confront him on this until I have formulated a plan. However, I will have him escort you to Madame Bettenfield's home and get you situated so he will not suspect we are on to his scheme. You can come to me with information whenever you feel it is necessary. Remember, we will keep our conversation entirely between the two of us. Don't speak about anything we have discussed to anyone. I will tell Colonel Thacher our conversation was about your seeking employment."

Washington walked out of his office and asked Colonel Thacher to return with him. He introduced Lomasi as the widow of one of his men who fought with him in the French and Indian War. He wanted to help her out as she had fallen on hard times. He instructed Colonel Thacher to take Lomasi to Bettenfield Manor and obtain employment for her as a cook.

Colonel Thacher stepped out of the room and summoned the sentry to bring the carriage to the back of the house. Lomasi followed Colonel Thacher from Washington's office and out the back door of the house onto the large porch. Another soldier brought a black carriage pulled by two large horses around the cobblestone coach path and pulled it up to the steps of the porch. One of the sentries helped Lomasi into the carriage. Colonel Thacher then climbed into the coach and sat across from her and the coach slowly began to roll forward. As they pulled the shades over the windows to shield themselves from the afternoon sun, the coach slowly moved along the cobblestone driveway in back of the house and out the large white back gate and into the road. As the carriage completed its turn, the horses broke into a full gallop and the driver snapped his whip and yelled them onward.

Lomasi had to chuckle. The ride in the coach was uncomfortable and it seemed to hit every bump in the road. But, the coach also had a gentle rocking motion to it. Although, her old truck also had a gentle rocking motion, she again chuckled. Lomasi thought that in other circumstances, the rocking was soothing to the point that she could actually go to sleep.

Neither Lomasi nor Colonel Thacher did much talking during the short trip. In ten minutes or so, the coach began to slow with the horses now moving at a relaxed gallop. The horses slowed to a walk and soon stopped. Lomasi could hear the driver of the coach climb down and the door opened and the driver was extending his hand to help Lomasi climb down. Once Lomasi had gotten out of the coach, the driver turned around and quickly ascended the wooden steps up to the porch and knocked on the door. Now, as Lomasi looked around from where she was standing, she found herself in front of an imposing and beautiful home, even more massive and grandiose than Washington's headquarters.

Colonel Thacher had now gotten out of the coach and stood beside Lomasi. Lomasi looked over toward the door of the house as she heard it open and a woman's voice greeting the driver.

The driver, returning her greeting, replied, "Colonel Thacher is here to see Madame Bettenfield, ma'am."

"Please bring Colonel Thacher into the sitting room," replied the woman.

This house was more elegant than any Lomasi had ever seen. Great wealth and influence resided in this place. Colonel Thacher and Lomasi walked into the sitting room of the expensively appointed home. In a short time, two very nicely dressed women arrived in the room. A larger woman walked into the room first, followed by the second woman. From the larger woman's demeanor and more expensive clothing, Lomasi guessed she would be the mistress of the house. And, she was truly an unusually large woman, both tall and broad shouldered. "She must weigh two hundred pounds," thought Lomasi. A massive white wig framed her heavily powdered face and generously painted red lips. She was as big as a man, thought Lomasi. However, Lomasi was quite sure she was a female, as evidenced by her large bosom and canyon like cleavage. Her clear blue eyes were also heavily made up. She wore a huge yellow silk dress, which Lomasi imagined could serve as a tent for six men.

The other woman, obviously subservient to the first, had coal black hair and was wearing a dark green linen dress and black shoes. She had on some make up, but made no great attempt to appear especially glamorous. That was probably a good thing, thought Lomasi. The woman was woefully unattractive. Her thin lips were painted with bright red lines. Her black or brown eyes, Lomasi could not decide which, were piercing and suspicious. Her expressions and mannerisms were severe and precise. She also looked like a man, thought Lomasi. But, once again, Lomasi was sure that she too was a woman. Together, the two women were frightening.

Lomasi, again feeling a sense of foreboding, feared they could not be trusted and were capable of great evil. She knew she must be very cautious and trust no one.

The larger woman spoke. "Hello, Colonel Thacher. It is so very nice to see you." Turning to Lomasi, she said, "I'm Madame Bettenfield, my dear. This is my head house servant, Lucretia Chattenborne."

Lomasi replied, "My name is Lomasi. It is very nice to meet you both, Madame."

Madame Bettenfield, flashing a brief and insincere smile, continued, "So, Colonel Thacher, what brings you and your guest to our home today?"

"Madame Bettenfield, General Washington is seeking employment for Lomasi. She is a very good kitchen servant, and he wishes that she secure a favorable position. I wonder if you might have any need for some additional help."

"Well, of course, Colonel Thacher," replied Madame Bettenfield. We can always make room for a friend of the General."

"Miss Chattenborne, would you please take charge of Lomasi and get her situated? The Colonel and I must discuss some other affairs."

Miss Chattenborne, in a sharp change of tone and civility, directed Lomasi to come with her and both women exited the room.

"So my dear Benjamin, how have you been?" Madame Bettenfield asked Colonel Thacher.

"My dear Rebecca, I have been quite well. I only wish that I could visit with you more often," replied Colonel Thacher.

Madame Bettenfield, moving closer to Colonel Thacher, responded, "You will be at our dinner four days from now. We will be able to visit more then."

Then, taking his left arm and walking with him toward the massive staircase, she whispered, "It was so nice to see you Benjamin."

24

Reunion

April 15, 1775   Philadelphia

David and Peter were able to find some shallow spots to cross the river then travelled most of the night on the old Indian path. They managed a few hours sleep along the dark, mosquito infested trail and arrived in Philadelphia at noon the following day. The day had warmed with the sun and they were in need of a bath, fresh clothing and food. They also needed to rest but there was no time.

As the men walked through the crowded streets they passed several taverns. Nothing they saw seemed overly inviting and they were also trying to guess which of the establishments might be favored by British soldiers. They weren't sure how to judge the likelihood of encountering British soldiers at particular taverns, however. And, they were very tired. "Let's just pick one," said Peter.

David agreed. "How about this one?" he said, pointing to the Croswell Inn on the corner of the street ahead of them. "Any port in a storm," said Peter.

The Croswell Inn looked inviting and offered both lodging and food. That a jovial man was standing in the doorway inviting people to come in added to the hospitable atmosphere. They took a room and the baths were out in back. A maid filled some tubs for them and they could eat and drink immediately. The innkeeper would also send a girl to the tailor to get some fresh clothes for them. It was too good to pass up.

After their experience on the Post Road with Jonathan, the last innkeeper they encountered, both men were suspicious of all innkeepers, particularly one so accommodating. They would need to keep their guard up for any shenanigans. But this innkeeper seemed to be genuine. As it turned out, this innkeeper's attentiveness had no sinister motive. His motivation for being accommodating was strictly monetary. While he fulfilled every need, he charged for the fulfillment of every need. This was only fair, but the man wasn't shy about the prices for his services. Fortunately, one gold coin from Peter's cache was very ample payment.

It was nearly two p.m. when the men, refreshed and rested, ventured into the busy streets of Philadelphia. Their new clothes and shoes were comfortable enough but, they were having trouble getting used to the breeches which reached just below the knee. Their stockings, which reached just above knee, were held up by garters.

As they walked past the shops and the people, David thought it would have been a very interesting tour were it not for the dire nature of their journey into this time. The innkeeper advised them of the location of General Washington's headquarters and didn't charge them for the information. As they walked, David and Peter were laughing about the innkeeper's "generosity" in giving them free information. In twenty minutes, their destination was in sight.

David talked with Peter about how to approach General Washington and present the important information to him. Would he believe them? David also wondered about Lomasi. Perhaps finding her should be their first task. They then concluded that they would simply lay out the facts to General Washington. They knew they couldn't trust Colonel Thacher and they would have to avoid him.

As they walked through the main gate on the cobblestone path leading to the Washington's headquarters, they saw the two sentries posted on the porch at either side of the large entrance door of the house. As David and Peter approached the front porch of the house, the sentry to the left of the door didn't lower his rifle, but challenged the men to identify themselves and state their purpose.

David gave their names and stated that they wished to see General Washington. The sentry went inside the door and in a few moments returned and informed David that Colonel Thacher must approve all General Washington's appointments and he could not see them until tomorrow at eight a.m.

"We shall return then," replied David.

Neither David nor Peter was unhappy about the delay in seeing Washington. It would give them time to return to the inn and get some rest and also scout around the area to see what they could learn.

As they walked through the front door of the Croswell Inn, David and Peter decided to have a beer. As they walked through a second doorway and into the tavern, they recognized a familiar voice coming from the back of the room. David and Peter walked further into the crowded room and spotted Contrary Walbridge, Phillip and John.

"What are you boys doing here?" hollered David as he and Peter walked up to their table.

Contrary, naturally, was the first to reply, "We needed a drink. What might you fellows be doing here?"

"We wanted to tell you boys to hold it down. We need to get some sleep," laughed David.

"Well, sit down then boys," replied Contrary. "A lad always sleeps better when he has a few drinks. Besides," he added laughing, "you fellas look a might haggard. Did you have a rough trip or something?"

As the five men sat at the table the conversation became more serious. Contrary, whispered he talked with several of his friends. The mood throughout the colonies was growing ugly. The Loyalists and the Patriots had gotten much more vocal. Rumors of rebellion and war were everywhere. People were suspicious of their neighbors. Something was going to happen soon, he thought. However, he couldn't quite put his finger on what that "something" might be. Then, Contrary started asking questions.

"You know, you boys never told me what you were doing in these parts. I'm guessing you don't like the British any more than we do, but you never did say. Why are you here?"

David turned and looked at Peter who was sitting right next to him. "Do I tell them, or not, Peter?" was his unspoken question.

Peter nodded his head "yes," and said, "We have nothing to lose, David. We can't trust Colonel Thacher and it's already April 15. Maybe these boys can help us and we can help them."

"Okay Peter," replied David. He then looked at Contrary who was sitting on his left. "Where we're from doesn't matter. What is important is that someone is going to try to assassinate George Washington very soon. We came here to try to stop them."

"Funny you should say that," replied Contrary. "I heard something to that effect myself but, I don't know where or when that will happen."

David interrupted Contrary. "We think the attempt on Washington's life will happen on April 19, four days from now. He is going to attend a dinner that evening and someone will poison him."

Contrary connected the dots. "That dinner will be at Bettenfield Manor, a big estate ten miles north. Madame Bettenfield owns the place. I learned about her when I visited Philadelphia before. She is claimed by both the Loyalists and the Patriots as one of their own. She has everyone fooled. I think she's a dangerous woman but everyone says I'm crazy when I say that about her."

"Hell, you are crazy, Contrary," laughed John. Phillip and Contrary laughed. Peter and David couldn't help themselves and also began laughing. Then Peter said, "I knew you were crazy when we first met you and you said your name was Contrary." That brought more laughs from the table.

"Anyway, if you boys can get serious for a minute," continued Contrary, "Madame Bettenfield is hosting a dinner for Washington and other high ranking people. Our leader Moses Brampton was supposed to attend but we haven't seen him yet so I don't know. If you think there's going to be trouble, maybe we can help."

Then Contrary added, "There is one other thing. I've heard several men have been staying in Madame Bettenfield's home for the last five or six weeks. And, there's thirty or forty men staying in the quarters at the rear of the property. They dress like farm workers however, it's said they appear to be some kind of special militia. They keep to themselves and stay inside the quarters or in the immediate area. Their presence is supposed to be a secret however you can't keep a large group of men a secret in times like these. Everyone is suspicious of what they're up to. Also, no one is saying much about the men staying at Madame Bettenfield's home. I guess they're supposed to be a secret too. I'll lay odds it's the damn British."

"That's bad news," replied Peter. "If there are thirty or forty men there, they're probably the backup for the conspirators who plan to poison Washington. If that's the case, they could try to kill Washington if the poison fails. That also means the men staying in Madame Bettenfield's home are probably Adolf Hitler and the Nazis. We're badly outnumbered because there are only five of us."

"Yes, but we can get help," replied Contrary. "I can get reinforcements and we can put an end to them if they're here to kill Washington."

Peter quickly replied. "Wait just a moment. We're getting ahead of ourselves here. First of all, these men may not actually be involved in this plot. We first need to determine exactly who they are and what they're doing here. I believe they probably are the men we're looking for but, we need to be sure before we take any action. We won't get a second chance if Washington is killed because we went after the wrong people. Contrary, can you get any more precise information?"

"The best way to do that is for all of us to go to Bettenfield Manor," replied Contrary. "We need to get close enough to these men to look them over."

"You're right," replied Peter. "We could find out pretty easily if we could just get a look at their weapons to see if they are a modern design." If they are World War 2 vintage, he thought, that would be all the proof we need.

"Contrary," Peter added, "you need to know something else. If these men are who we think they are, they will have weapons more dangerous than you have never seen. These men also have special training and are the most dangerous of killers. Your men are likely to be farmers and ordinary citizens. If your men took these people on, they would be slaughtered. We'll need to find a way to fight them that will make sure you win. Otherwise, you'll be throwing your men's lives away and these people will kill Washington anyway."

David gained a greater appreciation for Peter. His ideas were a sane approach to neutralizing these dangerous men.

"What do you mean by a modern design, Peter?" asked Contrary. "We have the newest guns ourselves. There's something you gents aren't telling me, isn't there?"

David and Peter looked at each other. Should they tell Contrary the whole truth, the entire story about coming from some other time? Could he handle it? Would he believe them? Once again, Peter took the lead.

"All right, Contrary, you want to know everything, so I'm going to tell you. But, I'll warn you, you're not going to believe a word of it."

Contrary interrupted Peter. "Well, I thought there was something a little odd about you boys when you stumbled out of the woods yesterday. Nobody takes the old Indian Trail because it's grown over and there's no bridge to get across the river. Everyone travels by way of the Post Road. So, you two seemed suspicious to me from the start because I knew you weren't traveling through the woods on that old trail."

"You were right to be suspicious about us, Contrary," Peter continued. "But, what I will tell you will make you even more suspicious, except, you'll be suspicious that we are not in our right mind."

"Let's hear it," insisted Contrary. Phillip and John, who had now downed more rum than they could account for, had begun singing, at least trying to sing. They weren't paying any attention to the conversation.

"Contrary," continued Peter, "we live in a future world. I live in the year 1945 and David lives in the year 2010. We are able to travel forward or backward in time. That is how we came to be here in your world in your time. A man named Adolf Hitler has come to your world also. He is the most dangerous of men and he's here to assassinate George Washington and insure the British defeat the Americans."

Contrary interrupted, "But why would he come back in time to kill Washington and help the British?" Why would he care about defeating the Americans?"

"Because by doing so," Peter replied, "Hitler will change history. Once Washington is killed and the British win the coming start war with the Americans, all events which come after that will also be changed. The reason Hitler cares about who prevails in the conflict between the British and the Americans is because in his future time of the 1930's, he shall initiate the most terrible of all wars. Millions of people will die. However, the Americans will turn the tide of that war and help defeat Hitler in 1945. If the British win the coming Revolutionary War, there will never be a country of the United States of America. Without the United States, Hitler will win World War Two and go on to rule the entire world."

Peter wasn't telling Contrary the entire story of World War Two because there wasn't time to further explain. Contrary would either believe him or not. If he did, he could become a valuable ally. If he didn't, he and David would have to figure out something else.

To Peter's and David's surprise, Contrary believed the story. "It's a crazy story gents," Contrary replied. "I would never believe such a story except you're just drinking your first beer and it's too crazy a tale to make up. So, it must be true. Nothing else can be said for it. But, I do have a question or two."

"Shoot," said David, not surprised to hear Contrary had questions.

Contrary looked at David with a quizzical expression on his face. "What do you mean, 'Shoot?'"

"I mean, go ahead. Ask your questions," replied David.

"So, you knew Hitler would try to assassinate Washington because of something you learned in the future. Is that right?" asked Contrary.

"That's exactly right," said David, knowing he should avoid telling him about Lomasi's visions.

"So, how do we stop these men?" asked Contrary.

Peter and David were taken off guard by that question. Both men realized they hadn't made a plan to stop Hitler from killing Washington. Yet, the man they were to confront was smart and focused. His closest allies were working with him, planning how to carry out the plot. He also had a garrison of elite SS Troops. And David and Peter had come to the year 1775 without a plan or weapons. It was time to figure out what they were going to do.

Always the one to face facts, David replied, "You won't like my answer, Contrary. The truth is we never made a plan. We never had time to think about what we would do when we got here." David realized it was the weakest possible answer however, that was the situation.

Surprisingly, Contrary understood their predicament, however, he wasn't gentle. "You two are crazy," he replied. "This man's a devil. Are you expecting some kind of miracle? You need to have a plan and you need to have help."

"We know that," answered David. "We were just a little slow figuring it out."

"No, you were real slow," laughed Contrary. "But, I'll tell you what. We'll give you a hand. It's to our advantage to help you because we have to win this war with the British. Like you said, it's real close to starting. I never thought about it, but if Washington is killed, there is no way we can defeat the British. You're totally right about that."

"But, there are only three of you," interjected Peter. "We'll need many more men than that."

"And, I'll get them too," said Contrary. "However, the first thing we have to do is scout out the barracks where that group of men is staying at Bettenfield Manor. We need to find out exactly how many men there are and what kind of weapons they have. Not all of us are farmers or businessmen, David. Both John and I have experience fighting in the French and Indian War. We know how to fight in the woods and we know guerilla warfare. John here may not look it, but he's a great scout. He can get into that barracks without anybody seeing him."

At that moment, John fell off his chair and landed noisily on the floor. It drew laughs from everyone in the tavern.

"Yeah, I can see John's our man," said Peter, laughing.

"He'll be fine in the morning," laughed Contrary. "Come on Phillip, let's carry him up to the room. We'll see you gents first thing in the morning and we'll make our plans. Then he said, "You know, you boys are lucky we ran into you again. If we weren't around to help you out, I don't know where you'd end up."

Peter replied, "Well, the first time we met you yesterday, you got us into a fight. Then you got us arrested by the British. And now, the British are looking for us to arrest us again. That doesn't seem so lucky to me"

"Oh yeah, I forgot about that. But, you need us now," laughed Contrary. Contrary and Phillip hoisted John off the floor. Each man grabbed one of John's arms and wrapped it around his neck.

David and Peter were exhausted from the day's events and decided to go to bed. Tomorrow would be a busy day.

25

A Face of Death

April 16, 1775   Philadelphia

First light came early. David and Peter rolled out of their comfortable feather beds. Their second floor room was small and dark and the single window above the stable area afforded a less than beautiful view. Neither the painful bites of horse flies nor powerful smell of horse manure stopped them from getting a good night's sleep. However, both men awoke with horsefly welts on their arms and legs. When will they invent screens? David wondered.

Neither of them wanted to begin the day, one they were certain would bring nothing but trouble. While they silently pondered their own thoughts each felt a growing apprehension. They would meet with Contrary Walbridge and try to develop a plan.

"Amid a multitude of projects, no plan is devised," Peter suddenly announced.

"What are you talking about?" asked David.

"Publilius Syrus," responded Peter. He lived a couple thousand years ago but I can't remember the exact years. Come to think of it, I wonder if I could have visited him when I was back in 48 B.C. What he means is we have too many irons in the fire and no plan."

"Yeah, you two should have had a beer together," laughed David. "Maybe he could come up with a plan. But, we'll figure out one today. I'll guarantee that."

David opened the door of the room and both men entered the poorly lit hallway and walked to the narrow staircase leading to the tavern on the first floor. It would be a short breakfast. As the men walked down the stairs, they spotted Contrary, Phillip, and John sitting at a corner table at the back of the room. Nobody else seemed to have gotten up this early as the three men were the only ones in the room. There was no heavy smoke in the air as there had been the night before.

"Good morning, boys," Contrary yelled. "Come on over and sit down."

The three men had already started on their ham and eggs. Both David and Peter were surprised that John, who had indulged heavily the night before, seemed to be in good shape.

"How are you boys doing today?" asked David.

"Well, Phillip and I are going to live however, John may not make it. He's looking a little green around the gills," laughed Contrary. John looked up for a moment, and then went back to devouring his food. He thought the cure for a hangover was a lot of food. If it was, he should be cured completely after he finished everything on his plate. John had done his best to drink all the rum in the place the night before and now he was trying to eat everything in the place this morning.

Contrary began the conversation. "Let's get down to business, men. We need to get our talking done before there are a lot of other people around. The city is crawling with spies and informants."

"David," Contrary continued, you and Peter are going to go to General Washington's office today, is that right?"

"Yeah," replied David. "We need to find our friend Lomasi. We've never met her but she is from our future time."

"Alright," continued Contrary, "while you're doing that John and Phillip will go out to Bettenfield Manor and see what they can find out."

"They need to be very careful," Peter cautioned. "Like I said, if the men quartered at Madame Bettenfield's are the ones we think, they are extremely dangerous and will kill whoever gets in their way."

"Don't worry about Phillip and John," laughed Contrary. "They can take care of themselves."

Both David and Contrary were shocked by Peter's harsh response. "Cut the crap, Contrary. John and Phillip aren't going for a walk down a country lane. In all probability they're going to spy on highly trained professionals, elite troops, with weapons more deadly than any of you can even imagine. If John and Phillip are caught when they're sneaking around, they will be tortured to obtain information on the people working with them, that being us. Then, they'll be killed. They will have sentries guarding their quarters and lookouts around the estate. I know I'm repeating myself but, you guys have to understand what you're up against."

Contrary, his lips pressed in a grim expression, replied. "I understand what you are telling me but, what would you have us do? We have no other choice."

Peter answered, "Just have John and Phillip look from a distance. If they get too close, I assure you they will be discovered. I know we must eventually fight these men but, it must be on our terms. If your men with their single shot rifles go up against these men from the future, they will be annihilated. These people have high caliber rapid-fire repeating guns they call 'machine guns.' Their machine guns can cut trees in half, cut down a forest in just a few seconds. Do you understand?"

"I understand," Contrary replied grimly. He looked at Phillip and John. "You heard the man," he said. "Stay low and don't be obvious. Be very careful. You're no good to us if you're dead."

David and Peter said they would meet with Contrary again in early evening after they located Lomasi. In the meantime, Contrary would try to locate Moses Brampton and line up some militiamen for the fight that was sure to come.

****

David and Peter arrived at Washington's headquarters at eight thirty. The sentry, recognizing the men from the day before, said he told Colonel Thacher they would be coming to see him today. He then disappeared through the doorway to see if the Colonel was available. He returned momentarily and motioned David and Peter to follow him into the large house.

David and Peter noticed the impressive appointments in the home serving as General Washington's headquarters. Luxury and wealth were on display everywhere. As they entered his office, Colonel Thacher introduced himself and offered the men chairs.

"And, how may I be of service to you gentlemen?" Colonel Thacher asked.

David knew the plot to kill George Washington could be a wider conspiracy and until all the players were identified, everyone was suspect. Abruptly, he decided to manipulate Colonel Thacher to see if he could get any information from him. "We were drinking at one of the taverns last night and we heard rumors to the effect someone might be planning to assassinate General Washington. We thought that we better report that to someone before we continued our journey south."

Peter was surprised at David's answer but assumed he had good reason for what he had said.

"Well gentlemen, I want to thank you for bringing this to my attention. I will act immediately to increase security for General Washington. You know, these kinds of rumors are circulating all the time. While we don't underestimate them, they generally don't amount to anything," Colonel Thacher replied.

"That's good news, Colonel," David replied, knowing Thacher was in the middle of the plot. "One question however. There are supposed to be a lot of men staying at Bettenfield Manor. Do you think they might be a danger?" responded David.

Colonel Thacher laughed, "No, not at all, gentlemen. In fact, I was there just yesterday taking a friend of General Washington's to fill a position on the staff of Bettenfield Manor. The only danger is General Washington's friend is a very beautiful Indian girl and those forty or so men out there will find her very hard to resist. You gentlemen might as well resume your journey. I will keep a close eye on things here and you need not concern yourselves any further."

"All right, Colonel," replied David. "We thank you for your time. We will be on our way then. It's been nice meeting you sir."

"It has been my pleasure, Gentlemen," replied Colonel Thacher. "I trust you can find your way out."

"Yes," replied David. "Thank you again, Colonel."

David and Peter walked out of Colonel Thacher's office and passed through the living room and front door, stopping on the massive front porch. The view from the porch was beautiful. The large trees and colorful gardens would make a good painting, thought Peter. David thought it would be such a nice trip if he were only a tourist. Unfortunately, the burden they carried made it impossible to enjoy any of this.

David turned to one of the sentries and asked, "Did an attractive Indian woman visit here yesterday?"

"Sir, we are not allowed to discuss those kinds of things," the sentry replied.

"But, Colonel Thacher told us such a woman was here yesterday. She is our friend and we neglected to ask the Colonel where she is located.

218

"What is her name, Sir?" the sentry asked.

"Her name is Lomasi," David answered.

"Yes, a woman of that name was here. When she left here, she went to Bettenfield Manor."

"Thanks very much," said David. "Maybe I'll see you boys later this afternoon down at the Croswell Tavern and buy you a few beers.

David and Peter walked down the steps and through the front gate onto the street.

While Contrary sent John and Phillip to check out Bettenfield Manor, neither David nor Peter thought they would learn very much.

"What do you think, David?" Peter asked. "Should we go to Bettenfield Manor to find Lomasi?"

"That's exactly what I'm thinking," David replied.

David and Peter walked north on James Street, a tree lined cobblestone lane west of Washington's headquarters. After two hundred yards, they turned east on a small, dirt street that ran between James and Old Church Road, the latter which ran along the east and back side of the Headquarters. Old Church Road was a busy, dirt-surfaced road that ran north out of the city into the country. It passed directly in front of Bettenfield Manor ten miles from where David and Peter stood. With no intention other than finding Lomasi, they began walking north on Old Church Road.

There were fields and woods on each side of Old Church Road. Though it was mid-April, some of the fields had turned light green with a cover crop. The woods were also green and had dense clusters of tall trees. David and Peter had seen all of the woods they wanted to see the night before last. "The woods are beautiful but lots of mosquitoes live in there, not to mention other interesting things," Peter remarked. While there were a few houses along the road, the further north they walked the fewer they saw. It was a pleasant, sunny morning, a great day for a hike, David thought.

Two women walking south were approaching. "Going to the city?" David asked, assuming from their coarse clothing they must be country people.

"Yes, that we are, Mister," the woman in the blue dress replied.

"We are looking for Bettenfield Manor," David continued. "Do you know where that might be located?" They knew where they were going, but David wanted to see if they could learn anything about Bettenfield Manor along the way.

The women looked at each other. The one in the blue dress, the more outgoing of the two, answered, "There is only one large house up this way. It is about nine miles distance." Again, both women looked at each other. "That would be Madame Bettenfield's home but, I would not go there without very good reason, Lads" she added.

"Why do you say that?" asked Peter. "Is there something about the place that is of interest?"

The woman doing the talking looked over at her friend who now had a serious expression on her face. "I just would not go there, Sir. It is a strange place and only for the wealthy, which it does not appear that you are."

Both women guffawed loudly at that remark. David thought to himself, they are easily amused.

"What do you mean?" asked Peter.

"Well," the woman replied, "one of me friends works there sometimes, she does. Madame Bettenfield has many visitors. My friend says they have all sorts of secret meetings. Oftentimes, some men stay overnight, they do."

"Do you mean Madame Bettenfield entertains gentlemen friends?" asked Peter, assuming the answer would be yes.

"No," replied the woman. "That's not why the men go there. There is no nonsense in that house. It is all business. The place scares me and all the rest of the people who live around there."

"When you get to Madame Bettenfield's home, you best keep a watch out for her head house maid. My friend said she is an evil person. My friend is very afraid of both women but she needs the money so she works there."

The women started on their way. "Just a moment," Peter started to speak. But, the women were finished talking and did not look back as they scurried away toward the city.

It was now nearly noon. The sun had drifted higher in the sky but the air was still cool. The farm fields had become fewer now and the woods had become thicker with trees growing right up to the side of the road. Madame Bettenfield's home was still at least five miles away. The men suddenly heard the sounds of a wagon coming up behind them. Looking back, they saw an old man sitting on an empty wagon pulled by two horses.

"Would you give us a lift?" asked David. The old man looked them over. Apparently satisfied, he said, "Climb aboard, boys."

It was another forty-five minutes before the old man said, "Bettenfield Manor is just over that hill there, boys."

"We'll get off here," said David. The old man stopped the wagon and David and Peter climbed down. 'Thanks for the ride," said David.

Old Church Road followed the contour of the land and a gentle incline, which crested at the top of a small hill. David and Peter walked to the crest of the hill and were now looking downward on the large home a quarter mile in the distance.

David and Peter decided they better not get any closer. They would hide in the trees and watch the place for a while. As the house sat on the west side of the road, they walked into the trees on their left. The fields of six-inch high early spring corn south of the estate extended from the home's gardens to the crest of the hill, bordering the woods in which they hid. From this vantage point, the two men had a perfect view of the house and its surroundings. They could also see the wall of the barracks, which sat in back of the estate behind a stand of large trees.

David and Peter sat in the concealed shelter of the woods on a fallen tree staring at the house for nearly an hour. It was nearly three p.m. Everything appeared quiet at the house. A group of a dozen uniformed soldiers had come from an area on the west side of the house and were walking in front of the house toward the east.

Suddenly, a lone horseman galloped wildly around the west side of the house toward the southwest, directly toward them. Just as suddenly, the soldiers came running from the east side of the house back toward the west, briefly chasing the horseman. As they ran, the soldiers held their rifles with both hands, positioned at their midsections crossways to their bodies. They were ready for action. When the soldiers stopped at the west end of the house, one of them raised his rifle and fired a single shot. The horse was killed instantly and fell away to the right, its rider crashing to the ground.

The rider freed himself from the fallen animal and ran to the edge of the cornfield. David and Peter watched the man two

221

hundred yards away. He suddenly threw himself on the ground and began crawling as rapidly as he could. He was coming directly toward them. The soldiers made no effort to stop the terrified man who was obviously trying to make it to the woods. He had gotten to his feet, bent over very low, and was running wildly. He was now less than one hundred yards away and was coming fast. The sound of a rifle shot, then another, signaled the soldiers were now attending to him. David and Peter could hear them laughing. It was a game for them. They knew they would shoot their man before he reached the woods. They were taking their time, making a sport of it. The running man was now fifty yards from the woods.

"My God, it's Phillip!" exclaimed Peter. "Come on, Phillip, you're almost here!" Peter shouted.

Phillip was forty yards from David and Peter, who were now lying on their stomachs. Several shots rang out. Phillip fell, hit once in the leg and once near his right shoulder. Half a dozen other shots whizzed directly by Peter and David. The "zings" of bullets splitting the air were ruthless reminders of death.

Phillip got to his feet and was running once again. Panicked because of his wounds, he disregarded caution and was running fully erect, making himself an easy target. David and Peter watched the soldiers as one of them moved to the front of the group and took careful aim. Peter was only a few yards from the woods.

"Dive, Phillip, dive!" screamed David.

Phillip, screaming and only a few feet from safety kept running fully erect. Blood covered the front of his shirt and soaked his left pants leg because of the bullet hole in his lower thigh. His face, contorted in pain and terror, was the face of death.

"Dive, damn you, dive!" screamed David. "Dive Phillip!"

Phillip's forehead abruptly exploded, showering David and Peter with pieces of skull and spraying blood. Then they heard the crack of the rifle shot. It seemed to hang in the air even after Phillip's lifeless body crashed to the ground inches from where they lay. Whoever made the shot hit a running man's head three hundred yards away. The bullet had not come from a rifle manufactured in 1775. It was obvious the soldiers weren't firing single shot flintlock rifles.

Peter said what David was thinking, "The Nazis are here."

Phillip had fallen less than a foot from David and Peter. Peter could reach out his hand and touch Phillip's shattered head. Phillip was lying with the left side of his head in the dead leaves on the forest floor. There was a small hole in the back of his head where the bullet entered his skull however the exit wound on his forehead was a crimson tunnel of red gore spilling from his brain.

The soldiers were running across the field precisely toward David and Peter. And they had dogs. They were coming to see Phillip's body but, they had heard the shouts as David and Peter tried to help Phillip.

"Come on, Peter!" ordered David, "We gotta get out of here fast!"

Both men jumped to a crouching position and started running south through the woods. After a few yards, they were no longer crouching. From the louder barking, they knew the dogs were gaining on them. The soldiers were probably over a hundred or more yards behind but the dogs would quickly catch them.

They were running down a small hill and the trees were large and stood close together. They were heading for the stream up ahead. The three dogs were nearly upon them. They sounded like hound dogs, probably weighing around sixty pounds.

"This will be fun," gasped David. "Peter, pick up a sharp stick or a large rock. We'll have to kill these dogs or they'll slow us down and the soldiers will catch us."

They reached the stream and ran across, the dogs plunging in close behind them. The first two dogs were coming fast. David had picked up a four-pound rock. As the first dog neared the bank, David ran forward to meet it. As the dog came up out of the water, David grabbed the dog's collar with his left hand and brought the rock in his right hand down hard on the dog's head. It split the animal's skull and a gaping wound was pouring blood. The dog was yelping and David again brought the rock down on the dog's head. It went limp and was silent.

Peter was struggling with the second dog while the third one had entered the water and was swimming toward them fast. David found a heavy tree branch lying on the bank of the stream. He picked it up and came up behind the dog Peter was fighting. David slammed the heavy tree branch across the dog's back, breaking its spine with a sickening crunch. The dog lay on the ground paralyzed and whimpering.

The third dog had his mouth around David's left ankle. The dog's teeth pierced his boot and sank a half-inch into his flesh. Again, picking up a rock with his right hand and grabbing the dog's collar, he pounded the dog's head as hard as he could. The first powerful blow killed the dog instantly.

"Come on, let's go," said David.

They were again running through the woods. The further in they got, the safer they were. After ten minutes of running, they turned east toward the Old Church Road. They reached it in a short time however, didn't come out of the cover of the woods onto the road. They stopped at the edge of the trees, staying out of sight of anyone who might be standing on the road. They looked north and south. The road had gotten busier with afternoon traffic but there was no sign of the men who had been pursuing them. They decided to chance it and walked out into the road and, in a few minutes, flagged a passing coach. The ride back to Philadelphia seemed to take a long time. It had been a bad day. One of their new friends had been killed.

They had no idea what happened to John. Had he also been killed? If not, where was he? They had to meet Contrary at the inn later in the day.

26

Confirmation

April 16, 1775   Bettenfield Manor

Earlier that day, John and Phillip had traveled by horseback to Bettenfield Manor. They left their animals in the woods west of Old Church Road. This was to the rear of the formal grounds of Bettenfield Manor, two hundred yards from the barracks housing the group of men on whom they were to spy. Phillip was to keep watch from the edge of the woods while John made his way across the clearing between the woods and the barracks area. Twenty five yards behind the barracks was a wooden rail fence, the zig zagging type with three layers of rails running at an angle and resting on the next three layers of rails which ran at an opposite angle, and so on. John had gotten to the fence and was lying hidden on the ground on the north side (woods side) of the fence.

He looked around the area, and seeing no one, made a run for the backside of the barracks. The barracks was a rectangular building running lengthwise east to west. Once John got to the back (north side) of the building he moved slowly toward the east end of the building where a door was located. Between the east end of the building and Old Church Road was the stand of woods where Phillip and the horses were hiding. John edged around the northeast corner of the building with his back firmly pressed against the white wood wall, slowly inching toward the door. There were two steps on the small porch in front of the door of the building.

Unexpectedly, the door opened and a uniformed soldier stood looking back into the building and laughing. He turned and stepped through the door and onto the porch. John stood frozen, his back to the wall, only a few feet from the porch. The man moved slightly to his right in the direction of the steps and then stopped. He stood on the porch and lit a cigarette. John had crouched down and couldn't move without attracting the man's attention.

Abruptly, he moved over to the single porch railing which was level with his shoulders, and put his arms on it and leaned forward resting his head on his arms. He groaned as if in pain, pretending to be hung over and sick. The startled soldier spun around and saw John, apparently very ill, trying to hold himself up.

The soldier, chuckling now, walked over to John and said, "Too much to drink, my friend?"

John looked up and smiled weakly, slowly moving his right hand to his stomach signaling he was ill. The soldier laughed again. In a lightning move John swung his right arm from his stomach up between the soldier's legs grabbing his testicles in the vice grip of his powerful hand. The surprised soldier, in pain and gasping for breath, was unable to call for help. John pulled the soldier down and under the single wooden rail of the porch, the man's body flopping like a rag doll in John's mighty arms.

Still holding the soldier's testicles in a crushing grip, John grasped the soldier's throat in a strangle hold with his left hand, and squeezed the life from the man. The soldier struggled briefly but in vain. From where he lay Phillip could see the soldier's face turn bright red, then purple and he struggled no more.

John looked at a leather pouch hanging from the right side of the soldier's belt. He pulled it open and saw a metallic object inside of it. The "pouch" was actually a holster containing a German Luger pistol, which John now held in his hand. He knew it was a weapon of some kind, a gun, but, nothing like he had ever seen. He pulled the belt off the soldier's hip and put the gun back in the holster and strapped the belt around his own waist. Having gotten what he came for, John ran back across the clearing toward the woods.

However, Phillip had seen a group of a dozen soldiers walking toward the west end of the building in the direction of the house. One of the soldiers spotted John when he ran across the clearing. The group started running around toward the front of the house and along its south side in order to head John off in the woods. Phillip had gotten onto his horse and raced right by a surprised John and around the rear (north side) of the barracks building from where John had just come. Phillip turned his horse south when he reached the west end of the building and headed directly southwest past the main house and toward the cornfield.

The soldiers, who had just reached the other end of the house, heard Phillip galloping away behind them. They ran back from where they had come on the west side of the house and stopped. One of the soldiers fired his rifle bringing the down the horse and Phillip just as they reached the cornfield. The horse fell on its right side but Phillip managed to pull his leg out from under the dead animal. The soldiers were shooting at him and he was crawling as close to the ground as possible. He started running, though crouched low, trying to get across the cornfield and into the woods. He almost made it. John watched it all from the woods where Phillip and the horses had been hiding. He quickly got on his own horse and rode out onto the Old Church Road and headed back to Philadelphia.

****

Lomasi, who had been working in the kitchen, heard the shooting and looked out the front door of the house. She saw the soldiers firing at a man who was running across the cornfield. She knew the poor man would never make it to the woods. When he fell the first time, she went back inside. The ruthlessness of what she had just witnessed sickened her.

Although she had only been working in the kitchen since the day before, Lomasi had learned a great deal. Adolf Hitler had often come to visit with Madame Bettenfield. Sometimes he stayed overnight at Bettenfield Manor. As was his habit when he was the Fuhrer in Germany, he preferred to move around and sleep at different places each night. He had done this because of fear of assassination. He could easily move back and forth between Philadelphia and Boston using the Chronometric Teleporter.

Also, there had been many meetings. None of the kitchen staff seemed to know what the meetings were about but they often heard the date April 19 mentioned. They assumed the conversations were in regard to the important dinner they were to have the evening of the nineteenth. However, Lomasi suspected the conversations had a more sinister purpose.

Lucretia Chattenborne, Madame Bettenfield's head house servant, had seen one of the maids listening at the door of the small library on the second floor where General Werner and Colonel Wolf were having a conversation. She had grabbed the woman by the arm and led her down the steps to the front door and told her she was fired. The woman would not get the balance of her pay because she was spying on Madame Bettenfield's guests. Crying hysterically, the woman ran down the cobblestone driveway to Old Church Road and never looked back at the house. Lomasi thought this was an extreme reaction to what was an innocent event. It was evident that something very secretive was taking place.

An officer came in from outside and was talking to Colonel Wolf. One of their soldiers had been killed and his pistol was missing. Either the man they shot hid the pistol in the woods or someone else was involved. Colonel Wolf concluded it was most likely a thief or else a Patriot who suspected their men were Hessians who would fight for the British. Either way, security needed to be increased. There were only a few days left before the nineteenth and nothing must go wrong.

Lucretia Chattenborne came into the kitchen demanding tea and pastries be immediately prepared. Adolf Hitler had just arrived and was meeting with Madame Bettenfield, General Werner and Colonel Wolf. Lomasi and several other women were working quickly to carry out Miss Chattenborne's directions. Once they had completed their preparations, everything was arranged on two large silver trays. Lomasi carried one of them and a woman named Alma carried the other. As they reached the downstairs library, Miss Chattenborne opened the door and went into the room ahead of the two women.

That was when Lomasi saw Adolf Hitler. He resembled all his pictures that she had seen. He was unsmiling, deliberate and brooding. There was a mysterious, dark aura about him. He momentarily glanced in the direction of Lomasi and the other maid, taking little notice of them. Colonel Wolf, however, was looking at Lomasi with a great deal of interest. She could feel his eyes examining her face and body. As she walked out of the room, she glanced in his direction. He was still watching her, a slight smile on his face. Lomasi felt great discomfort with this man's eyes following her every move. She knew the men sitting in the room were extremely dangerous and among the most evil in history. She must remember Shimasani's warning to "follow your instincts."

****

David and Peter reached the Croswell Inn just after six p.m. As they walked into the tavern, they had no trouble locating

Contrary Walbridge. His voice was easily recognizable and he could always be heard above the rest of the crowd. They walked over to where Contrary was holding court at a table in the back of the room. He was on his fourth beer and visibly upset. John had told him about Phillip's fate and Contrary was angry.

"Sit down, boys," he growled. "Phillip was killed," he informed them.

David told Contrary that he and Peter were there and had seen it happen. They tried to help Phillip but to no avail. The Germans had also chased them but they were able to elude them in the thick woods.

"There's something you need to see, David," Contrary said as he glanced downward. David looked at Contrary's hands just below the table top. Contrary was holding a German Luger. "John brought this back," he said, keeping the weapon out of sight. "He killed the German soldier who owned it. I don't know how to use this thing but, I think I can figure it out pretty quick."

David took the gun from Contrary's hands, and keeping it below the table, handed it to Peter.

"It's the Nazis," Peter said, holding the Luger in his right hand. "I can show you how to use it, Contrary."

"I don't take kindly to those bastards shooting Phillip," said Contrary. "I'll be paying them a little visit real soon."

"Hold on, Contrary," replied Peter. "We'll all be paying them a visit but we have to figure out how we're going to do it. We need to be smart about it. Remember, our first objective is to keep George Washington from being assassinated. Your revenge for Phillip's death will come in good time but let's stay focused on what's most important."

"Fair enough," replied Contrary. "But, me and John have a score to settle, and we will settle that score." John, with tears in his eyes, shook his head in agreement.

"I understand," replied Peter. "But, you need to remember your firepower is useless against the Nazis. This Luger pistol is a toy compared to their other weapons. You remember what we told you about them."

"Yeah, I do. And you're right," replied Contrary. "You fellows said everything takes place on April 19. What do we do until then?"

"Contrary," said David, "you told us you were going to get some men together. Did you do that?"

"Oh yeah, I didn't tell you about that. I'm so upset about Phillip it slipped my mind. I got over a hundred boys lined up. I can get more if I need 'em. I also got some cannons."

"Good," replied David. "The problem remains that we have to figure out a way to use them without getting them all killed before we get thirty seconds into the fight."

"These boys are all marksmen, David," Contrary replied. "They know how to use the cannons too, he boasted."

David could see Contrary needed another wake up call. "Contrary, we've become friends so I'm going to talk to you like a friend. You don't know what in the hell you're talking about. These men you would go against with your present day weapons are all crack shots themselves. Plus, like that pistol Peter is holding, all their weapons have multiple shots. Their guns can get off hundreds of rounds to your men's three or four. The bullets from their machine guns will cut your men to pieces before they get off one shot. And the bullets from these guns will penetrate everything but a rock. You need to understand the absolute superior fire power these men have. Otherwise, you're men will be of no use because they will die before they can fight."

"Okay, David, I got it," replied Contrary, now seeming to realize emotions and bravado couldn't defeat overwhelming firepower. It would be suicide to take on the Nazis in a one on one fight. He was also concerned about his men and agreed they would have to figure out another way to defeat the Nazis.

"Contrary," David replied, "you said you were suspicious about Madame Bettenfield. Do you think she's a spy or is there any possibility her sympathies could lie with the Patriots?"

An assertive voice abruptly interrupted their conversation. "Good evening, gentlemen." The four men looked up to find themselves surrounded by Major Tarpley and a half dozen British soldiers holding rifles leveled directly at them.

Peter, who was sitting closest to Major Tarpley, was holding the Luger pistol. In a move that caught everyone off guard, Peter immediately jumped up and grabbed the lapel of Major Tarpley's uniform and stuck the Luger underneath his chin. "Don't move, Major Tarpley," Peter screamed, spinning the shocked officer round to use as a shield. Standing behind him, Peter ordered the six soldiers to drop their rifles to the floor. They hesitated, confused and waiting to hear Major Tarpley give the order. Peter fired the Luger at a glass of beer on a nearby table. The mug exploded, showering two soldiers with beer. "Lay down your muskets, now!" he ordered.

Still, they didn't put down their weapons.

"Tell your men to put down their weapons, now!" Peter screamed at Major Tarpley.

Major Tarpley hesitated. "You fool," he smiled at Peter. "You have fired your only ball. Your pistol is empty." A soldier advanced toward Peter but, he shot the man in his right leg and he fell to the floor.

"I have seven shots left!" Peter exclaimed. "There's one for each of you."

Major Tarpley quickly obliged, ordering his men to put down their rifles immediately.

Suddenly, a roar of gunfire thundered through the room as an intoxicated Loyalist fired his pistol in the direction of Peter and Major Tarpley. Although Peter was the intended target, it was Major Tarpley who fell dead, a bullet through his heart. The situation went bad as two of British soldiers stooped and grabbed their rifles. Peter shot the soldier furthest from him in the chest, throwing the man backwards and crashing onto the floor.

The soldier nearest Peter had his rifle to his shoulder aimed directly at Peter. Peter buckled his knees, dropping down as the rifle discharged. The shot blasted through the room and lodged in the wall in back of Peter's table. Loyalists and Patriots immediately stormed toward one another and began brawling. Peter, David, Contrary and John hastily ran toward the back door.

27

Assassins

April 17, 1775   Philadelphia

Morning came early at Bettenfield Manor. Lomasi and the other twenty-two house maids slept in the white frame dormitory in back the main house. All of them were dressed and at work in the main house before first light. Lomasi had been working at Bettenfield Manor since the afternoon of April 15, which didn't give her much time to find out anything about the plot to assassinate George Washington. Since the assassination was supposed to happen in two days, there wasn't much time. She wondered if she should have returned to 1775 at an earlier date.

Lucretia Chattenborne, the head housekeeper, appeared after the women had been working several hours. She was a stickler for details and was checking to make sure everyone had done what they were supposed to do. She prided herself on being particular and took perverse pleasure in finding things not completed properly. Miss Chattenborne approached Lomasi and asked that she follow her into the dining room. Lomasi did as Miss Chattenborne had requested, although she thought the request odd because her duties that day were confined to kitchen area.

The dining room could have been the centerpiece for any fine house. In this house, however, it was just one of many magnificent rooms. But, it was breathtaking nevertheless. Large plaster relief medallions with designs of floral and angels graced the ceiling. Beautiful lace curtains framed windows, which themselves framed views of statuary gardens. Flowers of a thousand colors spilled over white marble walls and red brick paths. Thick trunks and muscular branches of large, old oak trees graced the green lawns spreading across the entire estate. Every window in the dining room offered a view of how heaven might appear.

"Lomasi," Miss Chattenborne said, "I have a special task for you today."

"Yes, Miss Chattenborne." Lomasi said.

"Colonel Wolf has requested you join him in his room this morning," replied Miss Chattenborne.

"What exactly does Colonel Wolf want?" asked Lomasi apprehensively.

Miss Chattenborne, her jaw jutting forward and her thin lips tightly pursed, said, "You shall have to ask him that question, my dear. Now, don't keep him waiting. It is our job to keep our guests comfortable. Do you understand me?"

Reluctantly, Lomasi began walking from the dining room. She understood Miss Chattenborne completely. Lomasi stopped as she the reached door and looked back, hoping the woman might give her an indication of what Colonel Wolf wanted. Miss Chattenborne dismissively waved her out of the room, and followed up with, "Go on, woman, and be quick about it."

Lomasi didn't want to think about what Colonel Wolf wanted. She remembered yesterday when Colonel Wolf blatantly stared at her, making no effort to not be obvious. She was wondering how she would handle an unwanted advance from him. She was sure that was his intent in summoning her to his room. She climbed the wide, circular staircase to the second floor. Colonel Wolf's room was the second door on the right. She walked down the hallway covered by a royal blue carpet with a gold trim of oak leaves. What a beautiful place this is, she thought. And yet, if my vision is correct, the most awful of murders shall occur here in just three days.

Lomasi reached the room and stopped, pausing before knocking on the door. She took a deep breath, composed herself, and tapped lightly on the door. Almost immediately the door opened and Colonel Wolf was standing before her. She had expected him to be in his nightclothes and thought that he would try to get her into his bed. Instead, he was fully clothed in his military uniform. His demeanor was formal and business like.

"Come in, Madame," he said.

"Thank you," replied Lomasi. Still not sure of his intentions, she asked, "Colonel Wolf, Miss Chattenborne said you wanted to see me."

"Yes, I do," replied Colonel Wolf. "Sit down, won't you please," the Colonel said.

"Alright," replied Lomasi, taking a chair next to the large feather bed.

"Madame," he continued, as you know there is a very important dinner here the evening of April 19. Since you are the newest member of the staff, I felt you would be the best person for a very important task that must be performed."

"What task is that, Colonel?" she asked.

"Madam, there are rumors suggesting that some harm could might come to one of our guests. Now, I myself don't feel there is anything to these rumors however, we must be very cautious just the same. What I would like for you to do, Madam, is to personally serve this particular guest. It shall be only you that serves him his wine, food, and whatever else he wishes. Do you think you can do that for me?"

Lomasi answered, "Yes, of course, Colonel Wolf. I will be happy to do that. Which guest do you want me to serve?"

"General Washington is the guest I'm speaking of, Madam. I want only you to serve General Washington to make sure his food and wine is safe and not tampered with in any way, if you understand what I mean."

Lomasi thought for a moment. This would place her into a position where she could safeguard General Washington. It was exactly where she wanted to be. This is a very lucky turn of events, she thought to herself.

"In other words, you want me to make sure his food and wine is not poisoned," replied Lomasi.

"You are very perceptive, Madam. That is precisely what I want. If you would agree to do that for me, I shall speak to Madam Bettenfield and assure you are given that responsibility. General Washington's safety is in your hands."

"Of course," replied Lomasi. "I will be very happy to do that for you." Again, she thought, I can now make sure that Washington's dinner will not get poisoned as the vision had prophesied. I can prevent this from happening.

"Good, very good," replied Colonel Wolf. "We will give you more instructions later. Remember, this is a very important task you are to perform. You must tell no one what you are doing. Everyone must be made to think that you are just a serving maid.

They mustn't know you are protecting George Washington from harm. It would ruin the evening."

Colonel Wolf, signaling the conversation was over, rose from his chair and walked across the room to open the door for Lomasi. "Thank you, Madam," he said.

Lomasi stood up and asked, "Colonel, may I ask why you have chosen me for this task instead of one of the more experienced house maids?"

"Simple," replied Colonel Wolf. "The other maids have been here for a while. They trust all the rest of the staff because they are familiar with them and feel that they know them. You, on the other hand, haven't had the time to form an attachment to the others. You will be equally suspect of all of them, as you most definitely should be."

"Thank you, Colonel," she said.

Lomasi walked to the door and Colonel Wolf put his hand on her arm and said, "Remember Madame, you are to tell no one about what we have discussed. Do you understand?"

"Yes, of course," said Lomasi. "I understand completely." She turned and walked out of Colonel Wolf's room and down the hallway toward the staircase.

When Lomasi reached the first floor of the house, the daily bustle of activity was well under way. The other maids scurried about preparing the morning breakfast and setting the dining room table for Madame Bettenfield and her German guests. When Lomasi entered the kitchen, several of the maids gave her sideways looks and a few giggles as they imagined what might have transpired in Colonel Wolf's room. Their imaginings irritated Lomasi, but she smiled back, ignoring their suspicions. It didn't matter what they thought. She would be gone in three days anyway and wouldn't have to think about any of this any longer.

In a short time, the German guests began descending the great staircase in the living room. Adolf Hitler and Martin Bormann came down together, speaking in whispered tones. The others, General Peter Werner, Colonel Helmut Wolf, and Dr. Wenzel Klein came down separately. Another man Lomasi had not seen before also had joined the group. She learned that this man was Colonel Dieter Kruger whom, with the aid of the Chronometric Teleporter, routinely traveled from Boston to visit with Hitler. While others on the staff were familiar with him, they never questioned how he could travel between Boston and Philadelphia so rapidly, given the distance between the two cities. Most of the staff had never been more than a few miles from their homes and never troubled themselves with the logistics of travel.

Four SS officers who normally had breakfast in one of the smaller sitting rooms also joined the group this morning. The fact that Colonel Kruger and the four other officers would be present at the breakfast this morning indicated that this would not be a routine meeting. Lomasi noticed the table was set for fourteen people. The Germans numbered a total of ten people. Madame Bettenfield, who customarily had breakfast with the group, was the eleventh person. But, who were the other three people would attend the meeting this morning? Two other officers, whom Lomasi did not recognize, now descended the stairs talking together in low, muffled tones. Lomasi learned that the British officer was none other than General Nigel Pickering, the British North American Army Commander. The other officer was General Gerhard Muller, the Commander of the Hessian Mercenaries.

Lomasi concluded these men were all conspirators who planned to kill George Washington. They had planned it and they were the ones who would carry it out. This meeting today would be extremely important. She must find a way to listen to what was being said at the meeting but had no idea how she could do this. But there was another piece to this puzzle. There were fourteen places set at the dining room table. She had counted thirteen people so far. Who was the fourteenth?

Miss Chattenborne, who was working with Lomasi and the other maids in the kitchen, must have seen someone coming up the driveway from the Old Church Road. Lomasi heard Miss Chattenborne tell one of the maids she would answer the front door. The kitchen was situated at the end of a hallway, which connected to the living room. As Miss Chattenborne left the kitchen area and walked down this hallway Lomasi followed her at a distance. Lomasi walked to the end of the hallway but stopped out of sight at a point from which she could see the front door. Miss Chattenborne now held the door open waiting for the visitor to come into the house.

Miss Chattenborne warmly greeted the visitor whom Lomasi could not see because he was standing behind the open door. However, she was surprised to hear a voice, which she'd heard before. Colonel Thacher stepped forward from behind the large white door and walked across the living room toward the dining room. Although Lomasi concluded from her vision that Colonel Thacher was involved in the plot to kill George Washington, his appearance at this meeting underscored the chilling reality of the rapidly unfolding events. Miss Chattenborne accompanied Colonel Thacher to the entrance to the dining room and as he entered, she closed the two massive carved, white wood doors behind him.

Miss Chattenborne walked from the dining room entrance back across the living room and toward the hallway in which Lomasi was standing. Lomasi quickly walked back down the hallway and returned to the kitchen. She knew she must find a way to listen in on the meeting.

She remembered a small sitting room was located next to the dining room. It was just large enough for a table with four chairs, and a few random chairs placed against the walls. Could she hear anything from this room? she wondered. She had to try.

Miss Chattenborne, who must have gotten involved in something else, hadn't returned to the kitchen. Lomasi again walked out of the kitchen and down the hallway to the living room entrance. No one was in the living room now. Lomasi quickly walked across the large room and past the closed dining room doors and scurried down the hallway leading to the sitting room. She hoped no one had seen her. When she reached the sitting room, the door was closed. She hesitated, wondering if someone was inside. She put her head against the door but heard nothing. Getting down on her knees, she put her eye against the iron fixture holding the doorknob and the key hole. She could see through the keyhole, but only a tiny portion of the room. Directly opposite the door was a window with a large tree just outside. Was there someone in the room, she wondered. She had to chance it and slowly opened the door, peeking around its edge to see inside. To her relief, the room was empty. Lomasi quickly stepped inside and shut the large, white door behind her.

She put her ear against the wall separating the sitting room from the dining room. While she could hear voices, she couldn't make out what was being said. The walls were too thick. However, there was a small alcove eighteen inches high designed into the wall. This architectural detail, a stylistic enhancement at the time, was constructed to provide a display space for vases of flowers or small paintings. The alcove was eight inches deep which meant its back wall was only a few inches thick.

Lomasi removed the large blue and white vase sitting in the alcove and placed it on the floor near one of the chairs. She put her head partly inside this alcove with her ear to its backside. With only inches separating her from the next room, she could hear the voices clearly and even identify who was talking.

The opening remarks were concluded and the group was settling into the business of the day. Hitler was speaking and had just asked General Pickering to once again outline the three directives of the King's Colonial Advisement Council.

Lomasi heard General Pickering slide his chair away from the table and stand up to address the group. "Gentlemen," he began, the three directives which are mandatory we accomplish are these? First, we must forcefully deliver a series of decisive strikes against the American rebel positions and overwhelmingly defeat them. Secondly, we shall incorporate the thirteen Americans into the separate country of Dorchester."

"Both of these events were in my visions," reflected Lomasi.

"And, thirdly," General Pickering continued, Madame Bettenfield shall become the Queen of this newly established country. That is the plan which we must execute within the coming days beginning on April nineteenth."

Lomasi hadn't realized Madame Bettenfield was to become queen of the new country of Dorchester. No wonder she was cooperating with the British and the Germans. She was an enemy.

General Pickering continued. "Our military forces are now lined up at various staging areas in the vicinity of Boston and will begin conducting operations against the Americans the morning of April nineteenth. At that time, they will march on Corcord, a large military supply depot owned by the Massachusetts Militia. General Muller's German Hessians shall also be moving against the Americans on April nineteenth. These surprise-attacks, combined with the assassination of General Washington the evening of the nineteenth will provide decisive blows against the Americans. They will take the wind out of the rebel's sails. Military operations on

April twentieth will simply be mopping up operations. The Americans won't have the heart for a fight once Washington is dead. The Loyalists will support the creation of the new country and installment of the Queen, Madame Bettenfield. That should also bring the Patriots back into line because they will have their own country and a queen to govern it.

Lomasi could hear General Pickering addressing Hitler now. "Sir, the success of our plan rests upon the success of your mission to assassinate George Washington. You are here, in the same location at which he shall be dining two days from now. I expect that you are prepared to fully carry out your part of the plan."

Lomasi could hear Hitler moving his chair away from the table and standing up to speak. In a tone Lomasi sensed was thinly disguised irritation, Hitler replied to General Pickering's questioning of the Germans' readiness and his British arrogance. "Sir, we are well prepared to do our job. It appears that you also are ready to do yours. But, remember this, Sir," Hitler added in a threatening tone," if you do not succeed, things shall not go well for you. Do you understand that?"

Lomasi heard a louder noise in the room as General Pickering assertively pushed his chair back and rapidly got to his feet. "Sir, are you threatening me?" he demanded.

Someone else, apparently General Muller, now moved his chair back and stood to speak. "Gentlemen, gentlemen," he interjected in a thick German accent, "we all have the same objective. Obviously, we have taken great care to prepare ourselves for the momentous events we shall initiate. Let us not sow discontent which shall detract from the success we can achieve. Everything is in place and we must work together in harmony. General Pickering," he continued, "Commander Hitler has as much at stake in these operations as you British. Both of you must win your own wars. Let us not forget that."

General Muller then addressed Hitler. "Sir, everything must be executed in concert. Once General Pickering's and my own military operations commence the morning of April nineteenth, there is no turning back. We are then committed to our own war if you should not succeed in assassinating Washington because the rebels will fight back. That will create formidable problems for us. That is why you must succeed at your end. I hope you understand that sir."

"Of course, I do," replied Hitler. "And, I understand both of your positions. Have no fear. I assure you, we shall succeed."

"I shall lay out our plan to assassinate Washington," continued Hitler. "We have even come up with a scapegoat upon whom we shall blame the assassination. We did that especially for you, Madame Bettenfield," remarked Hitler, in an attempt to return the conversation to a more conciliatory tone.

"That is good news, Adolf," replied Madame Bettenfield.

"Thank you, Madame Bettenfield," Hitler replied. "And, thank you also for your hospitality. Our stay with you has been most enjoyable. Now, gentlemen, and lady, I shall get on with our plan."

"Our main objective to assassinate George Washington will be an easy task. To assure success however, we have developed a simple plan with multiple redundancies. What I mean by that, gentlemen, is our plan has backup alternatives should the initial attempt on Washington's life fail. Washington will be traveling by coach with Colonel Thacher and that will assure that General Washington arrives here if he isn't killed on the Old Church Road.

"What do you mean by that, Commander Hitler?" asked General Pickering. "I thought George Washington was to be poisoned at dinner here in this house."

"That is the plan, General Pickering," Hitler said. "However, we don't want to chance the possibility that George Washington doesn't show up for some reason. His coach shall be escorted by half-dozen soldiers on horseback and that is their only security. We shall have six of our own men following them. If Washington should want to turn back or gets suspicious for some reason, our men will immediately move in and neutralize the six American soldiers on horseback. Colonel Thacher will have several pistols hidden in the coach and one on his person. If the coach begins to turn around, he shall immediately kill Washington.

Assuming Washington arrives however, the second part of the plan goes into effect. When the food is served, Washington's dishes shall be laced with a powerful poison. A few bites of any of the dishes in front of him will result in his death within minutes."

General Pickering shook his head. "That is a good plan, Sir," he said.

"As a further precaution, we shall have two of our men serving as attendants at the dining room entrance. They will be armed. Once Washington has entered the dining room, should he not eat the food with the poison, our two men will shoot him as he sits at the table. Colonel Thacher is also there as additional backup.

We also have the house surrounded by forty men with their modern guns we demonstrated for you. We also have four machine guns which you have also seen demonstrated. Once Washington is inside the house, our men shall quietly neutralize his six soldiers waiting outside. Should Washington attempt to leave the premises, he will never make it out of the dining room, let alone off the front porch."

"Gentlemen," Hitler concluded, "are there any questions?"

Both General Pickering and General Muller were both extremely impressed with the plan the Nazis laid out before them. It was impossible for this plan to fail.

"Commander Hitler," General Pickering, responded, "I must apologize. You and your men have been most thorough in your planning. It is no doubt the most fail proof plan that I have ever seen. There is no doubt in my mind this plan will succeed. Do you not agree, General Muller?"

"Yes, I agree, General Pickering," Muller answered. "It is a brilliant plan that has no chance of failure."

Lomasi, to her dismay, could not help but agree. Her concern greatly increased. She was alone in another time with no resources or weapons and a deadly force of armed men with a brilliant plan to kill George Washington. She thought she only had to worry about the poisoning of the dinner. The Nazi's complex plan was another matter.

General Muller spoke again. "There is one other thing, Commander Hitler. You mentioned to Madame Bettenfield that there would be a scapegoat on which the assassination would be blamed. Please clarify who that shall be."

"Yes, General. I was just coming to that but thank you for reminding me."

"I too am most curious about that detail, Commander," chimed in Madame Bettenfield. "Exactly whom do you plan to blame for the murder of George Washington?" she asked with a slight chuckle.

Hitler continued. "Our men have the perfect individual whom we can hold accountable for the assassination. We will plant evidence in this individual's quarters which will link that person not only with the assassination, but also with the French. We will make it appear that the French were behind the assassination of Washington. This will focus the American Colonies' rage at George Washington's assassination on France and make the prospect of the American Colonies forming an alliance with France completely impossible. This will also provide a stronger guarantee of a British success, perhaps without a shot being fired, because the Americans will now look to England as their savior while France would become the enemy. We shall leave a substantial sum of gold in this person's quarters with notes supposedly written by the French General DeRouelle instructing this person to assassinate George Washington."

"Well who is this unfortunate man, Commander Hitler?" asked General Pickering.

"It's not a man, sir. It's an Indian woman. This woman will be made to appear as someone whose husband, an Indian Chief, was killed by the Americans in the French and Indian War. What is an even more brilliant part of the plan devised by Colonel Wolf is this woman is to actually be involved in the assassination of George Washington. This will further insure she is clearly recognized as the assassin."

"But where shall you get this Indian woman?" General Muller asked.

Adolf Hitler replied, "Thanks to Madame Bettenfield's cooperation, the woman is now employed in this house. Her name is Lomasi."

Lomasi clearly saw where the conversation had been leading and wasn't surprised she was the one being framed for the impending murder of George Washington. However, the deviousness of Colonel Wolf and Colonel Thacher and the brilliance of the complex plan shocked her. The Nazis were as formidable as they were evil.

Colonel Wolf was now speaking. "Colonel Thacher and I must apologize to you, Madame Bettenfield. This is the first you are hearing that one of your employees is to be involved in Washington's assassination. Colonel Thacher and I decided to include her in the plan only yesterday. This morning I instructed Lomasi that she is to be the only person serving General Washington

242

at the dinner on April 19. When General Washington dies from his food being poisoned, Lomasi will be blamed because she will have been the only person serving him food."

General Werner now concluded the plan to create the scapegoat. "The final part of the plan assures there are never any questions regarding the fact that Lomasi actually killed General Washington. She shall never stand trial for the assassination because she will be shot while trying to escape."

This revelation did shock Lomasi. "These men are truly horrible," she whispered to herself.

"Absolutely brilliant!" shouted General Muller "That is absolutely brilliant. Gentlemen, I am delighted to be part of such an outstanding plan."

General Pickering seconded General Muller's remarks. "The plan to kill Washington is fail proof, Commander Hitler. I commend you for devising such a brilliant strategy."

Once again, Lomasi could only agree that it was a brilliant plan. Unbelievably, she was to be the one to kill the very man she had come to save.

Now she understood why Colonel Wolf wanted only her to serve Washington. If the poison worked, she would be the one who poisoned him. This isn't fun, she thought. For some reason, Lomasi took a moment to reflect on her garden in her backyard in a faraway time and place. It wasn't nearly as impressive as the gardens she could see through the windows of the sitting room, but she liked her garden much better.

But now, she had to get back to reality. It was Lomasi who now had to make a plan. To do what, she had no idea. But she had to act. It sounded like the meeting was getting ready to adjourn so she replaced the vase in the alcove. As she walked across the small room she was thinking how fortunate it was that she hadn't been discovered eavesdropping. She opened the door and peeked into the hallway. There was no one and the doors to the dining room had not yet opened. Lomasi walked quickly down the corridor and past the dining room to the relative safety of the hallway leading from the living room to the kitchen. As Lomasi walked toward the kitchen, Miss Chattenborne abruptly appeared from the shadows. Oh no, thought Lomasi.

Surprisingly, Miss Chattenborne walked past her simply remarking, "Needed a little break, did you, girl?"

"Yes, Ma'am," Lomasi replied," thinking how very odd that question was.

28

Firefight

April 17, 1775 Philadelphia

Once David, Peter, Contrary, and John ran to the back door
of the Croswell Inn they wasted little time. Contrary and John had
stabled their horses in the small barn in the back of the Inn. That
turned out to be a fortunate location because as the men ran out the
door they exited directly into the stable area. The horses were
already bridled but the men rode bareback as there was no time for
saddles.

Riding two men to a horse, Contrary and David on one and
John and Peter on the other, they raced their mounts from the corral
into the darkness of the back alley. In moments they reached Louis
Street, which was bustling with carriages and people walking in
every direction. That Louis Street was so crowded would slow them
down however, it was the best escape route from the city.

That it was dark would be an advantage, but they slowed
their horses to a walk in order to not attract the attention of other
British soldiers they might encounter. That was a smart move as
Peter noticed at least one British officer staring at them. However,
after walking their horses for several minutes, they suddenly heard
the clattering of horses' hooves on the cobblestone street. Contrary
turned and looked down the street behind them as they spurred their
horses to a gallop. It was a troop of ten British cavalry and they
were coming fast.

"Word gets around quickly," yelled Contrary. "Get a move
on John."

John yelled back, "We'll never make it out of town
Contrary."

"Yeah, I know," Contrary shouted.

Contrary looked back again. Although the coaches and
people in the street were slowing the British, they were gaining on
Contrary and John's animals which were carrying twice the load of

the British horses. Contrary, who was leading, suddenly steered his horse right down a dark street. John followed closely. Contrary turned his horse left down another street and again turned left at the next street. He was running the horse hard back toward Louis Street. This was good move however, as they rushed toward the intersection of Louis Street expecting to turn right on their original escape route, they spotted two mounted British soldiers with their swords drawn.

Peter screamed at John and Contrary to keep charging toward the soldiers. As Peter and John's horse pulled ahead of Contrary and David, Peter held the Luger in his right hand. John pulled their winded horse to a stop near the sword wielding British soldiers. Peter aimed the Luger and pulled the trigger, killing both horses. The first horse slumped to the ground, pinning its rider's leg beneath it. The second horse also collapsed however, the rider jumped away from the animal as it fell.

The soldier, sword in hand, was now running toward Peter and John, not realizing that Peter's gun could fire again. Peter aimed, shot twice, and the soldier fell backward to the ground with two bullets through his chest. Contrary and John galloped their horses around the corner of Louis Street to head out of town.

Once again however, they heard the British horses behind them. There were not as many now, probably because some of the soldiers were probably searching for them on other streets. But, there were five of them and they were gaining on Contrary and John's horses. This part of Louis Street was less busy because it wasn't near the main business section. However, there was no way they could outrun the British cavalrymen.

From the corners of their eyes John and Peter saw the powder flash of a musket as a thunderous roar reverberated off the walls of the buildings along Louis Street. Their horse instantly crashed forward onto the cobblestone street, blood gushing from the side of his head. John and Peter were thrown over the horse's head onto the stone street. Though stunned, both men quickly got to their feet and ran down a pathway between two buildings. They didn't know who fired the shot, probably a Loyalist, as they hadn't seen any red uniforms. But, it didn't matter. They were on foot regardless of who was shooting at them. They were also being chased by two British soldiers on horseback.

Contrary and David had no choice but keep going. The three remaining British cavalrymen were nearly upon them. David looked back as the tiring horse galloped down the less populated, darker Louis Street. One of the British riders was only a length behind them. An abrupt powder flash lit up the dark buildings and they heard the whistle of splitting wind as a ball shot passed inches from their heads. The other two soldiers were also getting close.

In a sudden move that nearly threw David, Contrary pulled back the reins back and turned the horse hard to race back from where they had come. The first soldier charged past them as Contrary galloped directly toward the other two British soldiers, one of whom was raising his pistol. Contrary pulled his pistol and shot one soldier from his saddle. The second soldier fired his pistol as he galloped past.

Contrary turned their horse left, heading down a darkened alley. They heard the two British soldiers charging hard on the cobblestone street. David told Contrary to pull up and he jumped from the horse. "I'll get the second one," he said, as he ran toward a pile of logs stacked near a doorway. Contrary spurred his horse forward as David crouched behind the logs. The first British soldier rode past with the second following closely.

"Hey!" David yelled.

The startled soldier abruptly pulled back the reins causing the speeding horse to rear upward, but he regained control and turned the animal around. Peering into the darkness, he tried to locate the person who called to him. David, who was hiding less than five feet from the soldier, had taken a log from the pile. He moved forward one step and threw the five pound piece of wood hard toward the soldier's head and heard a thump as it found its mark. The soldier tumbled from his horse onto the ground and lay motionless. David climbed on the riderless horse and rode further into the alley after Contrary and the British soldier pursuing him. He nearly collided with Contrary who was galloping toward him pulling a second horse. "That you, David?" Contrary yelled.

"Yes," David called back.

"I knocked the lad on the head and took his horse," Contrary said, laughing. The two men rode out of the alley to Louis Street.

John and Peter, who had been running down an alley between several large buildings, went into the first door that was unlocked. They found themselves in a faintly lighted hallway. They heard the British soldiers steering their horses through the alleyway outside the door through which they had just come. At the far end of the corridor was a stairway to the second floor of the building which apparently housed some type of business. They quickly headed toward the stairs. The hall on the second floor of the building was also poorly lighted. The only light came from the stairway they just climbed and a lantern at each end of the hallway.

John and Peter walked down this second floor hall toward the alleyway. The long corridor had many doors just as one would find in an inn. They stopped at the last doorway on the left and listened closely. Hearing no sound, they turned the handle and slowly pushed the door open and entered the room. It had seemed like a safe decision but turned out to not be so. A woman's hysterical shrieks suddenly pierced the darkness.

"Murder, murder!" she hollered. "They're killing me!" she bellowed. John and Peter bolted through the open door and ran back through the hallway and then down the stairs they had just come up. They turned to their right at the bottom of the stairs, running toward the end of the building opposite the alleyway where the British soldiers were searching for them. On their left was a door, which, judging by the yellowish orange glow in the space between its bottom and the floor, led to a well-lighted room. They stopped at the door, hesitant about opening it and creating another commotion which would reveal their position to the British soldiers. However, they thought this room, which was at the front of the building, would have a door leading into the street. They could hear the woman's screeches ripping the silence. Unless the British soldiers were deaf, they would also hear the screams that, for some reason, were increasing in volume.

As John and Peter stood with their ears pressed to the door of the lighted room straining to hear sounds, the howling woman charged down the staircase, stopping on the last step. She wore a tent like nightgown that made her large size appear even more enormous. While that dreadful sight was arguably interesting, what caught the two men's attention was the pistol in her left hand, which she was pointing directly at them. Up and down the hallway, doors began opening and men's heads began popping out to see what was going on. Concluding the street couldn't be any more dangerous than their present situation, they pushed the door open and ran through as her pistol roared and sent a ball through its thick wood.

They found themselves in a lavishly decorated room occupied by couples seated at numerous small tables that held tiny glasses of sherry or other libations. The crimson red chairs, velvet draperies and suggestively dressed women left no doubt about where they were. John and peter had stumbled into a brothel.

The screams, gunfire and the two men crashing through the room had startled the room's occupants. As John and Peter ran through the room filled with prostitutes and their customers, they saw the entire clientele consisted of red uniformed British soldiers, many whom were on their feet chasing after them. They burst through the front door into the street followed by a dozen or more officers. The two British cavalrymen were now rounding the building from the alleyway and joining the chase.

The officers who ran out the door after them stopped after a short distance realizing it would not be wise to be seen chasing intruders out of a brothel. They walked back up the street to the brothel to attend to more urgent matters.

However, the two cavalrymen were holding swords and pulled their horses alongside John and Peter, demanding the two immediately surrender. However, at that moment, they saw another dark alleyway and immediately ducked into it. Though the passage was very narrow, the soldiers spurred their reluctant horses into the dark passageway.

The horses became skittish and one reared up on it hind legs, refusing to go further. The alleyway between the two buildings was so narrow it was impossible for the British cavalrymen to dismount because there was no room. The mounted men either had to force the nervous horses to go further or slowly back out onto Louis Street.

The lead horse refused to move ahead. As the cavalryman tried to back the horse down the alleyway, the horse bolted and reared up, snorting wildly and panicking the other animal close behind. John and Peter heard the pandemonium but they continued sprinting through the narrow passageway. They reached the street running parallel to Louis and darted across and again into the alleyway and ran to the next street.

They slowed to a walk as they turned left on this less populated poorly lit street. This allowed them to catch their breaths and avoid suspicion. After walking nearly one block they saw two riders, one pulling a third horse. John immediately recognized Contrary by his characteristic posture in the saddle.

"Contrary," he called, in a loud whisper. "Contrary."

"Come on, John," came the reply.

John and Peter trotted over to the horsemen and mounted the third horse.

"Let's go," said Contrary, and the four men headed out of town.

Contrary had a friend who owned a farm four miles outside the city. They would be safe there and could plan their next move.

As they rode David said, "Contrary, we have to touch bases with Lomasi to see what she knows and make sure she's safe. We're running out of time so we better go to Bettenfield Manor in the morning.

"What do you mean, 'touch bases' with Lomasi?" asked Contrary.

"Yeah, explain that one to me too, David," said Peter.

David muttered back at them, "That's what I get for talking with two guys who are one and two hundred years old."

"Ha, ha, I agree," blurted out John. "I don't care for old guys myself, David. They can't drink and they move too slow."

29

Reconnaissance

April 18, 1775   Bettenfield Manor

Contrary's friend proved to be more of a convenience than intimate acquaintance. While he did remember meeting Contrary before, he couldn't recall where. He did recognize him however, and that got the four men overnight accommodations in the barn and a decent breakfast the following morning. More importantly, the man was a Patriot and willing to help.

During the breakfast Contrary talked with his friend, a man named Cass, and they agreed hostilities between the British and Americans would begin soon. Contrary asked the man what he knew about Bettenfield Manor and the situation there. Cass seemed to harbor a deep suspicion that something was not quite right at Bettenfield Manor. However, he could add little to what Contrary, David and Peter had already learned from John's visit to Bettenfield Manor which ended with Phillip's death. Cass was not certain if Madame Bettenfield was a Patriot or Loyalist. He said nobody seemed to know where her sympathies lay. It was true there were a large number of men housed at Bettenfield Manor but, Cass didn't know which side these men would be on if the Americans fought the British.

The reason for Cass' confusion was the equally confusing political environment at the time. People were divided into three main groups. The first group was those people who decided they were Patriots and wanted independence or Loyalists whose allegiance remained with Britain. The second group was those people who hadn't decided where they stood on the issue of independence for the colonies. The third group was a catch-all collection of individuals who, for political, business or personal reasons said they were one thing but were really another. The situation was nearing a flashpoint, however, and the pressure to take a stand grew more intense.

Contrary then shifted the conversation. "Cass," he asked, "if we wanted to pay a visit to Bettenfield Manor today, what pretext might we use for being there?"

"That's easy," replied Cass. "I could go along with a few of you gents and see if they want to buy any chickens. I've sold them a few in the past and it would be a good excuse to at least get on to the place."

"Okay, that sounds good," replied Contrary.

"Contrary," David said, "why don't Peter and I go to Bettenfield Manor with Cass? That way, you and John could try to find your leader Moses Brampton. If there is to be fighting, we'll need a lot of manpower."

"I was thinking the same thing," replied Contrary.

David continued, "Cass, could we borrow a couple of horses and some saddles when we travel to Bettenfield Manor? One of our horses doesn't have a saddle and I don't think we better be riding the British mounts because the horses and the British saddles will be obvious to anyone we meet along the road."

"I'll be glad to oblige," replied Cass. "Contrary, you and John will need a couple of horses too."

"Yeah, I was thinking David wanted us to do the walking," Contrary replied. "By the way Cass, when you and I first met, you were with the local militia which was led by Major Wellston. Are you still with them?"

"Sure am," responded Cass. "Major Wellston is a good man and a great leader. He has us boys ready to go at a moment's notice too!"

"How about tomorrow?" interjected David.

"What do you mean?" answered Cass.

"I mean are they ready to fight tomorrow?" responded David.

"Yeah, of course," said Cass. "They know trouble has been brewing and the fighting will break out anytime."

Contrary added, "Our leader Moses Brampton is staying at the home of Major Wellston. Cass, do you know where Major Wellston's home is located?"

"He lives in town and owns the livery stable at the edge of the city. It's only three miles from here. But, why are you talking about fighting tomorrow? No one knows when the fighting will begin. What makes you think it will happen tomorrow?"

Contrary looked at David and Peter. "Boys, we have to bring Cass into this mess. If what you think is going to happen tomorrow actually does happen, the British probably will coordinate an attack or several attacks to go along with it. That way, they catch the Americans completely off guard, and stop us in our tracks. When you think about it, it would be the perfect plan. It only makes sense."

David had never thought any further ahead than trying to prevent Washington's death. But the strategy Contrary described would be the perfect plan just as he said. Besides that, David knew from the history books the British attacks at Concord and Lexington would commence on April 19. If the Nazis succeed in killing Washington and the British launched a series of surprise attacks, the combined events could crush the Americans before any rebellion could begin. That would seal the fate of the Americans just as Lomasi saw in her visions.

"Okay, you're right, Contrary," said David. "Don't you agree, Peter?"

"I do agree," replied Peter. "Besides, it sounds like Cass is already in this mess whether we tell him or not. And with Hitler, Bormann, and the other Nazis involved, we will need all the help we can get."

David revealed to Cass the plot to kill George Washington at Bettenfield Manor on the evening of April nineteenth, the very next day. While David had to concede they didn't have a plan, he and Peter would try to make contact with Lomasi at Bettenfield Manor and see if they could figure out something. They could rendezvous with Contrary, John, Major Wellston and Moses Brampton later this afternoon.

The important thing is that Contrary request that Major Wellston have the militia ready to fight by mid-morning on the nineteenth, just twenty-four hours from now. With Moses Brampton's staying at Major Wellston's home, he could also support Contrary on his request to activate the local militia.

"Don't worry. That will be no problem," replied Cass. "They are always ready to fight with a minute's notice, just like the boys up north."

"Contrary, do you think it is safe enough for you and John to go into the city to see Major Wellston?" asked David.

Cass answered for Contrary. "Yeah, they can take a trail through the woods and come in on the Major's livery stable from the back. No one will see them."

"One more question," added David. "Peter, if you go to Bettenfield Manor with Cass and I, do you think there is any possibility that the Nazis might recognize you."

"Yes, there may very well be that possibility," replied Peter. "But, I have to chance that, David. Remember, I need to find my wife Johanna. Sooner or later, I shall have to confront Adolf Hitler to find out what he's done with her."

"I understand that," replied David. "But, today is not that day. I know how important Johanna is to you but you must remember stopping Hitler is our first priority. As miserable as he's made you, if he's not stopped he will create a world of misery for mankind. But, I completely understand where you are on this and I give you my word that I will help you find Johanna."

"Okay, let's get going!" exclaimed Contrary, who was fidgety to get on with things. "Come on John, let's go see Major Wellston and Moses. I'm spoiling for a good fight."

"Contrary," replied an alarmed Peter, "remember what we told you. Do not for a single moment underestimate the men you are going up against. I warned you about their weapons. Whatever plan we decide upon, it must not include fighting them head on."

"I got it," Contrary replied. "I just wanted to get a rise out of you Peter."

"Boys," he continued, "we have to plan a smart fight. Peter's right, we can't just overpower them with men and guns."

"Alright, Contrary," replied Peter with a slight smile. "I won't worry about but, I'll keep an eye on you just the same."

Cass, looking a little bewildered, asked the men what they were talking about.

Peter responded, "I'll tell you all about it on the way to Bettenfield Manor, Cass."

David and Peter picked out a couple of horses. David saddled his and then moved to Peter's horse to give him a hand as he had never saddled a horse before. Both men climbed on and, along with Cass, headed toward Old Church Road and Bettenfield Manor. Contrary and John saddled up their mounts and started toward Philadelphia to see Major Wellston and Moses Brampton.

Once David, Peter and Cass traveled the three miles to the Old Church Road, they rode north for another eight miles to where David and Peter recognized the rise in the road. They were south of Bettenfield Manor. As their horses reached the crest of the rise, Bettenfield Manor came into sight. David was afraid to look into the woods on his left because of his vivid memories of two days prior. He wondered if poor Phillip was still lying dead in the woods, or if someone gave him a proper burial.

"That's where it happened?" David remarked to Cass.

"Yeah," responded Peter. "That's where it was."

"Somebody's going to pay for Phillip's death, Cass," said David.

"I know," Cass replied.

From the start of the brief journey, the three men had allowed their horses to follow the road and walk at a casual gait. After the horses sauntered down the north side of the rise they pulled them left into the long driveway of Bettenfield Manor. When they reached the area in front of the massive home, an attendant came down from the front porch.

"Good day, gentlemen," he greeted them. "What brings you to Bettenfield Manor today?"

"Good day, Gerald!" responded Cass. "I just wanted to see if Miss Chattenborne needs any chickens in the next few days."

"If you will go around to the back of the house on the side carriage lane, I shall tell her you're here," responded Gerald. "She's probably in the kitchen area, although you can never tell with her. You know the way, don't you Cass?" asked Gerald in a teasing tone further enhanced by a sly smile on his face.

"Yeah, I know the way," answered Cass.

"What was that all about, Cass?" asked David, as the three men steered their horses around the driveway on the east side of the house.

"Me and Miss Chattenborne got a little thing going," replied Cass. "Gerald knows about it and always reminds me he knows about it when I come here."

The three men walked their horses back to the kitchen area where they dismounted and tied their animals' reins to the hitching post.

In a few moments, a woman appeared on the back porch. It was Miss Chattenborne. She is the most unattractive woman I've ever seen, David thought to himself. Cass, followed by David and Peter, walked over to the back porch and started talking with her. As it turned out, she did need some chickens later in the week, about four dozen in all.

While she had placed her order quickly, she lingered to talk with Cass. David politely interrupted their conversation and mentioned he had a friend working here named Lomasi. He asked Ms. Chattenborne if he might be able to see her. Surprisingly, Miss Chattenborne excused herself to go find Lomasi and let her know she had visitors. David figured her cooperative response was due to her desire to spend more time with Cass and also to get rid of him and Peter.

Cass chuckled after she left. "She wants me to stay and talk with her a spell. That will give you boys time to talk to your friend. When she gets back, me and her will go into the house. I'll meet up with you boys a little later."

"I guess we already figured that out Cass," replied David chuckling.

Miss Chattenborne returned and told the three men that Lomasi would join them in a few moments. Then she asked Cass to come with her toward the kitchen area and the two of them disappeared into the large house.

After they went into the kitchen, Lomasi came through the same door and out on to the porch. David saw Lomasi and immediately felt like he knew her. She was a beautiful woman with dark eyes and long black hair. She was dressed in a long floor length blue gown. She walked down the steps and over to where the two men were standing in the shade of a large oak tree.

"Hello," she greeted them. "I'm Lomasi. Miss Chattenborne said one of you men knew me. I don't see how that is possible as I have only been here for a few days. I haven't met many people and I don't recall meeting either of you."

"Lomasi," David interrupted, "I know who you are. I'm a friend of Tse and Shimasani. I've come here to help you. I know about your visions. This is Peter. He's a friend and is also here to help. Is there anyplace we can talk without being overheard?"

Obviously surprised, Lomasi said, "Yes. Tie your horses at the back of that white building and I'll meet you there in ten minutes. The maids live there but they are in the main house during the day." She turned and walked towards the back porch to go into the kitchen.

David and Peter walked the horses to the maids' quarters and tied them in the back as Lomasi instructed. She arrived several minutes later. David again noticed how attractive she was. Her calm and gentle demeanor added to her attractiveness. "We don't have much time" she said, "so we must talk quickly." Lomasi told David and Peter everything she heard during the prior day's meeting, including the brutally thorough plan to assassinate George Washington. "There's one other thing," she added, "they're having me serve George Washington at the dinner tomorrow so I will be blamed for his death."

"Very clever," replied David. "Unfortunately, it appears Madame Bettenfield is not a Patriot."

"It certainly doesn't sound like it," responded Peter.

"I need to go back to the house," Lomasi said, "but I need to tell you one more thing. I was trying to figure out how to save Washington. We could have him stay away from the dinner tomorrow, but the Nazis will figure out some other way to murder him. The only way to save Washington is to kill Hitler and his men."

David saw a group of four men in German military uniforms coming toward them. While Peter had the Luger, this was not the time for a fight. David grabbed Lomasi's right hand and dropped down on his left knee in front of her.

"Pretend that I'm asking you to marry me," David said to Lomasi. "Please, please," he begged in a much louder voice.

The four Germans walked up to the group and stopped.

"What are you doing here?" the leader asked.

David rose from his kneeling position and responded, "I am here to see my lady friend, sir. I would like for her to marry me but she does not think I would make a good husband. I am a hard worker and will take very good care of her. My friend is here to vouch for me. She should consent to marry me, don't you think?"

All four of the Germans laughed at David's feigned predicament. However, the leader ordered David, Peter, and Lomasi to go inside the maid's quarters to continue their discussion. The Commander would be walking around the grounds and didn't wish to be disturbed. They should stay inside until the Commander returned to the main house.

David nodded he understood and the three of them turned and walked to the door of the maids' quarters. Once inside, David looked through a front window and saw Adolf Hitler and Martin Bormann coming down the steps of the back porch of the main house. "My god, it's really him!" exclaimed David. "It's really Adolf Hitler and Martin Bormann. This is unbelievable!" he said, looking toward Peter and Lomasi.

"It is unbelievable," Peter agreed. "And, it's my fault. If it weren't for me the monster would be long dead."

Lomasi looked at Peter, a puzzled expression on her face. "Peter invented a time machine in the 1940's," David said to her, "and that's how Hitler escaped from the Fuhrerbunker." Peter shook his head, disgusted with himself.

"Don't let it get to you, Buddy," David said, trying to cheer him up. "Some good will come of it, I'm sure." He didn't tell Peter how the good would happen because he wasn't really sure it ever would.

While David assumed all along he would eventually encounter Adolf Hitler, actually seeing the man alive only a few hundred feet away was unnerving. This was the man who started World War Two and was responsible for the deaths of seventy million people. In a dark epiphany, David realized thwarting this man's ambitions and stopping him from assassinating George Washington was going to be a hellish undertaking. Hitler had survived countless attempts on his life and a World War. Would nothing stop this man? This was the most heinous murderer in history and he will stop at nothing to achieve his objectives. What in the name of god am I doing here? David asked himself.

"There he is!" whispered Peter, as he looked out the window. His voice conveyed excitement and rage. "Where's my wife you bastard?" he whispered loudly to himself.

"Calm down, Peter!" David warned. "Keep it under control! We'll get him, I promise! Let's figure out how we're going to do this, okay?" Peter continued glaring out the window at Hitler and Bormann.

258

Hitler looked down at the ground as he walked, apparently in deep thought. He seemed to be brooding. Bormann also appeared to be pondering something. But, he seemed less introspective and evidently appreciated the beauty of the gardens surrounding the two men.

Peter seethed as he watched the two men walking and chatting. He reflected that he had done everything Adolf Hitler ordered him to do. But, that was not enough. Hitler had demanded blind loyalty, which Peter refused to give him. Hitler took his wife Johanna prisoner and sent him into another time in the ancient past. Hitler had promised to use the Chronometric Teleporter to help mankind but was attempting to use the device to enslave others and force them to accept the Nazi doctrine. Peter truly hated him. The two men finished their stroll and walked back inside the main house.

Lomasi said she was late and had to leave, but she was still talking to David. Peter noticed they were getting along very well. David was holding her hand. "Be careful," he said. "Please." She turned and told Peter goodbye as she passed him.

After Lomasi walked out the door, Peter chided David. "Somebody's got a girlfriend." David's face turned red. He looked at Peter and said, "Yeah, somebody does."

While they waited for Cass, they tried to figure out a plan to save Washington's life and deal with Hitler. They decided they mustn't try to prevent Washington from travelling to the dinner by coach. They knew Hitler must be killed and if Washington didn't attend the dinner, Hitler and Bormann would immediately flee, knowing their plot had been found out. Also, as Lomasi said, if the coach turned back on Old Church Road, Colonel Thacher would assassinate General Washington.

Once Washington reached Bettenfield Manor, if Lomasi prevented Washington from eating the poisoned food, the two German soldiers disguised as attendants would assassinate him.

Then, there were forty German soldiers surrounding the house waiting to kill Washington if he were to attempt to leave. Finally, if necessary, the Germans would turn the machine guns on the house if Washington escaped death and were alive and inside the structure. They somehow had to save Washington's life and kill Adolf Hitler and Martin Bormann.

Abruptly, Peter said, "Lomasi told us the Germans store their machine guns and cannons in the large barn. Maybe we could disable the weapons and neutralize the forty soldiers."

"That's a great idea," David replied.

A wagon path provided access from back yard of the main house to where the barn was situated at the back of the estate. The barn was behind the woods and only the west end of the barn and its large entrance door was visible from the main house. Lomasi said she had seen soldiers entering and leaving the barn through this door. They had to unlock the door before they entered.

"Yeah, the barn would be the logical place to store the weapons," Peter surmised. "The four machine guns and two cannons would not need much space but the ammunition would require a good deal of room. Most likely, all the heavier weaponry was locked in the barn. We could burn the barn with the weapons inside. That would improve our odds a bit."

"Yes, that would help a great deal," David replied. "But, there are two problems with that idea. First, the Germans are not going to let us walk up to the barn with a match and burn it down right under their noses. And second, if the munitions are stored inside the barn and we burn it, the machine gun and cannon ammunition will be exploding for hours sending bullets and shrapnel flying in every direction. We'd injure or kill a lot of innocent people and Hitler and the others would escape before we get them. Remember, even if we destroy the machine guns and cannons, that still leaves forty German SS troops with rifles and pistols."

"You're right, Peter replied. And, they're all highly trained and deadly shots with far superior firepower. I don't know how to deal with them."

"But, if we could somehow neutralize those machine guns and cannons, it would be a pretty good start," said David.

Peter was looking out the window and saw Cass walk out on the back porch. "Time to go, David," Peter said. "I'll get the horses and you get Cass. I don't want to chance being seen by Hitler and Bormann."

Peter walked the horses to within fifty feet of the porch and stopped to wait for David and Cass. All three men were soon on their way down the carriage drive toward the main road. As they guided their horses out the gate of Bettenfield Manor and turned them south, Peter was the first to speak. With a sneaky smile he asked, "Did you enjoy your visit, Cass?"

Cass, shifting uncomfortably in his saddle and smiling, said, "Yes, I did, thank you."

That was the end of the conversation.

David, distracted by thoughts of Lomasi, snapped back to reality. "Cass," he said, "let's head to Major Wellston's house. We have to meet up with those guys to see what's going on at their end."

"That's exactly where I was going," replied Cass.

"Say, Cass. Why don't you ask David how he enjoyed his visit?" Peter asked.

Cass, understanding what Peter was getting at, looked over at David.

"Well?" he asked.

"Well, what?" responded David.

Peter and Cass looked at each other and burst out laughing.

"What? What is it with you two?" asked David.

Peter shook his head and looked at Cass. Both men again burst out laughing. David knew why they were teasing him and he looked at them and shook his head. Then his thoughts returned to Lomasi.

30

Major Wellston's Plan

April 18, 1775   Philadelphia

They reached Major Wellston's house in less than an hour. The three men tied their horses and walked up the stairs to the porch. Major Wellston had seen them coming through his front window and opened the door just as David was reaching for the iron knocker.

"Come on in, boys," he said. "I'm Josiah Wellston."

"How are you doing, Major," asked Cass. "Meet David Kelly and Peter Krause."

"Contrary and John told me all about you fellows," said Major Wellston. "I'm not sure I believe everything they're telling me but it sounds like we have a big problem we have to attend to."

"I'm afraid so, Major," replied David. "Tomorrow could turn into a real bad day for all of us if we don't act quickly."

"David, tell me about these men from the future who are going to cause us all this trouble," said Major Wellston.

David and Peter sensed from Major Wellston's cynical tone that he hadn't bought into Contrary and John's rendition of things. It was clear he didn't believe their story.

"David," suggested Peter, "why don't you show Major Wellston how the Luger works."

"Yeah, good idea!" replied David.

"Major," said David, I have a notion you don't believe what Contrary and John have told you about us. That's unfortunate because we don't have much time to convince you sir. And, we have to act very quickly with you or without you. Maybe you could come outside with us and I could show you a pistol from our time that may change your mind. Bring your pistol outside also, Major."

"Alright," said Major Wellston.

Contrary and John told Major Wellston about the Luger John had taken from the German soldier he had killed at Bettenfield

Manor. Major Wellston didn't believe a weapon with that amount of firepower could ever be invented.

When the men got outside, David showed Major Wellston the Luger. He also invited the major to set up a line of a dozen targets and they would see which man could hit the greatest number of them in the shortest time. Major Wellston, a good marksman himself, gladly accepted the challenge.

He went over to a stack of firewood and picked out some small kindling logs an inch in diameter and six inches in length. Major Wellston stood the sticks, on their ends on the top rail of the wooden corral fence in the back of his house. This would be a weapons competition rather than a contest to determine the best marksman.

The targets were fifty feet from where the men stood. It was agreed David would start shooting from the left end of the line of targets and Major Wellston would start shooting from the right end. Contrary would give the signal to fire.

Without hesitation, he yelled, "Fire!"

David carefully took aim and immediately began shooting from the left, hitting seven targets with his first clip which held eight shells. Major Wellston's first and only shot missed and he was re-loading. David quickly pushed the second clip into the Luger and fired at the remaining five targets hitting them in five shots. David hit all twelve targets before Major Wellston hit one. He was just finishing re-loading when David lowered his gun. Major Wellston's jaw hung open and his eyes were wide.

"My god, I've never seen anything like that," he said, flabbergasted.

"And you never will again in your lifetime," replied David. "Major, I hope this convinces you that we are from a future time. If you don't believe us and the Germans succeed in killing George Washington tomorrow, your thirteen American colonies will become a separate country forever governed by England. Can we count on you?"

There was much more to the story but, in the interest of time, David stopped at that point.

"We're in," replied Josiah Wellston, still astounded.

Contrary and John were laughing at Major Wellston's predicament. Cass stood staring and confounded at the scene.

"I'm sorry, Major," said Contrary. "It's not that we didn't warn you.

Major Wellston began laughing too, and so did David and Peter. Cass also began to laugh, although he wasn't sure why. He just thought he should laugh because everyone else was laughing.

But, Major Wellston's mood turned somber. "Boys" he said, "let's go inside. We've got to put together some sort of strategy to stop this thing." That was the reaction for which David and Peter were hoping. The men returned to the house and got seated around the large kitchen table upon which Mrs. Wellston set out some lunch.

Major Wellston had a reputation for being an expert military strategist. Like many others, including Washington, he was a veteran of the French and Indian War and had fought with great distinction.

He first asked David, Peter and Cass what they found out on their visit to Bettenfield Manor earlier that morning. Peter explained the Germans had four machine guns and two cannons. Major Wellston clearly understood cannons and their tactical utilization.

Peter, however, purposely went into great detail explaining the "modern cannon" and its repetitious firepower using self contained shells composed of both gunpowder and projectile. The type of cannon with which Major Wellston was familiar was a basic firing tube or barrel into which black powder and a projectile were separately added and then the black powder was manually ignited. The modern rapid fire, highly accurate cannon was far superior to the present-day cannons that were being used. Present day cannons would be useless in a direct confrontation.

Major Wellston had never heard the term "machine gun." Peter explained the weapon's massive firepower and deadly potential on the battlefield. Further, the Germans had rifles and pistols similar to the one David had demonstrated. Peter wanted to make sure Major Wellston clearly understood that taking on the Germans in any head to head battle would be suicide.

They also explained to Major Wellston that Colonel Thacher was a spy. The assassination plan would commence the moment General Washington stepped into the coach with Colonel Thacher to travel to the dinner. Should the coach turn around at any point, Colonel Thacher would be the assassin. If he failed, the six mounted

German soldiers would become the assassins. However, these were contingency plans. The main plan was to poison the General's food and wine at Bettenfield Manor. But, if that failed, he would be shot in Madame Bettenfield's dining room. As further backup, forty highly trained German soldiers would use their machine guns and two cannons if Washington attempted to leave the home. They are obviously taking no chances that Washington could survive.

"Boys, I understand what you're telling me," Major Wellston said. "I have a healthy understanding of what firepower can do on the battlefield. When one side is outgunned, particularly as outgunned as it is in this situation, there is no doubt about the outcome. For sure, we can't fight them head on."

"Major," Peter said, "we believe the machine guns and cannons are stored in the big barn near the woods at Bettenfield Manor. Our contact there, Lomasi, said the soldiers going in and out of this barn unlocked and re-locked it as they came and went. If the weapons are in this barn and we could neutralize them that would help considerably."

"You're right about that, Peter," Major Wellston replied. "Also, just so you know, Moses Brampton left shortly before you came and is rounding up a bunch of extra men. However, after what you've told me, I don't think extra men will be much help with the firepower the Germans have. In fact, I'm thinking the fewer the men the better off we shall be."

"What do you mean, Major? "Contrary asked.

"I'm still trying to figure it out," replied Major Wellston. "But, I know we can't win a fight with them on the open field. Peter, you said that Colonel Thacher shall be riding in the coach with General Washington."

"Yes, that's right," said Peter.

Major Wellston continued, "You know, I still can't believe he's a traitor. But, we'll worry about that later. Anyway, you said there would be six mounted American militia escorting the coach and six mounted German soldiers following about a mile behind."

"Yes, that's correct," replied Peter.

"Okay. Now, Moses Brampton will be attending that dinner tomorrow night. We will put him to work also," smiled Major Wellston."

"What do you mean, Major?" asked Contrary.

"I'm still sorting through all of this, Contrary," Major Wellston replied. "But, it's important to not only make sure Washington is not assassinated but to make sure these devils from the future do not survive the evening and return to haunt us at some other time."

"That was our intention," replied David.

"Wait a minute," Peter sternly interjected. "Major, I agree it is very important that their leaders Adolf Hitler and Martin Bormann are killed so they don't cause any other problems. But, it is also very important to me personally that I talk to Hitler before this happens. He is holding my wife prisoner and I must find out where she is. Only he can tell me. Also, I must destroy the Chronometric Teleporter which they have with them so no one else can travel to other times such as they have."

Major Wellston replied, "I understand, Peter. But, I may not be able to accommodate your request. There is much more at stake here than your wife."

Peter, in a rage, jumped up from his chair. "You have no choice, sir. I absolutely demand…."

"Hold on, Peter," David said, grabbing him by his right arm. "Major, Peter is right. He has brought us this far and we need to help him. Also, we must depend on Peter to find and destroy the Chronometric Teleporter. We wouldn't want to have to worry about someone else coming from another time now, would we? We need to work with Peter here if we expect him to help us. Do you get my drift?"

"Yes, I believe you've made yourself very clear," said Major Wellston. "Alright, Peter, we'll work the plan to put you in position to take care of your business with this Adolf Hitler fellow. David and his gun will accompany you. You two will be responsible for killing Hitler and the other leader. Did you say his name was Bormann?"

"Yes, that's right, Major," replied Peter.

"All right, boys, here's my plan," said Major Wellston.

First, we shall visit the barn tonight, just after midnight. We will try to get inside it and make the weapons inoperable. Contrary, you, John, David and I shall attend to that task. John, they will probably have a sentry. You shall see to him. Contrary, if there is a second sentry, he's your charge. I'm getting too old for that kind

266

of work. Remember, we don't want to kill them unless it's absolutely necessary. Boys, try to hit them over the head and knock them unconscious. Then, take their money, guns and boots. It will look like a robbery and not an attempt to sabotage their weapons."

"Peter, do you think that will spook the leaders?" asked Major Wellston. "And, what about if we have to kill them?"

"If men are killed, it might make them suspicious and they might flee. However, I believe we need to take that risk," responded Peter.

"I like you, Peter," replied Major Wellston, "temper and all. You're willing to take a risk."

Peter replied. "Major, I love my wife very much and I must find her. She means more to me than anything else. However, the only way to find her is to get to Hitler and I knew it wouldn't be easy. I see no other way than to take this risk."

"I understand," Major Wellston replied. "One other thing, if we do manage to get inside the barn we shall have to move fast. We have to disable those weapons without the Germans knowing they don't work. David, we'll leave it to you to figure those guns out. If you can do that, it would maintain our element of surprise for the other things we must do."

"Okay, boys," Major Wellston continued, "now to the unpleasant side of this party. Cass, you get the Indians out to the Old Church Road tomorrow night and take care of the six German soldiers following Washington's carriage. You should attack them at the second bend in the road because that's the best place for maximum surprise. It should be nearly dark when Washington's carriage passes. Cass, it must be done very quietly so Colonel Thacher does not hear any disturbance further up the road. He probably wouldn't hear any noise anyway, being a mile away and with the noise of the coach and horses. But, no chances must be taken here with Washington's life hanging in the balance. Also, no one must escape, including the horses. We can use the extra horses so have the boys capture them unless somebody is escaping on one of them. Cass, I repeat, be sure you kill all the men and capture all the horses. If either gets back to Bettenfield Manor or a horse runs past Washington's coach that will be a warning for the Germans and Colonel Thacher. No mistakes, Cass."

Major Wellston paused for a moment to tell David and Peter about the Indians. "This group is actually militia-men disguised as Indians, as was done at the Boston Tea Party," smiled Major Wellston. "We learned a lot from the lads up north. However, our men are expert marksmen with the bow and arrow. That allows them to attack quietly and by surprise. The attack I'm planning is exactly what they're trained to do. It's still very dangerous because the Germans have advanced rifles and pistols. If they see the attack coming, the results for us will be deadly."

"It's a good plan, Major," said David.

"There's something else, Cass," Major Wellston said. I shall ask to ride in the coach with General Washington tomorrow night. I shall request Colonel Thacher accommodate my request as I need to speak with General Washington. He will have no excuse to not let me do so because the general and I are good friends. My being there will be an extra measure of safety for General Washington.

"David, you and Peter shall ride to the dinner with Moses Brampton. You will tell Madame Bettenfield that General Washington is delayed but should arrive shortly.

Contrary, you will assemble one hundred men and slowly move them into the woods throughout the afternoon. Make sure they travel either singly or two at a time. We don't want it to appear that a force of men is forming. Send your scouts only as far as the edge of the woods to the south of Bettenfield Manor and keep them out of sight. They are to identify the positions of the Nazis surrounding the house.

The rest of your men shall not move up to the edge of the south woods until dark. Your full force shall be ready to attack from the south only. That will cause the Nazis to concentrate their forces south of the house. With fewer Nazis in back of the house, it will be easier for David, Peter and Moses to escape through the west woods. Once Moses, David and Peter arrive at Bettenfield, you should wait for one hour and then begin your attack on the Germans surrounding the house. This will be a diversionary attack only. The goal is not to kill anyone, just maintain rifle fire to keep their attention. We only want to distract them so David, Peter and Moses can kill their leaders inside the house and safely escape into the woods with General Washington."

"David and Peter, there is one other thing. You will also have to handle the two Nazi soldiers in the dining room. Moses can help you with that detail. You must also remember that Madame Bettenfield is an enemy. She and her staff may be dangerous. Going to that house is very dangerous. I hope you fellows understand that."

"We don't doubt that for a moment," David said. Then he added, "Major Wellston, it is a fact the Germans we are facing are from the future year of 1945. However, there's a little more to the story than that."

"Somehow, I knew there would be," replied Major Wellston. "Let's hear it."

"Yeah," Peter added, "I'd like to know what you are talking about also."

David continued. "Peter, as you know the Germans escaped to South America in the year 2010." That means they may have gotten hold of other more modern military inventions."

"Go on," replied Major Wellston.

"Major," David continued, "there is a device which allows soldiers to see at night. If the Nazis have this 'night vision,' your men will be sitting ducks. Contrary, if your men start taking what seems like too many hits, you must immediately pull back. That means the Germans have the 'night vision' and can see your men just like it is daylight. Do you understand?"

Contrary appeared shocked at this new piece of information however, he quickly recovered and shook his head he understood

"Well, boys, how do you like that plan? It's simple enough, huh?" smiled Major Wellston.

"I have to hand it to you Major," replied Contrary. "It seems to account for everything."

"Actually, I was being facetious, Contrary," replied Major Wellston. "The truth is that no military operation ever goes exactly according to plan. This is actually a fairly complex operation against a highly trained and lethal adversary. Lot's of things can go wrong. Also, you never know what the enemy is going to throw back at you. If everything goes okay, it won't be because of the plan but how well everybody does their part and also deals with those things that come up which we never thought about. Are there any questions? Does everybody know what they have to do?"

"Everybody nodded, 'yes.'

"Meeting's over, boys," said Major Wellston. "Contrary, David and John, we'll meet out on the Old Church Road at the second bend at eleven o'clock tonight. I hope you don't mind staying behind Peter but, if we get caught, it will fall to you to pick up where we left off." Peter nodded that he understood.

31

Night Raid

April 19, 1775   Bettenfield Manor

12:00 a.m. to 12:00 p.m.

Major Josiah Wellston sat on his horse as he hid in the woods on the west side of Old Church Road at the second bend. It was twelve midnight and Contrary Walbridge, John and David would arrive soon. The road was dark and the woods were darker. There was a moon somewhere up there but intermittent clouds kept its light sporadic at best. For the task they were to undertake, no moon would be even better. However, the few beams of light breaching the thick clouds provided enough illumination for the rider to keep his horse on the road. Without that stingy sprinkling of moonbeams the night would have been pitch black.

Major Wellston was contemplating tonight's mission. The risks were high. If they didn't stop the men at Bettenfield Manor, the course of the coming war and the future itself would be changed. He thought about Colonel Thacher, still shocked to learn he was a spy who had caused damage to the Patriots. Many good men had been arrested by the British, and large stocks of military materiel had been seized as a result of a spy's work. As he thought further about it, he realized it had to be Thacher. My god, he thought, this man sits in Washington's office. He must be dealt with before he causes more damage to us. The sound of galloping horses interrupted his thoughts. Here we go, he muttered to himself. Three horsemen reined in their mounts on the road directly in front of him.

"Major," Contrary called. "Major, it's Contrary, John and David."

"I'm here, Contrary," he shouted. "You boys ready?"

"All set, Major," Contrary replied, as Major Wellston guided his horse out of the woods and onto the road.

"Let's walk the horses," Major Wellston offered. "It's only a few miles and it will allow more time for people to get to sleep."

Thirty minutes later they reached the ridge south of Bettenfield Manor. There was a break in the clouds and they could see the house sitting on the small ridge on the west side of the road. Lights shone in some windows, but there didn't seem to be any obvious activity. The men quickly walked their horses down the ridge and past the carriage way leading to Bettenfield Manor. They soon reached the wooded area behind the large house to the northeast. The woods bordered Old Church Road and were also in back of several buildings located at the rear of the main house.

The barn, the target of their mission, sat behind a part of the woods one hundred yards west of Old Church Road. They saw the small road cut through the woods that allowed access to other areas of the estate. If a person stood at the front entrance of the barn and looked down this road through the woods, part of the main house was visible. Conversely, the front part of the barn could be seen from the house.

In order to reach the barn from Old Church Road the men would have to walk through the one hundred yards of thick woods separating it from the road. That there was some moonlight was helpful however but, if the moon became bright, it would put them in danger of being seen by sentries. All of the men but David were experienced fighters but he knew they were in great danger. This would not be easy.

The plan was to hide the horses in the woods on the east side of Old Church Road. They had done this and were now crossing the dirt road, which, because of the moonlight, shone a lighter color than the black woods and dark ground. The men crouched low as they quietly trotted across the road and into the woods on its west side. Each man carried a pistol and a knife, which provided good mobility and worked best in a close quarter fight. David carried the Luger. The watchwords of this mission were speed and quiet. They would avoid a fight if they could and the pistols would be used only as a last resort.

Major Wellston led the way as they crept forward through the dense growth and large trees. As they drew closer to the barn, they frequently paused to listen. They knew there must be sentries. They could hear nothing but night sounds of crickets and frogs. They

272

moved closer and were soon on the edge of the woods bordering the clearing where the barn was located. The barn was an enormous structure three stories in height, its peaked roof an ominous black silhouette in the night sky.

The four men were hidden behind a large tree. They listened carefully but heard no sound. "You two boys stay here," Major Wellston ordered. "David and I will see if we can get into the barn."

Staying low, Major Wellston and David slowly crept across the open area between the woods and the barn, angling toward the rear entrance to the building. There were no fences or wagons or other cover in the flat expanse. They moved more quickly as they neared the massive wooden doors on the barn's east end.

Suddenly, two bright lights shone near the front of the barn. Two sentries on opposite sides of the barn were advancing toward the back entrance where David and Major Wellston were struggling with the lock on the large wooden doors.

"Who's there?" a voice shouted.

David, who saw only one of the lights, realized it wasn't a lantern but a flashlight. It was carried by a man moving rapidly along the barn's south side toward the back entrance and coming straight toward them. From the woods, Contrary and John noticed the reflections of a similar light moving along the barn's north side toward Major Wellston and David. The carriers of the lights would soon be coming around their respective corners where the two men now lay on the ground.

John was the first to move. He quickly left the trees and ran across the open area toward the barn. Taking John's cue, Contrary followed but moved even faster toward the barn's northeast corner. Both men reached their respective destinations.

The first sentry, holding a flashlight and pistol, approached the back of the barn from the south. He was more cautious and moved out and away from the barn's south wall so he would not be surprised as he rounded the corner. John, anticipating this move, knelt on his left knee with his back pressed against the barn's back wall. As he heard footsteps approaching the corner, John lunged forward into the man's path, throwing his knife hard directly into the sentry's stomach. This was an old Indian trick he used many times. Once again, it worked. The soldier dropped his gun and the flashlight spun to the ground. The sentry gasped and dropped to his knees, clawing at the excruciating pain and cruel blade jutting from his abdomen. He fell forward causing the knife to penetrate deeper and cut across his stomach. He lay motionless, face down on the ground.

Contrary also had his knife ready. He too knew John's Indian maneuver. As the footsteps came close, Contrary jumped from his hiding spot and threw the knife hard. This sentry, however, had walked a wider arc and his flashlight had caught the glint of Contrary's knife blade as he was about to throw it. The soldier immediately dove to the ground toward his left side and Contrary's knife sailed harmlessly through the night air two feet above and well to the right where the man's head had been. Quickly, the sentry rolled over and jumped to his feet, holding his pistol and the flashlight, which were both pointed at Contrary, Major Wellston and David.

"Do not move," he screamed. "Put your hands in the air and stand against the wall."

John, realizing what happened, moved quickly. He assumed there could be more than the two sentries they had seen and he pulled his knife from the dying soldier's stomach and ran quietly up the barn's south side and around its front. He then ran down the north side of the barn toward the back where Major Wellston, David, and Contrary were now prisoners. As he reached the northeast corner where Contrary attacked the sentry, he heard the soldier order the three men to stand against the wall. The soldier had taken the pistols from all of them and was particularly interested in David's Luger. He also took Major Wellston's and David's knives.

"Alright, you three turn left and put your hands on your head," the soldier barked. "Now, start walking very slowly."

Peeking around the corner, John could see the soldier pointing a flashlight and gun at his three fellow intruders. The sentry and three men had their backs toward John as they walked along the barn's back entrance toward the small road through the woods. He was taking them to the soldiers' barracks, thought John. But, the soldier saw the second sentry lying on the ground and ordered them to stop. This would be his only opportunity, John thought. He slipped around the corner, and ran hard but quietly, straight toward the back of the soldier. John made no sound however the soldier cautiously turned his head to check behind him.

Glimpsing movement out of the corner of his eye, he turned to face John and brought the light around and raised the pistol.

Seeing the sentry's head move, John, who was five feet behind the soldier, threw himself toward the ground feet forward. Carried forward by the momentum of his powerful run, he rapidly slid across the ground toward the surprised soldier. Again John launched the knife with a forceful throw. As the knife left John's right hand, he knew it was off target. He always threw the knife at an adversary's midsection because that was the surest target. That was where he aimed. However, the moon had gone behind a cloud and he could only see the faint outlines of the sentry and his prisoners. The soldier's flashlight partially blinded John.

"It was a bad throw," John scolded himself, as his feet crashed into the soldier's crumpling legs.

Just as the soldier turned, but before he could bring the gun and flashlight fully into position, John's heavy knife struck him hard in the face. The blade penetrated at an upward angle below his right eye, slicing through the orbital bones and plunging into his brain. The violent impact of the knife and the collision of John's skidding body thrust the sentry two feet off the ground and knocked him backward. His lifeless body crashed into Contrary and David. "My God!" exclaimed Major Wellston, as he looked at the soldier lying dead on the ground.

Major Wellston and Contrary were experienced soldiers but as John directed the flashlight into the fallen soldier's face, the ghastly sight of him pulling his large knife out of the dead sentry's skull did not go unnoticed by either man. David was also unnerved by the gruesome sight.

Quickly regaining his composure, Major Wellston said, "We've got to move fast boys. We don't know when they change the guard. We need to steal the money, weapons, and boots from these two sentries to make it look like a robbery. If we have time, we'll take a few horses also to make the robbery even more convincing."

The men stashed the soldier's bodies and belongings in the woods. They would take the stolen items with them when they left and leave the soldiers' bodies where they would be discovered. Contrary was able to retrieve his knife which he viewed as a good omen.

They had to get into the barn to disable the machine guns and, if possible, also the cannons. Both the front and rear doors of the barn were secured by sturdy padlocks however, neither of the sentries had a key in their possession. There were several smaller doors on either side of the barn however they were securely locked from the inside.

Both Contrary and John were looking upward at a door high above the large main door of the barn's back wall. This door was used to bring hay into or out of the barn's second story storage area. While the door didn't appear to be open, it was their only hope of getting into the barn without a noisy break-in. Major Wellston, David and Contrary stood in front of the door in the barn's east wall and hoisted John up on their shoulders. This was a difficult task in view of John's size but they got the job done. John stood on David and Contrary's shoulders and asked them to raise him even higher, which each man did with great difficulty. They hoisted and then held his feet above their heads.

"Major, Contrary, throw me your knives," whispered John. "David, I'll need yours too."

David and Contrary struggled to hold John's feet above their heads. One at a time, Major Wellston threw the three knives to John. John, holding one of the knives in his right hand, moved his arm back behind his midsection and with a powerful slash slammed the knife's blade into the wooden wall just above his waist level. He took the other knives, one in each hand, and stuck them both into the barn's wooden wall at the highest point he could reach.

John held on to those two knives and hoisted himself upward while raising his right foot in search of the first knife he stuck into the wall.

"Higher and a little to the right," whispered Major Wellston

John found the knife and stood on it with his right foot while holding on to the other two knives. When he stood up he changed his grip because the knives were now at his waist level instead of above his head. He pulled the knife in his right hand out of the wooden wall and stretched high to plunge the knife into the wood once again. He repeated the same procedure with his left hand and pulled himself upward. From this position, he hoisted himself two more feet with his right hand and with his left, grasped the narrow wooden shelf underneath the hay door. He then pulled the knife out of the wood with his right hand and stuck it into the wood just below the wooden shelf.

Even with his great strength, John was tiring. Holding onto the shelf and the knife, he mustered every reserve of his strength and pulled himself upward to grasp the small shelf with the fingers of his right hand. He was now hanging from the shelf with both hands. He reached upward with his right hand and banged on the bottom of the "hay door." It popped open just a few inches, but it was ample room for John to reach in with his right hand and swing it open the rest of the way. With his right hand, he reached up and grabbed the vertical wall forming the right side of the door opening and did the same with his left. Though struggling, he pulled himself upward with both hands and swung his left leg inside the "hay door." He pulled himself the rest of the way in.

"That's unbelievable," gasped Major Wellston.

Even Contrary, who was never at a loss for words, was speechless. "Yeah," was all that he could manage. David was impressed. It was a remarkable feat.

In two shakes of a lamb's tail, as the saying went, the small door next to the barn's main back entrance swung open and John appeared. Major Wellston, David and Contrary stepped inside the cavernous, darkened room. John was still winded but happy with his feat.

Equipped with the two modern flashlights they had taken from the sentries, they quickly spotted what they had come for. Four wood boxes measuring two feet by five feet and eerily resembling coffins sat on a heavy wooden table. Each box was labeled "Maschinengewehr 42, MG 42, Mauser Werke-AG, Berlin.

Peter told David to watch for "MG 42" as that was the designation for the machine gun. Contrary and Major Wellston lifted the box nearest them onto the floor. The lids on all four boxes had already been pried off and then replaced however, not nailed down. The lids were left unattached so the guns would be immediately accessible when needed. As the two men removed the top from the box on the floor, John whispered loudly, "Major, come over here."

Major Wellston and Contrary immediately walked over to where John and David were kneeling on the floor. They were startled to see John holding his flashlight on an assembled machine gun with the ammunition belt feed inserted. It was a vicious looking weapon and was ready to fire.

The gun resembled a rifle in that it had sights on top its two foot long barrel housing however, it differed in that there were oval shaped holes along each side. Major Wellston, Contrary, and John didn't understand the purpose of the oval holes and David explained they were cooling vents. The holes added to the ominous appearance of the deadly weapon. The gun sat on bipods, which held the gun steady while it was being fired. An eight-inch trigger guard extending below the back part of the barrel beneath the body of the gun also served as a handle to hold the gun while firing. The stock of the gun protruded behind its main body and flowed into a graceful curve at the point where it met the operator's shoulder. Peter told them the gun would fire fifteen hundred rounds per minute, astounding Major Wellston, Contrary, and John. They had never even imagined a killing machine such as this.

Major Wellston and Contrary walked back to the box on the floor and stared at the machine gun cradled inside it. The gun's mechanism was advanced beyond anything they had ever seen, but David knew how to disable the firing pin. Pulling the trigger releases the bolt assembly, which provides accessibility to the firing pin. David moved swiftly, and within minutes, disabled all four machine guns by damaging their bolts and removing the firing pins. They were careful to make sure everything was put back where it had been and nothing appeared to have been disturbed.

The four men looked at the two cannons near the front door of the barn. They were mounted on carriages supported by two rubber tires. Having no idea how to disable them, David left them untouched. He realized he could make the guns inoperable by damaging them or stuffing dirt or some other object down their barrels, but that risked tipping off the Nazis their plot had been exposed.

They had moved to the small door through which they entered at the back of the barn. David showed the men how to turn off the flashlights and Major Wellston slowly opened the door and looked out the narrow opening. Everything seemed quiet and clouds had drifted in front of the moon. The intense darkness made for good cover but bad visibility. The enemy couldn't see them, but they couldn't see much either. Major Wellston listened but there was no sound. He and David moved through the doorway and peered into the darkness. "Let's go," Major Wellston said, and the two men sprinted across the open area to the trees.

Contrary carefully stepped through the door and quietly closed it. John re-locked the door from the inside and climbed the ladder to the loft. He would go through the hay door in order to close it so everything would look the same as it had before the four intruders arrived. There was a large pole with an attached pulley above the hay door. John made a noose-like knot at the end of a rope he had taken from the barn and placed it over the pole. With this type knot, he could pull the rope off the pole when he got to the ground. He descended by moving his hands down the rope as he "walked" with his feet against the barn wall. On the way, he retrieved the three knives he used to climb up the barn. Reaching the ground, he yanked the rope from the pole and it fell to his feet.

Contrary and John ran across the open area to the woods. The four men picked up the items they stole from the guards and headed for Old Church Road. They had decided against stealing horses because of the additional risk. It would have been a good move but they were becoming nervous and decided to get while the getting was good.

They cautiously moved through the small, dense forest, frequently pausing to listen. There was no sound. In a few minutes, they reached the east edge of the woods and the three-foot wide shoulder of Old Church Road. Intermittent shafts of moonlight loosed by the meandering clouds created random patterns of luminance on the dirt road. That helped them see, but also helped them be seen.

Major Wellston told Contrary and John to cross the road first. He and David would stay on the west side of the road to deal with anyone who might have followed them. They had made little noise as the men were Indian fighters and knew how to move through the forest swiftly and without noise. Contrary and John ran quietly, close to the ground. The moon disappeared behind the clouds.

"Major, run like hell!" screamed Contrary. "The horses are dead!"

Major Wellston and David strained their eyes but could see nothing. Was it Contrary and John crashing out of the woods onto the dirt road? A muzzle flash and loud blast from two rifles split the darkness. Gunshots screamed across the road and smashed through the trees. The moon peeked again. Contrary and John were sprawled in the middle of the road. Heavy footsteps of running men came toward them from the road. Someone was coming fast through the woods behind them.

"Get out of here" Major Wellston whispered as he turned to run north. Instinctively, David ran south on the shoulder of Old Church Road, staying in the woods to avoid the bullets streaking near him. However, the woods ended at the grounds of Bettenfield Manor and open area and David knew he had to run across the road to the larger woods to the east.

The moon was still behind the clouds, just as it was when Contrary and John were shot. They've got night vision, David realized. They couldn't have made those shots without night vision.

Abruptly, he turned and ran hard onto the road. He reached the road's center and dove to his stomach. Maybe it was the premonition of danger Tse said he would have. Maybe it was raw fear. He heard gunfire and the zinging of bullets in the air as he hit the ground and rolled over and over fast as he could. He quickly reached the dirt shoulder of the road and several bullets thudded nearby. Others flew past him and crunched into trees. Without stopping, he jumped quickly to a crouching position and dove forward, again rolling fast toward the woods. A flurry of gunshots smashed into trees and bushes inches from his head. He crawled behind a large tree as bullets thumped on its other side. Running footsteps were headed toward him and he wasted no time. He ran straight east, further into the woods, intent on penetrating deeply into them. As long as the woods were thick, the night vision would not help the Nazis. He thought he could lose them in the forest.

32

Spies

April 19, 1775 Bettenfield Manor

It was first light and Lomasi walked from the maids' quarters to the main house with two other girls. When they walked into the kitchen, they heard unusual activity in the living room. Adolf Hitler, Martin Bormann, General Werner and Colonel Wolf were sitting in the large chairs talking with one of the SS officers. Miss Chattenborne appeared in the kitchen and ordered the girls to prepare an early breakfast for the men.

Madame Bettenfield would also be joining them.

Miss Chattenborne told the girls two men were murdered on the property during the night. That made three murders on the property and there was great concern with their guests as to what was happening. Also, two intruders had been shot while trying to escape. Lomasi hoped that David was not one of the men killed.

Lomasi brought some tea to the men in the living room and overheard General Werner speaking with Colonel Wolf. Colonel Wolf maintained that the cause of the murders was robbery as poor colonials were stealing because times were bad. General Werner, however, asked Colonel Wolf if he had checked the weapons stored in the large barn.

"Yes, General," Colonel Wolf replied. "I have personally checked the weapons in the barn and everything is accounted for and nothing has been disturbed."

General Werner pondered his answer for a moment. "Colonel," he replied, did you check the operational readiness of all weapons?"

"What do you mean, General Werner?" Colonel Wolf asked.

"Just what I said, Colonel," General Werner shot back. "Have you checked to insure that all weapons are operational?"

"No, General, I have not," replied Colonel Wolf. "But, nothing has been disturbed sir."

"Colonel, do not upset me further," responded General Werner. "Check out all weapons immediately and make sure they are one hundred percent operational. Do you understand?"

Colonel Wolf stood up and saluted briskly. "Yes, of course General."

Hitler then spoke. "I am happy you persisted with Colonel Wolf, General. I have a feeling that something is not right here. I don't believe some poor colonials, as Colonel Wolf calls them, would face armed men to steal a small sum of money and some weapons. The question then becomes why did this attack take place?"

"I agree, Fuhrer," replied General Werner. "I shall keep you apprised of the situation as soon as I receive my report from Colonel Wolf."

The group adjourned to the dining room as Madame Bettenfield came down the stairs, ready to begin the busy day.

Lomasi lingered in the living room as long as she could without drawing attention to herself. As the meeting in the dining room was to begin, she wondered if she could again eavesdrop without being discovered. She looked for Miss Chattenborne to ask permission to be excused but was unable to locate her.

But, Lomasi decided that since this was the critical day, it didn't matter what she did. Whether the day turned out well or not, she would be going back to her own time. All that mattered was to make sure Washington survived. She walked out of the kitchen to the corridor and crossed the living room to the hallway leading to the sitting room.

Lomasi walked down the richly appointed hallway. Gold lighting fixtures pleasantly spaced along the light blue walls provided a serene setting for numerous paintings. As she walked, Lomasi glanced at the portraits of young children, idyllic garden scenes and several seascapes. It was as attractive an art collection as she had ever seen.

When Lomasi reached the door of the sitting room near the end of the hallway she stopped and put her head against its white wood and listened. She hoped she would be lucky and the room would again be empty. She heard nothing. Placing her hand on the gold handle on the left side of the door, she carefully turned it while gently pushing to create an opening through which she could peek.

Through the tiny opening, she could only see the room's west side to her left. No one appeared to be in the room. She cautiously opened the door slightly further and saw the table with its upholstered chairs and the dark stained wood chairs with their backrests against the wall.

She opened the door and quickly slipped into the room then gently pushed the door to close. As the door moved to her left revealing the east side of the room, Lomasi recoiled in shock as stared into the stern face of Miss Chattenborne. The door closed with a solid thump as the two women stood looking at each other in the small room.

Miss Chattenborne broke the silence. "Why are you sneaking around the house, my dear?" she asked.

"I didn't feel well and thought I could rest in here for a few minutes," Lomasi replied.

"I'm sorry to hear that, my dear," Miss Chattenborne replied. "But, I don't believe you. More importantly, Madame Bettenfield will not believe you either. I think you are a spy, and so will she."

"That's ridiculous," Lomasi replied. "Whom could I possibly be spying on and for what reason?"

"Never mind that," Miss Chattenborne replied. "Do you not think the men meeting in the next room think it quite odd that since you arrived at Bettenfield Manor four days ago three men have been murdered? That's nearly one killing per day, Lomasi. And the day is not over yet. Also, your friends came to visit yesterday. Two of the murders occurred only hours after that visit.

"I assure you that's an unfortunate coincidence, Miss Chattenborne."

Miss Chattenborne continued. "I told you earlier two men were shot trying escape. If you have any connection to those men, it will not go well for you. You are under a great deal of suspicion, my dear. Nothing like that has ever happened here at Bettenfield Manor and it has caused Madame Bettenfield a great deal of anxiety."

"Well, I'm not a spy and I'm not connected with those murders or the men involved. I abhor violence," Lomasi replied.

"Just the same, my dear, you need to be very careful. Even if you are telling the truth, you could be in great jeopardy. So, I will assume that you are being truthful and really do feel ill. I will leave you alone here to rest and when you feel better, you may return to your duties. I also suggest you lock the door. That way, no one will find you resting on the job. I have a reputation to protect, you know."

Miss Chattenborne pulled the door open and walked out, leaving a surprised, puzzled Lomasi alone in the room. She quickly locked the door and walked across the room to the alcove and removed the blue vase. As Lomasi put her ear against the back of the opening to listen, she was sure Miss Chattenborne didn't believe her story about being ill. Miss Chattenborne suspected she was a spy, but told her to lock the door. She must know I'm listening to the meeting. Miss Chattenborne is not naive. Could she be protecting me? That was a crazy thought.

As it turned out, the meeting was a review of the plan to assassinate Washington. Everything would progress as outlined in the original plan. The back up plans covered all possible contingencies. George Washington would never leave the house alive.

"Yes, what is it?" Lomasi heard Adolf Hitler ask.

It was Colonel Wolf. "Fuhrer, General Werner was correct in having me check the weapons. The machine gun bolts and firing pins have been sabotaged. The guns are inoperable. However, we can obtain replacements immediately. The ammunition has not been disturbed."

"Dr. Klein, will you see to that right away?" asked General Werner.

Apparently, thought Lomasi, they're going to get the new machine guns or replacement parts by using the Chronometric Teleporter to go back into the time in which they are now living. I must warn David and the others about this.

Adolf Hitler promptly ended the meeting. However, he asked that Martin Bormann remain with him in the dining room after the others left. The two men then began a whispered conversation that lasted nearly half an hour. Lomasi could hear nothing of that conversation.

What had Hitler and Bormann discussed, she wondered. This was a secretive conversation so it must have been very important. But, what was it about?

As she walked over to the door of the small sitting room, Lomasi wondered how she could warn David that the Germans would have operable machines guns. As she pulled the door open, once again she was surprised to be staring into the face of Miss Chattenborne. "You will please come with me, my dear," she ordered.

Lomasi closed the sitting room door and followed Miss Chattenborne.

"This is about the two men who were shot this morning while trying to escape?" Miss Chattenborne said.

"Alright," replied Lomasi, fearing the Nazis were going to question her.

As the two women walked across the living room, Miss Chattenborne directed Lomasi to go to the barracks building, which housed the forty German soldiers.

"What am I to do there?" Lomasi asked.

"You mentioned you were a doctor or some such thing and you knew about medicine and healing," replied Miss Chattenborne. "The two men who were shot need attention. I would like you to see to them."

Lomasi nodded that she understood as they walked toward the back door of the kitchen. Once the two women were outside and walking through the gardens and grassy area toward the barracks, Lomasi's thoughts turned to the events of the past several days. She worried she still didn't have a specific plan to prevent Washington's assassination.

Followed by Lomasi, Miss Chattenborne walked up the three steps to the small porch of the barracks. She pushed open the wooden door and both women stepped inside. The barracks consisted of one large room filled with forty beds, twenty on each side of the room, lined up perpendicularly to the walls of the building. There was a small window every ten feet. Organization and neatness prevailed. All the beds were made and each had a large box at its foot to hold its occupants belongings. Little else was in the room.

A German officer and two guards stood near the doorway through which the women entered. The men who had been shot lay on the two beds closest to the door. Lomasi walked over to the space between the two men's beds. From the blood stained dressings on the wounds of the larger of the two men, it was obvious he had been hit in his right side and in his right upper thigh. The second man had received a minor flesh wound in his right arm and appeared to be in good condition.

"They need to be brought to the main house," Lomasi said to Miss Chattenborne.

"That's impossible," the German officer interjected. "They must remain under guard here."

"I must be able to treat them properly and there are too many things I need which cannot easily be brought here. They both must be taken to the main house," Lomasi repeated.

"There is an area in the cellar where they may be confined and treated," Miss Chattenborne told the officer. "If you want these men looked after, they must be brought there." Lomasi was again surprised that Miss Chattenborne was supporting her.

"Get two other men to help you carry the big one," the officer ordered one of the guards. "This other guy can walk." Looking at the prisoner who was sitting up in the second bed, the officer said, "If you try to escape, you will be shot. And our aim will be more deadly this time."

That the two prisoners were not killed when they were initially shot was not an accident. Nazi SS troopers were excellent shooters and had they wanted to kill the fleeing men, they would have. Their intent was to disable the men so they could be captured and questioned. They captured the men but had gotten no information from them. They were to be interrogated again after their wounds were treated.

Lomasi and Miss Chattenborne walked back to the house to prepare the area in the cellar for the arrival of the wounded men. Miss Chattenborne helped Lomasi gather the items she needed and the two women descended the stairs to the cellar. The part of the cellar Miss Chattenborne had described was a large room with a solid wood door. In addition to the room being able to accommodate two beds, its door could be locked and it could function as a cell.

The German officer was satisfied with these accommodations. Two guards were stationed outside the room on either side of the door. When the women left, the door would be locked. The treatment of the two men did not take long. Lomasi quickly cleaned their wounds and applied a pasty cocktail of medicinal herbs to the more serious wounds of the larger man. For the second man, Lomasi had concocted a thick green potion, which she smeared on his wound.

With their work completed, Miss Chattenborne left the room. Neither the two women nor the wounded prisoners had spoken. As Lomasi stood up and began to walk toward the door, she turned around and looked at the two men.

"What are your names?" she asked.

"My name is Contrary Walbridge. This is my friend John."

****

Lomasi ascended the stairs leading from the cellar to the kitchen to resume her duties. She still hadn't devised a plan to prevent Washington's assassination, which was scheduled to occur within hours. Miss Chattenborne was working in the kitchen with the other girls. As she walked past Lomasi, in what seemed like an afterthought, she turned and asked Lomasi to come with her to help with another task. Lomasi followed Miss Chattenborne through the living room and down the hallway toward the same small sitting room in which she had listened to the meetings.

To Lomasi's surprise, when they reached the room Miss Chattenborne knocked twice on the door. Lomasi heard the door being unlocked, and it was opened by someone standing behind it. Miss Chattenborne entered the room followed by Lomasi. As the door closed behind them, Lomasi was shocked to see Madame Bettenfield turning the small latch on the handle to re-lock it.

Madame Bettenfield directed the two women to sit near her in the chairs at the west corner of the small room. She then looked toward Lomasi. "Miss Chattenborne tells me you have a great deal of curiosity about our guests and their activities, Lomasi."

While not surprised by this confrontation, Lomasi had not really considered what her response would be when it happened.

"Why would you say that, Madame? Are you not happy with my work?"

"We have no time for parlor games, my dear," replied Madame Bettenfield. "The three of us are all quite aware of the intentions of our guests. What is your position in this madam? And, be very quick about it. Our lives are in great danger as we sit here speaking."

Lomasi, who was re-assured by the knife within easy reach under her skirts, decided that her best option was to take the offensive and tell the two women exactly what her purpose was. She would confront them as they had confronted her.

"You are right, Madame Bettenfield. I am very aware of your guests' intentions. I have come here to prevent them from assassinating George Washington."

Lomasi was astonished at Madame Bettenfield's response. "Miss Chattenborne and I both suspected that was your purpose my dear however, in view of the gravity of the circumstances we felt it only prudent to confirm this. Preventing these men from assassinating George Washington is also our intent."

"But I thought you were to become the queen in the new country the British were to create," countered Lomasi.

"My dear, the Americans will never tolerate a queen. That is a British illusion. Besides that, while I am always opportunistic when it comes to politics, I am very loyal in my friendships. George Washington is my friend." Smiling slightly, she continued. "But then, from a selfish standpoint if Washington should die, the future of these colonies would be perpetual chaos. People who have a great deal of money do not always fare so well in times of crisis and civil unrest. Everything gets blamed on us. So I also find it much more profitable to support Washington and the Patriot cause.

"But, enough of that. We have sufficiently assured each other that we are working for the same objective of keeping Washington alive. The important question is how do we do this?"

Lomasi was not certain she could trust Madame Bettenfield or Miss Chattenborne. Madame Bettenfield's reputation was clearly that of a person who would always take the most profitable course of action. She didn't completely believe Madame Bettenfield would put her friendship with Washington ahead of her greed. On the other hand, she had plainly admitted that keeping Washington alive would be more profitable for her. Remembering Shimasani's advice, she decided to trust her instincts which were telling her that the two women were most likely trustworthy. Besides, she thought to herself, there is really no other choice and the time to take action to stop Washington's murder is getting short.

Lomasi was astonished with this surprising twist of circumstances and hadn't regained her composure. She replied in a dismayed tone, "I must confess I have not come up with a plan."

"Well, my dear, Miss Chattenborne and I have devised a course of action. It will involve a great deal of risk but if we are successful we shall prevent Washington's murder. However, you are an important part of this plan. You must be willing to trust me and do what I ask."

"I understand," replied Lomasi.

Madame Bettenfield continued. "We have very little time and if the Germans and British suspect we are working against them, they'll kill us. Do not doubt that for a moment. They are extremely dangerous men and the stakes are very high. You must go to General Washington immediately and tell him he is not to attend the dinner tonight under any circumstances. However, he must send a substitute so that the Germans think it is he who has come to the dinner."

"What do you mean?" interrupted Lomasi.

"One of General Washington's officers is a Major Abraham Rutledge. His physical appearance greatly resembles that of the general. Neither the British nor Germans have ever seen George Washington in person. You are to persuade General Washington that he must send Major Rutledge to the dinner in his place. Major Rutledge shall impersonate General Washington and this will assure there is no risk to Washington's life. Lomasi, I know General Washington quite well. He will not want to cooperate in this plan and will insist on attending the dinner himself. You must convince him to send Major Rutledge as a substitute. We shall do all we can to protect the major however, there is great risk and Major Rutledge must know this."

Madame Bettenfield continued. "It must appear that Washington attended the dinner because if he does not, the Germans will simply search him out and kill him. As you have seen, their weapons are far superior to ours and we could only sit and watch this happen. But also, just as importantly, the second part of our plan is to kill the Germans, at least Adolf Hitler and Martin Bormann. That way, they shall no longer be a threat to General Washington."

"I understand and agree," replied Lomasi.

Madame Bettenfield continued. "As incredible as this may seem to you, these men are from another time in the future. They have found a way to travel through the centuries and come into our time. For some reason, it is very important to them that Washington is killed. If they are not killed themselves, they shall again return to our time to kill Washington."

Lomasi avoided telling Madame Bettenfield she was aware these men had come from the future. She was also satisfied with the women's plan. It would achieve the most important objective, which was to prevent Washington from being assassinated. However, Lomasi had also realized from the beginning that Adolf Hitler and Martin Bormann must be killed. There was no doubt that if they were not successful in killing Washington within the next several hours, they would return to make an attempt on his life at another time.

"I completely understand, Madame Bettenfield. I know what I must do and I shall leave immediately. It's obvious that the most important element of this plan is complete secrecy. We must keep this plan entirely to ourselves."

****

A haggard Major Josiah Wellston stumbled into his house at eleven am. He had spent the night in the woods eluding his German pursuers. They were as difficult adversaries as he had ever experienced. Several times, the Germans nearly caught up with him. Several times he thought he would surely be captured. Somehow, he had escaped. He had gotten little rest during the chase, but he stopped to rest as he got closer to his home. He would freshen up and head for General Washington's Headquarters.

Several hours later Major Wellston arrived at General Washington's headquarters. The guards knew Major Wellston as he was a frequent visitor to both General Washington and Colonel Thacher. Today, both men were in an urgent meeting with two militiamen from Boston. The guard suggested that Major Wellston be seated in the foyer of the large doorway and wait for General Washington to become available.

Major Wellston persisted. "Tell General Washington I must see him at once," he demanded.

"Yes sir," the sentry responded. He turned and disappeared into the large home serving as Washington's headquarters.

The sentry returned shortly and directed Major Wellston to follow him into General Washington's office. Major Wellston walked into the office to find General Washington, Colonel Thacher, and two other men seated around a large meeting table.

Even when he was seated, it was obvious George Washington was an uncommonly tall man. With his stately demeanor and ample height, he sat straighter and higher in his chair, which conveyed little doubt as to who was in command. As usual, Washington's appearance was impeccable. He was perfectly groomed, with every one of his grayish hairs in place. His uniform was expensively tailored and he set the standard to which his officers and enlisted men aspired. The straight line of his lips enhanced the seriousness of his expression. His prominent stature communicated his demand for excellence, both from himself and any man who would serve under him.

"Good morning Josiah," General Washington greeted him.

"Good morning, General Washington," Major Wellston responded.

"Of course, you know Colonel Thacher. Let me introduce William Beacon and Richard Brown. They are from Boston."

"Good morning, gentlemen," Major Wellston responded. He nodded in the direction of Colonel Thacher who returned his gesture, slightly bowing his head.

"I'm glad you're here, Josiah. Please, take a chair," said General Washington. "William and Richard have been traveling hard for the last twenty four hours and have just arrived. They tell me there are large British troop movements up north and everyone is very concerned that war could break out at any moment, possibly even today. They also tell me men are coming into Massachusetts from New York, Connecticut, Rhode Island and New Hampshire. They bring their muskets but no ammunition, supplies or even food."

"Yes, I have also heard strong rumors that war shall commence very soon, General," replied Major Wellston.

"As everyone knows we have no American army organized," General Washington replied. "I myself can not act in any official capacity. Even my rank of "general" is presumed because I have not been given any authority or command. The Second Continental Congress is to meet in three weeks on May 10 and I expect I shall become an active general in the army then. I don't know what authority I shall have if that should occur."

Speaking in a tone of concern and anxiety, Washington continued, "There are many people in the colonies who believe that rebellion is not the proper course. Many wealthy landowners wish to remain under a British government. Many prominent citizens from my own state of Virginia are against rebellion. We have many people unwilling to act. Everyone wants to make speeches about the situation but no one will act. But, the time for talk has come to an end. People must decide which direction they wish to go."

Washington then shifted the conversation. "Josiah, I know you are to attend the dinner at Madame Bettenfield's this evening. I expect it shall be a very important gathering, particularly with the events which I have just learned from Richard and William."

"Yes, General," replied Major Wellston. "Also, I wanted to request that I accompany you and Colonel Thacher in your coach when you depart for the dinner tonight. I have several important concerns that I must bring to your attention."

"That would be fine," replied General Washington. "We leave at seven o'clock. Is that correct, Benjamin?"

"That is correct, General," Colonel Thacher replied.

"General, if you wouldn't mind, I shall leave now and return here at seven o'clock this evening," replied Major Wellston.

"Good," replied Washington. "We shall see you at that time."

Major Wellston then left the meeting to return to his home.

Soon after Major Wellston departed, the meeting with General Washington ended. Colonel Thacher penned a note and put it in an envelope with Washington's official seal on it. He called a sentry into his office and handed him the envelope. It was addressed to Colonel Wolf.

"I want you to immediately take this message to Colonel Wolf at Bettenfield Manor and deliver it to him personally. Is that clear?"

"Yes sir," the sentry replied, and he turned and left.

****

David had also managed to evade the Germans and found his way back to Cass' farm at nine o'clock. He relayed the early morning's events to him and Peter.

"I don't know if Major Wellston escaped the Germans or not," said David. "But, I'm sure that Contrary and John are either captured or dead. Oh, and this is important, the Germans have night vision on their rifle sights. I was lucky to escape. Cass," David continued, "you may have to assume command of the militia unless there is someone else who is second in command to Major Wellston. He was going to have Contrary take charge of getting the militia into position in the woods south of Bettenfield Manor."

"No, that's my job," responded Cass. "I'll round up the militia and cull it down to a force of one hundred men. I'll leave now to get them heading toward the woods around Bettenfield Manor."

"Cass," David reminded him, "Remember to wait for at least one hour after Moses Brampton, Peter, and I arrive before beginning the diversionary attack. Keep the men far back from the edge of the woods. The German's night vision will allow them to see your men after dark. There's one other thing. We damaged the machine guns so they won't fire however, the Nazis might repair them.

The machineguns look like oversize rifles and they would be resting on some supports under their barrels. If you see these machine guns, your men must break off the fight and retreat completely. If you don't see the machine guns before a fight begins, and they start using them, you will know instantly. Once again, break off the fight immediately and retreat or all your men will die. Is that clear?"

"I understand," said Cass. "Also, I'll have a man named James Chesterton lead the 'Indians' when they attack the six mounted Nazis trailing Washington's coach. He's a good man and can handle that task better than me. I can't hit anything with a bow and arrow anyway."

"Good," replied David. "I've got to get a little sleep now. Peter, when do we meet Moses Brampton?"

"We meet him at six thirty this evening," replied Peter. "He says that would get us to Bettenfield Manor early and give us a chance to check the layout of the place. David, I'll go with Cass and meet you back here late this afternoon. I don't want to sit around all day doing nothing."

"Okay," replied David. "I'm really exhausted so you'll have to excuse my sleeping for a few hours. By the way, Peter. We'll find out where she is today. Hang in there."

"Okay," replied Peter, "whatever 'hang in there' means."

33

Ambush

April 19, 1775   Old Church Road

12:01 p.m. to 7:00 p.m.

At six thirty, Major Wellston left his home on horseback heading for Washington's headquarters. The sun was beginning to slide downward in the west and a soft breeze cooled the evening. It would be a pleasant ride he thought, and he spurred the horse to a gallop. As Major Wellston rode south on Old Church Road toward the city, he wondered where the six mounted German soldiers might be positioned while they waited for Washington's coach to pass.

He had been riding less than five minutes when all went black and his lifeless body toppled from his horse and onto the roadway. He was dead before he hit the ground, a Nazi bullet through his skull.

Colonel Wolf had gotten Colonel Thacher's message.

****

Colonel Benjamin Thacher walked into George Washington's office as he prepared for the short journey to Bettenfield Manor. Thomas Tewkes, Washington's longtime coachman, had already pulled the stately carriage up to the back porch of the estate. The six mounted escorts were waiting on Old Church Road near the gate. A single pedestrian loitered across the road smoking a pipe, idly curious about the proceedings at the estate.

Colonel Thacher informed General Washington that Major Wellston would be late and not ride with them in the coach. Instead, he would see them at Bettenfield Manor later in the evening. As the two men walked out of the office, Washington paused, then turned to go back into his office.

"Colonel Thacher, please wait for me in the coach. I shall join you directly," ordered General Washington.

As Colonel Thacher walked down the stairs to board the coach the driver, Thomas Tewkes greeted him, "G'day Colonel Thacher."

"Good day to you, Thomas. General Washington shall be along soon," Colonel Thacher replied.

"That's fine, sir."

Moments later, George Washington came through the doorway and waved at Thomas Tewkes as he descended the stairs to board the coach.

"Good evening, General," Thomas called.

As General Washington pulled the carriage door open and climbed in, Thomas could hear Colonel Thacher speaking.

"Just a moment sir, what is this about?"

Thomas Tewkes snapped his whip and the coach lurched forward, moving swiftly around the circular garden in order to turn the carriage in the opposite direction to follow the cobblestone drive onto Old Church Road. The coach passed through the gate and made an immediate left turn to travel north to Bettenfield Manor. The six mounted escorts spurred their horses and fell in approximately fifty yards behind the rapidly moving coach.

The man across the road smoking the pipe walked away in the opposite direction. He would inform the other five mounted German soldiers that Washington was in the coach traveling to Bettenfield Manor.

Moments later, as Thomas Tewkes steered George Washington's rumbling coach away from the city, he heard a muffled gunshot from inside the carriage. A faint smile was his only reaction.

****

As his coach pulled into Cass' farm, Moses Brampton saw David and Peter awaiting him on the front porch of the wooden house. The big coach and its four horses rumbled to a stop but the accompanying cloud of dust kept going, enveloping David and Peter who were trying not to breathe it. They hurriedly walked down the porch's steps and pulled open the coach's door. The step underneath the door and a hand pull to its right provided easy access to the passenger compartment as the two men climbed aboard.

The driver cracked the whip and the big carriage lurched forward, rolling down the drive into the main road. As Peter had already met Moses Brampton, he greeted him and introduced David. Brampton was a heavy-set man with a ruddy face and friendly smile. He was also a man of intense purpose. He knew what had to be done and was focused on getting it accomplished.

"Major Wellston was getting ready to go meet General Washington and Colonel Thacher when I left the house to come and fetch you two gents," said Moses. "We'll meet him up with him later as soon as he takes care of the nasty business with Colonel Thacher and Washington returns to his headquarters. He'll be a big help in stopping these people and making sure they never return."

"I'm glad to hear Major Wellston is still alive," responded David. "I thought the Nazis might have captured him or worse last night. That he is alive is good news."

Quickly getting to the business at hand, Moses Brampton interjected, "Boys, we have to decide how we're going to handle the situation. It could get out of control very easily."

"Peter and I have to somehow isolate Hitler and Bormann," replied David. "We have to find out some important information from one of them, most likely Hitler. We need to do that very soon after we arrive because they'll know their plan has failed when General Washington and Colonel Thacher don't arrive."

The three men had no way of knowing that Major Wellston had already been killed. They also didn't know that Major Rutledge, who was attending the dinner impersonating Washington, had just killed Colonel Thacher in Washington's coach when he resisted arrest.

"Thank you, David," said Peter. "I'll wait outside until you tell me to come into the house. If Hitler and Bormann see me that will alert them something is wrong. If you can get them into another room away from the other guests, we could confront them there."

David intended to keep his promise to Peter that he would help him find his wife Johanna. David was a romantic at heart and he keenly empathized with Peter's love for his wife.

But now, he worried about the catastrophic aftereffects if he failed in his mission. The consequences would reverberate through two hundred years of subsequent historical events and jeopardize the future of the planet. Countries and populations would evaporate because they would never be born. Subjugation and suffering would be inflicted across the globe if it were dominated by the Nazis. My God, he thought, we just can't fail. It's not an option.

The weight of what he must accomplish bore down on him. How can one man carry such a burden? He couldn't answer his own question. He would ask Tse about this. But he already knew how Tse would answer. Tse would say he was feeling sorry for himself. David smiled. He realized the objectives were to prevent Washington's assassination, kill Hitler and Bormann, and destroy their Chronometric Teleporter. Peter told him there was a second Chronometric Teleporter somewhere and they must also destroy it. Peter's wife Johanna would probably be wherever that second machine was located.

Moses interrupted David's thoughts. "When we get there, we need to check the layout at Bettenfield Manor. There will be a large number of Nazis surrounding the estate and we need to have our escape route clearly in mind. We take Washington and exit the house through the kitchen and hightail it for the west woods. We need to make sure the area is clear or if the Germans are out there. The German troops will probably be positioned on the perimeter of the estate and away from the house. That would give them a good view of the open area around the estate."

Moses continued," David, your job is to get Hitler and Bormann into another room. When I see you do this, I'll have Peter join you. You must get the information you need quickly and these two men must be killed before the other Nazis become suspicious. When I hear your shots, I'll shoot the two attendants in the dining room.

Madame Bettenfield is another problem. If she senses trouble, she'll alert her staff and we'll have to contend with them. Keep in mind gentlemen, from a military standpoint, this whole thing is extremely messy. We don't have enough people, and we still won't even when Major Wellston arrives. We need to get our mission completed swiftly and make our escape. The men didn't know they had an ally in Madame Bettenfield. Things weren't quite as bad as they seemed. But, they were still bad.

"Our friend Lomasi will help," David replied.

"I'm sure she'll be useful," replied Moses. "We'll need all the help we can get. But remember, this plan remains very dangerous. There are far too many things that can go wrong."

The coach was drawing near its destination, passing over the rise south of the estate. Moses Brampton, David and Peter could see the manicured lawns and handsome buildings. Though it was still light, lanterns flickered throughout the imposing grounds. The coach turned left off Old Church Road and into the drive of Bettenfield Manor. The big coach slowed to a stop at the stately front porch of the majestic home. A footman scurried over to the coach to assist the men disembarking. As they climbed down from the carriage, the men understood the time to confront the world's most notorious murderer was upon them.

****

Throughout the afternoon, Cass had gradually marshaled one hundred militiamen in the woods across the field south of Bettenfield Manor. As Major Wellston and David had instructed, Cass positioned the men well away from the edge of the woods. This was to avoid detection and, when the shooting started, keep the men out of sight of the Nazi's night vision. He remembered David's warning about the possibility of the Germans having their machine guns operational.

Cass had sent several scouts up to the edge of the woods to identify the location of the Germans' positions. They spotted two well-camouflaged groups of three men each, both situated on the boundary created by the estate's manicured lawn abutting the farm field. One group was on the eastern side of the field, and the other on the western side. Both groups lay prone in their small clearings in the green corn crop. Each man appeared to have a rifle and pistol. Additionally, there appeared to be some type of other rifle placed on the ground and propped up in front of them. They had never seen a musket such as this but, when they reported back to Cass, he knew exactly what it was.

"It's a machine gun," Cass told the scouts. "It's a gun we're not going to tangle with."

As the sun moved lower on the horizon, Cass ordered his men to hold their positions. They would not be moving forward to get into a battle they all were itching to fight. Major Wellston, Moses Brampton, David and Peter must fight the battle alone. Cass didn't know Major Wellston had already been killed.

He realized the original intent of his attack was to create a diversion. He could still pull off a diversion by having several of his

298

sharp shooters move up to the edge of the woods and shoot a round or two into the Nazi positions. He could have the rest of his men positioned well away from the edge of the woods and shoot some rounds into the air. He could also set a fire. But, he knew that this wouldn't fool a sophisticated enemy for long.

****

George Washington's coach had just passed the second bend in Old Church Road and the six mounted militia followed fifty yards behind. Following one mile behind them were the six mounted Nazi soldiers whose job was to intercept Washington's coach should it turn back from its journey to Bettenfield Manor.

James Chesterton had been busy for several hours. He had assembled his force of forty Patriots disguised as Indians. These men were experts with the bow and arrow, one of many Indian skills they learned in the French and Indian War.

Chesterton positioned twenty men on each side of Old Church Road along a fifty yard stretch beginning just past the second bend in the road where it turned north. This would allow the Patriots to ambush the Nazis as they rode out of the turn. Sixteen men on either side of the road were placed at eight-foot intervals. The remaining four men on each side of the road were placed at the north and sound ends of the ambush area. They would prevent the Germans from escaping in either direction. All the men were hidden behind trees.

Additionally, Chesterton dug four shallow trenches across the road, two at each end of the ambush area. These trenches would hide buried ropes which were extended across the road and into the woods. The ropes were securely tied around trees on the west side of the road. On the east side of the road, the ropes were strung around pulleys on two separate trees. Two men stood ready at each of the trees. When the signal was given, the men would pull hard on the ropes around the pulleys and immediately tie them in a taut position around other trees. The double rope fence at each of its ends turned the ambush area into a deadly corral from which neither horse nor rider could escape.

The signal to yank the ropes into position would also be the cue for the forty "Indians" to commence shooting their arrows. The men had been trained to synchronize their shots in order that all of them fired together in volleys. They could each shoot twelve arrows per minute with consistent accuracy. They would unleash four hundred and eighty arrows per minute at their foes.

The waning light shone through the tall trees when Chesterton heard the galloping of horses. He had positioned himself at the north end of the ambush area and would give the signal to begin the attack. He could hear the horses going into the bend of the road. Within seconds, the six horses with their Nazi riders rounded the bend and were riding out of the curve and into the straight part of the road heading due north.

Chesterton waited another few seconds. The six riders rode two abreast forming columns of three horsemen. The first two horses galloped within ten yards of the north ropes when Chesterton yelled, "Now!"

The north rope fence flew up and the south barrier immediately followed. The moment Chesterton gave the command the first volley of forty arrows was shot. Three riders tumbled from their horses with multiple arrows sticking from their bodies. The other three riders pulled their pistols as the second volley of arrows found their marks and knocked two more men to the ground. Two injured horses lay writhing, their terrified gasps launching puffs of dust from the road's powdery dirt. Three horses, pierced by arrows and saddles empty, raced wild-eyed around the deadly corral. The last rider wheeled his horse round and spurred it hard toward the south rope fence, randomly firing his Luger into the woods. As he neared the south fence he spurred the frightened animal in desperate hope the horse could jump over the ropes, if he could even see them in the pale light. The panicked rider and his terrified horse ran at full speed, crashing head-on into the fence. The man was immediately airborne and sailed over the rope barrier. The horse reared and fell to the ground. In a moment, the horse got to his feet and shook himself. The rider had not fared as well, landing on his head and breaking his neck.

Of the other five horsemen, three were dead. There were two men still alive and Chesterton took them prisoner.

34

Assassination

April 19, 1775   Bettenfield Manor

7:01 p.m. to 8:30 p.m.

Moses Brampton and David Kelly walked up the scarlet-carpeted steps of the white staircase leading to the front porch of Bettenfield Manor. A doorman, elegantly uniformed in a long, gold trimmed black coat, black breeches and white stockings, welcomed then into the brightly lit living room of Bettenfield Manor. Peter Krause, remaining out of sight as planned, had lingered, and then walked up the steps to the porch. As the doorman greeted Peter and began opening the great door for him to enter, he responded that he wished to remain on the porch for a few moments to breathe some night air. He then slowly walked into the partial concealment of the dim light on the west side of the porch, taking a seat on one of the chairs backed against the wall of the house.

Moses and David, cautious about the food and drinks, could not risk raising suspicion by avoiding the dark red wine being served by the maids. Each man now held a glass in his hand. As they stood talking and looking about the magnificent room, Moses remarked that if Madame Bettenfield were to become a queen, this house could surely serve as her palace.

As David further surveyed the room he suddenly noticed Adolf Hitler talking to a woman he assumed was Madame Bettenfield. David also recognized Martin Bormann standing at Hitler's side. He then noticed that there were at least three other German officers in the room, a general and two colonels. Moses identified them as General Werner, Colonel Wolf and Colonel Kruger. The reason for all five Germans attending the dinner was presumably to sell weapons to the Americans. However, David and Moses knew their real motive. There were eight other dinner guests in the room, which included two Patriot militia officers from

Massachusetts. David assumed the two men standing near the dining room entrance doors were the two attendants, the backup assassins, of which Lomasi had spoken.

Lomasi, working as one of the maids serving the wine, brought her tray over to David and Moses.

"Would you gentlemen care for some wine?" she asked, even though they had full glasses in their hands. She quickly whispered to David and Moses Brampton that the German machine guns were again operational.

This was not an unexpected development and he had briefed Cass to be prepared for such an eventuality. David was not concerned the guns would be used against the militiamen because Cass would not attack if the machine guns were on the field. However, they would no longer have the diversion they needed to help in their escape. Maybe Cass would think of another diversion, David thought. Lomasi was about to tell David something else but was interrupted when the front door opened.

To the surprise of both David and Moses, George Washington walked into the room. Moses Brampton instantly realized it was Major Abraham Rutledge, not George Washington at whom they were staring. For some reason, neither Colonel Thacher nor Major Wellston was with him. David again realized the reality of Nazi's ruthlessness. If Major Wellston was not with Washington, he had to be dead. David and Moses Brampton both knew that. Peter, watching from the shadows of the front porch, also realized what had happened. Moses left David standing alone and walked over to greet the substitute General Washington.

He returned shortly to where David stood but he couldn't risk being overheard telling David it was an impersonator, not George Washington. He would have to play along with the deception and explain to David later.

Moses Brampton, knowing the machine guns were again operable, whispered to David that the plan to prevent Washington's assassination must be adjusted. Cass would not attack and create the diversion they needed to escape. Contrary and John had been killed. Major Wellston was dead. Also, Colonel Thacher......"

At that moment, a woman approached David and Moses. David recognized Miss Chattenborne as he had seen her on his visit to Lomasi.

"Sir, could you please come with me?" she asked David.

What is it? David wondered. We must act now. What could this woman possibly want?"

****

Moses Brampton remained at the reception in the living room and David followed Miss Chattenborne down the west hallway leading from the living room. She stopped at a closed door about midway down the hall on its left side. She knocked twice and opened the door gesturing to David to follow her into the room. As David entered, he was unnerved by sight of Adolf Hitler, Martin Bormann, and two German officers. Madame Bettenfield stood next to Hitler. Most disturbing, Peter sat in a chair against the opposite wall with an anxious expression on his face.

"I am Adolf Hitler," he introduced himself. "This is Martin Bormann, General Werner, Colonel Wolf, and Dr. Klein. Oh, and this is Madame Bettenfield. Of course, you already know Peter. Colonel Wolf invited him to join us."

Colonel Kruger was still in the living room at the reception.

Colonel Wolf, who had been holding his right hand behind his back, was now holding it in front of him, pointing a Luger pistol at David.

"Would you mind raising your hands and standing against the wall," he directed David.

David did as ordered and Colonel Wolf walked over behind him and moved his hand around David's belt, locating the pistol David was carrying.

"Now what would you be doing with a German Luger in the year 1775?" asked Colonel Wolf. "This is one of our guns, is it not?"

David, now turning around, did not answer.

Adolf Hitler once again spoke. "I understand you and my friend Peter are looking for me. Well, now that you have found me, what is it you want?"

"I am helping Peter find his wife," replied David. "That is all we want."

With George Washington in the next room, he dared not mention the real reason for his travel into time. Washington was already in an extremely dangerous position and there was no point in jeopardizing him any further.

"Of course, I don't believe you," replied Hitler. "Do you take us for fools?"

Martin Bormann, who had been silent, laughed as Hitler spoke. General Werner and Colonel Wolf also smiled.

Hitler continued, "You know why I am here and I know why you are here. You are the fool, an extremely presumptuous one at that. And you, Peter, of all people, should know the futility of trying to stop me. Had you remained loyal to me, you could have shared in the glory of the Third Reich when the Aryan race becomes the only race on earth. But, that is enough of this friendly banter, gentlemen. Before we kill you however, I want to know how you traveled through time. Peter, how did you manage to build another Chronometric Teleporter two thousand years ago?"

"Where is my wife you son of a bitch?" yelled Peter.

Colonel Wolf cuffed Peter on his forehead with the butt of his pistol, producing a cut and a trickle of blood.

"You're upsetting me, Peter," replied Hitler. "But, to answer your question, she is alive and well living in our compound in South America in the year 2010.

"Where exactly is she?" replied Peter.

"You shall never see her again, Peter," Hitler replied. "You betrayed me."

"I did everything you asked," Peter yelled at Hitler.

"Yes, but you were disloyal to me and you must pay the penalty for your sedition," Hitler replied. "But first, we must attend to the gentleman in the next room," Hitler continued. "As soon as General Washington is killed, we can talk again. Madame Bettenfield, is it time for dinner?"

"Yes, Adolf, I believe it is."

****

Lomasi had seen Miss Chattenborne leave the room with David. She knew that time was running out. The dinner would soon be served. She knew shat she couldn't monitor all the dishes being prepared for Washington (Major Rutledge) and there was no way she could be sure he didn't consume at least one of them. The risk was too great. Lomasi walked back into the kitchen and to the door, behind which were the steps leading to the cellar. She slowly descended the stairs.

The two guards were standing next to the door to the cell holding Contrary and John.

"I need to check their wounds for the night," Lomasi told the guard to the right of the door.

Without speaking, the sentry took the keys from his pocket and unlocked the heavy door.

"I won't be long," she told the guards, as they closed the door behind her.

Lomasi entered the room to find Contrary sitting on the side of his bed, his feet resting on the floor. John was lying awake on the other bed.

"I am Lomasi. David Kelly is my friend. I think they might be in trouble upstairs. They are going to assassinate Washington at any moment. Can either of you help?"

"I can," replied Contrary, "but, John's a bit under the weather."

"I'm okay," said John, even though he really wasn't.

"I will tell one of the guards to come into the room," Lomasi continued, "and come over to John's bed because I think he is dead. You two can jump him. He will scream for help. When the second guard comes into the room, I will handle him. Have you got it?"

"Yeah, we got it," replied Contrary.

"Okay, act dead John," said Lomasi.

Then she yelled, "Guard, come into the room!"

Unexpectedly both men rushed into the room.

"What is it?" the first one yelled.

"It's the big man on the inside bed. I think he's dead," replied Lomasi.

As one guard stood beside Lomasi, the second guard laughed and walked over between the two beds and looked down at John. "We're going to kill them anyway," he snickered.

Lomasi, who had moved to a position slightly behind the soldier standing next to her, purposely let a bandage drop to the floor. As she knelt down to pick it up, she quickly reached under the hem of her skirts to pull out her grandfather's large knife attached to her leg. Suddenly, John's body snapped upward, his large hands grasping the throat of the soldier looking down at him. Contrary jumped to face the sentry standing in front of Lomasi, however the soldier had immediately drawn his pistol and was angling for a shot at John as he struggled with the first sentry. Seeing Contrary react, the sentry swung his gun toward him just as Lomasi plunged her knife deep into the soldier's back.

John finished strangling the second sentry however, still suffering from his bullet wounds, he then passed out. John needed to rest. He could be of no further help this evening. Lomasi's knife had cut through the heart of the second sentry and he too lay dead.

Contrary and Lomasi climbed the cellar steps to the kitchen. Contrary had taken both Lugers from the sentries as well as extra clips of ammunition. David had shown him how to use the gun. Lomasi, who was woozy from stabbing the soldier, told Contrary to wait in the back section of the kitchen by the cellar door. She would check the living room to see what was happening there.

As Lomasi looked around the living room, she could see that General Washington's impersonator was still there, deep in conversation with the several Patriot militiamen. However, Hitler, Bormann and the other Germans were no longer in the room. Only the two Nazi attendants were still in the room, maintaining a close watch on their quarry. David had not returned to the living room. Lomasi wondered where all of the people had gone. She concluded that the plot to kill Washington was in operation just as planned, and those people who had left the living room were now involved in either carrying out the assassination or trying to prevent it. As she thought about where these people could have gone, she concluded that they had to be in the ballroom off the west hallway of the house.

Lomasi returned to the kitchen to find Contrary standing by the cellar door where she left him.

"The plan is in operation," she said. "Many people are missing from the living room. I am sure the ballroom is where they have gone. That's where we must go, however there's one small difficulty we must take care of first.

Somehow, Contrary knew this would not be a "small difficulty."

"What is this small difficulty?" he asked.

"There are two Nazis in the living room. Their job is to assassinate Washington if he doesn't eat the poisoned food. They're armed," replied Lomasi.

"So, if I ask them to have some tea with me, maybe that will get them out of the way?" laughed Contrary.

"That would be a good idea if you poison their tea," replied Lomasi.

While Lomasi was still very uncomfortable with the idea of killing another human being, she was reluctantly accepting the idea that at certain times, it was unavoidable. This looked like one of those times.

"On the other hand, if I walk in and shoot them, that will ruin dinner. I certainly would hate to do that," Contrary replied. "Do you think you could lure one of them into the cellar?"

"I can try," replied Lomasi.

"Alright, if you can get him down the stairs, I'll be waiting for him there," said Contrary.

Contrary descended the stairs to the cellar and Lomasi walked toward the hallway to living room. As she walked into the large room, the guests were engaged in conversation. She walked over to one of the two attendants and asked him if he could accompany her to the cellar. There was a problem with the prisoners.

"This attendant, a tall, muscular man with blond hair looked down at Lomasi and smirked.

"Yes, I will help you. Can't you Americans do anything yourselves?"

The man followed Lomasi back into the kitchen. She pointed the way to the cellar and the man walked over to the doorway leading to it.

"Come over here girl," he ordered. "You go down first and I shall follow you."

"I am busy sir," replied Lomasi. "Can you not find your own way?"

Obviously suspicious, the Nazi attendant gruffly repeated his order. "Get over here now, if you know what's good for you. You go down the steps first."

Lomasi had no choice but to go down the steps ahead of the man. As they got half way down the steps, out of the corner of her eye Lomasi could see the man pull out his gun. Obviously, he was no amateur.

They reached the bottom of the steps. The cellar was poorly illuminated and dark in its corners.

"Where is the problem?" the Nazi asked.

"In that room," replied Lomasi pointing to the closed door.

"Open it girl," he ordered.

As they moved closer to the door, the SS soldier moved his head back and forth, checking the entire cellar area for any surprise. Suddenly, they heard a moan behind them in the far corner of the basement. The soldier immediately turned and slowly walked to the area from which the sound had come. Lomasi followed the Nazi as he walked across the darkened chamber. Contrary was lying on the floor, face down, his right arm and hand under his body.

"Get up, you," the Nazi ordered.

Contrary didn't move and groaned once more.

"Get up or I'll shoot you," he again barked at Contrary.

Lomasi, who was standing in back of and to the left of the Nazi, took a small step to her right and positioned herself directly behind the attendant. She slowly raised her skirt and reached down, unsnapping the case and pulling out her knife.

"For the last time, get up," the Nazi growled at Contrary. "I'm going to shoot."

Lomasi raised her right hand, holding the knife to its highest point of her arm's reach. Her arm had begun its lethal thrust as the Nazi instinctively turned to check on Lomasi. Her intent was to put the knife into the Nazi's back however, when the man turned, the knife crunched into the center of his chest with a dull thud. The Nazi dropped to the floor next to Contrary. Lomasi, who hated violence, had killed a second time today.

An aghast Contrary could only say, "Damn, you're good with that thing."

"Do you think you can handle the second one?" replied Lomasi.

"Go get him. I'll get rid of this one," replied Contrary.

Lomasi quickly climbed the cellar steps and hurried through the kitchen. As she walked into the living room, she saw the other Nazi attendant looking at her. Maintaining her composure, she gestured to him to follow her and she turned back into the hallway leading from the living room to the kitchen. The attendant quickly caught up with her and she told him the first man needed help to carry a body out of the cellar. She directed this second Nazi to the cellar door. She followed him through the kitchen, grabbing a large knife off one of the tables. As the Nazi began to step through cellar door, she plunged the big knife directly into the left side of his back. The man fell forward, his full length crashing onto the cellar steps half way to the bottom and tumbling the rest of the way.

Lomasi went down the steps as Contrary stooped to check on the fallen attendant. He was dead.

Contrary looked up from where he was crouching and saw Lomasi. Neither said anything. Contrary rose to his feet and he and Lomasi quickly walked up the cellar steps. As they went through the kitchen and up the corridor leading to the living room, they heard screams and a commotion in the reception area.

****

In the ballroom, Colonel Wolf took a small cylinder from his pocket and attached it to the end of the Luger's barrel. It's a silencer, David realized. He's going to kill us. Peter got up from his chair and walked over by David. He could see what Colonel Wolf intended to do.

Madame Bettenfield, standing next to Hitler, spoke. "Adolf, I'm going to enjoy watching these two men being shot," she said smiling. "I'm going to enjoy it very much. In fact, I'd like to shoot them myself."

Hitler laughed. "Madame, if you wish to kill these two men, we are happy to oblige you. It would help repay you for your hospitality."

"But first," Adolf Hitler continued, let us have dinner to conclude our more important business with General Washington. Colonel Wolf, we will attend to them after our dinner."

At that moment, the massive doors abruptly swung open and Colonel Kruger rushed into the ballroom.

"What is it?" asked Hitler.

George Washington is dead!

35

Turncoat

April 19, 1775   Bettenfield Manor

8:31 p.m. to 9:30 p.m.

Colonel Kruger, assuming he was poisoning George
Washington, had slipped the deadly powder into his wine. Major
Rutledge drank it and soon collapsed, dying within minutes.

Adolf Hitler and Martin Bormann, along with Madame
Bettenfield, General Werner and Colonel Kruger hurried out of the
ballroom, leaving Colonel Wolf and Dr Wenzel Klein with David
and Peter. After Washington collapsed, he was moved to an
antechamber off the living room and reception area. The three men
and Madame Bettenfield walked into the room and saw George
Washington lying on a couch. He was surrounded by other guests.
A doctor stood near him.

"Doctor," Madame Bettenfield said, "what has happened
here?"

"George Washington is dead!" exclaimed the doctor. "He
collapsed and died. He went so quickly there was nothing I could do
for him."

"Check his pulse, General Werner," ordered Adolf Hitler.

General Werner walked across the room to the couch and
held Washington's left wrist. He looked toward Hitler and shook his
head. George Washington was dead.

Madame Bettenfield smiled and whispered to Hitler. "Your
plan was successful, Adolf. George Washington is dead and I shall
enjoy being a queen."

****

David and Peter, sitting in the ballroom with Colonel Wolf
and Dr. Klein, struggled to come to grips with the fact that
Washington had been killed. David was especially distressed he
failed to save George Washington's life and that realization was
overwhelming. I must kill Hitler, he thought. If nothing else, at

least people could live in peace. Although the United States of America may never come into existence, if Hitler was dead there would not be a World War Two and millions of lives would be saved.

Colonel Wolf, smiling, walked over to Peter. "You are indeed a fool, Dr. Krause. You're going to die, and for what?"

Peter looked at Colonel Wolf and remarked, "Adolf Hitler has changed. He seems more anxious, less confident. Even his voice seems to have lost some of its quality."

"Don't fool yourself, Dr. Krause," Colonel Wolf responded. "The Fuhrer is as vibrant as he ever was. The last two years have been hard for him but, he is doing fine."

"You wouldn't have a napkin or something for the little decoration you gave me in my forehead?" asked Peter as he put his hand on the cut from Colonel Wolf's pistol butt.

David, who was sitting next to Peter, sensed that he was trying to maneuver Colonel Wolf into a position where he could grab his gun hand. This would not be a good move because the gun would be facing Peter's body if the two men struggled. On the other hand, if Colonel Wolf turned to face Peter to give him a cloth for his wound, David might be able jump him from behind. If so, David would have to move quickly.

David looked at Dr. Klein who was sitting ten feet away. David sensed Dr. Klein would not be a participant if fighting should occur, but he wasn't sure.

Colonel Wolf walked over to one of the tables in the ballroom and picked up a napkin. He walked over to Peter and as he handed him the napkin, Peter let it slip from his fingers onto the floor. Peter expected Colonel Wolf would kneel to pick it up and he would then make his move. David hoped it would not happen because Peter would end up dead if he tried to surprise Colonel Wolf.

Colonel Wolf laughed, "Do you think I'd fall for a stupid trick like that, Dr. Krause?"

Peter, sitting in a chair, bent over and picked up the napkin. He blotted the napkin against his wound, leaving stains of red on the white cloth. With his right hand, he held the bloody napkin by its corner, dangling it near his face.

"How much blood was spilled by the Nazi's?" he asked. He threw the bloodied cloth toward a smiling Colonel Wolf who caught it in his left hand.

"Not enough, Dr. Krause," he laughed, as he moved closer to Peter. "And, after I kill you and your friend here, it will still not be enough."

Colonel Wolf was slightly closer to David, but not near enough for him to lunge at the colonel without being shot. Wolf looked like a tough guy and David figured he would move fast and lethally.

Abruptly, loud gunfire erupted outside. Machine guns were firing and there were crisp bursts of rifle fire at the front of the house. A startled Colonel Wolf glanced toward the front window twenty feet across the ballroom. In defiance of orders to not engage the Nazis if the machine guns were set up, Cass decided to initiate a diversionary attack.

Instinctively, David lunged at the colonel's back and the two men crashed to the hard wood floor. He grasped Colonel Wolf's right hand and as they struggled for control of the Luger, Peter dove from his chair onto Colonel Wolf's right arm. As Peter fought for possession of the Luger it fired twice, the sound of the shots muffled by the silencer. Colonel Wolf was a powerful man and Peter couldn't pry the weapon from his hand. Suddenly, the ballroom doors swung open and General Werner and Madame Bettenfield rushed into the room. They had heard the gunfire outside and were alarmed an attack was underway.

General Werner, seeing the men struggling, pulled his pistol from its holster and ordered the men to stop fighting. "You two," he said to David and Peter, "raise your hands." As David and Peter got up from the floor, General Werner ordered them to stand against the wall. "That's better," he said. "Now, we may get on with our business in a more civil manner."

The intense gunfire outside continued. David looked at Peter. Both men knew Cass' diversion would be of short duration. The difference in firepower of the Nazis and the colonial militia was overwhelming. Cass' men were probably retreating into the woods even now. They had no other choice.

"Colonel Wolf," General Werner said, "your silencer is on your gun, so make this quick." Colonel Wolf, nodded, and moved closer to David and Peter.

We blew our only chance, David thought. We're dead.

"Just a moment, Colonel Wolf," Madame Bettenfield said curtly. "Do you not recall that just moments ago, the Fuhrer said I could have the pleasure of shooting these men? Adolf said it would repay my generous hospitality. I should be very hurt if you deprived me of that pleasure."

"Madame," General Werner said, "surely, you were not serious about that request. This is not a job for a woman of your stature. Please get on with it, Colonel Wolf."

"General Werner," Madame Bettenfield replied sternly, "would you take it upon yourself to break the Furher's word to me. I insist that I be allowed to shoot these two men." Madame Bettenfield, visibly upset, glared at General Werner.

General Werner hesitated, and then spoke. "As you wish, Madame," he said. "I'm sure you shall regret your actions. Give her the gun, Colonel Wolf," he ordered.

"Thank you, General," Madame Bettenfield said smiling, as Colonel Wolf handed her the gun.

David and Peter stood with their backs to the wall facing Madame Bettenfield. General Werner and Colonel Wolf stood to her right. Both men were smiling, wondering if she would really be able to shoot the two men.

Madame Bettenfield raised the Luger and smiling, pointed it toward David and Peter. "Death is a terrible thing," she said. She suddenly turned to her right and shot General Werner through the heart. He fell backwards to the floor. Although shocked, Colonel Wolf instantly reacted.

Madame Bettenfield had already turned the Luger toward Colonel Wolf and as he leapt toward her, she pulled the trigger and he crumpled to the floor, a bullet through his left eye. His body convulsed for a few moments and then it was still.

David and Peter who only seconds earlier thought they would be killed looked at Madame Bettenfield. Once again she was smiling. "I never liked those two," she said.

"Madame Bettenfield," Peter said. "We thought you wanted to be a queen."

"The queen of America," she laughed, "now there is misconception. The Americans will never stand for a queen or a king," she replied. "I knew that when these men started talking about this incredible scheme. I cooperated with these men only so I could make sure their ridiculous plot was not successful."

"We were wrong about you, Madame Bettenfield. You are a true patriot."

Madame Bettenfield laughed once more. "Perhaps," she said, "however, I thought it would be more profitable for me to take the American side. So please, don't give me too much credit."

Unsure how to respond, David and Peter stared blankly at Madame Bettenfield. She walked over to where the two men stood and said, "Here is the gun, David. I've done enough killing for the day." Then she added, "George Washington is a friend of mine. Women like me have few friends. Perhaps that will help you understand."

"But, Washington is dead," Peter said.

The doors suddenly opened and Adolf Hitler, Martin Bormann, and Colonel Kruger came into the ballroom. "What is going on here?" asked a startled Hitler, as he looked at the bodies of General Werner and Colonel Wolf lying on the floor.

David, who had hidden the Luger behind his back when he heard the doors open, was now pointing the pistol at the three men. David told the men to move over to the wall and Peter quickly searched them, relieving each of a pistol. He also directed Dr. Klein, who had spoken little, to stand against the wall with the other Nazis. Peter recalled his friendship with Wenzel Klein and his respect for him.

David went over to the ballroom doors and placed chairs underneath the handles to secure the door from anyone else entering. Peter walked over to Adolf Hilter and asked the question he had waited so long to ask.

"Where is Johanna?"

Adolf Hitler responded that she was at their South American compound in the present year 2010.

"But where is that located?"

"We shall have to make a deal for me to tell you that," replied Hitler.

Dr. Klein interrupted. "Peter, Johanna is in the country of Tierra Verde."

As he spoke, he was writing something on a piece of paper. "Here are the exact coordinates," he said as he walked over to Peter and handed him the paper.

Hitler screamed, "I'll kill you for this you fool. We now have no leverage to free ourselves."

Ignoring Hitler, Peter asked, "Wenzel, are you sure about this? You are telling me the truth, aren't you?"

Dr. Klein, looking hurt, replied, "Of course, Peter."

"Peter, are you satisfied that you have your questions answered?" David asked.

"Yes."

"Alright," David replied, as he moved over to face Hitler.

"Fuhrer, or whatever they call you, you will have all of your men lay down their weapons and surrender immediately."

"You are also a fool," replied Hitler. "You shall surrender your weapons immediately or you and your friends and everyone in this household shall be executed within minutes."

David looked Hitler squarely in his eyes. He pointed his Luger directly at Hitler's heart.

"I'm ordering you for the last time to command your men to lay down their weapons and surrender."

"You go straight to hell," replied Hitler.

36

Fuhrer

April 19, 1775   Bettenfield Manor

9:31 p.m. to 11:59 p.m.

David squeezed the Luger's trigger and shot Adolf Hitler through the heart. Before Adolf Hitler's crumpling body had reached the floor, David had turned the weapon toward a visibly shocked Martin Bormann and shot him through the heart. He then returned to Hitler who was lying on his back. He pointed the pistol at his forehead and pulled the trigger twice, delivering two bullets into his brain. He then shot the very dead Hitler in his left temple, just to make sure. He repeated this series of gunshots on Martin Bormann's lifeless body. "Just to make sure, he said."

Colonel Kruger, appearing distressed, waited his turn to be executed.

"If you tell your men to stop shooting, I promise not to kill you," David said.

"I don't think that is possible," replied Colonel Kruger.

"Why not?" asked an angered David as he raised the Luger and advanced toward the colonel.

"No wait," replied Colonel Kruger. "I'm willing to order them to lay down their weapons, but they're all hard core Nazis. Even if they know the Fuhrer is dead, they will fight to the death."

Before David could speak, Peter interjected, "There is a way out of this. We may be able to have these men surrender and have this end very quickly."

"How is that possible?" asked David.

"Wenzel, come over here," directed Peter.

Dr. Klein rose to his feet and walked over to Peter. Dr. Klein had been Peter's protégé, working closely with him developing the Chronometric Teleporter. Klein had accompanied the Nazis into the future because Hitler threatened to kill his wife and family if he did not. Hitler promised Dr. Klein he could return to the present time of 1945 within one year. But Hitler broke his promise, renewing his threat to have someone go back in time to 1945 and kill Klein's family if he refused to cooperate. Klein had no choice.

"Are you going to kill me, Peter?" Klein asked.

"No, Wenzel, I'm not going to kill you," replied Peter. In fact, we're going to return you and all of the other men here to your own time in the year 1945 if they lay down their guns. Take me to the Chronometric Teleporter and we'll bring it to this room."

"Colonel Kruger," said Peter, "Tell your men Adolf Hitler and Martin Bormann are dead. The Nazi movement has ended. If all your men lay down their weapons and surrender now, they may return to their own time in 1945. If they don't immediately agree to do so, we shall destroy the Chronometric Teleporter and everyone shall be stranded in the year 1775 until you all die. There will be no chance for you or them to ever return to your own time."

"You mean you're just going to let us leave, walk out of here?" a surprised Wenzel Klein asked.

"Yes," replied Peter. "But, there are two conditions. First, all of the Nazis must surrender their weapons immediately and walk through your Chronometric Teleporter portal. Second, after we transport all of you back to the year 1945, David and I will destroy the Chronometric Teleporter."

Looking at David, Peter concluded, "By doing this, we can avoid further loss of life and remove the threat against the Americans."

"It's a good plan, Peter," said David. "Hitler and Bormann are dead. When the remaining Nazis walk through the Chronometric Teleporter portal the status quo will then be restored."

"What do you say, Wenzel?" asked Peter.

"Yes, I agree one hundred percent," he replied. I accept those conditions. That is very kind of you, Peter."

"All right, Wenzel, and thank you," replied Peter.

"What about you, Colonel?" asked David. Colonel Kruger, a professional military man and pragmatist nodded his head. "I shall tell the men to cease fire immediately," he said. "Under those conditions, it will make sense to them."

Peter walked out the ballroom with Wenzel Klein to retrieve the Chronometric Teleporter. Colonel Kruger went to front ballroom window and opened it. Yelling loudly, he ordered his troops to surrender.

Someone knocked on the ballroom doors. Madame Bettenfield walked over and removed the chairs David propped beneath the handles and the doors swung open. Miss Chattenborne and Lomasi entered the room. David smiled when he saw Lomasi, then asked Miss Chattenborne to have Moses Brampton come into the ballroom.

"David," Lomasi interrupted, "a man named Contrary is also here.

"Delighted to hear Contrary was alive, David asked Miss Chattenborne to also bring him to the ballroom.

"Lomasi," David asked, "was there someone named John with him?"

"Yes," said Lomasi. "John is hurt but he is alive."

In a few moments Miss Chattenborne returned to the room with Moses Brampton and Contrary Walbridge. The shooting outside had stopped. Colonel Kruger had managed to convince the troops that their mission was over. They could return to their homeland, but they had to leave now. The men agreed to surrender.

"You made it," said a smiling David as he shook Contrary's hand.

"Yep, they almost got me but Lomasi gave me a little help."

"Contrary," asked David, "can you and Moses make sure all the Nazis are sent through the Chronometric Teleporter? Don't ask," added David. "Peter will tell you all about it. Everything they've brought with them must also be put through the time portal. The weapons should be the last things to go."

Then he remembered, "Where is Colonel Thacher?"

Moses Brampton replied, "He was killed earlier this evening, David. Also,…….."

Moses Brampton was cut off when David abruptly turned toward the door and Peter and Dr. Kline. They had moved the Chronometric Teleporter from Dr. Kline's room on the second floor to the area outside the house just west of the ballroom.

"Peter, Moses Brampton and Contrary will help you get the Nazis through the time portal."

Within four hours, all the Nazis and their weapons had been transported back to the year 1945. Now only Dr. Kline remained to make sure everything had been completed.

David, Peter and Lomasi stood by the Chronometric Teleporter as Dr. Kline was about to pass through the glimmering portal hanging in the air.

"Peter, I want to thank you and David," and looking over at Lomasi, "and you too Madam, for your kindness. I wish you good luck in the future."

"Thank you, Wenzel," Peter responded.

David and Lomasi nodded farewell to Dr. Klein as he walked toward the portal. Just as he was about to step through threshold, he stopped and turned around.

"Peter, there is one other thing I must tell you. And I do so at the risk of my life," Dr. Klein said.

"What could that possibly be, Wenzel?" replied Peter smiling.

"Peter, I am surprised you didn't guess already," Dr Klein continued.

"Guess what, Wenzel?" Peter replied apprehensively. "Are you playing games with me?"

"I am not playing games, Peter," replied Dr. Klein somberly. "And, I'm only telling you this because you have treated us much more fairly than we could ever deserve. Again, I'm putting my life in danger by giving you this information."

"What is it?" asked Peter impatiently, no longer smiling.

"I thought you would have known, Peter," Dr. Klein sharply retorted. "I really did."

"No!" Peter screamed. "No! It cannot be!"

"What the hell are you two talking about?" interjected David.

"Do you not understand, David?" Dr. Klein said. "Surely a history professor......"

"David, for God's sake," Peter blurted. "Adolf Hitler and Martin Bormann are not dead! Those men lying on the floor are look-alike doubles, doppelgangers! Hitler and Bormann have escaped once again!

Note: This battle is remembered by a historical marker which reads: "Hallowed Ground-At this site on the 19th day of April in the year of our Lord, 1775, the Battle of Old Church Road was fought here by a militia company of one hundred American Patriots engaging a force of German Hessian Mercenaries. Twenty-six American soldiers gave their lives in the cause of freedom and are buried in this field. Lest ye not forget their sacrifice."

37

Checkmate

April 19, 1775   Bettenfield Manor

9:31 p.m. to 11:59 p.m.

This had been a very bad day. David still thought George Washington had been killed by the Nazis. Adolf Hitler escaped death once again, sending a look-alike double to die in his place. It was a well known deception he frequently practiced during World War Two. David was kicking himself for not remembering this trick of Hitler's. However, even Peter didn't recognize the double as an impostor, he told himself. But it didn't help. David still blamed himself for failing to accomplish what Tse had asked.

He looked over at Madame Bettenfield who was standing next to Miss Chattenborne and Lomasi.

Suddenly, Madame Bettenfield looked at David and said, "Why do you look so glum, Sir?"

"Obviously I'm unhappy that George Washington was assassinated and Adolf Hitler escaped. I have failed miserably."

Madame Bettenfield began laughing. "Sir, did Moses Brampton not tell you?"

Puzzled, David replied. "Tell me what, Madame?"

Madame Bettenfield and Miss Chattenborne were still smiling and Lomasi seemed very pleased.

"What is it?" asked David.

"David," replied Lomasi, "Madame Bettenfield has been working with George Washington all along. So has Miss Chattenborne. And, I'm sorry but I didn't have a chance to tell you that I was also working with George Washington. It's true Adolf Hitler tricked everyone and escaped. However, things have worked out very well anyway."

"How can you possibly say that?" replied David.

"Because," said Lomasi, "we have beaten Adolf Hitler at his own game."

"What do you mean?" asked David.

"George Washington knew there would be grave danger coming here tonight. He sent a look-alike double, a Major Abraham Rutledge in his place. Although we did everything we possibly could to prevent it, unfortunately Major Rutledge was killed. We deceived Hitler just as he deceived us. George Washington is alive!"

PART 4

TIERRA VERDE, SOUTH AMERICA

ARIZONA DESERT

MAY 16, 2010---MAY 17, 2010

38

Johanna

May 16, 2010   Country of Tierra Verde, South America

"Are you coming with me, David?" someone anxiously whispered from the dark.

It was Peter Krause, David's partner in the most extraordinary of events during the last several weeks. The men had gotten four hour's sleep after completing what they thought was an impossible mission until the evening of the prior day. They helped prevent the assassination of George Washington and the inevitable consequences for the country and humanity.

They should be celebrating, but they were too exhausted. They had slept in the back bedroom of Cass' farmhouse but wanted to leave immediately to find Peter's wife Johanna. David had promised to help him.

"David, wake up. We have to go now, the voice repeated."

"Okay, Peter. Okay," David replied.

Peter had gotten the coordinates of Johanna's location from Dr. Wenzel Kline. It was simply a matter of punching them into the Chronometric Teleporter and stepping through the portal. However, David was quite sure things would not be that easy. In the last weeks, he and Peter found going into other times and places meant facing dangers and unknowns.

Lomasi said she would also accompany them. Like David, she was eager to end her time travels however, she wanted to help Peter find his wife Johanna.

They were on their feet and dressed now. It was dark and difficult to see as they stumbled through the door into the main room of the farmhouse. David crept over to the couch where Lomasi was sleeping and put his hand on her shoulder, gently shaking her. She moved. "Okay, I'm getting up," she said.

Cass heard them talking and came into the room.

"I guess you people are leaving," he said.

324

"Yes, I'm afraid we must be on our way, Cass," replied Peter.

"We want to thank you for all you've done," said Cass. "You've saved our hides but I guess you know that."

"You saved our hides too," replied David. "If you hadn't started your diversionary attack, we wouldn't be standing here now. Thanks for everything."

Lomasi yawned, "Do you guys know what time it is?"

"It's time to go," replied Peter anxiously.

"Have some breakfast first, won't you," said Cass.

"That's okay," replied David. "Peter is in a hurry to leave. We can eat later if that's okay with Lomasi."

"Yes, that will be fine," said Lomasi. "I'm not awake yet anyway."

Peter now took the Chronometric Teleporter out into the yard in front of Cass' porch. David and Lomasi followed wearily. Although David and Lomasi could create their own portals to move through time, Peter insisted on using the artificial means of his Chronometric Teleporter because he could pinpoint the exact location of Johanna. Peter punched in the location coordinates provided by Dr. Klein and then flipped a switch, activating the machine. The six feet high by three feet wide orange bordered, blue portal hovered before them, appearing as a bright doorway into the black night.

Peter turned and looked at David and Lomasi.

"We're ready," said Lomasi.

The three weary travelers walked single file into the portal.

David, Lomasi and Peter, who was carrying his Chronometric Teleporter, stepped into the living room of a modest house. They were in Tierra Verde, somewhere in South America. The early sun was filtering through the spaces around the curtains, providing dim illumination in the room. David, who was the last to come through the portal, suddenly heard a noise behind them. He reeled to see a startled Nazi soldier rising from the couch. The man apparently had been asleep but was now crouching to reach for his rifle lying on the floor. David reacted quickly and kicked the man's jaw, stunning him. He pulled out his Luger and pressed his finger to his lips, signaling him to be very quiet. "Peter," David said. "We'll keep watch here. Go find Johanna. They knew we were coming."

There was not a sound and whoever owned the home must still be asleep. Peter tiptoed into the short hallway leading to the house's bedrooms.

On his left was the doorway of a small bathroom. On the right, a door opened into a small office. There were two bedrooms located across from one another at the end of the hallway. As he reached these rooms, the door of the one on the left was opened. The room was nearly empty, its only contents being a table, chair and some shelves cluttered with books. The door on the right was closed.

Peter listened and, hearing no sound, put his left hand on the doorknob and carefully pushed the door to open a narrow slit that enabled him to peek into the room. The bedroom was darker than the living room and he strained his eyes to see the person lying in the bed. But, he could only see the faint outline of the blankets covering someone. He gently pushed the door further and put his head into the room. He still couldn't see clearly, but there was a slight movement in the bed.

"Peter. Peter darling, is that you?" a voice whispered.

"Yes, it's me, Johanna" he shouted happily, throwing the door open and running into the room. Weeping with joy, they kissed, and held each other in a long embrace.

"I knew you would find me," Johanna cried.

"I knew I would too," replied Peter. "I didn't know how long it would take but, I knew I would."

"Peter," Johanna said, "we must leave here immediately. They know you're coming."

Suddenly, they heard the front door open noisily and David yelled, "Don't move." There was a pistol shot and someone fell to the floor.

David had expected there might be a second guard outside and he was ready when the man charged into the house. The soldier had his rifle raised to shoot but, David shot him with the Luger. The soldier fell backward onto the porch.

Peter rushed into the hallway with his own pistol raised, but saw everything was under control. "Johanna is putting on some clothes and will be ready in a moment," he said, as he set up the time machine. David dragged the soldier's body into the living room and shut the front door. They heard the noise of loud engines and vehicles racing toward the house.

"Come on Johanna," Peter shouted. "We must go."

In the excitement, Peter had forgotten about his two companions. "Oh, Johanna darling, these are my friends, David and Lomasi," whispered Peter. "If it wasn't for them, I wouldn't be here." The portal appeared and it was time to leave.

"Thank you both for bringing us together," Johanna said.

"Where are you going, Peter?" David said. "Will I ever see you again?"

"I don't know where we're going," Peter replied, nodding toward the Nazi soldier lying near the couch. David realized Peter didn't want to chance having the soldier hear his destination because Hitler would surely follow. "But, I will see you again, David. I promise."

There was a sound of men on the porch and a loud knock on the front door. Peter and Johanna hugged David and Lomasi and disappeared into the portal.

"Professor Neisner," a voice called. "Please open the door."

David quickly stepped to the front window of the living room and peered through one of the tiny openings in the drapes. He could see a military type truck, a cab with a canvas-covered platform for transporting men, parked in front of the house. There were four soldiers standing near the truck. He could only see the arm and shoulder of the soldier on the porch of the house and standing at its front door. Again, there was a vigorous knock on the door.

"Professor Neisner, are you in there?" the soldier called.

Lomasi raised her arms and thought about her little house and its beautiful view of the mountains. Immediately, the portal formed in front of her and David. As the front door of the house crashed open, they stepped through the portal.

39

The Return

May 16, 2010   Arizona Desert

Lomasi and David stepped from the portal and into the kitchen of Lomasi's house. Under the circumstances, there hadn't been time for her to ask David where he wished to go. Besides, for some reason she couldn't explain, she wanted to show him her home and the peacefulness of the desert around it. It was now early morning on June 2 and she was very happy to be back at her favorite place, in front of her big kitchen window facing the mountains and back yard with its small corral. Now, it was time for her favorite thing.

"Would you like some coffee, David?" she asked.

"Yes, please," he replied.

Then he added, "I take it this is your home, Lomasi."

Lomasi smiled back at him in a silent "yes."

Although he'd never been inside her house, he and Tse had come there before and he recognized her back yard and the mountains across the desert. David sensed the peace and comfort of her house. He liked it here.

While the house was modest, there was a tranquility he never felt before. The last time he felt such serenity was when he was young and lived with his parents. He walked a few steps into the living room and sat down on the couch. He could smell the coffee brewing as he leaned to his right side and rested his head on the pillow at the end of the couch. In a few seconds, he was asleep.

****

The soulful call of David's favorite bird, the mourning dove, woke him four hours later. With its spotted wings, tan and black coloration and portly body, the mourning dove wasn't the most beautiful of birds. Its small head, short beak, short legs and long tail didn't help much either. However, the mourning dove's song was gentle and reassuring. As he lay on the couch listening to the soothing calls, he stared at the bleached wood beams across the ceiling of Lomasi's living room.

He was reflecting on the recent events, if that was an accurate description of something that happened over two hundred years ago. He thought about Tse and how this whole adventure came about. He would find Tse right away and tell him all that happened. They were successful, for the most part anyway. They prevented George Washington's assassination and Tse should be happy about that. But, they failed to kill Adolf Hitler. David wasn't sure how that would go over.

David got up from the couch and called to Lomasi but there was no answer. He looked around the room. The clock on a table read three p.m. He stretched. The sleep refreshed him and he felt good. As he thought about the journey into the past, he struggled to comprehend the magnitude the extraordinary experience. If they hadn't succeeded in preventing George Washington's assassination by the Nazi's, the consequences for mankind would have been unspeakable.

On the other hand, the fact that he had actually gone backward in time was inconceivable. But, he wasn't dreaming. He had really done it. He entered the time when George Washington was living and was there the very day the Revolutionary War began, April 19, 1775. He shook his head in amazement.

But, his reflections turned to darker thoughts. One of the things Tse told him to do was kill Adolf Hitler. David thought he had done that but Hitler escaped death once again, just as he had so often done in his earlier life. That was a critical part of the mission and he had failed. A premonition that Hitler could return began to well up in David's mind. If Hitler did come back, what would be his objective the next time?

David walked into the kitchen and sat down at the table. He stared at the mountains, trying to get the thought of Adolf Hitler's escaping out of his mind. He worried about how he was going to explain his failure to Tse. He heard a noise outside the house and the front door opened.

"David," called Lomasi.

"I'm in the kitchen," he said.

"Hi David," she said, as she walked through the living room toward David. "You slept well I hope."

"Yes, I'm afraid I did," David replied.

"My aunt Shimasani wants us to come over to her house for dinner, David. Will that be alright with you?" Lomasi asked.

"Yeah, that would be great!" David replied. "I'm anxious to talk to her about our travels. But, I guess you already filled her in, didn't you?"

"Ha, ha," laughed Lomasi. "I did but I saved the good parts for you."

"Lomasi," replied David, "can we also go see Tse either today or tomorrow?"

"I remember you mentioned his name, David," she replied. "Now, who is he again?"

David was shocked at Lomasi's answer.

"You know, Tse," he replied.

"Who did you say he was, David?" she asked.

David was again confounded by her answer. Tse said he was a friend of Lomasi's and she didn't know who he was.

"Lomasi," David said, "are you telling me you don't know who Tse is?"

"No, I really don't, David," she said.

"Tse knew all about you. He said he was your friend," David replied.

"I'm sorry, David," she said. "I really don't know him. With what you've said about him he sounds like a good person. I'm happy to go with you to see him."

David was still surprised by Lomasi's answer. She was a shaman. She knew everyone within a one hundred mile radius. And, Tse lives right here in the area. David suddenly realized he never bothered to find out exactly where Tse lived. But, that wouldn't matter. Everyone knew him so it wouldn't be a problem finding him.

"If you're ready to go, we can walk over to Shimasani's home now," said Lomasi.

"Yes, yes I'm ready," David replied, still confused by Lomasi's not knowing Tse.

Lomasi closed the front door and they began their short walk to Shimasani's house. "I love the way the sun moves through the afternoon sky," she said. "The colors change in the afternoon desert. Greens, blues, sages and pinks turn to a deeper, richer shade. It's so

330

beautiful here. I like to watch the shadows get longer in late afternoon."

It was now after four o'clock but there was still plenty of daylight left. As they walked down the gravel road between the earth tone houses, David forgot about Lomasi not knowing Tse. He was enjoying their conversation and found himself increasingly attracted to her. About one hundred yards from Shimasani's house, David reached out his hand and gently clasped Lomasi's left hand. She looked toward him and smiled, squeezing his hand as she did so. David thought to himself, "It can't get any better than this."

As they approached Shimasani's house, she came out on her front porch and waved excitedly. She was happy to see them even though she just spent the afternoon with Lomasi. David and Lomasi walked up the stairs to the porch and Shimasani gave David a big hug.

"It is so nice to see you again, David!" she smiled. "You made it back safely."

"It's nice to see you again too, Shimasani," David replied. "I'm happy to be back."

"Come on inside. I'm making a nice dinner for you," she said.

As they walked through the front door into Shimasani's living room, David remembered when he and Tse visited. Tse sat in the small chair to David's right while he sat in the large green chair. Shimasani sat in a chair near the kitchen. The little table near a front window held the papers on which Lomasi had written the descriptions of her three visions. He remembered Shimasani opening the little drawer and carefully lifting out the papers for him and Tse to read. So much had happened that it seemed like such a long time ago.

"Please sit down," said Shimasani, as she came over and hugged David again. "Thank you for bringing my daughter back to me."

David remembered that Shimasani was really Lomasi's aunt however they were so close that they referred to each other as "mother" and "daughter."

"Lomasi can take care of herself," David smiled. "I didn't bring her back. She brought me back."

Shimasani, laughing, asked, "Do you want a beer, David?"

"I'll have one if you have one," David replied.

"You've got a deal," Shimasani replied.

As Shimasani got up to get the beers, Lomasi asked, "Mother, do you know a man named Tse? David wants to visit him and I've never heard of him."

"No, I don't know anyone by that name," Shimasani replied. "Does he live around here?"

David said, "Shimasani, you remember him. Tse was here with me when we came to visit you. You told us about Lomasi's visions." However, David suddenly remembered Tse said that Shimasani couldn't see him.

"David," Shimasani replied, "you were alone when you came to see me."

"You're right," said David. "I remember now. He told me you couldn't see or hear him."

Lomasi, realizing David's bewilderment, said, "Mother, David said Tse also knew all about me."

David added, "Tse was the one who brought me to see you Shimasani. When we left your house, he took me to the grotto and he gave me the power to go into time."

Shimasani, with her head resting on the back of the chair, smiled.

"What is it, mother?" asked Lomasi.

Shimasani knew the answer. "It has been a long time," she said.

"A long time for what, mother?" asked Lomasi.

Still smiling, Shimasani paused before she spoke. "David, Tse is a spirit," she said.

"What do you mean?" asked David.

"Tse is a spirit that watches over you and guides you," she answered. "That is what Tse did for you. He chose you to carry out a very difficult task and he counseled you on how to go about it. He guided you to me and to Lomasi. He knew she was in great danger by herself. But, with your help, no harm came to her."

David was speechless, shaking his head in disbelief. But then he remembered when he met Tse at the Trading Post there was no truck in the lot. How did Tse get there? Tse had just suddenly appeared.

"Tse is a spirit," Shimasani said again. "You will probably never see him again because his work is finished."

David looked over at Lomasi and smiled. Even though he slept all day he was weary once again. He had been through so much in the last few weeks. And now, he realized Tse was a spirit. It was all too much. David looked over at Shimasani's couch.

"Go ahead, David," Shimasani said. "I'll get you a pillow and blankets. You can't stay at Lomasi's house anyway. You're not married." Then, under her breath she added, "At least not yet."

"Mother!" Lomasi protested.

****

The next morning David was awakened as Shimasani quietly scurried about her morning routine. He smelled the coffee and decided a hot cup would be a very good idea. David sat up on the couch and, although the curtains on the front window had been closed for the night, he could see the faint light of the early dawn. David stood up and walked into the kitchen.

"Oh, I'm sorry, David," Shimasani said, as she walked into the kitchen from her back porch. "I hope I didn't wake you up."

"No, not at all," David replied. "The coffee smells good."

"Sit down, David. I'll get you a cup."

Shimasani opened her cupboard and brought out a large cup, which she immediately filled with steaming coffee.

"The bathroom is just past the living room," said Shimasani.

"Yeah, let me go splash some water in my face," replied David, who was enthusiastically sipping the coffee in front of him.

David had started his second cup when the front door opened and Lomasi walked in.

"Good morning, everyone," said Lomasi cheerfully.

"Good morning, Lomasi," replied David.

Shimasani, excited as usual, yelled "Good morning, Lomasi."

The conversation immediately turned to everyone's plans for the day. Shimasani had a full day of work in her garden ahead of her. David, who had not thought about the day, suddenly asked Lomasi to go to the grotto with him. He wanted to show her how he "found" the grotto by falling through its roof. Also, he wanted to visit there for no particular reason other than he was drawn to it. Besides, he left his truck at the corral on the day he and Tse returned to the grotto and he received the power to go into time.

After a breakfast of fry bread and some fruit, David and
Lomasi returned to her house. They climbed into Lomasi's truck
and headed north. After driving up the main highway for twenty
minutes, Lomasi turned left on the dirt road which sloped into the far
horizon. After another fifteen minutes of driving, David's truck
came into view. It was a long way off and was still parked by the
corral. In a few minutes they reached the corral and Lomasi pulled
her truck up next to his. David looked under the driver's seat of his
truck. His keys were still there.

They saddled two horses and started toward the grotto.
David never asked who owned the corral and the horses. He just
assumed it was okay to borrow them. As the horses walked toward
the massive red rock formations neither David nor Lomasi talked.
David was apprehensive about returning to the grotto because he
wasn't sure what he would find. He hoped he would find Tse, but
knew he would not. Lomasi sensed David's anxiety.

It was nine o'clock and the morning sun was warming the
desert. In another hour it would be very hot. David and Lomasi
reached the base of the large red rock formation that concealed the
entrance to the grotto. Although David didn't specifically remember
going through the hidden entrance, he instinctively knew where it
was located. That's odd, he thought. They walked up the narrow
trail winding behind the huge rocks and soon reached the big gallery
of the grotto.

As they walked into the imposing room, which was much
cooler than the desert outside, David looked at the grotto's ceiling.
He remembered the hole through which he had fallen was not there
when he came with Tse to the grotto the second time. When they
walked over to the far wall where the three black spectral images had
been painted, it was blank. There was nothing but red rock.

"Lomasi," David said, "you're going to think I'm crazy but,
this wall had three petroglyphs painted on it. Now, there's nothing."

Lomasi understood David's anxiety. Everything about the
last two weeks had been surreal. There had been one incredible
event after another. Lomasi didn't doubt David had seen paintings
on the wall, even though they weren't there now. She knew David
was disappointed because there had been no sign of Tse.

"David," Lomasi said softly, "please don't be concerned about these things. You must accept them as a part of the spirit world in which our people live."

David, who was firmly anchored in reality, had never really believed in the spiritual aspect of things. He accepted the actuality only of objects he could touch and events he could see. Yet, what had been unbelievable to him a few weeks ago was now fact. Traveling in time had been an impossibility which he discovered was a reality. But, the existence of spirits was a different proposition. He couldn't figure out how to think about Tse. Logic failed him.

Lomasi sensed David was struggling to make sense of the last two weeks. She walked over to his side and moved close, kissing him on his left cheek. David turned and put his arms around Lomasi and pulled her next to him. They looked into each other's eyes, and slowly, their lips touched. It was a gentle kiss. They kissed again, this time with more feeling. His lips moved to her neck and he kissed her again, and pressed next to her. Her breathing was faster and he felt an excitement he never had before.

"I love you," he said.

"I love you too, David."

Holding hands, they walked toward the narrow path leading from the grotto. When they got outside, it was close to one hundred degrees. Because of the heat, they walked the horses slowly and didn't reach the corral until eleven o'clock. David was looking forward to the air conditioning of his old truck. The heat never bothered David or Lomasi because they were desert dwellers, but when the temperature got this high, a little air conditioning was a welcome relief. After the horses were back in the corral, David and Lomasi shared a parting kiss. He would return to Ramona Springs and she would resume her shaman's duties. They would meet again this weekend.

As David followed Lomasi who was driving her truck down the dusty desert road, he couldn't stop thinking about what he experienced in the last two weeks. His routine hike in the desert had turned into a life-threatening journey. And a spirit named Tse had made it all happen. It's too crazy, he thought. But, then he muttered, "Where is Tse? Why isn't he here to meet me?"

The two trucks reached the end of the dusty road and stopped at the highway. Lomasi waved into her rear view mirror and turned right onto the pavement. David waved goodbye to her and pulled his truck forward and turned left. But, he really wanted to turn right and follow her. "I'm in love," he shouted out the truck's open window.

40

May 17, 2010   Ramona Springs

The drive back to Ramona Springs took thirty minutes. David drove directly to his small, white house and pulled into the driveway, waiting patiently as the automatic garage door went up. When it was this hot, the truck had to go in the garage. Although the inside of the garage was also hot, it was better than having direct sunlight on the old truck. It would be a little less hot the next time he drove it.

As the garage door came down, David got out of the truck and walked to the door leading into the kitchen. David's home was a three-bedroom bungalow with a living room, kitchen and three bedrooms. While the house was small, it was more than adequate for him. He went into the kitchen and closed the door behind him.

"Yeah, I think I will," he said, as he went to the refrigerator to get a beer. It was a little before noon but he figured it was noon somewhere in the world. It seemed to be an unwritten rule that a man couldn't have a beer before noon. A woman probably wrote that rule, he thought. Besides, he was in the Mountain Time Zone so that made it okay to borrow someone else's time zone to justify popping a beer. That was his rule.

He walked over to his old refrigerator tucked next to the doorway of his small kitchen. His mother had given him the ancient appliance when he was in college. Yeah, he could afford a new one he thought to himself. But this one worked fine. His father called it an "ice box" in a flashback to a time when blocks of ice stored in a "box on legs" provided the cooling for food and, probably beer, he guessed. He kept his beer in the very bottom of the refrigerator because the cold air was "colder" down there, or so he thought anyway.

The kitchen door next to the refrigerator led into the living room. On the living room's far side, another door led to three small bedrooms and a bathroom at the end of the hallway. David's house was not nearly as cozy as Lomasi's but it was comfortable. The house was painted "bland beige," as he described it, throughout the interior. Sitting at his kitchen table, David pulled the tab off the beer can and took a couple of gulps. He was in no hurry to go into the living room because there was probably a pile of mail lying on the floor below the postal slot in his front door.

As he sat at his kitchen table, he was still pondering the experiences of the last several weeks. He stared at the top of his wooden table that held his beer. Oh well, I might as well check the mail, he decided. I gotta do it sooner or later. As he walked into the living room he realized he was still tired. He gulped the rest of the beer and debated whether he wanted another.

"Yeah, I think I will," he said, answering his question as he walked back to the kitchen. David pulled open the door of his refrigerator and grabbed a second beer. He closed the door and stood in front of the battered refrigerator, staring aimlessly as if he expected it to tell him the meaning of life or something equally philosophical. Still looking blankly at the refrigerator, he popped the beer can. "Nuts, you don't know any more than I do," he said.

As he turned and walked into the living room, he gasped, dropping his can of beer to the floor.

"Hello David," smiled Tse, who was sitting on the couch. "Nice couch," he laughed. "You must have had to look real hard to find one this ugly."

It's past its prime, if it ever had a prime to begin with," David laughed, "I bought it because I knew you'd be visiting. So, after everything that's happened, all you can say is you don't like my couch?"

David was happy to see Tse, if for no other reason than to reassure him there really had been a Tse to begin with. But then, he knew there had been a Tse. How else would he have been able to go back into time? How would he know about Lomasi and Shimasani?

"Hold it, David," said Tse, who seemed to know what David was thinking. "Stop worrying so much. Everything that you remember really did happen. You didn't imagine it and you're not crazy."

That was a relief. He felt better knowing Tse appreciated his predicament. Shimasani and Lomasi took this kind of thing for granted. The idea of a spirit being some kind of supernatural presence which influenced a person was the natural order of things

338

for them. But for David it was a gigantic leap which, even with Tse sitting before him, was difficult to make.

"David, I know you're having trouble sorting things out," said Tse. "But, only you can do this. You must come to terms with everything that has happened and you must also understand your role in the future."

"Whoa, just a minute, Tse," replied David. "What do you mean by my role in the future?"

"David, I didn't come here today just to pat you on the back and make you feel better. I came here with a message for you. You need to understand and accept what has occurred and why it happened to you."

"You mean I need to get a grip?" replied David, smiling.

"That's exactly what I mean," laughed Tse. "David, even though Hitler escaped, you did a good job."

"Thanks, Tse," replied David. "I needed to hear that."

"Yeah, I know," said Tse smiling. Then he added, "after all, nobody's perfect."

"I'm sorry I didn't get Hitler," said David, reacting to Tse's teasing comment.

"Seriously, David, you got the most important thing done. I'm proud of you," replied Tse.

"Thanks again, Tse. Like I said, I needed to hear something positive. It's been a rough couple of weeks."

"Well remember what I said because I won't say it again. You need to be self-reliant, David. In the future, you need to figure out yourself whether you got done what needed to be done."

"Wait a minute, Tse," David said. "There you go again. What do you mean in the future?"

"Like I said, David, "I came here with a message."

David, still struggling to redefine reality and what was logical, didn't answer. But, he began to suspect what Tse was telling him. The job hadn't gotten done completely. Hitler was still out there.

"Don't be too hard on your self, David," Tse said. "You did everything right. Hitler escaped, but get over it."

"Thanks Tse," David said. "I hate to say it, but the guy was smarter than me."

"Remember, you must decide your future," said Tse, ignoring David's comment. "I won't be here for you every time."

"What do you mean by every time?" asked David apprehensively.

Tse stood up and looked toward the living room's beige wall, pausing before he answered. "I'm going to give you something," said Tse, and he handed David a small box he had been holding. "Open it after I leave."

Tse walked over and opened the front door. He smiled, then turned and stepped into the doorway. "Goodbye, David," he said, and walked out.

Holding the box Tse had given him, David walked over to the open door. Tse was gone. David closed the door and walked back to where he had been standing in the center of the room. The beer can he dropped lay on its side in a dark, wet circle formed when it emptied onto the carpet. He bent over and picked it up and walked into the kitchen.

Sitting at his kitchen table, David pulled the tan wrapping paper from the shoebox size package and laid it to the side. When he took the top off the box, he saw a rose colored rectangular slab of desert rock. He gently lifted the panel out of the box and laid it on the table to read the inscription.

"Everyone must find the Way. But some are chosen and are themselves the Way."
                    Tse

340

James Wharton is an Arizona author. His books include:

Detour
The Destiny Project
Deluxe UFO Tour Company
Invasion of the Moon Women
Strange Breakfast & Other Humorous Morsels
Ghosts of the Grand Canyon Country
Ghosts of Arizona's Tonto National Forest

www.jameswharton.net

www.ingramcontent.com/pod-product-compliance
Lightning Source LLC
Chambersburg PA
CBHW062018170626
46813CB00001B/211